Somebody in Boots

Nelson Algren

Somebody in Boots

New York, NY

Ig Publishing
Box 2547
New York, NY 10163
www.igpub.com

ISBN: 978-1-63246-030-1

PRINTED IN THE UNITED STATES OF AMERICA

10 9 8 7 6 5 4 3 2 1

Introduction

NELSON ALGREN WALKED into the Manhattan offices of The Vanguard Press on September 13th, 1933, and asked to speak with the person in charge. He was twenty-four-years old—5-foot eleven, maybe 150 pounds, gaunt and disheveled. For the past several days he had been sleeping in the back of a stranger's car as it raced east along state roads from Chicago to New York City, by way of Niagara Falls. He had one published story to his name— no appointment, no agent, no manuscript.

Vanguard's owner agreed to meet anyway. His name was James Henle and he wasn't put off by Nelson's lack of pedigree. Before he became a publisher Henle had been a journalist. He signed muckrakers after taking over Vanguard. And the press had published Karl Marx in the past, and jeremiads like *People Vs. Wall Street: A Mock Trial*. A scruffy drifter from Chicago was a stretch for them, but not much of one.

Henle invited Nelson into his office, and let him talk.

Someone from Vanguard sent me a form letter last month after my first short story was published, Nelson explained. It asked: *Are you working on a novel?* And I'm here to answer. I don't have a book, but I want to write one.

Henle played along.

What would you write about? He asked.

I spent last year on the road, Nelson said. I train-hopped from Chicago to New Orleans, and then spent time in Texas. If I were going to write a book it would be about drifting. I would hop freight trains into the Rio Grande Valley, and sleep in hobo jungles and eat at Rescue Missions and write about what I saw.

Henle liked the idea. The Great Depression was lumbering into its fourth year, but no one had written an account of the economic crisis like the one Nelson described.

I'll give you two hundred dollars to write that book, Henle said—half up front, spread across three months.

Nelson had been out of work since he graduated from a state college with a degree in journalism twenty-six months earlier. His family had lost their life's savings and their business to the real estate crash and bank closures. Unemployment was near twenty-five percent, so he accepted Henle's terms.

What will it cost you to travel south and begin working? Henle asked.

Nelson considered the question. He calculated the price in his head and began to answer, but then he checked himself. It would be prudent to ask high, he reasoned.

Ten dollars, he said. It will cost ten dollars to return to Texas and begin writing.

And then Nelson watched, in awe of his own cunning, as Henle reached for his wallet and removed ten dollars in cash. It looked like a fortune to him. The year before, he had harvested grapefruit for less than a dollar a day. He thought Henle was an idiot for parting with so much money.

"I really, really felt tickled with myself for taking that guy," Nelson said later.

•

Nelson hopped a freight train the next day and headed toward Louisiana along the South Pacific line. His plan was simple. He would retrace the route he traveled the year before—New Orleans, then west into the Rio Grande Valley—and collect material as he went. Characters would emerge from among the people he met riding box cars; dialog would drift on the air; scenes would flash past as his trains rumbled through dusty southern towns. The book would practically write itself.

It didn't work out that way. Nelson caught a westbound train in New Orleans as planned, but he rode it for a thousand miles—much too far. He drifted through southern Texas, then north through unfamiliar terrain until he reached El Paso. He stopped there to reassess, and because the border was so close he crossed it and visited Ciudad Juárez and found an arena and watched a bull fight. A toreador waved his flag; he slashed with his sword. A drunken American yelled—"He'll toss 'em all. This the bes' ol' bull ever was in these parts." And when the carnage ended, Nelson was as lost as he had been before it began. He hopped a freight rolling east then and headed toward the setting of the novel he was supposed to be writing, but he didn't make it far. The railroad police stopped his train outside Sanderson, Texas, and began walking the snaking line of its cars searching for hobos.

When the train pulled away, Nelson was stranded. It was October, and he was in the high desert. It would be cold when the sun set, so Nelson began walking along US 90. He had been on the road for three weeks and he hadn't written a word.

That night Nelson reached a little Texas college town called Alpine and decided to stay. There was a boarding house on the outskirts of town. A woman named Nettleton owned it, and she offered Nelson a room the size of a cell, a bed, a dresser, a desk, and one meal a day for ten dollars a month. Nelson accepted. He unpacked his things—two shirts, one pair of pants, pads, pencils. Then he went to work.

Nelson wrote by hand beneath the harsh light of the single bare bulb hanging from his ceiling, and his method was documentary. He created a protagonist named Cass McKay, and led him along a narrative path that tracks the one Nelson traveled himself the year before—away from home, into New Orleans and then Texas, in and out of Relief Missions, through traumas. McKay's world is a terror, and as he stumbles through it violence hardens him. A man slashes him with a knife outside a brothel. And he watches a freight burn and immolate the flock of sheep it had been carrying. He finds a child's body by the side of the tracks. And he becomes hardened to other people's pain.

Eventually Nelson approached the president of the local college and gained permission to use the school's facilities. He began typing his manuscript on campus by day, and revising by hand at night. The little money he had was spent on tobacco and coffee; he scrounged meals from trash cans. Local aspiring writers sought Nelson out, and sometimes he sat down with them over coffee or Coca Cola to discuss his work. They paid rapt attention when he held forth about literature but he didn't do so often. Mostly, he just wrote—day and night and day and night as the clock ticked down and his money ran low. "He worked like a dog," one student said later.

Nelson maintained a frenzied pace for four months, but then the last installment of his advance arrived and he spent it. The book was only half-written. He had to return to Chicago so he could finish writing but he recoiled from the idea. His parents' house was crowded with family members displaced by the Depression; everyone was out of work.

In late January, Nelson prepared to leave Alpine. He couldn't delay his departure any longer. He sent some letters north, and said goodbye to the students he befriended. He penned a home-sick poem—"All night one night I heard your voice, my city." Then he walked up to the college campus.

It was late and dark when Nelson arrived, and he began test-ing doors. Eventually he found one that was unlocked. When he did, he opened it and entered an office. There was a desk inside, and on it there was a typewriter. Nelson sat down and plunked out a few lines of text on the machine. Then he picked it up and car-ried it off the campus and down the hill to his boarding house. When he reached his room he sealed the typewriter inside a crate. And in the morning he mailed it to his parents, charges reversed.

A freight train passed through Alpine before noon that day and Nelson hopped on board and rode north. It stopped after forty miles, and Nelson stepped off and began warming himself in the sun by the side of the tracks. That's where the police found him. They asked his name. Then they took him into custody and brought him to Alpine where he confessed.

"A typewriter is the only means I had to complete a book which means either a few dollars or utter destitution," Nelson told the sheriff. "There is nothing that is more vital to my mere exis-tence as a typewriter, it is the only means I have to earn a living. If I write I can earn my own living."

And then the sheriff locked Nelson inside the Brewster County Jail.

A week passed while Nelson waited for his trial, two, three—his deadline came and went and he began to stew. He watched the clouds through the barred windows of his cell. Sometimes he played checkers. He pictured his future and saw the state prison at Huntsville, a chain gang—the end of a career than never began. The other inmates beat him with belts, and he caught hives and they covered his body.

He wrote a letter to a friend. "I'm halfway to hell," it read.

Nelson's trial began in February. The proceedings started in the morning and they were finished by lunch. First the lawyers made their cases; then the jury left the room to deliberate.

The foreman returned quickly.

"We, the jury," he began, "find the defendant guilty as charged in the indictment and for his punishment a confinement in the penitentiary for a term of two years." The foreman paused. Then he continued speaking: "Furthermore, we recommend that the sentence be suspended during the good behavior of the defendant."

The judge agreed, and Nelson was released—a felon, but a free man.

Nelson returned to Chicago after the trauma of his incarceration looking for allies and answers. A friend suggested he could find both at 1475 S. Michigan Ave. An arts organization called the John Reed Club met there—writers gathered in the group's meeting room, and painters. They had their own magazine, *Left Turn*. And close ties with the Communist Party. Nelson said he would visit.

He found the Club on the second floor of a dingy building hard by the freight tracks on Chicago's Near South Side. Murals covered the walls. Magazines published in the USSR were stacked on tables. And when people met to discuss literature or painting they didn't worry over technique. Art was measured by only a single criterion at the club: Does it serve the revolution? Meetings ended with a group rendition of the "Internationale."

Arise ye prisoners of starvation, members sang, *Arise ye wretched of the earth.*

Nelson was a star at the Club—one of the only members with a book in the works. And he became a regular. He attended Tuesday meetings that winter, and rabble rousing speeches. He even began making friends. Abraham Aaron was among the first. He was a young militant who had dropped out of college to help start the revolution. Richard Wright, a shy, moon-faced writer from Mississippi who had just published his first poems followed soon after. Then Nelson met a woman, and moved himself into her apartment.

For the next three seasons those were the corners of Nelson's life—the Club and its politics, drinking coffee into the early morning hours with Aaron, debating revolutionary literature with Wright, and plugging away at his novel in his girlfriend's apartment.

As Nelson worked, the new ideas he was being exposed to found their way into his book. His method changed. The observational, journalistic tone he employed in his early chapters faded, and anger seeped into text—politics, advocacy. Nelson wasn't content to describe the predation he had seen on the road the way he imagined he would when he pitched his novel to James Henle. He wanted to diagnose causes now as well, and propose solutions.

Nelson revised and expanded his book, and as he did the violence and crushing despair his characters experience in its early chapters transformed into a preamble to an argument for revolution. "The kewpie doll lay in a dark pool beside her, and people began running up to see," Nelson wrote. "Now came months that caught Cass up on a dark human tide. Whole families piled into cattle-cars, women rode in reefers; old men rode the brakebeams, holding steel rods above the wheels with fingers palsied by age."

Chicago, Nelson said, is "trying with noise and flags to hide the corruption that private ownership had brought it." "It's the big trouble everywhere," he proclaimed, and then he warned—"Get all you can while yet you may. For the red day will come for your kind, be assured."

When Nelson finished writing he submitted his manuscript to The Vanguard Press with the title *Native Son,* but they changed it to *Somebody in Boots.* It was a demand, not a request. More followed.

Vanguard felt the novel was not marketable and they used that argument like a cudgel against Nelson—he needed the book to sell, and they knew he did. Over the next few months, he removed some of the political content at their request, and transformed an interracial marriage into a union between a white man and a white woman. He cut some violent material as well. And then he resubmitted his book and waited.

It took Vanguard four months to print Nelson's novel—not much time, but enough for his dreams to develop outsized proportions. He began telling people he had written a sensation—a singular account of poverty, a piece of gospel truth bound to become a best seller. He was right, in part.

Somebody in Boots was released in March, 1935, to good reviews but tepid public reaction. It had no natural constituency. Some readers thought it was too violent, others too sexual. The revolutionary politics scared away the mainstream, but revolutionaries thought Nelson hadn't gone far enough. He introduced Cass McKay to the Communist Party in the text, but never allowed him to commit to the cause. For true believers, that felt like betrayal.

Three hundred people bought *Boots*, four, five, six, seven—then, nothing. It didn't even earn back its meager advance.

A few weeks after the book's release, Nelson's girlfriend returned to her apartment late at night and found him unconscious on the floor with a gas line shoved down his throat. She thought he was dead.

Nelson survived his suicide attempt, of course, but he was a phantom for several years afterward. He licked his wounds and fell in love and found a job; he killed one year working with the Communist Party, and another carousing. He carried a notepad everywhere he went but he never seemed to do anything with his material. Five years passed, six. Friends began teasing him. They said he would never publish again. An acquaintance mocked him. You're a "flash in the pan," the man wrote, a "mediocrity," "the almost-but-not-quite Algren."

Nelson shut them all up in 1942. *Never Come Morning*, his second novel, was released that year and struck his doubters like a well-executed hook—they didn't see it coming and after it found purchase they never felt quite so sure of themselves again. Critics adored *Morning*, and eventually it sold a million copies.

Thus began the second phase of Nelson's career—a period when he wrote books distinct from the text you're holding in almost every way. They saunter where this one stomps, and their characters dream and laugh. The worlds contained between their covers are alive with music, and thick with ideas. Even their titles set them apart. *Somebody in Boots* is a blunt declaration, but *Never Come Morning* and *The Neon Wilderness* and *The Man with the Golden Arm* and *Chicago: City on the Make* and *A Walk on the Wild*

Side move with the tempo of a good bar of blues when you say them fast.

After *Morning* was published, Nelson's books began selling by the hundreds of thousands instead of the hundreds. Fame replaced poverty. *Somebody in Boots* was forgotten, and Nelson was grateful that it was—of the eleven books he wrote this one "betrayed" him the most. So long as it survives so does an account of the worst years of his life.

Somebody in Boots slipped out of print for twenty-two years after its release, and returned then only because Nelson needed the money a paperback publisher promised him for a reissue. His agreement came reluctantly though, and he never got behind the second edition. Before the book went to press he cut the text to hell, and allowed the publisher to give it a new title. This book was called *The Jungle* in its second life, and it was available at newsstands for thirty five cents. The tagline on the cover read: "A Great Novel of Lawless Youth."

A complete version of *Boots* was released a few years later, but Nelson sabotaged that as well. He wrote an introduction that lacked even a word's worth of praise, and called it "an uneven novel written by an uneven man in the most uneven of American times."

Other editions appeared after Nelson's death in 1981, but they didn't fare well either. The eighties were the wrong decade for this book; so were the nineties. And fans and critics interested in tidying Nelson's literary reputation—I count myself among their number—never took it seriously. They accepted Nelson's comments on their face, and interpreted them as permission to read this book quickly and criticize it freely. And more nails went in its coffin.

But now the edition you're holding has resurrected *Boots* just as the world contained in its pages has begun to sound familiar again—a time when the man who feels "he had been cheated with every breath he had ever drawn," can be found walking the sidewalks, ranting. The voice of the bigot who proclaims, "Yep, niggers got all the jobs, every-where, an' that's why you'n me is on the road," echoes through the political system. And most of us— whether through hardship, disappointment or shrewd calculation—have developed an intimate relationship to the sentiment Nelson revealed when he wrote: "He could not trouble himself, one way or the other, about any better or happier world."

The country feels like it has come full circle since 1935, and maybe now, eighty-two years and eight editions into this book's long life, it will finally receive the honest chance it always deserved.

Here's to hoping.

Colin Asher

Preface

I WONDER WHETHER there stands yet, above an abandoned filling station a mile this side of the border, a wooden legend once lettered in red—

Se Habla Espanol

—that must now have been long washed to rose.

It hung between an autumn-colored tangle of mesquite and a grapefruit grove gone to weed on a stretch of highway where nobody drove. I'd lettered it myself.

And sat in its narrow shade shelling black-eyed peas below a broken sun.

Once in the dead of day a field of white butterflies came out of that sun, fluttered at rest like a single creature: then fled like a dream of white butterflies.

I shelled on.

The Sinclair Company owned the station. A Florida cracker wearing a straw kelly the color of an old dog's teeth was my partner. He called himself "Luther" and the one thing I knew about him for sure was that his name couldn't be Luther.

I'd met him working a small-time door-to-door fraud in New Orleans and he'd let me have a few doors. In no time at all we had had to leave town.

Luther owned a grapefruit-packing shed in the Rio Grande Valley, he had assured me—if I'd meet him in McAllen he'd make me a partner. In McAllen it had turned out all he'd meant was that he had a buddy who bossed a shed there—and now his buddy had left. Fired, dead, absconded or gone on the arfy-darfy, Buddy wasn't there any more. The only partnership Luther had left to offer me was in the station. Had he offered me half-ownership of a Southern Pacific roundhouse I wouldn't have turned it down. I'd *always* wanted more responsibility.

For I already knew that though wages were fine, spunk was better—and Sheer Grit was best of all. That was the stuff that enabled a young fellow to get himself a foothold on the Ladder of Success. There were deer in the chaparral and frogs in the ditch, if you didn't work for nothing you'd never get rich, I shelled on.

A Sinclair agent drove up with papers assigning responsibility for the hundred gallons of gas the company had let us have on credit. The man didn't pretend to think we could sell gas on that dreadful stretch. His suspicion was that we planned to set up a still in the brush. But keeping the station open made him look like a go-getter with his front office.

"It don't matter which one of you signs," he told us.

"Ah caint handwrite proper," Luther admitted humbly to the agent while handing me the papers, "but this lad here got more knowance 'n I'll ever have."

I signed the papers. Luther looked down at me from his six-and-a-half-foot height with a smile that drained cold glee. "You'll be the Filling-Station King of the Valley," he told me, like a reward.

I could hardly have been more proud.

Selling produce was THE PLAN. Every morning Luther boggled off in a beat-up Studebaker and returned each evening with a fresh load of black-eyed peas in the back seat, and a five-gallon jug of fresh water.

A store manager in Harlingen had told him that, if black-eyed peas were shelled and bottled, housewives would compete to buy them. Pointing out a Mason jar of peas, on display in the store window, that I personally had shelled and bottled, Luther rewarded me once more:

"You'll be the Blackeye-Pea King of the Valley."

I was shelling my way to fame.

In a land that seemed like an empty room furnished with fixtures of another day; when nobody knows where the old tenant has gone nor who the new tenant will be.

Nor what changes he'll make in the fixtures.

The land no longer knew what it was; so the men and women moving across it no longer knew who they were.

The youth with the outfielder's mitt on his hip, begging soap from housewives in backyards along the route of the Southern Railroad, thought he belonged to the Tallahassee Grays because he had a signed contract in his pocket. When he reached Tallahassee he'd learn that the league in which the Grays played had been dissolved. So all he belonged to was backyards along the route of the Southern Railroad.

The woman whose green years had been wasted in the tumult and din of a hundred speakeasies, now sat before a whiskey glass with a false bottom saying, "Don't get the wrong idea, Mister, I'm no whoo-er. But at the moment I don't have a place to sleep." And the tumult and din of nights without end kept dying slowly away.

I was a day-editor, night-editor, sports columnist, foreign correspondent, feature-writer and editorialist. At the moment, however, I was shelling peas.

Between a past receding like a wave just spent and an incoming tide, in a time-between-times, multitudes were caught in the slough of the waters. To be hurled, if they were young, strong and lucky, high onto the sands; others were carried topsy-turvy and didn't come up till they were far out to sea. Some were swept under never to rise.

There were snakes among the field stumps and lizards on the stones. Once a field of black butterflies came out of the sun, fluttered one moment and were gone: fled, like a dream of black butterflies.

I shelled on.

Huey Long was clamoring for redistribution of the wealth of those who were richer than himself in 1931, and the D.A.R. was demanding that all unemployed aliens be deported immediately. A cardinal was announcing, with contentment, that the nation's economic collapse was a spiritual triumph, because it brought multitudes closer to the poverty of Christ: the cardinal hadn't missed a meal in his life. Al Capone, on his way to the Atlanta Penitentiary, denounced Bolshevism. Herbert Hoover wanted somebody to paint his portrait. Huey Long threatened to vote Farmer-Labor rather than with the "Baruch-Morgan-Rockefeller Democrats." Alexander Meiklejohn observed that "American Statesmanship has come to a dead stop."

So had the cardinals, the rabbis, the ministers, the businessmen, the politicians, the bankers, the editorialists, the educators, the generals, the industrialists and the philosophers. Only the poets, the poets alone, saw what was building far out to sea.

Under the palaces, the marble and the granite of banks
Among the great columns based in sunless slime

The anonymous bearers of sorrows
Toil in their ancient march.

>*They look like men.*
>*They look like men.*

Whence do they come? How endure?
How spring from dragon's teeth in gutters of death?
Full-armed and numerous, where do they go?
To gather red lilies sprung from seas of blood.

>*They look like men.*
>*They look like men.*

They look like men of war.[1]

American statesmanship had come to a dead stop; and yet I kept on shelling.

It had been Herbert Hoover's land of Every-Man-For-Himself. It had also been Walt Whitman's land, saying, "If you tire, give me both burdens." Between the shelling of one sack and the next, I had had this flash notion: to show what had happened to a single descendant of that wild and hardy tribe that had given Jackson and Lincoln birth.

I had seen them riding the manifests and shilling at county fairs; whose forebears had been the hunters of Kentucky.

Where had the hunters of Kentucky gone when all the hunting was done? These were the slaveless yeomen who had never cared for slaves or land. They had never belonged to the plantations: they had seen the great landowner idling his hours while the blacks worked his cotton. So they'd put their own backs up against their own cabin walls and idled away their hours too: a cabin and a

---

1. From *They Look Like Men*, by Alexander F. Bergman

jug was all a man needed. If he had a fiddle and could fiddle a tune he was rich: Burns was their poet.

They had been as contemptuous of white mill hands as of black cotton pickers and for the same reason: they held all men in contempt who were dependent upon any owner. Nobody owned a man who owned a gun along the wild frontier. But, now that the frontier had vanished, where did the man go whose only skills were those of the frontier?

The struggle to preserve the great plantations was not their struggle, they knew: nor had they felt that "Mr. Lincoln's war" was their own. Putting a plague on both houses, they became hiders-out between armies who began moving southwest after Shiloh. Forced down to the border by the spread of great cities, their final frontier became the dry bed of the Rio Grande.

I hoped to show a Final Descendant: a youth alienated from family and faith, illiterate and utterly displaced, I thought of him always as a Southerner unable to bear scorn; who had yet borne scorn all his days. One who wandered through some great city's aimless din, past roar of cab and cabaret, belonging to nothing and nobody. A walker in search of something to belong to in order to belong to himself.

Where crossing-bells announced the long freight moving through the Georgia Pines, I had seen him riding shoeless on a boxcar roof. I had seen him with his face framed between the bars of the El Paso County Jail, looking out. I had seen him taking charity in a Salvation Army pew: a man representing the desolation of the hinterland as well as the disorder of the great city, exiled from himself and expatriated within his own frontiers. A man who felt no responsibility even toward himself.

"Keep things goin' *up*, Son," Luther advised me, "never inform on a sergeant to a private—inform on the private to the sergeant. Never inform on a lieutenant to a sergeant—inform on the sergeant to the lieutenant—*Up up up.*"

There were wild pigs below the station's floor. At night we heard coyotes cry.

Luther boggled off one morning but failed to return that evening or the next. Two nights later I heard a car wheel up—then no sound but that of the frogs in the ditch. Standing in the station door I discerned, dimly, a figure crouching. I called out but got no reply.

The next morning I discovered that Luther had siphoned the gas out of both tanks. I was stuck in the chaparral with nothing to drink but creek water, nothing to eat but black-eyed peas, and in debt to Sinclair Oil & Refining Company for a hundred gallons of gas. I started thumbing my way toward Mexico.

In the small-time vice-village of Matamoros I took a room in a hotel run by a woman who had entitled herself "The Mother of the Americans," though she didn't look like anyone's mother. There I wrote the first chapters of a novel I first called *Native Son*.

Reading, thirty years after, this attempt to depict a man of no skills in a society unaware of his existence, the curiously opaque face of Lee Harvey Oswald, alive one day and dead the next, comes through like the face of new multitudes.

Belonging neither to the bourgeoisie nor to a working class, seeking roots in revolution one week and in reaction the next, not knowing what to cling to nor what to abandon, compulsive, unreachable, dreaming of some sacrificial heroism, he murders a man he does not even hate, simply, by that act, to join the company of men at last.

My flash notion of the story of a Final Descendant now appears to be that of a progenitor.

This is an uneven novel written by an uneven man in the most uneven of American times.

Now I have to get back to my shelling.

—Nelson Algren

Somebody in Boots

PART ONE

The Native Son

The Miners came in '49,
The Whores in '51,
They jungled up in Texas
And begot the Native Son.

OLD SONG

1

WHY STUB MCKAY turned out such a devil he himself hardly knew; he himself did not understand what thing had embittered him. He knew a dim feeling as of daily loss and daily defeat; of having, somehow, been tricked. A feeling of having been cheated— of having been cheated—that was it. He felt that he had been cheated with every breath he had ever drawn; but he did not know why, or by whom.

The man was a strong man, yet his strength was a weakness. For someone kept cheating all the time, someone behind him or someone above. Somebody stronger than anyone else. And although he could never quite wind his fingers about his feeling, although he could never bring it out into light, yet he was as certain of it as he was of the blood in his veins. It was there just as palpably. It was there, at the bottom of all he thought, said and performed. At times the feeling was like an old hunger, sometimes like a half-healed wound in his breast. He was never without it.

In time he gave his pain a secret name. To himself he named it: The Damned Feeling.

Some of his fellow townsmen thought Stuart McKay half mad. In a border town, where even children drank and smoked, Stuart took pleasure in little but fighting and hymning. He used neither tobacco nor whiskey, he seldom swore, and he laughed almost never. Yet there seldom came a Saturday night that did not find him brawling, and he never missed a Sunday morning at the Church of Christ of the Campbellites. So he was hated, damned, and respected in Great-Snake Mountain as only a fearless man could be both damned and respected in that place.

A lean and evil little devil Stubby was, all five feet and five inches of him, inflammable as sulfur and sour as citron, sullen as a sick steer and savage as a wolf. A moody, malevolent little man, with a close-cropped, flat-backed head of bristling red hair, and eyes so very pale, so very slit-like and narrow, that the blue of them was scarcely distinguishable from their small sooty whites; so dust-rimmed, narrow-wise and cold that they seemed nothing but brief blue glintings beneath the cropped red bristles.

And although Stubby McKay was a good worker, yet because of his temper he seldom held any one job for a very long while. He was a section hand on the Southern Pacific a couple of months, he cleaned backhouses about the town for a time, then became a hostler's helper on the Santa Fe. After that he got work as a night watchman in the town's lumber yard, and that too he soon lost. Inevitably, in whatever capacity employed, high or low, he would be discharged for fighting. He would strike some yardman, or buffet a boilermaker, or insult a foreman. He was arrogant, insolent, and disrespectful toward his employers, and therefore earned very little when he did work. The townsfolk called him "catawampus," meaning that they thought him violently cross-tempered. "Som'un ort to clean thet Stub McKay's canyon up proper for him jest once,' the folk agreed. "Mebbe thet'd learn him to be so derned catawampus all the time. The man's that mean he ort to be muzzled."

No one ever succeeded in cleaning Stubby's canyon for him, however. For all his brawling, he was never soundly beaten once.

When hard-pressed he would draw a knife, pick up a brick or a bar of iron—anything within reach. Once, upon being chided for having employed a four-foot length of rubber hose to knock down a Mexican section boss, he explained himself half-apologetically:

"Well, y'all see, when ah fight a man ah jest go all-to-pieces-like, so sometime it happen ah don' rightly know exacly what is it ah got in mah hand. This Spik straw boss now, when he commence givun me all thet boss-man talk, ah gotten god-orful nervous-like an' straighten up mah back to see does he mean it all—an' 'en all o' suddent there ah was, alarrupin' his arse with thet ol' rubber-hose line; an' ah s'pose ah'm right fortunate it weren't his haid 'stead of his arse, 'cause ah swear ah caint recall where ah picked up thet hose. Ah swear, ah jest caint recall."

And his favorite hymn, which he sang with clenched fists, was number thirty-six in *Hymns of Glory*:

> *The son of God goes forth to war, a kingly crown to gain*
> *His blood-red banner streams afar—Who follows in his train?*
> *Who best can drink his cup of woe, triumphant over pain?*

He lived with two sons and a daughter in a three-room shack in Mexican-town, and most of his neighbors were Mexicans. The shack faced a broad dust-road that led east to the roundhouse and west to the prairie: a road hung with gas lamps leaning askew above lean curs asleep in sun, where brown half-naked children played in ruts that many wheels had made. Within the home, poverty, bleak and blind, sat staring at four barren walls. Ragged dish towels hung, in a low festoon, from the damper of the stove-pipe to a nail above the sink, and the sink was a tin trough salvaged from a dump heap. Unwashed dishes and pans lay in it.

Stuart's living room was used for both dining and sleeping. In its center stood a table built solely of orange crates—a creation of Bryan McKay's. It was unsteady, inclined to totter, as Bryan had been the morning he built it. A faded strip of green oilcloth covered it. A smoky and cheerless place, this room, with but one small window. On one wall hung the shack's sole decoration, a dusty piece of red cardboard bearing the simple legend:

CHRIST
Is the head of this house
THE UNSEEN HOST
At every meal
THE SILENT LISTENER
To every conversation

One room was a mere hole in the wall, a little sloping window-less cavern in which the sister Nancy slept, partitioned off from her men by a strip of dark cheesecloth nailed above the cavern's opening.

Slantwise behind the home ran the Santa Fe railroad; between the tracks and the house stood a lop-sided privy.

The privy was loathsome within. It stank fulsomely. Scraps of torn paper lay strewn across its floor, flies swarmed in the place, no one had ever cleaned it. Its door hung creaking and half-unhinged, a thousand nameless dark weeds grew about it.

The red dining-room legend one day found its way onto the privy wall. Stubby found it hanging lop-sidedly there, and came back into the house with one suspender unbuttoned. He laid the cardboard on the table, clutched a tuft of his close-cropped scalp with one paw, and rapped the legend fiercely with the knuckles of his other hand. Although he was very angry, yet his voice held a complaining ring that was like a plea beneath a threat.

"Bry'n," he said, "were you-all a well man today, ah swear ah'd beat yo' fo' this."

Bryan tittered slyly, girlishly, half to himself, and Stubby turned away. He could not bear to hear womanish giggling in a full-grown man. And Bryan would not admit that he had done the thing, although everyone knew that it could have been nobody else. Later on the younger brother asked Bryan if he were not just a little afraid of Christ Jesus.

Bryan tilted forward on his chair in the corner till his shoeless feet found the bare dirt floor.

"Not me, ah'm not afeered o' Jesus. Why, ah'm Jesus little wooly lamb, ah am. Me'n Jesus git along jest like this—" He crossed two fingers, one on top of the other, and thrust them under Cass's nose. "See, young scapegallers—this is how me'n Christ Jesus git along. Oney the one on the bottom, that's me every time, an' him on the top—that's Christ Jesus." Then he tittered girlishly, and crossed and recrossed his fingers.

Cass was a sickly thing, and Bryan had left his health in France. But Nancy was strong, her girlhood was happy, she had always been gay.

As a small girl, walking alone in the tiny garden on the mornings of those early days, days as yet undarkened by any shadow, she would laugh at everything she saw, red zinnias and blue morning-glories, tall dahlias and the wild daisy. Of the sweet purple clover she wove herself garlands, she made herself crowns of lilac and rose. Then, dressed like some little brown Mexican flower-girl, anklets of marigold, wristlets of grass, she would dance through the garden singing in sunlight, till she frightened the sparrows and caused them to scold her. For sheer delight she would dance, laughing, leaping and twirling, whirling about with her brown arms stretched wide; then, laughing and gasping, half-dizzied and toppling, she would throw herself down in the long grass of summer; laughing, laughing, weeping with laughter.

In all bright things she took deep joy: in gay-colored birds, in pictures and ribands; in gaudy new dresses, in flowers and songs.

Nance had been mischievous, too, as a child, always fighting with street urchins, chasing the chickens, or stealing white grapes off honest folks' vines.

All day one day she coveted a great white blossom growing in the yard of neighbor Luther Gulliday. It was a wild chrysanthemum, she had not seen one before in her life; so she begged Luther for it, and he gave her instead—an apple. Nance went off quite humbly—an excellent actress. But when dark came she strolled again toward her flower, saw no one watching, plucked it and ran.

So all her days passed, unreckoned, fast-fleeting. She plucked wild plums, in the sunlight she found them, and her days were like these: she grew in light, unattended.

Sometimes after supper, while undressing for bed, she would press her hands slowly down the white bow of her loins. A great wonder would fill her, she would stand looking down. She would lie still in the darkness, her breasts like twin spears; and she would feel then as though she lay on a pyre whose flames were already beginning beneath her. The girl would be afraid, though she did not know of what. And her face in the dark would change to that of a woman.

Then she would sleep, and in sleep too she laughed. She was three years older than the boy Cass.

So the house stood, and so were the McKays, in the pre-depression years, on the West Texas prairie. Their home stood like a casual box on the border; it was wooden and half-accidental. It had no roots in the soil, it stood without permanence. Although it was old and unpainted and rotting, yet it appeared somehow to have been in its place for but the past few days. So with the people within—Texan-American descendants of pioneer woodsmen—they too had no roots. They too were become half-accidental. Unclaimed now they lived, the years of conquest long past, no longer accessory to hill and plain, no longer possessing place in the world.

They too were rotting.

On the edge of the town grew the jungle. Fathers warned sons not to go near it. Mothers intimidated their six-year-olds with tales of bearded men lying in wait in the long grass down by the Santa Fe tracks. But to a boy like Cass McKay, who was a lonely child, the Santa Fe jungle was not a fearful place. To a boy like Cass, who feared his father and had no mother, the jungle offered companionship.

Boys little older than himself lay idling about in long sun-shadows there, talking, jesting, eating, sleeping, waiting for one train or another. They boiled black coffee in open tins or ate beans with a stick; they rolled cigarettes single-handed and sang songs about far-away places. Cass never listened without wonder, he never watched without admiration.

"Ah'd like to git out of this pesthole some day," he mused to himself. "Ah'd go to Laredo or Dallas or Tucson—anywhere ah'd take fancy to go. Ah'd git mah right arm tattooed in New Awlins, ah'd ship out f'om Houston or p'raps f'om Port Arthur; ah'd git to know all the tough spots as well as the easy ones. Ah'd always know jest where to go next. Ah'd always be laughin' an' larkin' with folks."

Cass listened to the boys and older men, and he learned many things:

That Beaumont was tough, but was loosening up. That Greensboro (in the place called Car-line)—that that was a right bad little town to ride into. That Boykin, right below it, was even worse. That toughest of all was any place that was anywhere in Georgia; if you were caught riding there you were put on a gang, and you worked on a pea farm from sunrise till sunset, sweating along in a chain for sixty-one days or until they caught someone else to take your place. But they gave you fifteen cents every week, and a plug of tobacco on Sundays besides. "So *that* part's not so bad," Cass thought.

He was a red-headed shaver in blue overalls and bare feet.

"Stay 'way from Waycross," an old Wobbly warned him, "less you want to do ninety days in a turp camp." And a young man sang an old tune for the boy, beating on a tin can in time with his song.

> *Turp camp down in Gawgia,*
> *Cracker on a stump,*
> *Big bull-whip he carries makes them blizzard-dodgers hump.*
> *Watch 'em flag it out of Gawgia when they've done their little bump.*
> *Oh boom the little saxophone, rap the little drums;*
> *We'll sing a little ditty till the old freight comes.*

Southern Texas, but for Beaumont and Sierra Bianca, was simple; the Rio Grande valley was a downright cinch—you could ride blind down there without any penalty just so long as you got off on the side away from the depot when you got into McAllen. You could get through Alabama all right—provided you didn't stand up on the tops like a tourist, so long as you stayed out of sight at division points, provided you stayed off the A. & W.P. Those A. & W.P. bastards utterly discouraged a man, for they made a point of putting you off at a spot in the woods forty-four miles northeast of Montgomery—a water-tank in the wilderness entitled Chehawee. And you walked to Montgomery then unless you had a fin. You could stay on for a fin, cash down on the barrelhead.

Look out for that town in Mississippi called Flomaton, 'cause that's Mick Binga's hole. Binga, even when he had both arms, was plenty-plenty tough. One night he licked two niggers for riding and they came back an hour after and shoved him under the wheels so that he lost his right wing—but he shot and killed both niggers while they were running away. Since then he's a devil on whites, and death to blacks. Since then he's killed and crippled so many niggers that even his railroad has lost count. Some say he's killed twenty. Some say more, some less. Some say that when he gets fifty even he's going to quit to give his boy the job. His boy is majoring in French philosophy now at Tulane, but everyone knows how well such stuff will pay him.

> *The roundhouse in Cheyenne is filled every night*
> *With loafers and bummers of most every plight;*
> *On their backs in no clothes, in their pockets no bills,*
> *Each day they keep coming from the dreary black hills.*

Look out for Marsh City—that's Lame Hank Pugh's. Look out for Greenville—that's old Seth Healey's. He'll be walking the tops and be dressed like a 'bo, so you'll never know by his looks he's a bull. But he'll have a gun on his hip and a hose-length in his hand, and two deputies coming down both the sides; your best bet then is to stay right still. You can't get away and he'll pot you if you try. So give him what you got and God help you if you're broke. When he lifts up that hose-line just cover up your eyes and don't try any back-fightin' when it comes down—*sww-ish*. God help you if you run and God help you if you fight; God help you if you're broke and God help you if you're black.

Old Seth Healey at Greenville—there's a real bastard for you. Someone ought to kill that old man one of these days. The only way you can tell he's a bull as welt as a brakie is by his hat. He wears patched blue overalls and keeps his star hid. Lean as Job's turkey and twice as mean. The hat's a big floppy affair with three holes in the top, and it's the only way you can tell that the fellow coming down the tracks is Healey. Sometimes he's bareheaded, then you can't tell for sure—till he cracks you over the side of the head with his pistol-butt. Then you're fairly certain. He once hit a boy in the belly with his fist so hard that the boy died, in the grass by the tracks, half an hour after. A black boy. So look out for Greenville, it's right above Boykin, and it's Seth Healey's town. Look out for Lima, too—that's in Ohio. And look out for Springfield, the one in Missouri. Look out for Denver and Denver Jack Duncan. Look out for Tulsa, look out for Joplin. Look out for Chicago—look out for Fort Wayne—look out for St Paul, look out for Dallas—look out—look out—look out—LOOK OUT!

Most of the boys felt that they belonged. They were, definitely, underdogs. Between themselves and those above they drew a line for all to see. It was always "We" and "Them." People who lived ample lives, who always stayed in one place, who always had a roof over their heads—these were "Them." In judging a man, Cass learned, the larger question was not whether the man was black, white, or brown—it was whether he was a transient or "One of them 'inside' folks." Inside of a house that was to imply.

Cass sensed the strong "we"-feeling among these men and boys. He learned that in jails where the food was inedible, as most often it was, the men bought their own food by levying upon each newcomer to the extent of whatever they could find on him. Kangaroo Court was held whenever a new vagrant was brought in, and assessment was always justified as being a fine imposed for breaking into jail without the consent of the inmates. Oldtimers always paid, if they could, and without hesitation; they understood the fine as a loose form of insurance. A man was assisting those of his own class, and when he himself was down his class would help him. But whether he was able to pay or not, he usually shared in the supplies bought outside the jail.

Kangaroo Court was an institution which pleased county judges and chief deputies, for it enabled them to pocket money which otherwise they might have been forced to spend on supplies. One jail in southern Louisiana had established a treasury with a fund of over two hundred dollars, so that the turnkey and sheriff were dined once a week by the prisoners. At the Grayson county jail in Sherman, Texas, the prisoners printed a weekly paper, *The Crossbar Gazette*.

All tales seemed strangely wonderful to Cass when he heard them told in the jungle. These men seldom spoke of the terrible hardships they endured. Hardship they most often bore in silence. It was of the infrequent and wholly accidental bits of good fortune they had happened upon of which they spoke: how one had found a new corduroy jacket with a wallet in the pocket when he had climbed down into a reefer one night in Carrizozo; how another had been taken into a Methodist minister's home one time, and had been fed and clothed for three straight days; how another had come upon a drunken woman in an empty cattle car.

Of the pathetic effort to keep clean, merely to keep clean, they had nothing to say. They were always begrimed with coal dust and cinders, always begging soap from each other; and at every junction they sought water for washing so soon as thirst was quenched. They hung shirts to dry on fence-posts by the tracks or on bushes in the jungles; they put clothes on damp rather than dirty. Most carried combs, and pocket-mirrors and toothbrushes were not uncommon. Sometimes one would reveal a small fetish to Cass that he might not have shown a full-grown man: a woman's glove or a woman's handkerchief, found perhaps on a bench in a city park. One showed Cass a photograph of Mary Pickford and said, "Mary's my aunt."

Of the darker side Cass could not know, of this they did not speak. Of long cold nights when you walked unlit streets, hungry, ill, alone. When the wind cut so that you gasped with pain, and so tired you were you scarce could stand. When you knew you had either to beg or die; and the hate that is yellow and springs from shame rose within you and made numb your heart till you could think of nothing save how sweet it would be just to kill for the simple pleasure of killing. You felt how easing to your own hurt would be the sight of another man's blood; you knew then that to vent your own pain you must see another man suffer too. Yes, a freezing marrow could be well warmed just by watching fresh blood flow—this, when you had not a penny for drink, made you forget fierce cold. The escape was called "jack-rolling." Men fought then for the sheer sake of fighting. Two hungry men in an alley, at night, clasped in each other's arms amid garbage and ashes, biting, kicking, sweating in terror—so that one could laugh in relief when the other lay senseless; so that one could look down and see dark blood bubbling above torn lips, and know that it was he who had brought the blood up in that throat, and that it was he who had torn those lips. But the men of the jungle never spoke of jack-rolling save in jest. Hunger had taught them silence as well as haste.

Oh I met a man the other day I never met before,
He asked me if I wished a job a-shovelin' iron ore.
When I asked him how much he would pay, he said twelve cents a load,
I said, go 'long old feller—I'd ruther stay on the road.

"Ah'd like to get out of this pesthole," Cass thought. "Ah'd like to see Fort Worth an' Waco."

Cass was fifteen in 1926. He was lank, like his brother Bryan, red-haired like his sister, and he was already somewhat cave-chested. When Cass walked, he slouched. When he stood stiff he sometimes cocked his head to one side, like a long-legged fighting cock, and then he looked as though he had not laughed four times in all his life. A gaunt and lugubrious lout. He had gone to school long enough to learn how to read and write, but then the school board had hired a teacher who was half-Mexican, and Stub had taken Cass out in protest. The teacher was still in the school, so Cass had never returned.

Cass could feel his body growing, it was groaning and straining and stretching. There was a great travail within him, a great toiling and laboring, as though an oak were sprouting in his vitals.

Sometimes strength would surge through him in a tide, and then he would run aimlessly and shout at nothing at all.

In his mind, too, was a growing. A sudden light would flash within his brain illuminating earth and sky—a common bush would become a glory, a careless sparrow on a swinging bough a wonder to behold; and then the light would fade and fade, like a slow gray curtain dropping.

Some moments were irretrievable.

One day in March he raised his eyes from play and saw a solitary sapling on a hill, bending before the wind against a solid wall of blue; and it seemed to him that it had not been there before he had looked up and would vanish as soon as he turned. Many times after that time Cass looked at the same slender shoot; never again did he see it so truly.

In a sense it *had* vanished.

At times he could catch Nancy in one of these strange life-glimpses. One second she would be moving about the kitchen, his sister about her familiar tasks, and the next she would be a total stranger, doing he knew not what. There would be a picture of her in his mind then—not moving, but rigid, tensed with life and still as death. He would be afraid and bewildered.

And then there was the lilac—that spring-time when it bloomed. It grew by day against a fence, and it bloomed at night, in rain. Cass waited each day for its blooming; each night he smelled it from where he slept. Every morning he brushed its buds of soot that trains had left in the night; each day he watered it. He had watched it every day, and he had seen:

That it grew out of dust and yearned toward sky; that it seemed half-asleep in the early morning, but that it became restless as day grew toward night; that when east-wind passed it shuddered in joy as though unseen hands were stroking its buds; and that whenever the sun was directly overhead the whole plant, even to its tiniest twigs, seemed bending a little in pain.

And one night Cass awoke, and heard a small rain on the dooryard dust, and he smelled a velvet-dark smell. It came to him on the smell of rain, and he heard the tapping of drops on the roof overhead. Behind a thin curtain he heard his sister's low breathing; and knew she slept with her hair for a pillow.

Then the velvet smell made a purple image in his brain; his throat seemed to swell with the wild-dark odor. In the yard dust caught between his toes and the light rain flecked his face. Above his head night-clouds hung, heavily brooding. And the smell from the dooryard's corner drew him as powerfully as though a woman waited him there: he traced the texture of lilac leaves as though touching a young girl's breasts for the first time. He closed his eyes; his fingers wandered wantonly, to stroke that delicate blooming.

The lilac was blooming in the night.

Cass buried his face deep in lilac-leaf that time, and his heart pained, first trembling a little, then swelling slow.

That was in the springtime when the lilac bloomed, but it never bloomed for him again.

Often in the evenings of that spring and summer he would become uneasy and restless; he would begin to walk because, of a sudden, it would seem hard to stand still. His spindling shanks would start clipping along like a great pair of shears, ever faster and faster, till the walk became a run and the run became a race— then something would give within, and he would be tired, tired. He would return slowly, feeling troubled and strangely dissatisfied. Utterly exhausted, he would climb into bed with his brother.

Then such dreams as he would have! Once he was atop the utmost peak of the highest mountain on earth, clouds and storm winds breaking about him, snow-gales sweeping down. He was naked, and he was laughing—he was not cold among these snows. And everything was so wild and strong that when he woke in the morning he was sickened by the sights and sounds and smells of the house: the stains of Stubby's spittle and Bryan's cut-plug tobacco juice dried in brown globs against the wall; the sweaty, yellowish smell of unclean bedclothes beneath him, and the sour smells from the kitchen. The work-a-day world was a sorry place compared to what Cass knew in dreams.

Yet once he dreamed he was walking softly down a dark and narrow way where little blue lights burned all in a row. Black-cowled children stood in darkened doorways as he passed, and he walked ever softer and softer, for everything about this street seemed strange. Then all the little blue lights went out at once, there was no light anywhere in the world, and he woke. And that time it was good to see the work-a-day world once more; Cass felt, somehow, that on that night he had come close to death.

He did not always dream. Sometimes he lay awake beside his sleeping brother, wondering, filled with an adolescent yearning, imagining all manner of far-away places. He saw broad blue waters and woody places, pleasant cities where children played. Sometimes as he lay so Nancy would laugh lowly out of sleep, and he would be recalled from wonder. Then he would think of his father, how Stuart rode switch engines all through the mysterious night. He would think of his father, how, in the chill, smoky mornings, he would come in while Cass was dressing by the wood stove, tracking soot and cinders and sand into the kitchen on his pointed little brown Spanish boots, dangling an empty tin dinner pail from his hand.

In after years Cass never heard the long thunder of passenger cars over a bridge in the dark, but he caught a brief glimpse of a smoky dawn through an opening door; never saw the white steam whistle in the light, but he saw his father stretched, mouth agape, on the disarranged cot in the corner, brown boot-toes pointing upward.

And in after years Cass always feared a night of storm or wind. On such nights, as a boy, he heard something, or someone, come stealing through darkness out on the road; he heard cold fingers tap along the west wall, wind-fingers trying the knob, then, whispering something quickly, something running like the wind in haste away, driving all small things before it.

Yellow and black, yellow and black: these came, for Cass, before he was grown, to be the colors of sun and blood, the hue of life and the shade of death. To think of living was to see yellow; to see blood was to think of black. He could never in all his life see blood as crimson—it looked too dark for that. When Cass thought of blood he saw a black rivulet running a rail that gleamed in sunlight—an iron rail gleaming yellowly, as though smiling while it drank.

This was because of a thing which occurred when Cass was not quite sixteen.

All one bright windy morning he had worked in the dooryard. (Stuart had forbidden him to run with Mexican boys.) He had built himself a tire-swing; he had turned a clothes-wringer for Nancy for an hour, and had helped her hang out the washing; he had carried in kindling; he had patched a frayed kite.

And all about him, on the roofs of the houses, aslant the old privy, across the small garden, through air, earth and water—over all things streamed the strong yellow sunlight. As though coming like rain from atop Great-Snake Mountain, the deep yellow sunlight. The good yellow sunlight; and the mad March wind.

He had heard the whistle of the noon freight on the Southern Pacific to Houston—three long and two short blasts—and swiftly, as a thing done every day, he hopped down from his tire-swing and raced toward the S. P. tracks. Even though this train would not be hauling coal, as he knew it would not be, yet it remained a duty to watch it pass. To see the 'boes that would be riding the tank cars, to exchange hand-waves with them, to share the excitement that all there would feel—this would be the event of Cass McKay's day.

He was almost too late. The engine itself was a quarter of a mile east of town when he arrived, and he was only in time to see the last half-dozen gondolas roll by; she was fast picking up speed, and the brakeman was already back in the cab. Two Mexican section hands and several town boys were standing about a thing atop the cinder embankment. A thing huddled. Yes indeed, it wasn't often that one could come into town without seeing a sight or two for one's pains. Eagerly Cass clambered up, small stones slipping beneath his bare feet, stepping over the sagebrush that grew up through the cinders: then he pressed himself roughly between the two Mexicans and saw what they saw.

Face downward in the sand beside a clump of thistle a boy was lying, his right arm flung across his eyes, a boy in a brown shirt and blue corduroy slacks.

Over him a tall man stood looking down as though understanding this all to himself.

The left arm was spewed off slantwise at the shoulder, the jaw hung limp. This Cass saw first. One eye hung out of its socket by one long thin wet thread, the filament rising and falling a little straight up and down as it hung. Someone had pitched a small bundle of clothes to one side and strewn it over with sand.

At the waist, between the dark shirt and a broad bright belt, the side began to tuck in and out in short quick violent little jerks. In—out. One of the Mexicans called shrilly. "Look! Look! See what he do now! In and out he going!" Two of the town boys walked toward the bundle and went off down the tracts with it dangling between them.

And all down the gleaming yellow rail there ran the warm wet blood—warm wet blood running black and slow beneath the unpitying sun; black and slow down an iron rail, darkening small stones as it spilled and seeped, into ties; the blood of heart and brain and sinew wetting a thistle in the sand. And black, black, black; black as darkness on the bright sun's face.

The thunder of the morning freight faded to a low singing of rails through heat, to die at last in the east into silence.

There never came, in later years, a sunny, windy day in March, but Cass would feel the heart within him pumping, pumping momently; and he would be faintly sickened and half uneasy and somewhat afraid.

Yellow and black, yellow and black—these were the colors of sun and blood, the hue of life and the shade of death, the symbol of flesh and the sign of dust.

In August of 1926 Cass saw blood again. Bryan killed an old housecat that had been around the home for seven years; and he killed the creature by wrenching off its head.

Bryan McKay was easy-natured enough when sober; yet when drunk he could be as cruel as malice itself. One day he noticed the old cat chase one of the hens off the porch, but he paid little attention and went on his way. He knew the old tom never killed anything, not even mice. But three days later, drinking tequila in the town with friends, he remembered, and put his bottle down.

Cass was in the kitchen that morning, painting a shoeshine box for use in town. The old tom was curled on a chair beside the sink, pulsing evenly, after the manner of most good cats. Cass heard Bryan's voice approaching, and he put his brush aside.

"Chicken-chasin'! Bird-killin'! Sly black egg-suckin' son-a bitch . . ."

Cass grabbed a newspaper off the stove and threw it over the cat as it slept. Had he not done so Bryan might never have caught him. At Cass's touch the tom vaulted to the floor and raced directly into Bryan's hands as Bryan lurched into the doorway. Bryan scooped the cat up and whirled him about like a flywheel, first this way and then that, while his mouth fixed into a hard and crooked grin.

Cass pleaded hoarsely, "Bry'n! Yore *hurtin'* him"—then the body, claws still outspread, whanged like a small pillow against the wall above the stove, and the head remained in the hand. Bryan flung this at Cass, and the sun from the doorway was in Cass's eyes. Fur brushed his shoulder and dampened his cheek. He screamed in fright, in hoarse terror, and in hate. He stared at a ragged head on the door at his feet, saw dark blood seeping into dust there, and touched his cheek with his finger. He stood looking down for minutes after Bryan had left, hand on cheek touching blood. Then, slowly, his hate drowned his fear.

He ran up the road after Bryan, and pounded Bryan's back with both fists till Bryan whirled and caught him. He held Cass fast, with no drunken fingers, white dark-shawled women paused as they passed and Mexican children gathered to see. For one terrible second Cass thought Bryan was going to twist his head off as he had the cat's.

"Combate! Combate!" sang the little brown children, leaping and skipping in the sun.

Bryan did not strike. He stood looking down and holding Cass tightly, with all the drunkenness gone out of his fingers. Yet when he spoke Cass thought him still drunk, for what Bryan said made simply no sense at all. Although Cass was squirming and writhing and twisting, yet he heard each word clearly.

"Nothin' but lies—nobody told nothin' but Jesus-killin' lies. Told us it was to fight fo' this pesthole—told me . . . Oh, ah didn't believe all they told, none of us did, but we laughed an' went anyhow. Now, look at me. An' they won't never speak truth to you-all neither."

He released Cass as suddenly as he had seized him and went on his way toward the town, walking slow.

Mexican children trailed Cass all the way toward the house, mocking and inquisitive. "What goin' on, red-son-of-beetch—eh? What trouble you sons-of-beetch make t'day?"

Back in the kitchen Cass made a coffin out of his shoeshine box and buried the tom within the lilac's shadow.

Toward the end of that afternoon he was in the living room watching a hawk wheeling in dusk far over the prairie as the prairie night came down. He saw night come walking between the little low houses, down through the winding Mexican alleys. Wind came, bearing sand between houses and trees. He saw sand on the broad road rise, in whirling night-spires, to spread over the roof tops. For a long hour he watched the approaching storm, till all was utterly dark. Wind struck against wall then, whispered something quickly, and passed on, driving all small things before it.

Cass wondered if he would ever have to be outside, to be driven before darkness as a small thing before wind.

2

DURING THE RAINY months of winter, after the wagon-wheels of autumn had left long knolls and low ridges far over the prairie, when rooftops were sometimes white of a morning, then talk of a coal train coming through would spread like wildfire in the town. Some would say it was coming on the Southern Pacific; others would have it straight from the station-master himself that it was due on the Santa Fe: and this made a difference, for the trains took water at different points. Usually the majority of those who sought the coal were driven off by brakemen or detectives before they secured so much as a single lump, but there were times when a coal train did come through and neither brakeman nor bull came near. These times were rare in Great-Snake Mountain, and they were remembered for long weeks after as a holiday is remembered.

One morning in February of 1927, there came the usual afternoon whisper—two coal cars were coming through on the Santa Fe at three o'clock! Clark Casner, the ticket agent, had just let the cat out of the bag. There wouldn't be so much as one bull riding, Clark had said. The train would stop fifteen minutes for water, and the coal cars would be toward the tender. Fifteen minutes! No bulls! Could such a thing be? Then someone, of course, had to refute it—the car, this one said (and he too had it straight), would come through on the S. P. about four in the morning—"An' when it do y'all best be in yo' baids, 'cause thet man ain't gonna stop fo' fifteen secon's—ain't gonna stop ay-tall—he's gonna come thoo heah shoutin' lak th' manifest t' Waco." Rumor and conflicting rumor rose then and strove, and only the actual arrival of the train on the Santa Fe put an end to argument.

Cass and Johnny Portugal, a halfbreed boy who lived near the roundhouse, went down to the tracks together that afternoon with a gunny-sack between them. It took two boys, working swiftly together, to fill such a sack.

They found a dozen children huddled on the pumping station with chapped blue lips. All carried gunny-sacks, and one held a clothes-pole besides. This man was Luther Gulliday, the McKays' next-door neighbor. The clothes-pole had a purpose.

Beside Luther Gulliday stood a little Mexican girl in a long black shawl, clutching behind her the handle of a wobble-wheeled doll buggy. In the bottom of this carriage Cass observed a carnival kewpie doll that had no head lying sprawled on its back with arms outspread.

It looked somehow odd to see such a doll, so helpless and headless in cold and wind.

The girl surveyed Cass and Johnny with an Indian antagonism in her eyes. When Johnny greeted her familiarly, in Spanish, she did not reply. Merely stood waiting in mute hostility there, bare baby-knuckles clutching a doll buggy's handle.

"She's half Osage," Johnny whispered. "Her folks come down from Pawhuska last week."

"Osage or Little Comanche," Cass replied, "she won't git enough coal fo' two nights in *that* contraption."

Cass wondered what the child would do if he stepped over

and lifted the doll out of the carriage as though he intended to take it from her. Then he looked at her, out of one eye's corner, and concluded immediately that she would do plenty. No one was getting very far ahead of *this* girl on *this* trip, that was plain enough to be seen.

"She don't have to look so fix-eyed at everyone," he thought. "If that man really comes through like they say, there'll be a-plenty fo' all us. Why, ah cu'd fill that dinky buggy out o' this heah sack an' hardly miss me a lump. How perty she look tho'—My!"

Cass had never, heretofore, seen such beauty in a child.

And when the train came toiling painfully around the base of the mountain three miles distant, Cass saw her step back just an inch. He saw that she was already afraid. Then the cars were lumbering past, someone cried, "*Carbón! Carbón!*"—and the first of the coal cars was going by. Rolling slow.

What a bustling about there was now! Nobody stomped cold feet or swung his arms now. Nobody stood slapping his palms together just because a couple of thumbs were cold—there was something better to do with cold fingers now. Cass and Johnny Portugal were among the first to get into the coal car, but a dozen others followed, like so many buccaneers swarming over the sides. Johnny held the sack while Cass filled it; they filled it between them, right there and then, laughing and swearing all the while. Everyone laughed and swore, working frantically.

Only Luther Gulliday worked slowly.

Luther Gulliday loved order and system in his work. He too climbed into the car, but he did not, like the others, begin an unmethodical hurling of coal into a sack or over the side of the car. Luther did all things differently from other men. He went about now picking out the largest lumps he could lay hands on, placing them carefully, one by one, along the iron shelf that runs the length of a car on the outside above the wheels, all the while counting: "One! Two! Three!"—until the iron shelf was lined to its full length. Then he hopped down, held the pole like a lance against the first lump and stood stiff as a statue, his gunny-sack open and waiting. Should anyone have presumed to take one of his lumps before the car began moving, Luther would have cracked him smartly with the pole. And as the car started rolling again the lumps fell neatly, one by one as they met the pole, into the open sack. He counted aloud as they fell in the resounding accents of a man counting votes for his closest friend, "One! Two! Three!"

When their own sack was almost full the boys heaved together and got it over the side—and someone shouted "Jump!" The brakie was coming. Cass saw him running toward them far down the spine of the train. He saw too that there was plenty of time, so he threw one more lump over just for good measure; then he felt the car moving faster under his feet, and jumped. Johnny followed, and stood grinning and pointing at Cass because a thick coat of coal dust filmed Cass's face. Cass heaved impatiently at his end of the sack. He did not like anyone to laugh at him, especially a half-breed.

"Nancy'll sho' feel good to see this," Cass assured himself as they toiled along under the heavy sack. She couldn't tell him *this* time he was sinning—not after they had been without coal for so long;—even his father would have to smile! Why—here was almost enough to last through till March! Think!—Were it filled with *potatoes* instead, would his sack be then one jot the more precious? Well, could one burn potatoes and keep a house warm with them? And how heavy it was! But how warm they would be! No more going to bed after freezing at supper now! And all because of *himself*, that was the main thing. In the pride of his exploit the boy's heart exulted. Why couldn't every day be just like this one? Why couldn't something like this happen every day? Johnny Portugal shifted his end of the sack and paused to look down at his feet; a doll buggy lay in a deep rut there, turned upside down with its wheels in the air, wobbly tin wheels turning this way and that like toy windmills in the wind. Beside it lay the Mexican child, her bare arms outspread. The long black shawl was drenched scarlet now, and one finger clutched one dark crumb of coal. She lay on her back, and her head had been severed from her body. The kew-pie doll lay in a dark pool beside her, and people began running up to see. "She must of got anxious an' got up too close," Luther Gulliday said, "she must of just slipped a little."

That coal was the last that Cass ever brought home. Before it was gone Stubby had lost his job on the Santa Fe, and this time there was no other job to be found. Stubby had come to be known throughout the county as a "bad hat," and jobs for "bad hats" were not plentiful in a place where even tame men would work for a pittance. To make matters no easier for Stuart, the man who was taken on in his place by the Santa Fe was little Luther Gulliday. Stuart saw Luke coming home every morning, an empty tin dinner-pail on his arm; Stuart saw him passing down the road toward the roundhouse every night. He never saw without growing white with fury.

Luke was a little man, smaller than Stuart; but in the town he was as well liked as Stubby was hated.

And Stuart's mind was dark. Within his head inconstant fleeting shadow-shapes passed and repassed, without cessation, all day, all night. All day, all night lights flickered there. He had always been aware of his own darkness; now he began to fear it.

The man had had so many cruel tricks played on him in his lifetime, he had hurt so many other men, that sometimes now he became afraid of the darkness growing within him; it too would deal him a scurvy back-handed slap one of these days, he felt, if he didn't strike out first. Often while he slept he became aware of something that a passing flash, like a brief lightning, had revealed within his brain; had revealed clearly there against the black, yet too briefly to be discerned. So briefly that he saw only that there was a *thing* there—a thing growing, a thing wholly evil. And sometimes some ancient fancy or some feeling not his own laughed within a cavern in his brain—he knew the laugh because it was mocking. Laughter was mockery, Stuart knew.

Powerful suggestions and willful persuasions of people he could not see clamored within him as he dreamed. Memories of ancient wrongs, cruelties perpetrated otherwhere, some other time, all came thronging to harass him. Sussurant dark whisperings of night, low-muttered half-tales of murder and trickery; always they spoke of trickery. Sometimes he felt that he, too, would like to trick someone or something, sometimes the voices aroused within a desire to kill so that his throat became dry with that desire. Like the craving for strong drink that comes on a man, clutching his throat so that he must drink or fall dead.

Stubby did not understand. Always his thought evaded his mind. He could only go his hard way dumbly and alone, without wonder, without knowledge, with only pain for friend. He could only know a dim feeling as of daily loss, as though all the blood of his body were spilling momently from a broken vein and his eyes had been curtained that he might not find where.

The feeling of having been cheated—of having been cheated—that was it!

And now came the hard West Texas times, the charity-station days and the hungry nights. This was spring of 1927, but to the McKays it was little different than spring of any other year.

For days when the town was troubled by tourists Cass acquired the approach sibilant, the whisper sudden, swift, and clear: "Yo' like Spanish gal, boss? Fifteen-year ol' jest stahtin' business? Come, ah show yo' where to, she treat jou all right. Not rush, jest take yo' time. Come, ah show yo' where to." Cass's speech at this time was a curious congeries of West Texas idiom, Southern drawl, and Mexican intonation.

Back of the Mexican pool hall dark girls stood in doorways, waiting. Cass knew Pepita by sight, Teresina and Rosita. Little Pepita sought to tease him whenever she saw him pass: "Look— there go my ugly red-hair boy." She would raise her voice as he began to run: "Ugly red-hair boy!—you got no dollar for Pepita today?" Once she gave him a five-cent pack of tobacco for showing a tourist to the back door: he took it and fled without so much as a single "Gracias, Senorita Pepita." He smoked that package out with Nancy in one evening, but he did not tell her how he had earned it. Often after that he came home with fifteen cents or a Mexican quarter in his pocket, and would tell her that he had earned it by shining shoes on the streets.

In May Bryan killed the last of the hens, and for two days they ate meat; after that it was black coffee and okra. Stubby got a few backhouses to clean, but his own privy remained, as ever, a vile hole. Before the summer was out they were on charity.

Fortunately for her own good health, Nance had been reared in happier days. Between 1919 and '24 Stuart had worked almost regularly. She had not suffered from hunger in her adolescence, as Cass now did. She realized this to the extent of placing on his plate, before they sat down to table, a part of the pitiful daily portion that was hers. Always Cass saw what she had done; secretly, he compared portions at every meal. He always saw, but he never protested; he would pretend that he didn't perceive his portion to be the larger. He would wolf down his share and stare at what Bryan had left, his tongue cleaving to the roof of his mouth with hunger. Bryan would push the coffee remaining in his saucer toward him, or shove over a half-eaten crust; then he would smile to see the boy gnawing like a dog, holding the piece in both dirty paws.

"When yo' gonna grow up to eat like a man?" Bryan would ask. "Yo' don't eat like sixteen any more than as if yo' was nine."

Once, for five days running, they had nothing to eat but oatmeal: gray, lumpy, utterly tasteless. Then came a day with nothing at all. For the five days following that day it was rice—without milk, without sugar. Oatmeal and rice were all they could get from the relief station. Cheap as milk was, the cattlemen who ran the county feared to make it cheaper by pouring it out to charity. They poured it out to their hogs instead, and thus bolstered falling prices. Their consciences they salved by putting dollar bills in the collection plate of the First Baptist Church on Sunday mornings; and they gained the sanction of every truly patriotic Baptist in the town in the process.

Bryan sat all day in shadowy places or wandered aimlessly about the Mexican streets. If not ordered to do anything he would perform small tasks about the home; but if, openly, Nancy told him to build up the fire or chop up some kindling, or plant a few beans, he would give her a blanket refusal. He had no time for women's tasks, he would say, and would walk off toward the town. She had learned never to ask anything of him, and by this method sometimes won his help. He would pull a few weeds out of the garden, pare a few potatoes, or begin fussing with a couple of planks and a hammer in the dooryard. Few tasks that he began ever saw completion. He tired easily, he lost patience or thought of a joke that he had to tell Clark Casner right away. Once, while building a small chair, he began drinking in the midst of his work. Despite his wobbling legs he got a back nailed onto the chair, and, after a fashion, three legs. Then he sat down on it, feeling the task well done. It collapsed in a heap, and in the middle of the heap he sat, giggling like a ten-year-old. He had many friends, and they were all roaring boys. Usually when he returned from town he had a pint of tequila on his hip.

He would sit in some dark corner of the house, tippling half-secretly. Often no one would know that he had returned from town till they heard him tittering to himself, or humming through his teeth from some nook. Sometimes, when well in his cups, he would sing. He would wail a half dozen lines over and over again, each time with a different rhythm:

> *They say I drink whisky; my money is my own,*
> *And them that don't like me can leave me alone.*
> *Oh whis-key, you vil-lain, you've been my down-fall,*
> *You've kicked me, you've cuffed me,*
> *But I love you for all.*

Then he would titter. He had been gassed at St. Mihiel.

Stuart alone remained outwardly unaffected by these days. All day he slept, each meal he ate alone just as though he were still working on the Santa Fe. Promptly at six PM, as ever, he would pull on blue overalls over his boots and leave down the road toward the roundhouse.

Once there he kept to deep night-shadow, he encircled the wide glare of the floodlights, he avoided anyone whom he saw approaching him. Standing concealed behind some dead engine, he watched the man who had taken his job.

Every night Stubby watched Luther Gulliday. Just before dawn he would start back, and Cass would be wakened by the flare of a match in the early dark. Stuart would be bending over the living-room table trying to light the old-fashioned lamp; but the wick had been dry for a long time, it would never light, the match would burn out on the bare dirt floor. Every morning Stubby tried to light the lamp, he never seemed to remember that it was dry; he seemed unable to understand why the wick would never flare. And Cass would see the fierce gash of his father's mouth in the match's glow, the straight line of the lips and the long jaw below it; the flickering flower of fire on Stubby's high cheek bones made the face look like a yellowing death's head, suspended in space.

"How ugly my father is!" the boy would think then, wondering whether he himself had a face that looked as long as a small horse's, all bespattered with freckles and soot.

With Nancy there was more than hunger. There was shame, and a growing despair at the meanness of her daily tasks, unrelieved by little save hymning on Sunday nights, or by small gossip with some other ragged girl after the pans and pots had been cleaned. On the streets she became so bitterly conscious of her outworn dress and her run-down heels and her stockingless legs that she ceased altogether to go into the American quarter of town. Only rarely would she leave the house to go farther than the dooryard.

Even to go to the relief station for supplies she disliked to leave the house. It became Cass's duty to go there because of her dislike for the task. Bryan had friends in the town to feed him, and he cared little whether Nancy ate or not. But once, when black-eyed peas were being distributed by the charity station, Cass became stubborn and refused to go. He said that it was now Bryan's turn, and said it so peremptorily that, at the last, Bryan made a pretense of going. He returned very shortly, empty-handed, saying that the agent had refused to help them any longer. Cass became uneasy and went to inquire, and so learned that Bryan had not been to the station.

Cass used to wonder about Bryan, watching him. He wondered how it would feel to be Bryan just for one day. Was there no way to learn how someone else felt? What was it that went on inside of heads all the time? Cass watched people, wondering about all of them. Could no one else know how he himself was inside, what went on inside *his* head? Sometimes in the morning when he arose he was sick almost. For was there never anything else but killing and cursing, sleeping and eating, drinking and fighting and working and cheating, day after day, for all men? Was this all that poor peopie did? Did everyone, everything, cats and hawks and men and women—did all of these live only to eat, fight and die? Even if no one chased them, kicked them or wrenched off their heads—did all of these die just the same? And when would he himself come to death? All through his boyhood Cass was never quite free of a sense of imminent death. All his boyhood he asked himself, "What else is there? Why?" It seemed to him then that in being a man there might be something more.

"Ah'd like to get out of this pesthole," he thought. "Ah'd like to see New Awlins."

And there came a morning in late October that Cass never forgot. Above the roof the sky was gray, and clouds like hands were pressing down. Stuart was sitting on the back porch when Cass got up that morning. Bryan had not come home the night before-hand Stubby was watching the road for him. He had not been to bed yet, and he had not eaten his morning oatmeal. Sometimes as he sat he would look down at the toes of his boots, then he would scuffle the toes together, regard their scarred leather a minute, and raise his eyes toward the road once more.

Cass was eating bread and rice when he heard Nancy's whisper: "When y'all git through eatin', go awn up the road a space an' head off yo' brother, do y' see he's again cornin' weavin'-like."

Cass toyed with the water in his coffee cup, and arranged crumbs in a pattern about the rice-bowl. Then he heard the porch door slam, and he thought that his father had left—till he heard his voice. And because his father's voice held a strangely complaining ring, Cass knew that he spoke to Bryan.

"Now where y' git it this time, eh? Ah tell'n thet Luke twicet now not to give it yo' any mo'. Who give it yo', eh? Give me over thet devil bottle." Cass heard his brother bawling, "Ah'll eat when ah'm hongry, ah'll drink when ah'm dry"—and the song was broken by the tinkling of glass breaking against a stove-lid. They were both in the kitchen then.

"Ah've *right* t' drink, ah have. Ah *needs* drink. Ah'm a sick man an' ah *works* fo' mah whiskey."

Cass didn't know what Bryan meant when he said he worked to get whiskey. And when Stuart spoke it was as though he did not realize that Bryan was drunk at all.

"Yo' elegant lyin' son-of-a-bitch, y' ain't done lick o' toil goin' on eight year. Ah knowed yo' was wuthiess first time ah seed yo', yo' weren't never nachrai. Yo' was bo'n with a caui an' been off plum evah since."

Bryan chuckled warmly, as though he and Stuart were sharing some excellent jest together. Bryan felt joyous inside, he was bubbling there, he felt as though he and his father ought to laugh over something together. He walked into the living room, flopped down on the chair in the corner and tilted leisurely against the wall.

Stubby followed, and Cass sat frozen over the careful pattern of brown crumbs on the faded green oilcloth.

"Ah ast yo' what yo' mean—yo' *works*?"

Bryan laughed boyishly up. Then he put his hand in his pocket and withdrew a dollar bill and a quarter. He wagged the bill under Stubby's nose, and tossed the quarter at Cass, and laughed so unrestrainedly that Cass had to raise his eyes.

He saw how smoky it was in the house. Smoky and dark. A dry wind whimpered about the east corner, like a child whimpering in sleep. Cass remembered being wakened in the night by the sound of low sobbing. He heard Nancy come into the doorway behind him, heard her feet pause there, knew that she too was afraid for her brother.

Bryan tilted forward in his chair and went to the center of the room on legs that knocked against each other like a pair of bone clacking-sticks. Stubby stood with legs spread wide, following Bryan now only with his eyes. Bryan leaned against the table with one hand and waved his dollar with the other, cheering it as though it were a flag; then his supporting hand slipped an inch, and the water in Cass's coffee cup slopped over the cup's brim onto the table.

As though seeing his father for the first time, Bryan began trying to focus his eyes upon him, wagging his head foolishly from side to side in the effort.

"W-well h-hell-oooo there," he stammered,—"Ol' nigger-finger." He extended the dollar to Stuart.

"Heah, Mex. Go git yo'se'f a gypsy whore."

Cass saw all the blood of his father's face drain out, he heard his father's breathing. He saw that Stubby was swaying a little, as though he too were drunk. Stubby's eyes were almost closed, and his mouth hung wider than it did in sleep. Suddenly he seemed a big man, a tall man, bigger and taller than Bryan, even though Bryan was really inches the taller. He put a hand on Bryan's shoulder so slowly that one might have thought he was going to speak to Bryan in friendly reproof—had it not been for his eyes being almost closed that way, and for the odd way that his mouth was hanging open. Stubby shook Bryan back and forth a little at first then, just a little at first; he didn't want to hurt Bryan, he just wanted to shake him a little—Cass could see that by the way he was doing it. He just wanted to shake Bryan a little, for being drunk all the time.

Yet, just for a minute, Cass was so afraid for his brother that he thought he was going to cry. Then Bryan began giggling while Stuart was shaking him, and Cass saw how really funny it looked to see a person going back and forth through the air like that, in and out of a loose blue coat—back and forth through the air like a white-faced jack-in-the-box in a ten-gallon hat. Up and down, back and forth, in and out of a flopping blue coat.

Outside the wind came muling down.

Perhaps it was the laughter, the fool's giggling that did it, for Stuart could not bear Bryan's unmanly laughter. Smash between the eyes with his fist like a hammer he hit him, and Bryan only said "Ooof- oof."

Cass smelled the terrible life-smelt of warm blood flowing;

he faced around and saw Bryan's features running together like water. Bryan wasn't chuckling to himself anymore. He was just standing there with his nose squashed in, and with his back to the table, while Nancy tried to get in front of him before Stuart struck again. But Stuart shoved her away with his right hand and hit Bryan again with his left.

Stuart didn't hit Bryan every time after that; his fists seemed to scrape and glance as though he could no longer see clearly. And Bryan just stood there trying to walk backwards like a craw-dad, and one eye was closed and one white piece of tooth showed obliquely through his lower lip; blood came bubbling over that lip, and he couldn't go any farther back because of the table behind him that wouldn't quite fall over, so he dangled his wrists in front of his face as though thinking that this might keep Stuart from hitting him between the eyes like that again. Cass couldn't hear a sound come out of Bryan's mouth; it looked to him like a fish's mouth, opening and closing. He saw Nancy trying to hold her father's fist, and he saw that she was saying something to Stubby; but Cass couldn't hear her words. Then Stuart hit Bryan twenty times ah at once; for just a moment after Bryan kept dangling his wrists in front of his face. Then the table slid slowly from under him, and he went over backward as it slid.

Cass saw him fall. He fell with the back of his head against a crate that had a faded picture of an orange on it. Cass saw this yet heard no sound. He saw Bryan struggling to rise and perceived that the left lapel of Bryan's coat had been burned, sometime in the past, directly beneath the collar. The label bore a little round brown hole there, the kind of a burn that is most often made by a cigar or a cigarette stub.

And suddenly now his brother looked so terrible, Hopping in

drunken helplessness there on the earthen floor, that Cass could bear to look no longer. Yet for one minute he could not tear his eyes away, for Stuart was not finished. He kicked Bryan in the groin with the toe of his boot. The flesh ripped, and tore. Cass saw it. Bryan lay with his head lolling against the sunkist orange, his knees bent and his legs wide. Between them Stuart's boot had torn the cloth of the suit so that Cass saw clearly what Stuart had done. Stuart did not see. He kept kicking, kicking mechanically.

Cass's mind went black and blank; he never remembered leaving the house.

When his senses collected he was walking slowly toward the S. P. water-tank with a resolution already reached in his mind never to go back. Even before he realized precisely where he was he had determined not to return. He had had enough of fighting and blood. He had had enough of cruelty. Always the sight of blood, or the mere thought of inflicting pain on another had revoked him. And now to see one man beating another, that man his own father, to see a helpless one beaten unmercifully, that one his own brother—this was beyond bearing. He was going somewhere now where men were somehow fess cruel. Some place where he would never see human blood helplessly spilling. He feared all blood; he dreaded men who spilled it.

Cass never became hardened to fighting. He was never to learn total indifference toward it. He was to live all his life among fighters, yet himself fight not once. He was to see men fight with guns and knives, with bare fists and with their teeth. All his manhood he would live with evil: with men who hated and mocked and fought, with strong men who were cruel to the weak, with men who were weak but were yet more cruel, and with men consumed with a wanton greed. Yet not once in his young manhood was he to see the shadow of pain cross a human face without being touched to the heart. He was never to see a blow struck or a man beaten, in all his young manhood, but he would be sickened almost to fainting.

3

CASS RODE ATOP a boxcar, watching the Texas hills roll by. "Leavin' them hills now," he kept telling himself, "lieavin' 'em fo' good an' all—leavin' paw an' po' Bry'n an' sister." And when he thought of Nancy his heart pained. But he was going to San Anton' now, that big city where the army lived, and he wasn't coming back. He was headin' from San Anton' to New Awlins, 'cause that was even bigger than Houston. Oh, he'd go everywhere now, everywhere he'd always wanted to go—Jacksonville, Shreveport, Montgomery and Baton Rouge. He'd see all the strange places he'd always wanted to see. He'd get tattooed like a sailor, all over his chest and arms.

As the train gathered speed and the night wore on the cold began to reach him; he climbed down into a gondola loaded with iron rails, seeking warmth there.

From sleep he woke with a sudden start, a warning heard in the jungle many months before ringing in his brain: "*The wheels slipped on the track an' two rails jolted loose an' damn ef one didn' go clearn through that Po' boy's belly . . .*"

He climbed once more atop the boxcar, but his body had cooled from his brief nap and he could not bear the biting cold. Carefully then he worked along the spine of the cars, afraid to stand upright because of the wind. When he reached a box with a loose hatchway he crawled inside. It was an empty cattle car, the door was covered with straw. Cass heaped several dusty armfuls in a corner and fell to sleep with a wadded yellow newspaper under his head for a pillow. He was very tired.

When he awoke it was morning, and slant light was flashing past into the gaps between the car's boarding. The train was approaching the yards in San Antonio, and he climbed out as it began to slow down.

Cass was gladdened and surprised to see a full twenty more 'boes come off with him, from several parts of the long van, and he fell in with them as they walked. All seemed headed for the same destination. Down the track a hundred yards they came to a frame house resembling a stable. Near the place, hunkered over wood fires, a dozen-odd men with empty faces waited. Cass paused before a sign on a fence, and spelled out a warning there; his lips moved as he read:

FREE SOUP KITCHEN AND CITY SHELTER—STAY
OUT OF TOWN AND KEEP OFF ALL TRAINS
NOT IN MOTION

He was suddenly aware that he was ravenously hungry.

As he was standing in line someone tapped his shoulder gently; he turned his head, and such a man as he had never before seen in all his life stood before him. A tall man in khaki, in glistening black boots, with badges and buttons, with red stripes and gold braid. And this apparition was speaking to *him*, Cass McKay.

"Boy, don't you know you're wasting your life?" it asked.

Cass cocked his head; he hadn't known. He wanted to reach out one finger, to touch that bright braid.

"Riding the rods I mean—that's wasting your life, ain't it? The army makes men out of green kids like you."

Cass grinned a half-grin with one side of his face. His nose was running, so he licked up with his tongue.

"The government wants men to send to China, the Philippine Islands, Cuba, Haiti—you couldn't ever get to Haiti by riding the rods, now could you, son?"

Cass wasn't very certain; but someone in back barked at the sergeant: "No—and he couldn't get a bullet up his arse in Nicaragua if he stayed at home, neither."

A few of the bums laughed, but the sergeant seemed only annoyed. "Well, he'll never lose a leg under a freight train by joinin' the infantry, wise-guy back there," and he turned again to Cass. "Don't never listen to wise-guys, son. They'll poison your mind against your own country. An' I'll bet you're straight from the Big Bend country, aren't you, son?" He asked this last with a friendly white smile, and placed one friendly hand on Cass's shoulder. Cass drew back from that hand; he remembered his father's hand, on his brother's shoulder.

And he looked down, and he saw that this man wore pointed boots.

"Ah guess ah don't want to join no army today, mister," he said.

The sergeant put one gloved finger under Cass's chin, and lifted Cass's face to his own. "Why not? You have no physical defect, have you? You haven't got anyone dependent on you, have you, son?"

Cass stared, he didn't know what all those *lawng* words meant. "You haven't . . ."

The man in the back iet out a warning whoop—"Don't listen to that army-pander, kid—Uncle Sam is a old he-whore and that guy is his youngest pimp."

A few laughed faintly, moving up an inch. The sergeant blinked and feigned not to hear. "Have you any physical defect, son?" he persisted quietly.

"Yeah, ah reck'n," Cass said.

The sergeant frowned, spat fiercely toward earth to conceal a self-doubt, hesitated a second and passed on down the line, surveying prospects. Cass heaved a long sigh of relief. To the man in front of him he whispered, "Is that some gen-rel? Do he git paid much?"

"Five dollars for every kid he recruits, that's all he gets."

Cass drew in breath in amazement. "Gawsh a-mighty," he gasped. Then he thought, "Why, hell—that old feller was a-doin' the same thing ah used to do fo' Pepita back home. Oney ah didn't get no five bucks apiece, ah just got a sack o' terbacco or a Mex nickel."

When he got inside the doors something within his stomach's pit took a cold little slippery flop, nauseating him momentarily—each man in the line ahead, he saw, was writing his name in a book before receiving food. Fear strove with hunger then. He became afraid that he might not remember how to write his name, for it had been long since he had learned how. But he was shoved ahead by those behind until it was his turn. Then he thought wildly, "Ah'll make a stab—ah'll just bluff the whole bunch—mebbe ah'll be able to do it agen if ah do it suddent-like." He picked up the pencil, felt eyes on him, made a long swift scribble and grabbed for a plate. Although no one seemed to see, it was not until he was safely seated at the rough board table in the dining room that he again drew easy breath. On his plate was a square of cornbread afloat in black molasses.

The smell of unclean bodies mingled in the heavy air with the smell of beans boiling in the kitchen. All about him men were eating, and the doors and walls were smeared with mud and scraps of food. One place at the bench whereon he sat was vacant because someone had vomited there, in an orange-ed puddle.

Cass watched those about him as he ate, wondering about each of them. Most were boys. One or two gray-beards, but only one or two. Not half a dozen out of thirty, all told, who even approached middle age. Three Mexican boys, sitting at a separate table; eight Negroes, ranging from twelve years to twenty, on a bench equally segregated; and the rest sitting at the table where he sat, with faces American and much like his own. High-cheekboned, thin-lipped, blue-eyed faces. Several he thought younger than himself.

One had a face as fruity as a cherub's, a rosy, soft and smiling face that had not yet lost the rounded contours of its infancy. When the counterman asked this boy his name, the lad replied swiftly, "I'm Thomas Clay; I'm thirteen-and-a-half-goin'-on-fourteen—gimme an extra lot o'beans an' two cups o' misery an' I'll tell you some more."

A little stout man with a huge breadth of chest and shoulders and a small bent nose in a perfectly circular face appeared in the doorway and roared jovially at everyone:

"Directly yo' all finish eatin', couple you boys step out heah an' give me a han' with a bit of kindlin'—takes kindlin' to cook yo' all cawnbread yo' know."

He said this so smilingly, so pleasantly, that three who had already finished rose immediately to help him. Then the others were set to cleaning dishes and making up the wooden bunks on the second floor. Cass wanted to bathe, he was caked with coaldust; but he saw no sign of a shower or a tub and he lacked the courage to ask. With a dozen other American boys, each with a pan and a bucket, he was set to sorting raw beans; letting these trickle through their fingers, a handful at a time, the boys picked out small stones and foreign matter.

Cass found himself working beside the lad of the cherubic aspect. In an undertone the boy confided to Cass that the information he had given the counterman was false; his real name, he said, was not Thomas Clay but Thomas Clancy, his true age not twelve but sixteen, and the time he had spent on the road nearer four years than four months.

He had run away from a reform school in Cleveland, he added, when he was twelve, and had been on the road ever since that time. Cass did not know which tale was true and did not greatly care.

The long afternoon wore on; as soon as one sack was picked through the counterman brought out another, and Cass's eyes began to burn with the strain of keeping them fastened on his palms in the darkness of the place. There were no lights, the place was damp as a tomb. The counterman told them that when night came they would have to double up on bunks upstairs.

Shortly before dark—Cass was again feeling hungry—the friendly fellow of the forenoon came in. He stood in the doorway as he had done in the morning, shutting out the gray October light with shoulders so square that he gave the impression of wearing a two-by-four plank under his coat. For a minute he said nothing. Then he planted his feet wide beneath him, and drunkenness pumped out in his voice. And he spoke hard—hard as a fighting man might speak, after a hard defeat.

"Git to thet woodpile now, ye tramps, ye goddamned pesky go-about bastards—y'all been eatin' an' crappin' roun' heah sence mo'nin' now—git t' thet woodpile o' git yo' arse in the in-fun-tree, one o' the other."

His right hand kept jerking over his shoulder to the lumber yard.

"Woodpile o' in-fun-tree, one o' the other."

He repeated this several times, then cursed them all once more and abruptly walked away. The counterman began to laugh; but even as he did so he checked himself, for, surprisingly enough, the little man had returned.

"Git in th' army o' elts git t' thet woodpile, ah says—tha's what ah says. Shet down th' goddamned charity-suckin', bum-feedin' bean'ry racket—that's what ah been tellin' 'em all. Put the sonsabitches in th' army or put th' sonsabitches to work—tha's the idee—sweat the bastards' balls off—teach th' pesky go-abouts to keep out o' Texas—tha's what ah tells 'em all, uptown."

He cast a challenging eye about the room, saw no one uncowed, and left once more. This time he did not return, and the counterman finished his laugh, albeit somewhat sheepishly now. None of the men at the tables joined with him; somehow, absurd as the little man had sounded, not one felt like laughing. All sat silent at their idiot's task, letting the little brown kidney-shaped beans run through their fingers, looking morosely down at their palms. Such a ring of authority had there been in that drunken voice that it had left every man and boy of them inwardly agitated. The words had sounded too much like an alternative offered by one perfectly sober. It had left them troubled, resentful, and fearful of they scarcely knew what. It had made each man too sharply aware that he was an outcast—an outcast sorting pebbles out of small brown beans on the sufferance of society, an outcast whose next job might be that of shooting down outcasts in other lands—on the sufferance of society. The feeling was not good.

An hour before midnight the man to Houston whistled past. Cass and Thomas Clay crouched under an embankment until the engine passed, and Cass ventured the guess that there would be but few empties in the string, judging by the engine's hard straining. They could not find even a cattle-car unclosed; everything rolling was sealed. Cass became a bit afraid that the entire string would go by and leave them behind for another ten-hour wait; but Clay insisted on an empty, and Cass wanted companionship. Clay could not be hurried. "I'm kind of pooped out t'night," he complained. "You kin grab anythin' you feel like grabbin', but me, I want an empty so's I can sleep. These S. P. reefers feel like you're settin' 'top a wobbly waffle iron—Jeez, they make dents in my fanny so's I can't walk straight all next day." An empty ore car came rolling by. Since the cab itself was but six cars behind this, Clay had to consent to hopping it. He went up first, and Cass ran with the car till Clay was on the last rung of the ladder before he himself hopped.

Clay clung to the side, peering down into the darkness. He would not jump till he could see into what he was jumping. He saw that the car was unloaded, that its sides sloped steeply to the center, and that there two chutes gaped wide. Beneath the chutes he caught the glint of rolling wheels; and he turned his head to say that they would have to find another car.

Cass was already coming up—when he reached the top he leaped past Clay, with a victor's shout, and flung himself over the side onto the slant steel floor. Clay swung over swiftly, saw a white hand sliding downward in darkness, and mashed his shoe down on its knuckles. He felt Cass fumbling at his heel, felt him clutch his leg—and for three long miles it was thus they rode, the one clinging fiercely to the car's steel side, the other clinging no less fiercely to the leg he could not see. In those brief minutes Cass saw the wheels below his toes, and remembered in terror a boy in a dark shirt sprawled in sand among cinders; he saw again a Mexican girl who had come for coal with a doll carriage.

When the train went into a hole for a passenger engine Clay gave him his hand, and Cass hitched himself up to safety. He was caked with coal dust, his face was bruised in a dozen places, he had lost his cap and skinned the knees out of his overalls; but he shouted, "Ah'm obleeged, fella." The other made no reply. Cass began to laugh then, uncontrollably, at nothing at all; he laughed until his knees were shaking and his eyes were wet, and he could not stop even when he saw Clay looking at him in amazement. He became so weak with laughter that when Clay left him to seek another car he could not follow his friend for several minutes. By the time that he felt able to follow, Clay had disappeared somewhere down the spine. Cass was too shaken to follow far. He found an oil tanker, and sat all night with his back braced against the rounded side and his legs against a coupling, watching the Texas hills go by.

In the morning, in Houston, he found Clay once more; they went uptown to the Sally together. After eating they snuck out the rear entrance to avoid work, and returned to the Soupline tracks. Before dark they were on their way to New Orleans.

Cass could not sleep a wink that night for thinking of New Orleans. "Ah'll bet there's places to git tattooed on every corner, an' showhouses an' whorehouses with Creole gals." Twice he saw small yellow lights gleaming in distance, and both times he had to rouse Clay, thinking he saw the lights of New Orleans. One city was about the same as another to Clay, however, and he merely rolled over, grumbling, "Fella, I've told you nine times now we can't hit New Orleans before light. Them lights is still in Texas. You'd best be gettin' yourself some rest whiles you still can get it."

But Cass could not sleep. He sat in the open doorway of the swaying box, his legs dangling over the side, trying not to remember Nancy.

Great dim forests rose out of darkness, rose and fell to rise again; stretches of field where he smelled cane-soil, cone-shaped hills of high-heaped rice-husks that even in daytime would have looked like soft-coal mounds. The car roared through tiny hamlets darkened and steeping, and Cass fancied he smelled the wind off the Gulf. Sometimes sudden valleys opened beneath him—so deep that he drew himself back in brief fear; and just before dawn he grew very tired and curled up beside Clay to take a short nap. When he woke Clay was standing above him, sullenly digging him in the ribs with his toe.

The car was rolling very slowly. Cass blinked out into sun-lit fields. Then he jumped to his feet, brushed straw off his coat, and rolled a cigarette with Clay. How long he had slept! He saw by the sun that it was well past ten o'clock.

When they leaped to the ground Cass thought to see people— thousands of men and women, all rushing, all shoving and mauling and pushing each other; he thought to see towering buildings and streetcars roaring like trains through the midst of the press. But to his dismay he was still on the prairie, with only the long steel track ahead, and only the back end of a retreating caboose to amaze him. After walking a few miles they came to the houses of the Negro suburbs—little one-story shacks much like his own had been. Clay informed him that they now were in Gretna and that New Orleans lay west across the river. They turned down a pleasant street called Copernicus Avenue. A shaded, quiet little street lined by clean white cottages on either side; from porches and lawns Negro children paused in play to watch them as they passed.

"Goddamn," Cass swore, "Ah nevah did see so many jigs in all mah life befo'—where ah come from we have lynchin' bees to keep the population down." He spoke loudly, in order that Clay would think he was tough.

Clay grunted assent. "Yep, niggers got all the jobs, everywhere, an' that's why you'n me is on the road. Up north they's six dinges for every telygraph pole. A white man don't stand a chance no more, anywhere."

When they reached the ferry a nickel apiece was required. Clay paid for both without hesitation, but was irritated to see Cass take no apparent notice—Cass walked straight ahead onto the boat as though he owned half the wharf.

The truth was that Cass had really not seen, it had not even occurred to him that a fare might be required. And when they were half way across the river he turned to Clay and inquired, without even blushing from shame of ignorance, "Say, what ol' river u this anyhow, fella?"

Clay looked at him to see if he were joking; he himself knew every large river from coast to coast. He saw that Cass was in earnest, and he saw too that Cass looked as dull as an ox with its jaw hanging open.

"The Hudson," Clay said, and spat over the railing.

Cass only said "Oh." He did not doubt for a moment, and did not sense the other's contempt.

When the ferry docked Clay left him alone, walking off swiftly without a word. Cass was hurt, yet was not surprised. He merely thought to himself, "He just sees ah'm not like most others, that's all. Reck'n ah'm a queer cuss one way or another." It had happened often before, back in Great-Snake Mountain; so often there that he had grown up to expect others to go off from him, sooner or later. He did not understand this, he merely resigned himself to it.

He felt dreadfully alone.

He was not deeply concerned about eating or sleeping; yet he did wish to bathe, and he had no money. Seeing nothing which looked to him like a Sally, he asked the way of a fat fellow who stood about doing nothing. The fat one pointed silently straight down the street, and Cass went to a building bearing the sign: "Volunteer Prisoners' Aid Society." He could not read every word of this sign, and thought he was entering a Salvation Army home.. The man at the desk shook his head sadly—there was a fee here of twenty-five cents. If he didn't have that he'd best go somewhere else. "Six blocks to the left and four down is a place. You'll see the sign, bub."

"Six blocks to the left and four down" proved to be twelve to the left, and ten down. Cass walked from one side of the city to the other before he finally found the place, and then recognized it only by a line of men waiting in front.

It was the Jesus-Saves mission.

Here he was given a little pile of something made from shredded cabbage and carrots, and a cup of cold chicory-coffee. While eating, he learned that there was a shower in the basement. The coffee gave him the courage to ask the commandant's permission to bathe. But a blank had to be filled out before this could be done—and when the commandant gave him a pencil and paper in the office Cass almost wished he had not asked at all. It had been so long since he had teamed to read and write that now it only came with an effort. But he labored manfully with the pencil, and succeeded in writing his name again, after a fashion. As the official led him to the head of the staircase that wound down into the basement, he warned that the shower was cold. Cass cared not a button. Not even the descent into the chill cellar could dishearten him.

To get under the shower he had to wait some minutes for his turn. An old man stood under the feeble stream, scrubbing painful old joints. Cass waited in the doorway for him to finish. The light was so dim, the old man's belly was so large, that its navel looked to Cass like a small incurved tunnelling into gray flesh such as he had seen small mole-things make in gray earth.

There was one other in the tiny room—the louse-runner, a lank and pockmarked man of perhaps sixty years. Cass watched this delouser, and he began to feel ashamed that he would have to undress and be naked before such a man. The fellow had a shameless eye, and a searching manner. And Cass was ashamed to be naked before anyone, for he felt that others could read too much of his life in the scars of his body, in his rounded shoulders, his pigeon chest, in the thinness of his arms and legs. His blood was still unquiet from the shame he had felt at being unable to write more than his name when the commandant had given him the pencil.

The louse-runner was crouched now over the old man's clothes like a vulture hanging over a dung-heap. Holding his hands before his face beneath the little light, he rose slowly, with deliberation, studying his cupped palms as he rose. They were running with lice. He kicked the bundle off to the side without taking his eyes from his hands, and the old man held his head wistfully to one side, like an intelligent parrot.

"Extryord'nary," he piped, "extryord'nary."

The louse-runner brushed him from under the shower and stretched his hands under the water, rubbing his palms like cymbals together, as though to crush to mere pulp whichever lice might be so fortunate as to escape death through drowning. Then he shouted over his shoulder to someone unseen, and a pimple-faced youth with black rubber gloves came tearing down the stairs, took up the bundle in over-nice fingers, and carried it away to be fumigated.

Cass began to undress then. Slowly. How sorry he felt for that old man! How ashamed he had looked! But what if he himself should be found to have lice on him? The very thought made him desire retreat, even at this late hour. Better go dirty or wash in some river somewhere than to risk such shame! He felt the louse-runner watching, and he undressed more swiftly. Why must the man stare so? Did he think he might be a girl?

No socks to take off, no underwear. Dirt was frozen on him. The flesh of his arms and chest was blue-white, hairless and goose-pimpled. How ashamed he was to be so ugly!

The shower was as cold as the commandant had warned him, but there was plenty of a strong brown soap; by diligent scrubbing he got most of the dirt off, albeit in the process his fingers became numb with cold. He felt the louse-runner looking closely again, as he scraped at his ankles. "Ah'd do some better if he'd quit a-lookin' at me like as if ah was some cold-shouldered colt," Cass thought to himself.

The ordeal finished, he was given his clothes. For a moment Cass had the illogical notion that the louse-runner was disappointed at not having encountered a single louse in his overalls. When he was dressed Cass asked him for a cap, for it was cold in the place. The louser brought the matter before the commandant, in the latter's office. There the commandant placed the entire responsibility back onto the louser's shoulders. After some rummaging then, in the depths of the office clothes-closet, Cass was awarded a cotton cap that fitted down snugly over both ears and shaded his eyes with a peak so large that it lent him the aspect of a frequently-defeated jockey.

Observing himself in it in a little cracked tin mirror hanging on the clothes-closet door, he said to the commandant, "God *damn*, don't it look jest *fine*, mister?" The commandant stiffened, Cass became afraid, the man was standing up and pointing to a red and white card on the far wall. Helplessly Cass looked at him, wondering with increasing fright what thing he had said or done to provoke this man's anger.

"Ah caint read all that, mister—them's too *lawng* words." The commandant read for him, still pointing with outstretched arm.

IF YOU MUST USE PROFANITY PLEASE
STEP OUT IN THE ALLEY

Cass began to feel a little better, and under his breath cursed both commandant and louse-runner roundly.

Later he wandered past the old French graveyard on Basin Street, and strolled, for curiosity's sake, in and out of stores on Canal. In the Southern Railroad depot he found a fountain where water ran cold as ice. Then he walked back to Canal, remembering the wharves. He found the Desire Street wharf deserted, hung his shoes on a beam, padded his cap into a pillow, and slept. When he woke the sun was beginning to slant, and the river had turned from brown to cold green. Cass rose refreshed, and resumed his strolling.

All that late November afternoon he walked New Orleans in unconcern, caring not in the least which way he wandered. He passed by houses great and tall, stone mansions with strong iron gates; gates which barred wide paths winding through pleasant lawns. He looked through windows and saw white walls with pictures hanging; dimly Cass envied those within. He came, too, to houses much like his own had been: poor, unpainted, wooden … He saw black children who played within sight and smell of unmentionable filth, in alleys where gray rats ran. He saw the clean children of the rich, that they were quick and bold. On Melpomene Street he saw a young Negress with a baby on her back, pawing in a garbage barrel like an angular black cat. All afternoon Cass wandered.

Then it began to grow dark, and he forgot all that had happened at home and all that he had been on the road, for the lights of New Orleans came on, and he had never seen any lights quite so bright.

The lights of the city! The sounds of the street! It was just as though somewhere a switch had been thrown, making all things of a sudden gay and brilliant and beautiful, just for him. Canal Street thronged with men and women, a thousand gay faces passed him by. Signs went on and off. Everyone was happy and laughing, everyone was talking, everyone hurried. The people were almost as he had imagined—but such lights he had not dreamed of. Cass had never heard such sounds. Green and blue and red the lights, flashing on and off and dancing; loud and soft and strange the sounds, all wonderfully confused. Directly above his head an orchestra blared through open windows into the southern night, and Cass stood long with neck upturned and mouth agape. And after a while he walked on, and he came to a quieter place. Signs went on and off. Then he came to a street where there were no signs.

Cass came to a street that lay all deserted and unlit by any lamp or little window-gleam, and he went down a walk so narrow that on it but one could pass at a time. And he felt that all houses here were evil and old, that all their shades were drawn for shame; and that though the street was deserted and dark, yet there were women behind the shades; and that though the street was so soundless, so sad, behind the curtains men were laughing. So he walked on, and walked always more softly.

A girl stepped out of a doorway he had not seen, hooked him by the arm and looked up smiling. A foolish smile, weak. Then she pursed her lips that were pale as death, and spoke in a blurred Alabama drawl. "Look daddy, y'all like to sleep with me tonight? Ah'm clean as cotton, daddy, an' y'all kin take yo' own good time." They were almost to the corner, where streets were lit luridly. The girl spoke swiftly, urging him to walk slowly. "Y'all don't have to pay me till yo' see what yo' gettin'. Don't have to pay me till after-while, hon, if yo' don't want to pay me right off."

She placed his hand on her breast, and he paused. Wonderingly Cass touched her, pressing her breast half fearfully. How soft that was! Cass had never touched a woman before; as in a haze now he remembered the dark girls in back of the Poblano Cafe. She drew him aside and let him explore her until she felt that he was aroused; then she led him back to the doorway from which she had hailed him. She led him easily. His heart began zig-zagging wildly, desire and daring sent warm waves through his flesh. Should he? Should he take the chance—without money? Well, hadn't she said he didn't have to pay until after while? Maybe he'd only . . . maybe by then . . . His head was whirling, his thoughts raced crazily. When they reached the doorway he put down desire for a moment and drew back to tell her he had not a penny. But she caressed him into the passageway before he could speak three words.

Somewhere in the back a man was laughing, a young man, judging by his laughter. The doors of the passage were numbered; against No. 14 Cass set aside his misgivings. He took her about and kissed the pale lips. The girl knew every trick to arouse him, and he pressed her against the door with all the thin strength of his loins. She laughed, a metallic little laugh, then struggled free and opened the door against which he pressed her.

After the lock clicked behind her she lit a small lamp. Its glow lit faintly on the wall a picture of a bleeding heart in an oval frame. The girl went to the bed and sat on its edge, fingering a small silver cross at her throat. Seated beside her, Cass put his arms about her; sweat began rolling down the inside of his shirt from under his armpits. The girl rose and turned down the lamp till its flare was small as a match's glow . . .

Cass slept only briefly; when he woke it was still dark. He woke with a start, with a fear at his heart. Fear that the girl might waken before he got out. He became so afraid that he could scarcely breathe in his anxiety to get through the door.

Yet he knew he had to take it easy, rise softly, step softly, go soft as a cat across the floor, softly as a young cat just half way across the room. The door was locked. He turned the knob all the way around twice without making a sound; he put all his weight against it without making a noise. It was locked, but he knew where the key was. He'd seen it on her dresser, saw it now in the dimness from where he stood. But when he reached the dresser what he had thought was a key proved to be only a small silver nail file. He opened a drawer, it had to be in there since it wasn't on top. The dresser squeaked, and behind him he heard the whore jump up; in the dresser mirror he saw that, naked as she was, she stood at the door to block his way out. Cass turned about slowly, a half-grin smeared over half his face, his hair hanging in his eyes. He was faint with such fear as before he had never known.

How savage she stood! All naked and snarling!

"Nancy! Nancy!" Cass wanted to shout, "Nancy—come help me now!"

But there was no room in his throat for a sound; his throat seemed closed with fear. It was the girl who called out.

"Jack! Jack Gaines!" she shrilled like a magpie, "Jack! Jack Gaines!"

Cass heard heavy feet come pounding through darkness, a side-door opened and a half-clad blond came in. He was breathing heavily; the hair on his chest seemed matted with sweat. Cass watched the chest, saw its yellow matting moving, rhythmically up and down, the while the fellow regained his breath.

"The fartsnatcher ain't give me a dime yet, Jackie, an' he tried to heel out with mah ring on top of it. Ah'm gettin' tired of gettin' rooked by every punk who comes along—see what he got an' whatever yo' gits."

Cass saw the rouster coming toward him in a half-crouch, like a professional wrestler. For just one moment then it seemed to Cass that someone was tickling him in the pit of the stomach with a blood-tipped feather—and he was on the floor beneath the man, and the feather was a sharp-pointed stick jabbing and splintering in his gut. He found his voice with his face thrust nose-deep in carpet.

"Ah got nothin', mister—ol' girl tol' me ah didn' *have* to pay nothin'—ah was but lookin' fo' th' key—ah was but—"

A short swift blow with the heel of the palm caught his tongue full between his teeth and sent red waves of red pain into his brain; so that of a sudden he saw Bryan lying flat on his back and Stuart above him, kicking. Such strength did fear then give him that he threw off the heavy rouster with a single effort of his back, struggled crazily to his feet and raced in blind panic to the hall door, forgetting that that door was locked. Straining at the knob, he heard the rouster coming up behind him, turned and dodged the fellow, and tore across the room to the side-door standing wide.

The last thing Cass recalled was the white blur of the girl's body beneath the red blur of a bleeding heart. She was in that doorway with her legs spread wide, she was holding the bed-post with her left hand—and some dark and heavy thing hung straight down out of the right.

Pain wakened Cass. A long, slow-starting, zig-zag pain that began in his viscera and ran jaggedly upward with gathering speed until it flashed like an orgasm beneath his heart, and left him sick and sweating. Twice it went through him like an electric bolt, leaving him each time sicker, number.

Cass did not open his eyes; he did not wish now to waken. He was cold, and frightened by the severity of his pain so that, as he sweated, he trembled a little. He did not wish to wake up. He wanted to sleep now. He wanted to sleep so long that he would never wake up. If once he opened his eyes, he knew, he would have to start living all over again. He would have to get to his feet and see men and women, would have to be tired and cold and alone. He would have to go begging, be mocked, shamed and beaten.

So he lay long, in the place where he was, and he would not

open his eyes. And he could not return to sleep because of the pain in his belly. Then he began to feel cold, so cold; so cold that when he touched the roof of his mouth with his tongue he thought that, whatever was wet there, was frozen.

And because he was so utterly wretched, being unable to sleep or to rise, he whimpered. Tears forced his eyes open, he saw where he lay.

He was lying in an open lot that appeared to be chiefly a dumping ground. It smelled of dead flesh. The first thing he saw clearly was the head of a dog whose body was gone. That head smiled amiably, there were ants in both eyes. He rose stiffly, wondering that no one had seen him lying there. New Orleans was already gray with morning.

Cass did not know where to go, he did not know quite where he was. And he didn't care greatly, one way or the other, and walked on only to avoid the stares that strangers would give him should he stand still. He could think only of Nancy, could only wish that he were not alone now. Nancy would tend him, tend him out of love. He touched his face, gingerly, and he felt dry blood beneath his chin—blood dried into clots like great rough scabs there. And down from the corner of his mouth ran a deep furrow into the flesh—his mouth jerked sidewise when he tried to touch the wound. Apparently the devils had tried to cut his throat.

He was too ill to walk very far at a stretch. Every few hundred yards he sat down on curbstone or step. He was glad that it was still early morning so that there were not many people—strangers—to stare at him as he rested. People—strangers—to stare as he sat. All people were strangers, he was born to be stared at. His belly burned for water.

Resting on a wooden bench in front of a little Italian grocery,

Cass watched two children at play. Black children, skipping. For a minute he almost forgot his own wretchedness in watching their joy. But the man from the grocery came out, looked at him twice, shrugged his shoulders, and told him he would have to sit somewhere else. The bench was for customers, he had no room inside for it, his customers came out here and ate breakfast upon it. He might have a customer any minute now. Perhaps the customer would like to sit on the bench. Perhaps the customer would like to sit on the bench with nobody near him when he ate breakfast.

When Cass rose that time he felt as though somebody had just turned on an electric fan in his belly that whizzed hot dry air in long ripples down his stomach's lining. Long dry ripplings, all the way down, with a whirring there as of many blades. He felt the fingers of one hand with those of the other: they were cold. His head: it was hot. People were passing, morning was blue-gray again; and he needed a drink of water.

He walked till he saw a filling station, and he looked about for a hose. There was no one about the station that he could see. A fuzzy ball of a police pup lapped water from the tank wherein inner-tubes were tested. Inside, between a safe and a rack of colorful road maps, Cass saw water in a tall glass barrel. Paper cups were hanging above it. But before he'd taken two steps toward it, a voice behind him called him back.

"They's nothin' inside for you there, bub. The can is around the rear."

Cass turned and saw the attendant, a dashing fellow in white overalls. He was cranking gas swiftly into the tank of a maroon roadster with frosted-sugar headlights.

"Ah oney want a drink is all," Cass said turning half way around.

The attendant made no reply. He kept cranking endlessly, bending a little as he cranked and watching the hand of the pump-clock swinging. Cass watched too, while little tongues of flame singed the roof of his mouth. The mission would be on the other side of town—and he had to drink *right now*. The puppy lapped noisily at his feet; Cass had an urge to kick it and run. The attendant walked around the other side of the roadster to inspect its oil; no one was watching.

Carefully, cautiously with averted eyes, he lifted the pup off the ground with his shoe, holding it by its furry middle, and flung it hard as he was able toward the cement base of the pump. It landed softly, sprawling against stone, yelped once as it regained its feet, sneezed and went off sneezing.

That made Cass feel a little better; as though the boot had been put on the other foot for a change. As though he had just outwitted an enemy. And then it seemed to Cass that he could *smell* all that water standing so near, with all the clean white paper cups hanging right above it. He could smell it while his throat shriveled for one wet drop—he turned, ripped cups down, caught one after dropping three; and then, in using both hands to turn on the water, crushed the cup flat between his palms. As he stooped to retrieve one which he had dropped, the water began flooding the floor; he forgot about cups in a desperate effort to close the faucet before he was caught. In his haste he jammed the handle; the floor was littered with paper cups, it seemed to him, before he finally slammed the faucet off—paper cups afloat in a flood like a back-flooding sewer.

"Whew!" he gasped, stepping back, having in his excitement almost forgotten his thirst, "Whew! Ah shet it jest in time."

But it hadn't been in time at all.

"Well, isn't this nice now, I must say. Couldn't you leak a little on the desk for me too before you have to be leaving?"

This voice was a whip, contemptuously coiling. Cass flinched as though he were about to be spat upon—then a hand on his collar, he was reel-spinning through space; he was going face-forward; he felt the boot bite in deep, deep at the base of the spine where his father's boot would have bitten, sending him onto the concrete of the driveway with his wrists straining stiffly in front of his face to save himself a bruised nose as he fell. Then he picked up and ran, dodging crazily in and out of Canal Street traffic, fancying the attendant hard on his heels. He ran along the steep curbing, while passersby stared for two full blocks. Then he could go no farther; he could have run not one step farther that time had there been a whole mob of attendants at his heels all shouting "Law that guy!"

And his throat, if it had known thirst before, was now varnished with it, like an asphalt road smoking in sun. He could not even spit now, he could not dampen his lips with his tongue. Hard hands were wringing his stomach out, as Nancy would wring out a gray dish rag. And his stomach was nothing more than a dark furnace for his thirst. Traffic was picking up down South Rampart; from an unseen corner a peanut-whistle twittered tinnily.

No one had spoken of thirst in the jungle. He had not been told about being kicked. Nobody had said much about shame and mockery.

He went into the first restaurant he saw and found it crowded with men eating oatmeal. The waitresses were too rushed to say "No," so Cass just stood there, a little inside the door and a little off to the side, shifting uneasily from one loot to the other. And when he became too ashamed to stand and shift that way any longer, he left.

On the corner of Camp and Felicity people were thronging out of a church. Dimly Cass wondered whether Catholics would drink holy water if they were as thirsty as he was and had no other water to drink. Then the hands on his stomach were hard and callused, as Nancy's hands had become; he walked on while they wrenched and wrung, thinking of Nancy and Nancy's hands. Till he came to a second gas station. The water-tank here was enamelled white. A slender bronze statue stood on its peak, a little naked man with wings on both heels, standing on tiptoe as though preparing to glide off the tank and by out the door into the sun above the Camp Street palms.

Cass looked about a little more covertly than before. This time he would do differently; this time he would plead so piteously that he could not be denied.

The attendant was a Negro.

"What is it, son?" he asked just as though he really thought Cass might reply, "Ten gallon o' gas in mah lawng maroon roadster."

The black face was smiling like a full moon in eclipse. It looked, somehow, kind.

"Mister, kin ah git a drink heah?"

"Sho! Theah!"

But he wasn't pointing straight at the ice-water tank with the little bronze man on its peak. He was pointing off to the side a little. He was pointing, in fact, to the radiator hose. Meekly Cass went there and drank from a rusty nozzle. The water was warm, with the warmth of stale urine, a sticky, sweetish-sour warmth like that of sodden pickles. When it trickled through his fingers it trickled dark amber; in the palm of one hand it left small specks like the specks that flies leave in summer in milk. Perhaps, Cass thought, such specks were only soot. "Just good ol' root, that's all.

Mebbe them little speck-things'll just make it meaty-like, sort of, so's ah wont have to hunt up that derned Jesus-Saves joint all over town agen."

After he had swilled down almost a pint of the muddy stuff, he washed the dotted blood off his mouth and dried his lips on the back of his hand.

He didn't feel any better, somehow. He felt sick. He felt sick and lonely. He didn't want to go to Jacksonville after all. He didn't even want to see Baton Rouge. He wanted to go home.

And with no further ado he turned toward the wharves.

4

WHEN CASS CAME to the ferry he saw that a fare was required, and he formed the hasty opinion then that the ferry was free were one going west across the river, but cost a nickel when one went east. He stood at the side in his tattered overalls with blood on his mouth half-coagulated, while hot bolts of pain tore him and thirst came anew, and he begged. He begged humbly, with one palm outstretched. An elderly woman put a nickel in the box for him, and he limped out onto the boat.

It took him two hours to retrace the streets he had walked with Clay on the previous morning. When he reached the S.P. tracks at noon, he lay down in spare and cindery grass, and slept with his shoe for a pillow. He did not waken until the freight to Houston roused him; it took all his strength to swing up a ladder. As soon as he found an empty he fell once more to sleep, this time to waken only to change freights in Houston, early in the morning hours. On the outskirts of San Antonio he ate at the same beanery where he had eaten with Clay the week before. for had his name really been Clancy?) That same night he was on his way back to Great-Snake Mountain.

Slouched down in the cool dark of a fruit-car reefer, he smelled thousands of ripening oranges all night. All night long he smelled them. He could see them dimly, stacked high as the roof, only a few feet from his finger-tips. He would have liked to suck on one for a while, but because of the reefer's steel screening there was no reaching them at all.

He had learned that for him, Cass McKay, there was no escape from brutality. He had learned that, for him, there was no asylum from evil or pain or long loneliness. It might be that for others there was something different; but for him lonely pain and lonely evil were all that there was in the whole wide world. The world was a cruel place, all men went alone in it. Each man went alone, no two went together. Those who were strong beat those who were weak. They who said they loved Jesus wore little spiked boots, and those who kept silent ran swiftly away. There was only one God, and he was a devil; he was everything that there was in the world, for he was all pain and all evil. He was all that was secret and dark and unclean. There were only two kinds of men wherever you went—the men who wore boots, and the men who ran. You must not try to take that which belonged to another unless you were strong enough to keep it when that other found out. Otherwise you would be kicked into a jailhouse. If you could get much you were strong, and therefore good; God gave to the strong and took from the weak. He was on the side of the ones who rode in autos, who lived in white houses: he was as big as County Sheriff Shultz, as rich as Judge Bankhead from Presidio, pious as the Reverend Benjamin Cody, and fierce as the rancher Boone Terry.

He, Cass, was on the other side, because he himself was so weak. He was weak, for his father was poor and his brother was sick, and his sister was ragged and his mother was dead, and he lived in Mexican-town.

Somehow now Cass felt that he was walking in darkness, below a high dark wall, a shadow among many shadows. He didn't know whose many forms walked before and behind him. They too were crouched in night-dark, below a high dark wall.

The house was silent when he arrived. It was late, and the town slept. In order to avoid waking his sister he lay down in the door-yard, in the long buffalo grass by the fence. The air smelled of punk.

Toward morning he was awakened by the straining of a freight engine; he rose and went to the swing on the garden side to wait until dawn.

Although it was scarcely a week since he had left, yet it seemed many days to Cass.

Above the house the first slant rays of morning touched Great-Snake Mountain. As the light grew there he saw low clouds across the prairie, in a long moving mist crouching toward the green mountain. Slowly the long mist moved toward the high mountain, like a sleek gray cat approaching, then it lunged forward swiftly and ruthlessly, and all the great peak was enwrapped from his sight. As though claws of fog had pierced an earthen heart.

Sitting in the lop-sided tire-swing, Cass thought to himself then that could one but come close to a shining star it might look much as the great peak did now: just a dim height curtained by roiling cloud, with all the shining vanished away. The peak did not look beautiful to him now. It seldom had. Even after the mist dispersed and Great-Snake Mountain stood up clearly and tall, like a stately woman standing alone robed in purple and gold and green, not even then did it appear even pleasant to him to see. Cass was hungry, and more than anything else it looked to him like a huge and green-streaked heap of ancient horse-dung that had lost most of its odor. To a man who had just eaten well the mountain no doubt would have appeared beautiful; for the sun was on it and the sky was behind it—and humbly now in its high white mist three quiet sheep were grazing. But to Cass they appeared much like himself: just lour somewhat hungry-looking sheep atop a hungry hill, their fleece bitten by frost in the morning air and their heads hanging a little out of too-long loneliness.

He heard movement in the kitchen, went to the back door and tapped like a stranger there. It was Nancy. She came to the door with her hair undone; it cascaded in an auburn torrent half-way down to her waist. She gave a cry half surprise and half joy, and caught him into her arms.

For very emotion Cass could not speak, his affection swelled his heart till his throat felt dry. He could only cling to his sister, and run his hands through her hair, and try not to whimper again. Nancy's hair held a red-brown sheen; it was tawny in the light. It held the odor of the dooryard lilac that long ago had ceased to bloom.

Being taken unaware by emotion made restraint difficult for Cass. Nancy ran a finger over the cut on his mouth, traced it down from his mouth to his throat. There was guilt in his eyes when she did that, and he winced. He averted his eyes. "That hurts, Nance," he said, and he took her finger away.

"But Lawd—how'd y'all git cut that away? Look at me."

He faced her. "Slipped an' fell on a railroad spike. How y'all been gettin' on with the charity-folks?"

"Tol'able."

He saw the raggedness of his sister.

While eating clabber and combread over the kitchen stove he asked, "Where's Bry'n?" Nancy did not answer for a minute.

"Bry'n's stayin' on uptown some'eres," she hnally replied, "Paw thrashed him so's he won't walk all by hisself for a spell. Luke nex' door tuk him on uptown; so now he's at Clark Casner's place, ah s'pose."

Cass asked for his father only to inquire briefly, "He'll be home directly, y' reck'n?"

Nancy did not reply at all this time. They had finished eating and Cass was clearing the dishes when Stubby strode into the kitchen. He tossed his empty tin dinner pail into the sink, and went on into the living room without giving any indication that he had so much as seen Cass. His whole bearing was that of a man either returning from a hard night's work, or of a man walking in a dream. He went directly to the bed, stretched out on it without removing his boots, and to all appearances fell to sound sleep the moment his head touched the pillow.

The brown boot-toes pointed sharply to the roof.

Cass looked at Nancy in bewilderment. He had never seen his father like this before, and he was frightened. But Nancy would not answer his glance, she would not turn her face to show that she saw. Instead, she turned her face away. Cass saw that she was ashamed of their father.

And in the weeks that followed it seemed to Cass that Nancy never once looked directly at him; she seemed to be forever shifting her eyes or turning her head or walking abruptly away. He could not understand how the week of his absence could have wrought such an irreparable change.

Yet, it had split life in two.

He remembered how often Nancy had waked him out of sleep with low laughter. Yet now she laughed not even when awake. All day now she went about the empty house, puttering, fidgeting, tight-lipped, dry-eyed. Cass had no inkling of the conflict in her heart. After the joy she had evinced at first seeing him she seemed to recoil, so that at times he was reminded in her of his father. She too would walk past him as though not to see. And she never learned how severe a gash he had suffered down the side of his mouth, for he tended it himself, at night, half-secretly. He did not want her to see it, he did not wish now that she tend it: he was ashamed of that wound. He never told her how he had gained it. And a wall began growing between them.

He washed the cut late at night, at the dooryard well. He picked it and daubed it with unclean rags. When the scab was half-formed he tore it off, and it bled anew. And when it was finally healed he looked in a mirror, and he saw a little road of gray scar tissue running like a loose gray ribbon out of his mouth's left corner.

Cass resumed his trips to the charity station. And January came with rain, mountain days were gray again. And outside was the gray Texas winter.

To Cass it seemed that the town was coming to be full of men like his father. Not until he had been away from the town and had returned did he really see how many idle, swaggering rogues there were in the place. The fear of blood and fighting seized him whenever he passed a group of men on the street. For blood and fighting were on their minds, and he sensed it as he passed.

On hot afternoons through June and July he saw them lounging about on the courthouse steps, or in front of the pool hall or domino parlor. They wore great gray hats and dusty blue overalls, they were cold-eyed even when smiling. Sullen men, sharply dissatisfied, and quick to cross in their mood. Vain, ignorant, native; and cunning as the mountain wotves.

Although all were troubled by the same sharp discontent, some could free themselves of the feeling by fighting. Some hearts, like Stubby's, were consumed by a flame that burned steady and hot, demanding blows and the feel of flesh cringing. Something there was within such men that burned like a fever; they turned to fighting to escape feeling: to a cock-fight, a bull-dog fight, a bull-fight across the border or a human fight near at hand. They turned to drink and to gambling and to the Mexican whorehouse, or to a lynching.

In the middle of July, nine months after Cass had returned from New Orleans, there were two killings on the streets in a single week. One boy was stabbed, and a second was lynched for the stabbing. Two brothers, sons of a small tenant-rancher named Ross Kilbane, started the trouble. Kilbane, a harmless little man and a widower, had had trouble with his boys ever since the death of their mother. Cass knew both boys, and ran when he saw either. They called him a Mexican because he lived among Mexicans, and they chased him with added fervor because he was red-haired.

The precious pair were sitting together near the watertank on the Santa Fe one boiling Tuesday afternoon, waiting for a freight to take them to San Antonio, when the quarrel began. A young Negro transient who had been waiting a short distance away for the same train later told what he had seen of the fight.

He told it standing on the courthouse steps, with Sheriff Lem Shultz standing on one side and a gang of idlers on the other. Cass, nearby, heard every word.

"This un, th' little un, he was settin' cross-leg first *ah* seen 'im, chawin' a straw 'tween he teeth; but *this* un, he were layin' down on he back all th' while. This un, the little un, he kep' sayin' how hongry he feel, but this other, he kep' layin' down an' don' say how *he* feel atall. Then this un, th' little un, he say he so hongry now he could chaw he tongue, had he oney pinch o' salt, an' ask me nigger has ah got any grub. Ah tol' him no, 'cause o' co'se ah ain't, an' he call me ol' name lak he think ah lyin' an' commence chawin' at ol straw agin. But other boy don' say is *he* hongry atall. *He* jes' keep layin' still all th' while, lak he deep asleep; oney ah seen o' co'se he werent.

"Well, ouah man didn' come an' didn' come, an' he were due at two an' it were after fo', an' this un, th' *little* un, he commence gittin' the' all-ovah fidgits again. He chaw at ol' straw real rapid. Then he ask me what time is it nigger, an' ah took me a guess an' say qwata to five an' he say does they feed yo' in th' army an' give yo' money beside, nigger, an' ah say ah reck'n so, white boy. He don' say nothin' fo' space then; an' 'en he say suddent-like what time is it nigger, an' ah tuk me a guess an' say qwata *afta* five, white boy. An' 'en he spit out he straw an' get up an' say sort o' low, 'Clyde, 'at man ain't comin' this day no mo' an' yo' damned well know it all this time— yore a lyin' little turncoat, Clyde Kilbane, it kill mah soul jest t' call yo' kin."

"'At's jest what he say—an' 'en this other boy kep' layin' right still fo' minute like he deep asleep an' caint hear nothin' atall; an' 'en he open one eye jest a mite an' look up an' say, 'Speak out loud why don' yo', Homer?' An' this un, the *little* un, say right back, 'Reckon ah spoke pert 'nough fo' *you-all* to hear—th' man ain't comin'—so you is a liar on top o' thievin' from yo' pappy.' 'En this boy, he were layin' down, he open other eye jest a little too an' say real siow-hke, 'We-el, ah nevah figged a Terry Ewe back o' barn'—an' 'en he got up so quick ah nevah seen 'im rise an' they was at it with th' big- ges' longes'jack-knives ah evah did see—an' 'en him what jest riz up he were layin' down agen jes like befo', an' ah see he were cut perty bad awright 'cause it keep comin' down from right undah he arm, an' this un, the *little* un, he seen where he cut him an' he git all white-face an' kneel down ovah; but ah didn' know he was cut some his'ef. Ah jest stahted thinkin' 'bout time ah staht mindin' mah own bus'ness; an' so 'at was when ah begun t' go 'way.

"So's o'co'se when y'all brung me heah t' show me this boy plum *daid* ah just might astonished, folks." He paused to look at Sheriff Lem Shultz beside him. He was a big youth in a ragged red sweater, and he looked like a Lake Salvador Negro—"An' that's all ah kin tell y'all." He smiled then, a wide sweet white smile.

The second killing of the week occurred four days later, on a Saturday night, when the Negro was dragged through the streets behind an automobile, and burned.

Into the middle of August of 1928 came days hot beyond any in the memory of the town. Every morning the sun rose red as blood, as though intent on scourging every living thing off the earth before it set. The cotton growers along the river saw their crops wither before them in the red heat. In the town none ventured out save him who must; the streets were deserted. On the ranches the cattle sought escape by lying all day in the long shade of the barns. But there was no escape, the great green blood-fat flies of summer tortured the beasts as they lay. On the surrounding ranches dozens of head were lost through the milk fever. The cows' bags became caked and heavy, and dried up; then their bags had to be amputated to save the animals' lives.

Every night a foolish small breeze would come skipping and hissing out of the east, running like an evil little buffoon from doorstep to doorstep, as though to tell those within of the coming of rain; but every one knew that the small breeze lied, even the cattle mocked it with lowing. So it would whisper away to the west, like a cat racing out from under a henhouse with feathers in its fur.

Into the limitless yellow sky the steam from the roundhouse rose slowly, slowly; straight up into the air it rose, more like a pillar than the tossing white plume that one always saw there when there were clouds and wind. But there were no clouds, there was no wind—day after day the sky yawped hungrily for them, yellow and threatening.

Watching that white pillar rise against that yellow wall, Cass remembered a proverb the Reverend Benjamin Cody once had spoken:

"There are three things that are never satisfied, yea, four things that say not, 'It is enough': the grave; and the barren womb; the earth that is not filled with water; and the fire that saith not, 'It is enough.'"

So Cass thought, "When the sky is yellow and has no clouds, it is like the earth not filled with water."

Fires broke out in the town, and on the ranches.

One night during this spell Cass passed the old county jailhouse and paused, for always it held a peculiar kind of dread for him. At the barred window, draped in slant silver moonlight, a sleepless old man stood looking down, his fingers wound whitely and tightly about the bars. An old man—gray, unclean, unshaven, dangling his head out to get a breath of air. His skin was drawn so tightly over his cheek bones that the flesh appeared to have been drawn down and then tied tightly under the chin like a woman's bonnet-strings, for under the jaw hung long turkey-folds of flesh that left his cheek bones jutting out from beneath his eyes. He saw the boy staring up at him and waved one thin hand down, like a hand waving out of a dark crate. Cass did not wave in return, but he came closer and whispered with head straining up, "Did y'all steal somethin'? Did they get y'all fo' gittin' drunk? What y'all do *wrong*, mister?"

The old man appeared startled. He put his hand over his mouth and stepped back out of sight; Cass heard him coughing. And from behind the bars, in the darkness there, one breath of the oppressive heat of the place came down to Cass as he stood. When the old man came to the window again he looked down and answered. His voice seemed very tired.

"I never did but one thing really *wrong* in my life, sonny—I was born in Texas with a hungry gut, an' that was my big mistake. You got no terbacco on you, hev you, sonny?"

Cass had none, and the old man disappeared from the window.

On that same night a boxcar loaded with sheep caught fire while standing on a siding on the Santa Fe. For some reason everyone thought it had been fired deliberately. In the middle of the night the frightened bleating of the trapped beasts and the glow in the sky brought the townsfolk out half-dressed and tousled from sleep; two shirtless men unsealed the doors of the blazing box with pokers. Then, in panic, the foolish animals blocked both escapes with their lunging bodies so that all but half a dozen or so were burned to death. One old ram butted his way out with his fleece on fire. Racing crazily through the dust of Nevada Street, bawling blindly, he thwarted every attempt to throw water on him until he fell and was unable to rise.

Cass saw Luke Gulliday's wife standing atop the railroad embankment, and he climbed up to ask her whose sheep they were.

"Boone Terry's," she told him, and she laughed when she said it. She was a strapping young wench who cuckolded her husband at every opportunity.

"Did you say Boone Terry's, Beulah?" someone asked her from below, and she called down assurance that she had.

And after that, somehow, a holiday spirit crept into the night, and a strange half-religious air. Cass had the same feeling as he had had once while watching a reunion of Holy Rollers, an air as of something half-supernatural took hold of him. Down on the dust of the street below a living beast was struggling in its own flame, and the fronts of the stores on Main and Nevada were all aglow with the reflected flare of the fire, like pagan temples burning there. The glass of their windows was shimmering in molten green-gold streams; and all about him the panicky bleating and screams of the animals mingled with the hard laughter of mountain men and women.

"Boone Terry's! Are y'all right sure in the face o' thet?"

"Saw the seal on the car when they opened the door."

"Say now, the Jesus-God, wouldn't ever'one feel downhearted if Boone has let his insurance lapse?"

Boone Terry had a great many enemies in the town, because, although he was the richest rancher in the county, he gave no milk to the charity station. He gave, instead, money to the churches, and the churches though it wiser to save souls with money than to buy milk. He gave to every church in town save the Catholic Church, which was Mexican. To the Mexican Methodists, however, at the *iglesia metodista*, he had once given an organ.

From where he stood now Cass could see that the hindquarters of the ram were already burned black. As he stood listening to the beast's last screams, watching its last convulsive kicks, he became conscious of a tall figure beside him, and he looked up; it was the Reverend Benjamin Cody of the Church of Christ, Campbellite. Cass shied away, for he had not gone to his church for a long time; the tall man did not even notice him. He stood looking down from under bushy brows at the ram struggling in the dame below, and he spoke in such a deep and Biblical voice that the laughter about him died. In the town he was regarded, by the Campbellites, as a prophet of the Lord.

"Behold—the fire and the wood, and also the lamb, for a burnt offering. Did not Abraham say unto Isaac, his son, God will provide the lamb for the burnt offering? And behold, behold—"

A minute of silence followed this; then the tall man turned on his heel and strode away, leaving his silence behind him. He walked the streets all night, people said, and communed with Christ Jesus. Big Beulah Gulliday shattered the odd silence that the preacher had left by calling down to her husband below. Luke was pouring water on the hindquarters of the dying animal, and Beulah shrilled out, "Might as well let 'em burn the whole way now an' pour the rest down yo' own arse instead, you Luke, 'cause that need some coolin' too."

Luke glanced up and called back in the accents of the Reverend Benjamin Cody, "Woman! Be holed. Be holed."

Everyone laughed at Beulah and Luke for a minute. Then a Mexican came up from the roundhouse with an ax, and ended the ram's suffering with one blow; he stood astraddle the animal and with a single swing cleft the skull cleanly in two.

"Don't take that haid home with yo', spik,—y'all hev to buy Boone a new ram tomorrow if you do," Luke Gulliday warned.

When Cass passed the carcass the next day, where it still lay in the road, he saw that out of the unburned flank several steaks had been cut. Before evening the dogs had the rest. And that was high noon when he passed, and so still was the air that he could hear the tapping of someone's hammer on wood away over on the other side of the arroyo, two miles distant. All things seemed to be standing still, holding breath, everything was waiting for no one knew what; yet nothing dared to move, nothing dared to stir, everything waited . . . and into this calm there burst, with incredible violence, a dry hot wind from the west. Everyone heard it when it was yet miles off, and ran to hide. Then it tore through the town hissing and screaming, tossing sand as high as the rooftops, hurling sand with an insane malice against the windows, smashing panes and whirling in clouds into the rooms where the people hid. And the sky came down so low, that, although it was noon, the day was as dark as a starless night. As a night when a thousand Indian demons whirling in black and yellow robes rush screaming from doorway onto doorway, dashing themselves against the houses, shaking the boards and the beams and the rafters the while they shriek in a red mad rage.

That was the beginning of a whole year of storms. Cass and Nancy sat huddled about the stove in the kitchen all that day. Somewhere outside, they did not know where, their lather walked through the storm. He did not come in till late that night, after the wind had passed. They did not ask him where he had been, for they knew well that no one in town would willingly take him into a house.

In the morning five houses and a dozen windmills had been blown down, and every west-facing windowpane in town had been shattered. The streets were littered with chicken feathers, cinders, cotton, and aged yellow newspapers.

Yet there had been not a drop of rain.

5

ALL OF OCTOBER was cool that year. It rolled into November with pleasant days. But in mid-December winter set in, and there was no coal for the stove.

The windy months were beginning.

Every evening then, so soon as the dark sun had set, there came a tow rising keening over ail the gray prairie, like the crying of many small birds before storm. A million small birds far off, lost in dusk before storm. The low calling would merge slowly, and mount, until it was a single indrawn howl all on one key; the very foundation of the little house trembled with it, the dishes rattled on the shelf. The windmill in the dooryard would flash about, pause tentatively, and then whirl on once more like a toy pinwheel in the blast. Sand rose in torrents. The windy months were beginning, and there was no coal for the stove.

For hours each morning Nancy sat bent above that stove, reading in dimness with moving lips. She sat with her knees propped high toward her chin, reading the Bible. The Bible was all that she ever read now. It was a big book, built for family use; sometimes her hands tired from holding it as she sat. Then she would brace it against a stove-lid or a pot. The stove-lids were cold and the pots were empty. Sometimes she trembled a little; sometimes she twisted her fingers through the auburn coil of her hair.

Cass resented seeing his sister so, but he wasn't certain just why. It was not that he knew she fought hunger in silence, nor that he knew she was cold as she sat; it was the great book that irked him. He came to think of it as a part of that wall that had risen between himself and Nancy; its covers were large and dark, they seemed like small walls in themselves.

Cass saw the helplessness of his sister.

"Mebbe warm weather come early this year," she said, on one of the first cold days of November. "Mebbe the wind'd die down early this year."

"More'n likely another norther'll hit us t'morrer mo'nin'," Cass made reply, resenting dimly his sister's baseless optimism.

"Mebbe, if we could jest move down valley-way, you'n' me jest, y'all could git work pickin' oranges or grapefruit aroun' some packin' house an' ah'd find me a job sortin' 'em or packin' or somethin'. Anyhow, it's wa'm down by them towns, they say . . . if we could git down there jest."

"Ah'd rather stay on here," Cass answered. "Mebbe, did we even git down thar, we couldn't find no jobs. What we do then, if that happen? In this place folks knows us, anyhow. Ain't nobody knows us down valley-way."

"What good's it do fo' us to know folks or fo' folks to know we? All folks us knows is plum harder up 'an we. Ah ast Beulah Gulliday fo' few chunks o' coal, 'cause her Luke got Paw's ol' job, but Beulah say she ain't got a single solitary lump, nor kindlin' neither, on account Luke's been buyin' drinks fo' the boys uptown agen. What we gonna do fo' winter's fuel, brother?"

Cass knew in that moment what he was going to do; but he forebore to say because of the Bible beneath Nance's hand.

It was almost two years since he and Johnny Portugal had

last stolen coal; detectives rode every coal train that came through now, both on the Santa Fe and on the Southern Pacific. But Cass thought he knew where he could get some heavy wood. Down in Boone Terry's lumber yard he had seen pine logs from the mountain stacked as high as his head.

At the charity station he consulted with Johnny Portugal. After dark they met on the corner of Chihuahua Street under a lamp that looked, in the windy cold, like a bright teardrop from a nose hanging by one dark curved hair.

They walked around the lumber yard twice, casually, but met no one. Then Cass, because he was slightly the taller, boosted his friend over the fence; he followed over, dropped to earth in darkness. "Listen!" he cautioned. But there was no sound.

A tarpaulin had been stretched over the logs and then tied tightly to two rows of stakes in the ground, as a tent would be tied. There was no way of getting a single log out. Johnny would have surrendered the project, but Cass was obdurate.

"Let's look around," he whispered. "Let's look in all Boone's barr'is. Y' caint never tell—mought be coal-oil in 'em."

The boys heaved against a barrei till one end tilted; when it settled back on end they heard a liquid swishing in its depths.

"Mebbe ees kero*seen*," Johnny suggested, and he went off in search of a railroad spike and a housebrick; Cass reclimbed the fence, headed down the tracks to the Santa Fe jungle, and returned with an armful of rusty tomato cans.

"Some of'em mought leak a mite," he said, aligning the cans in a rusty row across the frozen earth. "We'll have to watch it when we spill 'er."

Johnny wound a cotton bandana about the spike and Cass tapped it tentatively against the iron of the barrel. Despite the cotton rag, the small sound rang clearly in the still night air. The boys waited. Rigid and listening and ready to run, they waited for feet that come swiftly in boots. Feet of the law, coming swiftly to strike.

The last barrel against the fence had a wooden cover. Johnny prepared the spike again, and Cass held it while he tapped. It sank in deeply and softly, like a steel chisel into cheese. When the hole was almost through they heard someone coming across the road on the other side of the fence, and they dodged into shadow. But it was only a half-drunken half-breed rolling by; they heard him singing as he passed:

> *En la cruz, en la cruz*
> *Do primero vi la luz*
> *Y las manchas de me alma you lavé*
> *Fué alli por la fe do vi a Jesus*
> *Y feliz para siempre seré.*

His song was lost around the corner of the *iglesias metodista*; they returned to their task and in a few minutes the hole was completed; when Cass put an eye to the opening he saw that the barrel was full to its brim. In the night air the stuff was almost odorless. The boys took a firm hold and heaved together again—and when they got it lying flat on its side on the earth, like a beer keg on a bar, the cover came off. It had been loosened by their chiseling and forced by the sudden upsurge behind it. In the flood-freshet that followed both boys were drenched. They were bending over aligning the cans in front of the barrel when it burst like a brief tidal wave over their heads, smashed down the cans and set them to floating, spread over the ground and flowed under the fence— made islands out of groundswells and small lakes out of ruts.

Dripping and horrified, the boys stared at the kerosene swirling about their feet, and then they stared at each other. In that moment Cass felt a trickle coursing down the back of his right ear . . . Johnny whooped like an Indian, Cass grabbed a can, with one scoop filled it to overflowing, and raced for the fence at Johnny's heels. This time Johnny needed no boost. When they came down on the other side of the fence Cass saw that half of what he had secured had spilled in the climb, and that the remainder was leaking fast. So he wadded his cap, already sodden, around and below the tin, and ran like a mad boy before the rest was lost. Johnny's footsteps pounded far behind.

On the next night, after dark had come down, and Stuart had left the house, Nancy and Cass enjoyed the luxury of a lamp. They sat together over the precious glow, set on the living room table between them, trying to warm cold hands over the flame.

Somewhere in the room a fly without wings kept knocking itself against the wall, oppressed perhaps by the sharp smell of the lamp.

Outside of the window Cass could see the barren boughs of the sycamore, where his tire-swing had hung, stretching cupped hands to the wind, like lean old fingers cupped for alms; he heard the wind rush past without stopping, without seeing, without heeding the little tree.

Nancy and Cass.

They did not know each other very well, this brother and sister. He was almost eighteen years old, but he did not yet know his sister very well. He thought, "What is father doing? Where does he go?" And he had a sense as of an impending disaster; his heart pained a little, and felt tired of beating.

"Bryan is drunk," he told himself. "He's layin' back o' the Mex cathouse mebbe, or back o' th' filling station with Clark Casner. He won't come back 'cause he's too scared of paw now. Nance is hungry, oney she don't say it 'cause thet'd jest make us both hungrier. Nance is colder'n me ah guess. But down at the yards there's logs eight foot high, an' every freight fo' the last six weeks has been haulin' coal through here. Seems like a little mought come our way, oney it never do."

On the ceiling flame-shadows from the lamp flowed endlessly, like moving lights on a river at night; the shadow-pattern here was that of having no pattern, ceaselessly. Nancy's face in the lamp's bronze glow looked almost like an Indian woman's face, half turned away.

Her eyes were dark and her cheekbones high, and her hair was like a helmet. When he looked close Cass perceived the turmoil in his sister's face, he saw there the joylessness of her life. Her eyes seemed to be smoldering; he studied their sullen flare unaware that she knew he studied her. And he had the peculiar notion that her pupils might roll back in her head any moment— rolling back till only the blind whites showed—that then, screaming, she would rise, seize his throat and try to strangle him, the while her hair hung in her eyes like a madwoman's hair.

Cass shuddered his odd thought away. He did not know why he thought of such things so frequently. He only knew that of late he was often hungry.

"It's gittin' low," Nance said.

Cass thought, "She used to laugh lots. Now after she gits in bed she cries sometimes."

Nancy cried for the utter joylessness of her life.

The wick began sputtering, and Nancy rose. Cass heard her undressing behind the dark curtain and resolved to sit by the flame until it had died entirely. Nancy had pretended that she noticed nothing when he had come in with a pint of kerosene leaking out of a rusty tin can held in a sodden cap.

"Shore don't smell like y'all been rained on," was all she had said.

After Cass had climbed into bed he was unable to restrain his tongue any longer.

"Are yo' hungry, sister?" he asked.

She did not answer him. Within him hunger worked up and down through his bowels.

And then slowly, terribly, Nancy began to sing. Cass had heard her sing hymns a thousand times, but never before sheerly out of pain—he tried to close his ears to the shrill madness of her voice.

> *Have you been to Jesus for the cleansing power?*
> *Are you washed in the blood of the lamb?*
> *Are you fully trusting in his grace this hour?*
> *Are you washed in the blood of the lamb?*

"Shet up!" he howled miserably, for it racked him horribly to hear.

> *When the bridegroom cometh will your robes be white?*
> *Pure white in the blood of the lamb?*
> *Will your soul be ready for the mansions bright?*
> *Are you washed in the blood of the lamb,*
> *In the soul-cleansing blood of the lamb?*

"Do yo' al'ays sing when yore that hungry?" he asked, wishing in some way to hurt her now, somehow to mock her with her own pain, and yet not knowing quite how.

For reply Nancy only sang more shrilly.

Are your garments spotless? Are they white as snow?
Are you washed in the blood of the lamb?

She did not finish. Sobs checked her. He listened to her catching her breath between her teeth till he could bear it no longer; then he rose and went in. She was lying face down on the pillow, and the tattered quilt had been tossed aside; Cass stood in cotton underwear, his feet were bare on the bare dirt floor; he shivered with wet November chill.

"What is it, Nance?" he asked. "Caint ah help some way? Ah'll git rice in the mo'nin' at the station, we'll have that, sister."

She only sobbed into the pillow for reply, and he sat down beside her on the bed, put his hand on her naked shoulder, and stroked the silken carpet of her hair. She turned her face to him then, streaked and hollow-eyed, and pressed his hand so fiercely in hers that she hurt his fingers. He saw a long shudder run through her as she lay, and he put the quilt back about her. Her voice strained with the effort to keep out pain.

"Ah been tryin' to pray, Cass, like Maw used to tell me to do. 'Member Maw, Cass? She uz good to me. She used to tell me an' Bry'n to pray to Christ Jesus in 'diction an' want, an' not to leave off goin' to the Church o' Christ no matter what. We shouldn't never left off church-goin', Cass—an' now ah'm so shamed for Paw an' Bry'n an' all . . ."

"Y'all think it'd do good if we stahted to church agen, an' prayin' like we used?" she asked.

For the first time in their lives then, Cass felt stronger than his sister. He saw in that moment how strangely helpless Nancy was, in all things; he spoke with an assurance that was new to him.

"God ain't never fed us, Nance—not wunst he ain't. When Paw ain't workin' we beg our breakfast, that's all. Elts we go without. He never fetched us kindlin'. But mebbe it was him what fetched me a beatin' f'om a Santy Fé dick when ah tried to cop us coal to burn, an' it bled all day an' left me a mark on mah neck fom it too. So ah reckon he jest don't give a damn, if he's anywhere ay-tall. Elts he's actin' plain orn'ry."

"Mebbe we been sinnin' an' he are punishin'. Y'all been sinnin', Cass?"

She looked up. In the darkness Cass traced his scar furtively. He recalled the old man in the jailhouse.

"Reckon the wrongest sin we done, sister, was just bein' bo'n hungry in a pesthole in Texas."

She turned slowly toward him, looking at him somehow wildly, as though she had not heard, and almost as though she did not know that he had been with her these many minutes.

"Git back to yore baid"—her voice was strange. "Git off'n mah baid! Caint yo' see ah'm 'most *nekkid*?"

She jerked the covers up high over her shoulders, looking at him with eyes empty and burning like two lamps already fading to darkness—"Go awn now"—ah know what your aimin' at well enough."

Stunned as though he'd been struck between the eyes, Cass groped back to the other side of the curtain. He could not understand. For hours he lay awake, trying to understand. Then he concluded, "She was jest actin' smart, that's all. Derned if Nance ain't gittin' as catawampus as the ol' man sometimes."

But what was it then she murmured into the night as though to speak between clenched teeth? Every night now he heard her. Low, troubled words; confused pleadings, and a half-told despair.

He had heard her, and he had not understood. He was too hungry to think it all out into a clear understanding.

He was too hungry to understand what hunger wrought in his sister's mind.

Cass and Nancy did not have fire four times that winter; and that was the winter of 1928–29. It was a good winter for the tourist trade, and Cass pimped boldly for the Poblano Café. What few pennies he earned, however, went to the table. Before spring came Nancy knew he was pimping. She said nothing. But she could not forgive it.

All one April afternoon Stuart McKay had been lying, eyes tightly closed, on the disheveled cot in the corner. When he thought no one looked, he opened one eye. From the kitchen Cass had watched furtively, had seen his father breathe heavily, feigning sleep, and he had been afraid. The slant sun climbed the wooden walls, dropped slowly down behind the mountain, left the room to final night. When its reflected rays had paled from the window Stuart sat up, stretched as though after long sleep, and swung his legs over the side of the bed; then silently, as one upon whom many wait, he passed out into the deepening dusk. Cass saw his shadow pass the door, heard the quick little boots tapping over the dust of Mexican-town . . . then pity replaced fear in his heart; and he could have wept tears of blood for that poor man, his father.

Stuart walked up the Santa Fe toward the roundhouse. On either side stood workers' homes; dark, unpainted, unlovely even in the dusk they stood. So many boxes, all in a row. One after another, all the same, each one alone, every one dark.

Somehow to Stuart McKay they seemed to be standing

without shame, just because they stood all in a row like that. He did not see the little low houses now, yet he felt shame like a wind on his cheek as he passed. He had gone this way a thousand times, each time it was the same. It was the same; he felt that always as he passed houses watched him with small squint eyes, that each squat hovel was naked and black.

"Like nigger whores," he said to himself, "sinnin' nigger whores thet'd give a man clap jest to look at 'em wunst."

So on this night Stubby did not turn his eyes to where the little low houses stood.

The odor of tamales frying came to him mingled with another smell, as of a dead burro or cow lying somewhere close by.

He passed the jailhouse, waiting quietly like a thick-necked wrestler who watches an opponent and knows his own strength to be the greater. He followed the tracks over an embankment between gardens where grape-vines hung, lifeless and dry and dinging in wind. Stubby heard their leaves whisper crisply as he passed. Without turning his head, without clearly realizing what sound he had heard, he spoke to himself, "Drought done fo' thet grape patch. Dry as a guinea hen's arse since way last August. Good. Now the rest'll go too . . . the cotton, the corn . . . the cows . . . good."

Ahead of him signal towers burned yellow, red and green. Down from the roundhouse floodlights came slanting so brightly that their glare defined cinders between the ties. The night freight from San Angelo had come in and waited, panting and throbbing like a thirsty beast, beside the dripping watertank. There would be steel on that man before it pulled for Presidio, Stuart knew—steel bars upon steel bars. Long fierce cold rails that would lie quietly in darkness, but could flash blue death like any lightning flash; that would flash blue light when the sun came upon them. He liked the thought, and let the picture of long sharp bars roll about in the back of his brain. Iron—that rusted. Not steel. Steel was a trickster. Steel killed men.

He passed between two sidings of sealed boxcars and came to a shadowed corner of the powerhouse. This was his corner, his secret place. From here he could see the man whom he came every night to see, but the man could not see him. He would watch this little devil that gave whiskey to others, this runt-devil who stole other men's jobs. He would see that the devil worked well, that he did not shirk, that he did not drink when he should be working. Damn all runt-devil's whiskey that made men drunk.

The Damned Man—Stubby had to call him that.

He crouched in darkness almost an hour before he saw anyone other than Mexican stokers. Then a hostler passed within a few feet of him, and behind the hostler came Gulliday. Stuart saw Luke clamber up the cabin and into the fireman's seat. He saw him climb over the tender to the watertank as soon as the engine rolled under the standpipe. The tender was standing with its tank under a spout like a colossal camel's nose, projecting. Standing on his toes there, Luther reached up, yanking against the great counterweights, shoved the spout into the tank, and opened the valve. Water poured down so last that in less than a minute the 8,000 gallon tank was full. Stuart knew that it was full. He heard the water rushing over Luke's boots, slopping all over the rounded deck, drenching Luke's gloves and his sleeves and the knees of his trousers. He saw Luke shut the valve and ding the spout upward— and Stuart felt, on seeing this, that had it been himself atop that tender the valve would have been shut a second sooner. Small as he was, he was bigger than Luke. Luke was too timid, too uncertain in his movements; uncertain and none too strong; whereas he, Stub McKay, was fast as a rabbit and strong as a burro; and always cold sober.

The engine rumbled off to the coal station, and Luke walked back to the roundhouse, shuffling his boots as he walked.

Stuart waited till Luke had reached the roundhouse before he dared to follow. On his way he paused to peer between two sidings of boxcars. Mexican mechanics, blackened and half-naked, scurried under the droplights.

"Heatherns, every one," Stubby muttered, peering. "Heatherns cleanin' Amerikun road-hogs."

An S. P. express locomotive crashed past him, hurling up great sparks to the brooding sky, hauling its string of pullmans as though they were toy carriages. The great drivers thundered by, boiler-lightning flashed spasmodically across the maze of tracks, the earth shook under Stubby's feet, and a long smoke went up against the sky. Then the windows of the pullmans raced by, every one darkened but the last, where lights and silverware were flashing. Stubby glimpsed a woman all in white sitting with a spoon in her hand, laughing, with her head thrown back.

"She'll be in San Anton' by mornin'," Stubby told himself, fingering soot out of his eye.

Over a dead locomotive he saw heat-lightning cleave the sky. It glowed and quivered ominously, a three-tined fork far, far to the north, silhouetting momently against the night the tall, encircled smoke-jacks of the great roundhouse. In just that way once, he remembered, heat lightning had silhouetted to the north a distant wood hill; it had illuminated trees there that time, tall and encircled, so that he had stayed up late that night to watch, and to wonder. Then he had walked, with someone in white, down a dark way between two fields of ripening cotton. He had walked and talked with someone in white that time; Where had that been?

Where had they walked? Who? He had forgotten so many things. Everything now seemed long ago. He only remembered a dim place, and a lost thought, and a half-seen figure waiting where two white fields of cotton met beneath heat-lightning in the sky.

He walked on till he could see Luke again. Luke was pulling down the iron spout of a standpipe once more; again he was fighting with a coal chute that was too heavy for him, but that was not too heavy for a better man. Stuart heard him panting with his effort—Good! He was breathing in dark dust! Might he soon breathe in dark death!

The cars far behind the engine started slowly, their wheels slipping, jerking, slipping, jerking. Then wheels were turning, wheels were straining, wheels were shrieking with gathering speed. Stubby came slowly out of shadow when he heard their turning sound. He could not help but come, for wheels were steel, and wheels were rolling. Directly into the flood-beams' glare he walked, and he did not wince once in their fierce light; he was unaware of light, he did not know why he had come out of shadow. He heard only wheels, felt only an old fury, saw only one man.

The Damned Man. The Damned Feeling. He smelled nothing but smoke, felt nothing but hate, heard nothing but wheels.

He saw only—The Man.

A brakie walking the tops saw Stubby coming up swiftly behind the little hostler, and something in Stuart's stride caused him to point one finger and call out.

Little Luke Gulliday did not see, he never heard that warning shout. Stubby caught him at the waist and raised him above his head high into the glare of the floodlights, held him high for one long moment there—laughing. Luke struggled once, and then, as though suddenly realizing what hands held him, screamed wildly above the din of the passing cars. And Stuart hurled him so far under that the last of the scream became a brief part of the roar of wheels turning with gathering speed.

A mob has a face with a single mouth. Opening, closing. It has one long hand with a thousand fingers, it points at a house, it weeps and hisses.

"Yeah," said Mob-Mouth, "Stuart McKay, the very same one as acts sech a bad hat, an' that there is the house, the very same house. He been actin' bad-hat-about-town goin' on fifteen year, an' the Jesus-God hisself don't know what's gone on behind them walls in alt these years. They say Beulah Gulliday jest won't believe. *Poor, poor* Beulah."

A boy with a dog-like mane wormed swiftly out of the crowd's very center, ran to the kitchen window, tapped twice at the pane, whirl-stumbled about and disappeared once again into the heart of the gathering throng.

Cass heard that tapping there, and woke to a sense of horror. Even in sleep a stale horror had held him. He woke with a fear that had not left him since seeing his father leave the house with eyes unseeing and fixed in the twilight. His fear was like another being in the room, and he did not know what he feared.

He saw Nancy standing in the kitchen with her back turned toward him, stirring something on the stove. With the tears of his terror already starting he went to her, and she turned to face him.

For one brief moment Cass did not recognize Nancy—he stepped back, gasping, and his hands caught his throat.

She was looking at him out of his father's eyes, cold and sullen and hostile.

Cass understood in that moment that his father had done some terrible thing, but he didn't know what. In that moment whatever it was did not seem at all to matter. He could only see that this was not Nancy at all, and could not think of his father. Like one in a dream he turned slowly to run, lifting leaden feet toward the door—she caught him before he had taken four steps. He struggled, and his arms were strengthless things. He tried to cry out, but his voice was choked. He wanted only to get outside to the safety of the broad dooryard where there were no corners in which to be caught — but she caught him as his father might have caught him, struck him cruelly across the teeth as his father might have struck him; and then she held him fast. He had to listen, and as she spoke her fingers twitched spasmodically, like ten little white snakes eager to strike once more. And she spoke hard. Hard as a spent harlot speaks.

"Pussy-faht, yo' stay in this house. Caint yo' see out of window? Yore Paw pushed Luke Gulliday under a freight, an' half the town seen him do it. He done it a-pu'puss too he did, an' took a cut at Lem Shultz when Lem come to take him. Oh, ah hope they stretch him now till he faht blue ice—ah swear ah hope they stretch him out this very night on co'thouse square. Oney whether they does or not, we're both murderer's kids jest the same." Her voice did not soften. "Say, pussy-faht, how do it feel to be a murderer's kid this mo'nin'?"

Outside someone shouted and threw a stone; it zoomed against the east wall and then tinkled away as though, in rebounding, it had struck another stone. Cass returned to the living room, lay down once more on his disheveled bed, and stared up at a long slit of light in the ceiling. It was through that slit that rainwet came, sometimes at night while thunder rolled; tapped down onto the floor at the foot of the bed or splashed onto the bedclothes till he felt it on his feet. Then he would have to rise to bring a basin from the kitchen. He closed his eyes, and shut out all light, and tried not to hear any sound from the dooryard. He whimpered to himself in fear.

The sheriff drove up to the house late in the afternoon, swerving into the dooryard in a small cloud of dust. He parked his little gray sedan under the sycamore and called to those within to come out. He drove Cass and Nancy to the courthouse then; till evening Cass answered questions there. He had to answer most of those which were put to Nancy sitting beside him, for she seemed reluctant to reply. Cass wanted to see his father, but he had not the courage to ask by the time the questioning was done. It was almost dark by that time, and the sheriff drove them back home.

It was the first time Cass had ridden in an automobile.

The next morning Lem Shultz drove up again, and this time, after the questions were done, Cass saw his father.

"Y'all tell him 'hello' fo' me," Nancy said.

Lem Shulz walked beside him all the way up the winding stone staircase to the cell. "Ef yo' wants to be alone with yore pappy ah'll hev to frisk yo' first," he said.

"Ah'd ruther be alone," Cass replied, and Lem searched him before unbolting the heavy door. "All you McKays is bad hats," he said, "an' a sheriff has got to be keerful."

Then Cass was alone with his father.

Stubby lay on a blanket in a five-foot cell, his left leg cuffed to a ring in the floor. Two Mexican boys were playing cards on the floor of the run-around, and someone unseen called out, "Is that the nut's kid, Sheriff?" At the end of the bull-pen water stood in a puddle. Cass looked through the bars and said, "Hello"; but the man on the floor did not reply, and Cass had no other words to say.

Stubby looked at him a second without recognition; then he rose and went to his window, dragging his chain behind him.

He stood at the window with his side turned to Cass, looking down into the dusty road below. Cass did not want his father to stand in plain view like that; all day men had been moving about the town. Some curious, some sullen, some angry.

There were men looking up from under that window now, Cass knew. He could hear laughter from the street, and someone calling up.

In Stubby's eyes was nothing of fear. He stood looking down at those below, with the old lawless look in his eye. It occurred to Cass that not once in his life had he seen fear in his father's face.

Stubby returned to his blanket, and Cass asked him to try to sleep.

"Jest close yo' eyes an' fo'git it all," he asked, "It'll come out awright sho' 'nuf. Y'all didn' mean to hurt Luke, we know. Jest foolin' 'round was all y'done, an' Luke tripped up an' fell. We know. We ain't worryin'. We jest want y'all to shet yore eyes an' sleep a while now, that's all."

Surprisingly then, Stubby obeyed. He closed his eyes tightly, like an overly-obedient child, and appeared soon to sleep. The face looked strangely untroubled then; it looked almost quiet, as though it had lost all old bitterness. Cass looked long at his father, at the face so still after years of malice, at the fierce old jaw and the hollows long hunger had forged in the cheeks. Then Lem Shultz rattled his keys and Cass passed again through an open door, and he never saw his father again.

Lem kept jangling his keys till, midway down the stairs, Cass paused. He could not see clearly, and he felt ill. Lem put the keys in his belt then, and Cass felt a bit steadier. Downstairs, in the county clerk's office, Nancy waited. Lem drove them back home, back across the S. P. tracks into Mexican-town down Chihuahua Street and around the corner, into their own small dooryard. All the way Nancy did not speak once.

But once they were back in the house and alone, she laughed a sly little laugh to herself and spoke in the flat hard voice that Cass had already come to fear.

"See them boys by the spik pool-hall when we druv by? What yo' reck'n them boys was figgerin' on, standin' there that-away? Figgerin' on goin' to Divine Service t'night? Them was ever' one friends o' Luke Gulliday's, that's what they was, an' you'n Bryn mought do right well to get out o' town direc'ly. Y'll know that, pussyfaht?"

Cass could have struck his sister in that moment. "Ah might do that yet, sister," he heard himself saying. And then he said a thing that all his life he regretted.

"Ah'll take out o' town direc'ly, an' then y'all kin go down valley-way like you said wunst, to get yo'self a job in a spik whorehouse in La Feria. There's lots o' houses south of La Feria, sister. Y'all might try it over at the Poblano a spell."

It was the last word that Cass spoke to his sister.

And he could not yet know, as he never would know, what simple thing had wrought change in his sister. He could only know, lying in bed and remembering lost laughter in the little dooryard, that to him his sister had been lost. For his father Cass felt little more than a sigh of relief and a sigh of pity. It was almost as though he had known for long that a day would come when his father would kill. It was not this that left him filled with shame. The change in Nancy alone served to shame him. It was for her, despite the words he had spoken, that he felt the larger pity, and the deeper fear. It was Nancy, not his father, who remained inexplicable. It was his sister that was gone, not his father.

Half that night Cass lay awake, his heart filled with remorse for what he had said. Yet he could not, despite all his desire, go to his sister and say he had not meant his words. She was no longer Nancy to him. The wall between them was too high. His thoughts plunged and swerved, remembering hostile men. Under the blankets he clenched his thin fists.

He heard a freight engine switching in the distance, and he wondered if Nancy would go on living here. He ran his hand under his chin, and he felt the ridge of a running scar that would never disappear in all his days, like a ridge of deep-encrusted dirt there that would not be scraped off no matter how often he plucked it. Down from his mouth's left corner to his throat's beginning it ran; and he realized slowly, picking at it there in the dark old room, with his sister's breath coming softly from behind the dark curtain, that, of itself, the time to leave had come to him at last.

This time there would be no one to turn back to. There would be no place waiting for him now. Neither waiting love, nor patient peace, nor help for daily shame. No shelter when a night was cold. No running now from loneliness and fear of stronger men; only the pain of being ashamed, and the pain of being alone.

Alone, with his shame. On the streets, people pointed. So

long as he stayed folk would point as he passed. So long as he stayed, each day would bring shame.

Cass turned his face down into the pillow. Fear made his face white, but no tears would come. Some dim knowledge of what was yet to be forced them down his throat. He stuffed the ragged comer of the pillowcase into his mouth, and held it there till he no longer had need of crying. Then he rose quietly and dressed; and he felt no need of saying good-bye.

In the dooryard a million crickets sang; he looked at the lilac as he passed, and he wondered when it would bloom again.

PART TWO

The Big Trouble

"Harlots and Hunted"

BAUDELAIRE

6

Now came months that caught Cass on a dark human tide. From city to city he went now; there was no standing still and there was no turning back. No place to go, and no place to rest. No time to be idling and nothing to do. He moved, moved, everything moved; men either kept moving or went to jail. Faces, like fence-posts seen from trains, passed swiftly or slowly and were no more. They raced for one moment by, they faded, they changed; they became dim, darkened, or ran blackly in sun. From day to day faces appeared and passed, from hour to hour dimmed and died. Finally they seemed to Cass like faces seen in dream. They were no longer real then, they were no longer living. They were things then formed of death-flesh, as dark and as dead as the fence-posts flying.

And there were always such faces. In a sullen circle they stared for an hour, neither hostile nor friendly nor kind. They too were of the hunted. They moved aside to make place for him or silently turned away; he stood among them in silence; he then, too, stared unhostile in his turn. Then it was *move, move—Don't come here any more*—and the faces were gone again.

A summer passed, suns passed, clouds passed, rain fell; he begged, he cringed; he lived within a ragged throng.

Sometimes he wondered what it would be like just to lie

very still in a house somewhere and be well and clean once more. He slept, he walked, he lived in fear; beside him others slept and walked.

Sometimes he stole; pennies off a newsstand, a pear from a fruit store (this while waiting to beg the store's owner for over-ripe bananas); and once a shirt from an old man sleeping, only to find it alive with lice the minute he put it on. In Brooklyn he waited in front of the subway for newspapers which men and women dashing for trains dropped or discarded. When he caught a full paper he peddled it covertly. Some papers would be stamped: "If this paper is offered for sale it has been stolen." He could read all of these words, and he knew what they meant, but he took the chance just the same. By keeping every paper tightly folded until he received his three pennies for it, he was never caught. He learned to watch penny peanut machines for salty crumbs left up the slot after a buyer had walked away. He thrust muggy fingers up a machine and licked off what stuck to his fingers. Once, in front of a candy store in New York, two girls were giving away samples of fudge, and from each he got two pieces before he was refused more. Once he stole a bottle of milk off a door-step, but a dog started barking beneath the step and he dropped the bottle and ran. In a ten-cent store in Harrisburg he picked three chocolate bars from a counter and walked without haste toward a revolving door. On the other side of the counter a white-frocked flapper began walking without haste also, keeping just even with him toward the door all along the long counter. Past multi-colored gum drops, chocolate peppermints, Lafayette mixture and licorice cigars she went, watching him out of one eye's corner. Outside it was snowing, she caught his arm just as he reached the door. He knew that the jig was up then, of course; he got so scared that his heart slipped and fell briefly, making him cough a small cough as he stood, her hand restraining his. But she didn't speak loudly, she only whispered.

"I seen you take something. You put it in your pocket. Better fish it out quick and go."

Cass thrust the candy into her hand, and ran. The sidewalk was filmed with ice thin as paper, and in trying to run too swiftly across it he slipped and fell; as his heart had slipped and fallen.

And even though there were faces always about him, some moving north and some south, yet he himself went alone.

He learned how to sleep on a boxcar roof when that roof was swaying from side to side. He became used to park benches, and fugitive unlit places; he lay down on wooden floors in the flops of great cities, and found brief rest on the tile of strangers' hallways. Yet sometimes when he was tired he had no place to sleep or was too afraid to lie down. Once at night in October, on a bench in a park in Chicago, a man came and stood looking down quietly, paternally. He wore a furry dark coat with a belt. When he spoke Cass saw a warm small mouth; it was rouged and moved roundly; its lips were sweet berries. And when this man saw that Cass was tired and yet had no place to sleep but a bench, he sat down fatherly beside him.

"You want a job tonight, sonny? *I'll* give you a *nice* job. Easy. Soft. You know? Soft as sugar-titty. You like sugar-titty, sonny?"

Then he laughed like a girl and gave Cass a long cigarette and moved uneasily nearer, till Cass smelled perfume on the coat and could see white spittle on the little red lips. Cass thought of boys who became slaves to men, and he wanted to run from this man. Yet he dared make no move, fear wrapped him 'round. He sat very still and smoked the cigarette swiftly, feeling colder and colder within with each draw. About him the lake-fog came creeping alive; the man put one hand about him possessively and with his other hand stroked Cass's thigh. And as he stroked he spoke slowly, in rhythm with his hand.

"Come on, kiddo, you got me now. You'll love it, honest you will. It's fun for you too, and we'll have a drink first, and we'll take a long ride."

He showed Cass a bill then, and Cass had never seen a bill that big before. He stared at it, all dumbyokel curiosity, till the cigarette began suddenly to taste as sweet as Texas sugarcane—he flicked the butt, in one brief arc, away into nightgrass and creeping lake-fog. Then he took the bill in his hand the better to see it (though the man held tightly the other end all the while), and he counted the number of times it had "twenty" printed upon it. Then he let it go, the man took his hand away and stood up abruptly and walked briskly off down the gravel bridle path, his pearl spats a twinkle in the arc light under his long dark coat. And after a while Cass got up too, to look for some other bench.

He could not find another, and to the one he had left two other 'boes had come; the benches were filled with sleeping men. He was too tired to look for long that time. So he lay down in the aged October grass with a newspaper about him to keep off the damp.

For two months Cass lived in Chicago, in the fall of 1930. He walked up and down West Madison Street every day, one ragged bum among ten thousand ragged bums. He lived on what he could beg off the streets, and he went with a mind that was dark. Sometimes, for one day or one morning, he had a friend, but only for one day or one morning. He was always half-hungry; he slept in parks; he knew shame and cold. He was often afraid.

Curled up on the editorial page of the *Evening American* one afternoon, within the lengthening shadow of some butcher-on-horseback's statue, he wakened just as the sun was setting behind the city; when he brushed aside paper his eyes met the sunset, a thin red line between two darkening towers.

Lying here among other men now, starving and thirsting daily with other men, being now part of this life led by so many other men, Cass thought, in his moment of waking, that "Civilization" must mean a thing much like the mob that had threatened his father. For this too was a thing with a single mouth, this too mocked with pointing fingers. And as it had threatened his father, so now it threatened him. Through hunger, cold, and shame it had pursued. "We have no work for you" (he heard familiar voices); "We have no place for you. This is our world, louser. We do not claim you, you have no right here. We are *The Owners*. We Own All. Get out, get along, go somewhere else—keep moving till you die."

Along the broad boulevard a thousand men raced in automobiles toward food, warm fires, homes and wives. This was the fecund and darkening city, its towers, its terror, its threat.

"If once we catch you begging *openly* we'll stick you in jail. If you ride our trains you'll land in jail. And if once we catch you *stealing*—then to the pen you go. Get out, move along, go somewhere else. And stay out of sight till you die."

Cass walked down the I. C. tracks, for it was time to be getting on. Nights were growing cold again, and so he was headed south.

Once, two weeks later, as a train neared Marsh City in East Texas, Cass was wakened. A big man stretched on straw at the other end of the car was warning everyone fiercely, in a big man's voice.

"If Hank Pugh opens up the doors when we gets in, jest y'all stay right where yore settin', at now. Don't go hoppin' out the side or runnin', 'cause they jest ain't no sech thing as runnin' here. I been here befo'; I know. They shoot in this man's town." The big man rose clumsily, like a small elephant rising, and added quietly, "Jest set tight till he says, 'Awright, lousers, come awn out now.' An' then y'all want to say to him right back, 'Aw, come awn up in, Tuffnuts'—like that." The big man made a long face at the wall and spat tobacco out the door.

Parrotwise, another repeated the warning. Cass sat up. "When ol' Pugh say, 'Come awn out, lousers,' y'all say to Pugh right back, 'Aw come awn up in, Tuffnuts,'—like that. Don't fergit now."

Once the car leaped forward, front wheels two inches off the track, thunderously to lunge its steel into steel ahead; then it found the track again, wheeled with slackening speed toward the city. The men waited. Those lying, touched by sun and soot in sleep, rolled uneasily as they lay; they rumped each other suddenly as the long car buckled, and sat up blinking. Swearing then, and sweating from their sleep, they clung to walls, beams and boarding. The big man and the boy with the parrot's cackle slammed the great doors shut. In the darkness heat crawled down Cass's throat.

"Half a mile to Marsh City now, boys. Better start tightenin' up them guts, all you what's gonna hold *this* man down. They's gover'ment bulls here now beside Hank Pugh—but if y'll stick right with me, we'll sail right on through. They stops fo' water in this pesthole, then they tear right on fo' Shrevepo't. That's where ah got a job waitin' fo' me. Ah'm a Wob is why. It takes a old-time Wob to get jobs in these times."

From a dozen unwashed bodies a cloud of sweatstench rose into Cass's nose. Bits of straw blew into his mouth, tickled his throat, and worked into the cracks of his body until he had to keep scratching himself as though he had lice. He felt like a scarecrow stowed away, in autumn, in some dark old barn.

Jolt upon jolt, the car began slowing; then it jerked once and stopped, boards all quivering. All down the line behind him then, Cass heard each car buckle once and stop, beams all quivering. Sudden footsteps overhead warned that it was time to screw up courage. The men waited, till their car seemed still with waiting.

"When Pugh says, 'Come awn out, lousers,'" warned the parrot-voice, "Y'all say 'Aw, come awn in, Tuffnuts'—like that. Now don't y'all fergit." Cass surmised that this must be a friend of the Wobbly's.

"They won't cut this car off us here, will they, Mr Wobble?" someone asked. The Wobbly answered with contempt in his voice.

"Marsh City ain't no division point fo' *this* train. Don't yo' know what yo' ridin', kid?"

The kid didn't know. "Mr Wobble" let in a beam of light that cleft his face from forehead to jaw. Cass, standing in a corner, saw it. It was a bulging forehead and a bulging jaw, with a chin like a jagged rock outthrust. Then somebody was coming, and the fellow closed the slit he had made in the darkness. Somebody in boots. Cass heard him crushing cinders as he advanced swiftly, stepping over ties and scuffing against the rails. The door was flung wide.

Over the Wobbly's shoulder the boys peered down at one small man peering up. A little man, with a pale pointy face. Someone in an awed undertone asked Cass if this were Hank Pugh, and Cass nodded his head that it was, although he did not know. The man did not stand as though lame, but his face looked ugly enough to be Pugh's. When the little brakie spoke, the Wobbly only spread his legs wider in the doorway, folded his arms across his chest, and spat toward the earth.

"How many crawdads you got in that hole, big fella?"

"Oh they's plenty more'n jest me in here, Buttons—nigh onto twenty men ah reck'n." Behind him then as though to prove their numbers, the dozen-odd boys and men bestirred themselves noisily.

The little man below smiled knowingly, and turned away; Cass heard his boots moving faster and faster, back over the same wooden ties over which they had come. Such boots were two despisers of small things; they were high-heeled, sharp-pointed, imbedded deeply with spikes, shining with sun or bright with rainwet. Stuart had kicked Bryan at the base of the belly, but that had been long ago.

"Now, you ones what ain't of a mind to stick close to me'd best hit the grit right now, whilst you still got a chanst. That little shack has went to git Pugh."

Two ragged waifs with fatuous eyes hopped out and left at a long gallop down the ties. Rags streaming in the wind behind them, they looked like two bounding black colts with upright tails. A lank fellow leaned out and grinned after the pair, pointing a finger out of an unclean sleeve.

"Farm kids never do learn—they won't git two mile afore they're snatched. An' they won't be gittin' back on the road agen so easy neither, what with Marion County payin' sixty cents a day for every yokel in the jailhouse. No, them farmers won't be runnin' far, an' they won't be thrashin' oats next August neither." Hate like a sudden memory smothered his eyes and split the thin mouth into a snarl—"Goddamn 'em—Don't *I* know?—Don't *I* remember? Handcuffed me to the bars on my twenty-eight' day and I held cold steel till the month was out. Ninety days I set in that hole, an' for nothin' at all so help me God. Them ninety days was ninety years an' I'll never get 'em back."

"Horse—. You ain't never seen a *real* jail." A Northern voice was speaking. "I got vagged in East Florida an' got put to stompin' sileage. Grits, gravy an' cornbread every day an' two meals by lanternlight. Eighty-five men in one room an' not even a sheet of newspaper to sleep on. Hell, man, you ain't seen a real jail till you've stood up in a East Florida sweat-box a spell."

Cass could not see the man who said this, but he had known about Florida, and he had not gone there. It seemed to him now that no one in the car was as afraid as he himself was—till a voice now familiar spoke again, and then he knew he was not alone in his fear.

"When this Lame Hank Pugh says, 'Come awn out lousers' y'all want to say to him right back, 'Aw come awn in, Tuffnuts.' Don't ya'll fergit now."

It was the parrot-voiced boy.

The men crowded the doorways, shoulders brushed, hands touched, electrically a pleasant current passed from man to man. Cass ceased to be afraid for a moment; behind him someone began singing "Casey Jones."

Then down the tracks came a tall man, limping. Immediately, to buoy sinking spirits, the men set up a chorus of jeers, catcalls and mockery.

"Hulloo—thar come ol' Casey Jones hisself, with his whole danged army an' the town clown behind him, an'—"

> Ol' Casey Jones was a son of a bitch
> He backed his engine in a forty-foot ditch

The boiler busted, and the smoke-stack split
The fireman farted and Casey . . .

They broke off, for the detectives were now within hearing. Silently they waited now, those in front wishing that they had been a bit less impulsive, those behind edging uneasily back. In front of them all stood their leader, the big ugly Wob. But whenPugh came up it wasn't the Wob who spoke first, it was his squeaky-voiced companion.

"Will y'all let us ride, Mr Hank Pugh?" he pleaded, "We aint a-aimin' at trouble ay-tall."

The tall man stood with his hands on his hips looking alert and unamazed.

"Awright, boys, come awn down out now, an' come out one at a time. Trespassin' private proppity y'know," he paused to smile warmly; "an' when we're all through y'all git breakfast uptown—how'd that strike all you boys?" He kept his smile.

"Breakfast uptown"—the men knew what that meant, and those that moved at all moved only toward the car's corners. For one moment the special agent's eyes walked swiftly from face to boyish face; then they settled on the Wobbly's, the only full-grown man he could see.

"You-all come out first."

The Wob raised one eyebrow, and remained unmoving.

"That's right—stand still when I say come out! Don't make a move when I *tells* ya to move! Stand gawpin' like a figgin' ijit at me! Well by Christ *all* you sons-of-bitches'll wish you *had* of moved!" Pugh's mouth snapped shut, he came swiftly forward and the boys heeled back. As though the wheels had leaped suddenly under their feet, they fell against each other in a rush for the corners; then the door whirred past and was locked from the outside.

The boys laughed nervously, wondering why the agent had not come in after them; their other door stood wide as daylight.

"Don't let 'em lock this door, kids," the Wobbly warned, "that's what he's figgerin' on. He ain't got time to pull us out, so he figgers on keepin' us in."

Above their heads the boys heard men clambering over the spine and coming down the sides. When they reached earth Cass saw that there were now five deputies. They looked like farmers and hill-men just come from their farms and hills; they bore clubs and their faces were hard.

The Wobbly remained alone in the doorway, legs wide and arms akimbo. Although he spoke not a word, all there took his meaning as clearly as though he had said, "You'll have to get *me* before *this* door comes closed." From far ahead came two brief blasts, he braced his arms on the door's jambs in the second before the wheels pulled forward. In that second's fraction the man appeared like a great bird poised for flight over the heads of the little men threatening him from below. His arms seemed long dark wings outspread, and his shoulders hunched with tension. Then, like a gaunt buzzard, he was spinning downward through space. Cass saw him yanked head-first into the arms of the deputies. There had been no shot, only arm-wings flailing a brief pattern through sun, and legs flailing space into upreaching hands. Then there came hard laughter, and the sudden terrible rushing sound that is made when many men go swiftly against one. It was like a brief cold breeze, that sound. The door crashed past, the car jerked forward, and a small lock clicked as it jerked.

Dark now, utterly dark. Pugh would telegraph ahead to Waskom, the next division point. There, unless they broke out in the interval, everyone in the car would be held for trespassing on private property, and for resisting the officers. Or for vagrancy, or disorderly conduct, or, quite possibly, for vandalism or malicious mischief. Unless they broke out. "What a bunch of punks—to let Pugh git away with a stunt like that. Lawd, they aint 'nuf guts in this whole gang to stuff a . . ."

The voice checked itself abruptly. It had sounded much like a woman's voice. Men sucked in breath in an indrawn silence.

"Say! That sounds like a woman back there!"

In the darkness Cass heard an eager forward-jostling; then came silence again, till the car seemed rocking with its silence.

"Damned if it ain'ft boys! Say—whyn't you tell us afore, nigger gal? What y'all got in them pants anyhow, nigger gal?"

"Nigger gal, fellas! Say, nigger gal, where'd y'all come from anyhow? How long you been ridin', eh? Where y'all think yer goin' to? What's yore nasty name, nigger gal, anyhow?"

The girl's voice was a hung thing, oblique with thin fear.

"Charlotte Hallem. Goin't' Noo Awlins. Comin' f'om . . ."

"Whoops! She's a-goin' to Noo Awlins to work on *Franklin* Street—Step right up, gen'lmen, meet Charlotte, the little travelin' girrul. Which way y'all taken it t'night, gen'lmen?"

Simultaneously, two voices from different parts of the car struck up the same tune, wailing it out until others joined in,

> *Oh Charlotte the harlot*
> *The queen of the whores,*
> *Scum of the east side*
> *Covered with sores.*

They sang this jeeringly over and over again; they all knew the tune of *Long, Long Ago,*—till a voice spoke out strongly to bring them back to realization of their predicament.

"Get that nigger gal off yer mind, you kids. Start figgerin' how yer gonna get out of this hole before we hit Waskom."

Cass thought: "That's that derned Nawtherner again, talkin' like he was the engineer. The air's gittin' kind of close all right though. Unless we staht workin' last it'll be ninety days fo' me too, in Marion County jail."

"Okey, Yank," someone said.

In the whole ragged crew there was but one jack-knife, and that belonged to the Negress. But she gave it over when asked by the Northerner, and the baiting ceased for a time. Yet something of lust unquelled remained in the air.

They took turns whittling at the wood; when one hand tired the knife was passed on. Came Cass's turn, he expected to feel a deep hole in the two-inch boarding; instead there were only a few feeble scratches to show what had already been accomplished. The wood was too hard, the knife was dull as a tin spoon; in the hands of the boy who followed Cass the blade snapped in two. This was the boy who had aped the Wobbly's orders; when the blade broke he said, as though its breaking had jogged his memory, "When they pulled John out sudden that way we should o' got right out an' pulled him back in. Then I would of said, 'Aw come on up in,' Tuffnuts'—jest like that."

Once in the night Cass woke, and did not know where he lay. Stooping gray figures came and went all about him, he felt as though he were caught somewhere, deep down. Then he remembered: he was lying on a creaking nightdoor with his cap for a pillow and straw for his bed, and Nancy was nowhere near at all.

"Ah shouldn't of said such words to sister that time," he thought.

And he slept once more, and he dreamed. He dreamed he was

walking beneath a wall that stretched in a rising curve over prairie. It was evening, the end of the wall was dusk, and in vastness above him a great hawk wheeled; dimly, sweetly, from very far, a church-bell chimed and chimed toward night. Cass clung close to the long dusk-wall, he feared the wheeling hawk; it seemed that the bird had been searching for long, over the whole dark prairie for him. The church-chimes paused, there came the thunder of wings down-whirring, wing-thunder became the roaring of wheels—and he woke to his own heart's pounding. In the corner men were piling something. He rose and saw that they were preparing to burn their way out. Rags and straw and paper were piled against the wall.

"Aint y'all feared of it cotchin' th' other cars?" Cass asked of nobody in particular.

"Naw, they's a steel gondola ridin' in front an' a iron dumpcar in back," the Northern voice replied, "an' anyways the crew ought to see it 'fore it goes too far." The man lit a match and leaned over; in the glare Cass saw that he had a hare-lip.

"I burned outen a box once before," the hare-lip moved, "on the Central of Georgia, outen a wood reefer. You got to be careful that it don't spread." The men stomped the flame down wherever it threatened to catch the floor.

What a joke this would be on those Waskom bulls, when they opened the car to get a load of bums at two dollars a head—and found nothing inside but four charred walls! As they stomped the dame the little Negress came out of a corner and helped to beat dame back with her cap; her frizzly hair, brushing Cass's cheek, excited him a little.

"Ah hates fire," she condded, "cause fire made me a widder oncet—an' not so long ago neither."

It was long work, the work of burning out; the flame ate up air that they needed for breath. The men coughed. The black girl opened her collar, and her throat seemed darker than the night about them. Cass could see its outline in the dimness, black as a pillar of black baleen. When there was a hole in the boarding big enough to let two hands through, the Northerner and Cass tugged and yanked together, gradually loosening the boards. Then the train began slowing and they had to leave off out of fear of the shack. Cass heard the engine taking water far ahead, and heard the brakie testing the air. The shack would know where they were all right, and would listen and look as he passed. Being afraid that the man would see the ragged hole in the car's side, the Northerner hung his cap over the hole until he had passed. Then the car rolled on again, and they yanked anew at the boarding. When fingers tired there was someone else's to wrench and strain in turn. But three or four of the 'boes lay in sleep and did not care whether morning found them free or in a cell on a vag charge.

Cass was tired. He was always tired now, and ready at a moment's notice to doze anywhere. He didn't know why he was always so tired; he only knew that his months on the road already seemed years. When he looked back in memory it seemed almost as though there had never been anything but the road, the long American road, all his life.

His eyes had scarcely closed when it seemed to him that some voice that had spoken now was still, or something that had been moving had stopped very quietly. He sat up and saw blue moonlight running through a crack in the boarding as high as his head. A low range of hills stood limned against night, prairie was rushing past like sea. The men were crowding toward the open place, anxious for the train to slow again in order to leap.

Cass breathed in nightwind off those hills, the low range passed as he stood watching; a line of tall steeples came in its place. Like cathedral-skeletons against the breaking light. Oil wells. Far, far to the east, over the very brim of the veering world they stood. Then over a distance of half a mile the train began to slow and the men began to go off, one by one, the most daring first. They hit the dirt running, some staggered and fell; it was hard in the dimness to see just where one was jumping. The boy preceding Cass caught his foot against something just as he jumped, he fell head downward toward the wheels and saved himself only by sheerest luck, plus some presence of mind: he caught the last rung of the side-ladder as it swung by, and dragged, dangling, for seventy feet. Then he shoved himself free, and rose from earth with the knees gone out of his trousers and one side of his face raked with cinders in furrows. Cass jumped after. Then the black girl. Behind them for half a mile they saw dim shadow bums, walking slowly. Then someone pointed and someone called out: Cass turned his head toward the train they had left.

Around a curve against black sky the moving boxcar in the night went blazing toward false dawn; tall flowers of fire spilled in the dark, orange-wanton blossoms burst the black. From the long curve then, as the whole train straightened, one flat and pointed sheet swept down. And in one moment the entire car was enwrapped in flame. So vivid was that long caravan, in that moment of straightening by dame silhouetted, that Cass could discern two of the train-crew moving microscopically down the spine of the cars toward the box that was burning.

"Ah hates the sight of fire," the Negress said, watching next to Cass. "On account of it made me a widder oncet."

The men were afraid when they saw. They huddled together in

little groups, till the train in distance seemed to be stopping. And each man in his mind added one word then to the list of his crimes and felonies of the past five hours; here was something to reckon with more serious than all their previous offenses put together. This was arson. Some looked accusingly at Jones, the Northerner, but Jones looked right back and said nothing at all. He took no blame, not from any man, his look seemed to say.

As they scattered Cass found himself walking between Jones and the black girl. With two others they headed for a little copse of scrub cedar. Not until they had put the scrub between themselves and the tracks did they feel a degree safer. Someone would be caught, Jones said. Someone always was.

The boy who had been the Wobbly's companion walked directly ahead, munching a sandwich; when he had consumed half of it he returned the remainder to his pocket, for future reference. Cass, watching hungrily, suddenly hated the boy; he was lanky and pimpled and walked slinkingly, like a thief. On his bindle Cass read his name, sewed on the pack with red thread, in large letters: *Claude Burrus, The Smilin' Kid.* The black girl took a bar of chocolate out of one pocket and a pack of ten-cent cigarettes out of the other. After both had been passed around there was not a great deal of either left for herself. Claude Burrus took some of both, thanked her for neither, and walked on ahead chewing and smoking alternately.

The girl laughed and joked with them all as they walked. Cass saw that she was no longer afraid, because she was now in the open. And she told them of herself, of the place she had come from and where she was going; she had come from New Mexico, she was going to Louisiana. She had lost her husband, was going to work now in a laundry owned by the late husband's brother. As she talked and smoked the breasts under her overalls rolled hugely. These appeared to weigh perhaps four pounds apiece, and thus betrayed her otherwise masculine aspect.

Jones thwacked her on the rump with the flat of his palm.

"Say, if y'jest lost yer husban', you'd best to marry me now, black gal. I'm a good pervider, I am. Come on out in the scrub wid me an' I'll pervide y' some right now." He glanced at the others for approval, and Claude Burrus laughed.

"Go ahead, nigger gal. Marry the Yank."

"Kin I be best man at yore weddin', Yank?"

"All o' you kin be best men," Jones offered magnanimously, "soon as Lizah-Jane say the word. Oney you'll have t' take at bein' best men, an' we ort to chip up right now fer a gift fer our littl' bride—fifteen cents apiece ort to do, ain it, Lizah-Jane?" He kept trying to suck his hare-lip down, to conceal it with his under lip. The habit gave him the impression of having two mouths; a big and oblong cross-cut one, and a little triangular hairy one right on top and growing out of the other. In his narrow eyes glowed a devil of cruelty.

The girl ceased to joke and to chatter. Once she dropped a little behind, to let them all pass on; but Jones wound his arm in hers and would not let her go.

"Ain't time fer no divorce yet, Coconut-Tits—wait'll we gets married first."

Claude Burrus took up the joke immediately.

"Ain't time fer no div-orce yet, Coco-nut Tits—You'n me is gonna git married t'gether in Waskom." He took her other arm.

When houses began to dot the prairie, at closer and closer intervals, the men turned north to skirt a town.

To the east gray light rode down between the hills. Then the sun like a bucket of blood spilled over, and grayness became a running red. The homeless rested.

In a small valley they lay down, five ragged men and a girl. A red-buttressed mesa went all about, there came green pine-smell down from the mountains. The 'boes spread out their coats and slept. The grass was touched with early dew.

Cass slept with his back against a small tree, sharing the tree's trunk with Claude Burrus. How tired Cass was! He slept till he heard a crow over the prairie let fall a single caw; the sound waked him, but he did not open his eyes until he heard someone walking off. The black girl, stepping quietly away from Jones; the Northerner lay purring in sleep. Obeying a passing impulse, Cass nudged Burrus. The boy jumped up and called the girl sharply. "Lizah, where you-all goin' to?" Jones awoke, stretching.

Sleep had refreshed them; they were ready for deviltry.

The girl paid no heed to Burrus until she heard him coming up swiftly behind her. Then she whirled, all defiance, her voice a threat, and a plea—then a sob.

"Puppy, yo' keep awn a-pesterin' me an' sho' as shucks ah'll beat yo' eahs down. Sh-sho as sh-shucks."

Standing so, her body thick in some sharecropper's overalls, short arms akimbo, she tooked fully capable of thrashing the gangling, pimpled youth. Yet, her eyes were wet. Behind her a clump of dead mesquite stood against the light of noon, its boughs blackly barren against the sun; like the form of something from which the spirit had fled. A meadowlark rose in a swift white blooming, bright tail splitting the sky in two. The men barked laughter. One egged the girl on and another the boy.

"Nervy black heifer," Olin Jones grumbled. "They're whores every time. Why don't he push her black puss in anyhow? They all

yell some, but don't believe *that*, they like white boys to do 'em that
way. That's what they're for, y'know."

Then he laughed lowly, a faint half-laugh; they all had to
laugh then at what they saw. Burrus, with his side turned toward
them, was urinating on the girl's overalls; when she stepped back
he followed. And when she could go no further back, because of
the mesquite behind her, she screamed and struck out at him. He
caught one arm and imprisoned it, laughing, but her teeth found
his wrist and his laughter broke—"Oooooo"—he yelped like a
lashed pup—"Oooooo, now I will git yo' fer *real*."

He advanced slowly, the girl's voice rose to frenzy.

"White! White! Mah Joe you burnt!"

She came forward like an outraged cat, and her fingernails
screeled deeply down his face. In a panic of surprise and pain, he
recaptured her arm and twisted until she screamed darkly, like a
cat with its throat cut trying to scream. Twisting thus slowly and
using both of his own hands, enraged by the feel of blood on his
cheeks and encouraged by sharp cries behind him, he forced the
girl to her knees and to earth. He was not quite strong enough,
however: though he pinned her arms deep in sod and kneeled hard
on her breasts, yet she writhed so that he could no longer control
her. Had Olin Jones not run up swiftly, still feigning faint laughter,
she would have escaped them all. Jones squatted heavily down on
her legs in the very moment when it seemed she was finally free;
holding her firmly with one hand, with his other he ripped her
overalls down the middle. Laughing faintly.

Cass saw. The other boys saw. They all came laughing forward to see.

And the girl's cry went up like a silken thread into air till a
hand like shears cut it down. A hand over her mouth as laughter

died. And there was no sound then save the sound of five indrawn breaths, and somebody who said, "Ah—ah."

Jones spoke steadily.

"Free ride t'day, gentlemen. If you want it, come an' get it."

Now there came into Cass's heart a dark and terrible desire. Drawn by a power more strong than himself, like a strong hand pushing him from behind, he went closer and closer. About him others moved slowly closer. All moved slowly, in silence, toward the black woman. The air became charged with the smell of the woman, they all smelled the dark woman, her thighs and her womb: womb, belly and breasts, her thighs flexing in fear.

They were all of them men; they were men without women.

7

CASS AND THE man called Olin Jones stood on the corner of Common and Cotton Streets, in Shreveport. For the first time in many months Cass did not feel alone in the world. He had a friend, one who was wiser than himself. They had been drunk together the night before, and they were hungry now. Unwashed, they stood in rags.

"I kin mooch a dime out of anything with pants on, male or female," Olin boasted to Cass; "you watch my smoke an' all you'll see is ashes." Olin knew when to whine, when to cringe, and when to beg boldly; he knew when to come fawning with a "Jest three cents fer carfare, mister, so's I kin get to work?" And he knew when to wink broadly and say, "Be a sport, pal, I'm a vet an' I ain't had a drink all day. Let's have a dime for a shot, waddya say?" He had taught Cass that sheer stick-to-it-iveness was the larger part of successful mooching.

"Come on, Red," Olin offered. "They's a jernt on Market Street belongs to a guy used to be a pal of mine in the field artill'ry. He'll set us up to coffee an'. He's a Greek, an' his misery's the hottest stuff in cups. Come on."

Walking swiftly and turning odd corners, they passed the courthouse on Milam Street; a block later they passed the jail. Olin jerked his thumb toward its upper windows.

"Put sixty-one days of my life up there on the second floor an' I ain't yet found out why. They kep' me two months, an' then they let me go. No trial, no hearin', no show-up, no nothin'. Just settin' up there fer sixty-one days, askin' the jailer every day 'Why?' An' I never did find out."

"Ah never really been in jail 'cept to sleep overnight up north sometimes. Ah like Sallies better."

Olin spoke crisply. "I never stand up fer Jesus. I'd ruther go to jail fer a week then sing one of them chicken-dribble songs jest fer a crumby cot. I don't trust no holy bastard, livin' or dead. The holier they look the quicker they'll rook you."

They turned down Texas into Market Street.

The little white restaurant was crowded, and steaming; buttocks in trousers warmed every stool greasily. The owner was a monster, a Greek with a belly; under his egg-stained apron he strouted out somehow awfully, like a woman come too late to her time. He saw what they wanted before they begged it, and a middle-aged blonde came bearing two cups of coffee in one hand and three bowls of soup in the other. The soup was for paying customers, the coffee for Cass and Olin. She bore bowls and cups on her fingertips in a mechanical unconcern rather baffling to Cass. They drank leaning over the cigar-case, and drops spilled onto white business cards face-up under the glass; the first sip made Cass wish for sugar. He made a wry face. Olin was bolder. He reached down the counter, returned with a bowl, and Cass spooned out one timorous helping. But Olin turned the bowl on end and sugar avalanched into his cup. His coffee overflowed onto the counter and still he poured sugar, grinning faintly. "Ah guess he's as hard as he says he is," Cass thought uneasily, looking about to see whether the owner were watching.

Olin drained his cup in two gulps; he did not trouble to replace the bowl. The glass beneath his elbows became a running farrago of coffee, drifting sugar, and two smoldering cigarette butts; he leaned over the mess unashamed. Half-covering it with his unclean sleeve, he hissed at the waitress:

"Ssssssss—sneak us a sugar doughnut, Blondie."

The woman refused to hear, and when she returned he took a petty vengeance on her for her deafness. Whispering just low enough to be heard by her clearly, he said, "That blonde scurve ain't young no more, Red. Jest look at her, what she's doin' now. Say, don't she look jest like a old slut gettin' set fer her last big Sattiday night?"

Cass cautioned, "Be still, Olin, be still. Y'all won't git nothin' talkin' thataway."

The woman was placing a long platter of steak and potatoes before a man with a milk-driver's badge pinned onto one side of his cap; a slow-surging flush across her temple showed only too clearly how well she had heard. Olin laughed his faint laugh, being well-pleased. Then Cass, feeling the milk-driver's eyes on him, himself reddened. The driver's look was insolent; he too had heard Olin's whisper. Cass's cap was ripped at the side, his shoes had only strings for laces; and that impersonal look kept walking over him. The man chewed an onion as he surveyed, to add to the quiet insult of his eyes. Olin saw that look and came to Cass's aid.

"Jeez," he gasped in an awed undertone, looking straight at the driver, "Didja ever see a mug like that before, Red? Say, Red, don't it look sort of like somethin' you throw sawdust on an' sweep out quick 'fore it smells up the whole barn? Don't it look sort of like somethin' like that, Red?"

The driver turned his eyes away, and Cass said, "Shhhh." The

Greek was coming with a bag, and the bag's open throat revealed butter-rolls and sugar doughnuts. Cass received it in both hands. Then the kind Greek monster gave Olin a dime, and they mooched out arm in arm.

Olin held the bag, but Cass could eat faster because he had no hare-lip. Olin's deformity worked obscenely in and out as he ate, all brown and hairy and bristling. When the sack had been emptied Olin puffed the bad lip into the bag, twisted its throat, and burst it with a "pop" disappointingly feeble. Then, hanging over a white stone parapet, they watched the ripped paper drift zig-zaggedly down into Red River far beneath.

For the first time in many days Cass did not feel hungry. He launched a slow nodule of spittle after the sack and leaned far over to follow its course. "It'll go clear down to the ocean now, that little hunk o' spit," he informed Olin.

When Olin Jones laughed his mouth looked like two mouths, a big one and a small.

Down Market Street, in the business district, they paused in front of a little burlesque house to gaze at the pictures of girls displayed in front. Cass thought of the black girl violated on the prairie. Yet he said, "Say, this looks hot enough to scorch mah pants off, Olin. Let's go in, Yank ol' boy. Let's us pling fo' bits apiece an' go in here. What yo' say?" Cass spoke in bravado, to drown secret shame.

Olin Jones laughed faintly. He was always ready.

"That's how I like to hear you talkin', Red. Like you got some life in you, like you was a real man. What side the street you want? I'll take this an' you take that. Watch out fer cops an' preachers an' do like you been seein' me do. Don't take no Mex nickels, don't stand in one spot, don't get scared of nothin'—an' I'll meet you here in an hour."

Left atone, Cass's courage drained out of him. A hundred white faces passed him by every minute, and he let them all pass. Some faces were young, with round, meaty cheeks, and others were gray as winter with age. And all, young and old, were going somewhere in a hurry. It seemed to Cass that everyone had something important to do in the world save himself. He himself had nothing to do, so the least he could do was to stay out of the way. He was like some lost burro, he thought, a young burro who walks riderless all through a dark night.

"Ah'd like to do somethin' *big*," he thought; "Ah'd like to be in one hell of a hurry like other folks."

Lounging against a wall, he waited long for some likely seeming prospect. Half a dozen times he sidled up beside strangers, only to lose his voice the moment they turned to face him. Finally, however, he resolved to be bold. He slipped up beside an old woman who dangled a silver mesh bag from her left arm, and he whispered. She screwed her eyes up one moment inquiringly; then fear like a curtain clouded them and they looked like an aged sheep's eyes: sick old sheep eyes pleading timidly, "No. No. Please go away. How terrible you seem, how ugly and fierce!" She tightened the mesh bag about her wrist, drawing it swiftly closer up. Cass stopped dead in his tracks; he had frightened her badly. Watching her retreating figure, his fingers found his scar and traced it. Next time he would try a man. Some young man. When red traffic tights stopped eastbound pedestrian traffic on Marshall Street he stunk abreast of a stim fellow in a seersucker suit.

"Gimme a dime, mister," he asked, "Ah'm hungry as hett."

Surprising even to himself, he was demanding. He heard the sound of his own voice, and its sound was encouraging. It rang true, like the voice of a man who wouldn't take "No" very easily.

The slim fellow slipped on the sidewalk, and turned angrily on Cass.

"Beat it," he snarled, as though Cass were somehow to blame for his slipping.

"Did' y'almost fall, mister?" Cass inquired, with hair hanging in his eyes. Olin wouldn't have retreated now, he knew, so he tossed his hair back, and he stood his ground. "Well, a nickel then," he persisted, coming closer. Hell, he was half an inch taller than this fag and *twice* as tough; even if he wasn't wearing white flannels. His shoulders were as broad, almost; even though they weren't wrapped in a silk-striped shirt.

A mole on the fellow's cheek began bristling, his face seemed to darken under the eyes; then the red traffic lights flashed to green, he brushed Cass aside with a cool contempt and paced away with the crowd.

Cass hesitated only a second, but the fellow had reached the opposite curb before he'd gathered the courage to follow. Halfway down the block, singling out a straw hat among many straw hats, he fell into step again with the seersucker suit.

"Well, mister, y'all gonna gimme that nickel? Jest tell me what yore gonna do, that's all."

He felt as tough now as Olin Jones himself. Tough as a bull-whip and twice as mean. No ice-cream-panted college bastard was going to shove him, Cassy McKay, off the sidewalk.

The fellow was keeping his eyes ahead, pretending not to hear. "Ah know how to git a rise out of this kind," Cass thought, and aloud he said, "That seersucker suit look just like a sea-sucker's suit to me, mister."

The other did not reply; he was thinking, "By right I ought to call a cop on this lout. He ain't hungry, he looks strong as an ox. Still, he is kind of cave-chested at that. And he sure ain't had a haircut since Hoover won Arkansas.—Oh, hell." He dug for his change. Cass, bending over with one hand outstretched, saw three quarters, a dime, and four pennies. He saw all that lying there in the clean soft palm, so close that he could have snatched one of the quarters and run. In anticipation, he cupped his palms. When he received in them only the four pennies he didn't say, "Thanks." A devil rose to his tongue and said instead, "Ah deserve more, mister. Honest to Jeez, ah'm really deservin'." He grinned, feeling himself wholly clever now. "Ah guess ah'm workin' mahself through somethin' too." But the seersucker suit was gone.

Cass was strangely well-pleased with his four little pennies. He felt he had worked hard for them, he felt that he'd earned them. Above all he felt that he could now get money again almost any time he wished, just like Olin Jones. He felt that he had overcome that shame which, many times since he had left Great-Snake Mountain, had kept him from begging. Cass did not yet know how temporary is the courage which the simple fact of food in the belly loans a man. For twenty-five minutes he begged and he wheedled, plinged, panned, mooched and pursued; and with such force that he amassed sixty-eight cents. Then he stopped a tall man bearded like a physician, a man with a cane and a waxed goatee, one dressed like a duke who strode like a king. Cass thought, "Ah'll bet that's a millyunaire sho' 'nuf, an' jest fo' plain orn'ryness ah'm gonna give him a mooch." The answer came smooth-smiling and soft: "I'm on the stem too, son. Sorry as hell."

"Well anyhow," Cass reflected, cocking his head to the side in puzzlement, "anyhow, ah got mine." He wished, as he began working back to the little showhouse on Market, that older men would quit calling him "son."

He hoped that Olin had not done too well. Olin brushed past him before he reached Market.

"I'm goin' in, son; I got mine."

Cass was proud then that he too had plinged enough for an admission. In the lobby he bought two packs of gum, to show his appreciation of Olin, and they went inside chewing five sticks apiece.

Now Cass had never been to a show before, any kind of a show. After his eyes had adjusted themselves to alternate darkness and glare he saw a stage thronging with beautiful women, and he heard a voice trilling sweetly as any lark; albeit there were but five rouged wenches there and a contralto who quavered her voice in weepy songs by seizing her windpipe between two fingers. The girls danced without any semblance of rhythm, sometimes one scratched herself as she plodded. When there was nothing else to do, and all five moppets were out of step together, they stopped, one by one, and waggled their breasts loosely, like half-filled water bottles. But for Cass the air rocked with beauty, and angel-voices sang. The cheap tinsel hangings had, for him, a high magnificence. He was lifted wholly out of himself.

And, wholly, wonder overcame him. Once, from far away, he thought he heard Olin Jones say something about the air being stuffy or stale. Cass was not even conscious that there was air about him, however; then, after a timeless interval, he remembered hearing faint laughter near; he turned toward Olin then, but Olin was gone, leaving behind him only his faint echo. How long he had been gone Cass never learned, for he never saw Olin Jones again.

He sat on in the front row, bending toward the stage with mouth unhinged, till lights came on, and an usher started toward him. Cass rose at the usher's touch—and how he envied the fellow!

"Lawd! To work in such a place as this! To come heah every day!" In that moment Cass could imagine nothing on earth more desirable. At the door he turned and looked once more at the stage, but there was nothing there now save a sheet of cheap shoddy hanging crookedly over some dark and barren boards.

Cass never forgot the Market Street burlesque house, and the desire to attach himself to burlesque was to remain with him until simple circumstance would bring him to such a place.

Outside it was raining, soft autumn rain of Shreveport midnight; the long unlovely Southern street glowed wetly under round street-globes. The wavering line of light running the column of each lamp made each globe seem a little Southern moon, tethered to the Southern street. Cass walked on as in a dream; he could not waken. Women in vision raced his brain. They whirled, they bowed, they rose in pairs; they sang, and, bending sweetly over, spoke low and lustful for his ears. Then they danced in a wanton circle round, paused one moment, and were gone.

And the fierce frenzy Cass had known three days before with the Negro girl came blazing afresh in his blood—when the singers in fancy came again their flesh had turned from white to brown. Then their legs twinkled darkly, brown breasts quivered, slender brown arms reached warmly up for him.

The brown girl's arms had fought him fiercely. Cass looked around.

He was sitting on a bench facing the river, and the rain had stopped—and in one moment all the dim faces and brown breasts of fancy, the far away sound of swift music—even the scent of the perfume still in his nostrils—these in one moment became crystallized, hardened, grew smaller, came closer, became one solid thing. It was no longer fancy then, no longer vision, but hard hot lust. He rose quickly, and his loins were stiff with his desire; his brain held nothing but his desire, and his blood was storming with it.

Through a park and down a flowered way he passed. On a bench a woman lay under an overhanging bough, protected from its dripping by yellowing comic-strips. Her bare legs stuck out from under the heaped paper like two thin white clothes-poles out of a damp laundry basket; Cass saw, in their protuberant veining, that the woman was very old.

He had lost his cap somewhere, he didn't know where, and his head was uncombed for days. Sweat stood on his forehead; his hands twitched in his torn pockets. He could not sit down, although twice he tried. The same hand that five days before had thrust him from behind now made him rise and walk on. He tried telling himself that he was only looking for a place to lie down, but his heart knew better. His veins ran with fire and his heart cried out. His brain and his heart, and more than his heart. As in a mist of memory he remembered his brother Bryan, and a secret vice Bryan had often practiced. Cass didn't want to do that.

Although he had not slept for hours, had not eaten since the morning, hunger and weariness had no part of him now. He began to plan crazily.

"Back o' town. Where's back o' town? Ah'll do like ol' Olin do, when *he* want it bad enuf. Give her a nickel when yore through an' if she don't like it tell her to stuff it. Where's back o' town? If she raises a fuss beat hell out o' her. That's what ol' Olin does; that's what black gals is made fo'." He fumbled in his coat and found a dime and four pennies. It did not take him ten minutes to be accosted.

In a yellow sweater with an upturned collar a mulatto girl stepped out of a slant alleyway as he passed, holding a newspaper over her head in lieu of an umbrella. Cass stooped under the paper with her, and in silence they walked to an old frame house with a musky negroid smell all about it. It smelled heavy and sweet inside, as tropical flowers smell at night. Up a winding stairway they went, then down a dim passageway lined with doors. Smelling that heavy purple smell, Cass recalled a dooryard lilac blooming.

One door stood open as they passed; Cass saw cards littered across green carpet, and he heard a woman singing.

> *O fill mah casket with sweet marijuana*
> *Let me dream mah life away*
> *Ah ain't gonna marry or settle down*
> *Ah'll cook me up pills till some bull shoots me down . . .*

The odor about the old house was more than negroid, more than lilac. Cass had never smelled anything quite like it before. It smelled like punk, and it smelled like disease. It smelled like patchouli. It smelled like fernol.

While the girl was unlocking a door a white man came out of a room far down the hall; he paused, buttoning his trousers, and passed on, whistling. Out of memory where it had slept came a shrill and savage cry into Cass's brain.

"Jack! Jack Gaines!"

Slowly Cass turned about and slowly walked back toward the winding stairway. When he reached the head of it the yellow girl overtook him.

He couldn't bluff it through as he had planned. Like a child caught in a small lie he held out his hand, and all he possessed in its palm. "Ah ain't got so much as ah thought ah had," he said, and his heart dragged darkly when he said it. She peered through

dimness into his palm; he hoped against hope that she'd take fourteen cents—then she laughed very softly and slapped the palm
upwards. The dime rolled silverly down the stairway, the four pennies rolled into darkness; and the yellow girl was gone, laughing
mulatto laughter.

On his hands and knees down the staircase then, Cass recovered three pennies; but the other penny was lost, and so was the
dime. He looked for them until he heard someone at the head of
the stairs. Then he picked up and ran, a big country lout out of a
Shreveport whorehouse, three pennies in his fingers and his hair
in his eyes.

Cass knew where he was going to spend the pennies, too. He
went straight for the arcade off Fannin Street. There, on moldy
postal cards from 1912, he saw, first: a girl sitting in a bath tub;
second, a girl plunging into surf wearing a bathing suit; and third,
a mere blank grayness. He stared at this mere blank grayness till
the owner came by and said, "Machine's out o' order—caint yo'
read?" Cass went hurriediy out of the place, carrying with him the
wanton leer of the girl he had seen in a tub; he had seen her breasts
and her thighs, he kept assuring himself.

But it was not enough. The thing would not let him be.

On the corner of Fannin and Edwards he almost ran into a
girl or a woman, he couldn't tell which, walking alone. Face pow-
der smell came to him strongly, and he turned to follow. She had
smelled just like the girls in the show. And though the streets here
were unlit, yet he seemed to perceive her whole body clearly, only
twenty yards in front of him, saw all its movements beneath a dark
dress, sensed all its whiteness, felt all its warmth.

And because he had already learned that life gave no good
thing fairly, that all things go to those most cruel, Cass put down

in himself what there was of ruth, and he walked faster. When he was only a few feet behind her he broke into a run, the girl turned her head, and he stifled her scream with one long arm that went like an ape's around her mouth. He saw her mouth opening whenever he looked, opening and closing without any sound. But he did not know he had struck her till he saw her lower lip bleeding. He did not know where he was till he saw they were no longer on a street; somehow, they were in an alley and she was beneath him. "Why'nt she pick up an' run off from me?" he wondered, unaware of his knees that pinned her.

Cans and ashes lay strewn about them; he saw all things standing out in sharp detail, as though roundhouse floodlights were shining down from directly above him. He whipped off the hat that concealed the girl's eyes. "Say, ain't you Nancy?" he whispered, running fingers through her hair to see. But it was not thick hair like Nancy's. It was thin and fair. Slowly then he understood, touching that head, that this was only a little girl struggling beneath him. A little ten-year-old wisp of a thing.

"No, *yore* not sister," he said and he saw her lips moving.

"Please . . ." (he saw the moving child-lips say it, and he felt himself waking).

"Please . . ."

And in shrill terror Cass rose and ran.

Before morning came he was out of Shreveport. He never went there again.

8

THE PEOPLE WERE moving about, moving about. It seemed to Cass that no one knew why. Sometimes it seemed to him that men were all, somehow, blind; that they went from city to city in darkness.

By the winter of 1931 Cass knew that disaster had come to the world above him. For all through the South that winter, East and West, the trains gathered people like flies. Whole families piled into cattle-cars, women rode in reefers; old men rode the brakebeams, holding steel rods above the wheels with fingers palsied by age. Several times Cass saw pregnant women riding in empties.

"It's the big trouble everywhere," a girl told him. Wherever he went men spoke of "the big trouble."

And even though there were now faces always about him, some moving east and some west, yet he himself went alone. All men went alone; no two went together.

Faces changed. One spoke of Seattle, one of Memphis, another of ripening wheat in Kansas. But whatever they said, Cass felt that they were lying; he felt somehow that these faces had never seen the cities and fields, that they only thought they had seen them.

And the voices always lying, always boasting or lying voices, they all came to sound alike to him, as voices sound in rain. Their words were encrusted with a thin film of white spittle, like the spittle on the lips of the pervert in the park.

Wherever he walked that winter, whether in New Orleans along icy docks or on Railroad Street in Baton Rouge, he saw the vast army of America's homeless ones; the boys and old women, the old men and young girls, a ragged parade of dull gray faces, begging, thieving, hawking, selling and whoring. Faces haggard, and hungry, and cold, and afraid; as they passed, booted men followed and watched. Springfield, Decatur, Little Rock, Fort Smith; Beaumont, Houston, Austin, San Marcos. Then, San Antonio.

Cass got into San Antonio on the third night of January of 1931; and 1931 hit San Antonio with rain, sleet, and hail. He slept under newspaper that night in a wheelless S. P. passenger coach standing on a siding outside the S. P. yards. It smelled foul within, but its windows were boarded and its floor was dry.

All night rain tapped against the windows; a timid rat came to nibble something at the far end of the coach, and Cass rustled his paper to scare him away.

When he rose in the morning he felt hunger like a wound behind his navel; so he came to his feet slowly, having learned that hunger spun his head like a top whenever he came too swiftly to his feet. Outside a false dawn was breaking over a dripping water-tank, and beyond the tank lay the city. He tied his shoes standing against a pile of carwheels through which stunt burdock was still trying to grow; then he pushed through fields of buffalo grass knee-high and stiff with frost, until he came to a street.

Nogalitos Street.

"If ah could rustle me up two bucks in this pesthole," he promised himself, "ah'd get me tattooed all over."

He decided to look for that beanery where, three years before, he had eaten with a boy named Thomas Clay. Or had it really been Thomas Clancy? Cass pondered this ancient question as he walked.

Night-clouds hung heavily, threatening snow. A child's face peered wanly from a window as he passed, like the face of a sick child peering. As he passed the false dawn died, the streets became black as pitch once more. He could not find the old beanery, nor any similar place, though he sought along the streets for long.

When he turned down Pedro Avenue into Navarro it was seven o'clock—and three blocks away, unevenly scissored there from a gray mist, a soup line seemed a thousand-humped serpent winding. Regularly and minutely the dark line jerked, was still with waiting, then wormed six convulsive inches through one narrow door. Its humps were the heads of homeless men, centipede legs were arms in rags. Its hungering mouth was a thousand mouths; even from three blocks away Cass felt that dreadful humility with which homeless men wait for food. A feeling as though of some disgraceful defeat came to him. On the curb gray sparrows flirted their tails, and pecked where horses late had passed.

Once, far ahead of the place where Cass stood in the queue, at the place where the queue found the door, someone shouted something in anger or pain, and a mocking response came from within. A little flurry of excitement ran up and down the line, many laughed together and a single cry went up, weakly and thinly striving up into the unseen sky. Fog wrapped the cry, and Cass saw the bum who had cried out: he was walking swiftly away down Navarro. At the corner his angry figure turned, Cass could see it only dimly, the voice came muffled by mist.

"Do a man have to wait all mornin' in line to git a tin plate o' cow-donick? I kin get garbage out o' any old can."

But even Cass knew better than that. He knew that once a week, on Saturday, all open garbage was sprayed by the city. (In order to keep paupers from poisoning themselves on Sunday, which was the Sabbath.) So to the sullen shoulders in front of him, to a flat-backed head on a hairy neck he said, "They're puttin' stink-oil on the grab-cans now. That guy won't find even crap left clean. Ah seen 'em sprayin' it on last summer, back o' Commerce Street in Dallas. It was green kind o', looked like to me."

The flat-backed head did not turn to reply. But three sparrows rose in a single flight and the head turned then slowly to follow that rising. Cass's throat contracted when he saw the man's face. Disaster or disease had torn or eaten the nose away until only the nostrils now remained. Cass had seen faces beaten expressionless by defeat, faces hungry and hopeless and sick with long shame— but this was the mask of death itself. He touched his own nose and found it running. He smeared phlegm off on the back of his hand and looked down at his wrists. They were blue-black with dirt and cold, and the reddish hairs on the backs of his fingers seemed frozen around the roots.

"That stuff they're puttin' on the cans is coal-oil, bub," a voice behind him informed. "*I* read about it in the paper, that's how I learned. Coal-oil, so kids'll quit gettin' sick from eatin' slop."

The noseless man spoke nasally.

"Yeh, they want the kids to starve healthy-like is why they doin' it."

The fog began to lift above the mission. Two of the sparrows returned to the curb.

When Cass was only a few feet from the building, a door opened and a smell from within came billowing out. It sugged up his nostrils in one thick and sticky woosh. In one moment hunger went out of him. Like blood through a bag, hunger drained out. Had it not been for remembering coal-oil on the cans Cass would have followed the bum who had cried out in protest. Instead he tried to close his senses when he came into the place. He reached for a plate, found an empty place at a bench, and sat down among a dozen other ragged once-men.

"I Am The Way And The Light," a wall-sign informed him. "Christ Died For Your Sins," said another.

Cass looked down at his plate. The thing upon it was formed like a meat-ball and it well might have been all of that; but it wambled about in a thin yellow swill, a kind of diarrheal brown gravy. Cass thought of cow-dung dropped thinly and long. "Cow-donick" the man in the fog had called this meat, and the recollection did not help Cass greatly. After moderating its odor with salt and hot pepper, he yet could not down the stenchful stuff. One bite, wholly vile, convinced him that the man had been right. He swallowed, retched halfway, and paused one moment to reflect: the meat was as rank as something a half-starved street-cur would have to regurgitate twice before downing. The coffee had been ground out of chicory and some cheap dry cereal; he swashed it down hastily to cleanse his mouth of the meat, found it both hot and good. It was bitter as medicine, but invigorating, and he felt a little stronger after drinking. When he learned that he could have a second cup he reached for it eagerly.

Over the brim of his cup he regarded a squat and foreign appearing fellow valiantly struggling with that with which he had himself struggled. For some reason the man kept tilting his plate on a level with his eyes, first to one side and then to the other, as though unable to make up his mind about something. He did this three times while Cass watched, till the brown-yellow soup began stopping over the edge and the thing in the middle began walking, as though on very short legs, about the periphery of the tin. He set it down quite carefully then, and with a deliberated accuracy spat in the plate's center. Then he rose from the bench to flee for coffee, belching hugely as he fled.

Cass drained his cup and rose to ieave the Jesus-Feeds-All mission, but at the door he learned that to pay for his meal he would have to chop wood in the yard for a while. This did not take him longer than twenty minutes; when he was through his hunger had returned. He resolved to give the alleys a try before returning to the mission. He could only get one more meal in the place anyhow. The "Jesus-Feeds-All" mission served no one man more than twice, if he were transient. After two meals you went somewhere else. And "somewhere else" was down the nearest alley.

Beside Cass, as he found the street, the squat-necked man fell into step. He walked with his fists jammed in his pockets and his cap pulled low over his eyes; for a minute he said nothing.

"Looks like a hunky," Cass thought. "If it weren't fo' furriners times'd be better."

"Are you a hunky, fella?" he asked.

The fellow replied in a voice so broken and guttural that at first Cass could not quite understand.

"No, not hunky. Litvak from Memel is all. You know? Carl Jusitska, that is my name."

Then Carl Jusitska spoke of his life as they walked. He had once been a steel-worker in Latvia, a place somewhere in Europe, and there he had had a wife and four boy-children. Today he did not know where this family was, because of a red-haired man who had come one day to the rolling mill where he had worked. The red-haired one was an American, and the foreman brought him into the yard where Carl was sitting among other workers, all eating dinners from tin dinner pails. The foreman had told his men that they must all listen hard, for this was a wise man he had brought, even though the wise one did not use the tongue very well. So each man listened hard as he was able; and the American told them young workers were needed in *Dee*-troit, a place somewhere in America. AH workers who came there would receive such fine wages that very soon after they arrived each man would send for his wife and his family and all his small brothers to come to Dee-troit also. And when he told how much money each man would earn in that far place the men were a little suspicious; they could scarcely believe. Carl had been a little suspicious too, but the more he thought it over the truer it all had sounded. Then the red-haired one had finished speaking abruptly and had gone swiftly away; no one knew where to exactly, he was not seen again anywhere. And the more Carl had thought it over the truer it all had sounded. He had come to America, and had sent for his family.

"For one year I am scab," he said, "I get reech. Not unnerstan'. Then unnerstan': I am scab. I join oonion. I strike, I am fire. No joostice. I am poor once more." He pushed back his cap and pointed to a line of gray about his temples. "See, I get old in thees America. No monies anymore, anywhere. You tink Mary gone home? You tink where I could find she?"

Cass walked a little faster. He didn't like hunkies.

To their left, for a block, loomed a long low factory, silent now where machines once rumbled. Its windows had been broken out, there was nothing inside now save silence and rust.

"Mebbe Matvey Karskoff send Mary monies to come home to Memel. Mebbe Mary take such monies an' go. Matvey like Mary for long long time."

Cass was hungry. He was cold. He didn't like hunkies. He wiped his nose on the back of his hand.

"*Look*"—Carl took his shoulder so fiercely that he had to stop. "*Look*, ked—we eat togedder, leev togedder, sleep togedder— everee night for twelve long year—an' now no more. Wonse in ol' time, long time, time afore we marry, Mary say, ''Oney you is what I lof.' Because Mary say thees ting to me we marry. Now— no more. Now when it get night I tink Mary in bed wit Matvey. I look in many windows to see. In same bed I tinkin'—windows, houses, rooms inside wit' beds. So walk, walk, all night walk. Same bed, Mary. Same bed, Matvey."

Cass took the hand off his shoulder. He wanted something to eat, right away. He saw the swart alien face a foot from his own, and for one second he wanted to hurt it, to strike it between the eyes so that it would cry out quickly and strike back blindly. He wanted to kick it till it bled. He wanted to see its mouth broken in with pain.

"Git along, bum," he said. "Whyn't you go back where you come from?"

Carl Jusitska turned swiftly and went off in the opposite direction. His hip bumped and scraped the bricks of the factory's wall as he went, as though he could no longer see clearly the street whereon he walked. Cass's eyes followed till the man from Memel was lost in an eddying swirl of traffic. Then Cass tightened the thin and greasy cord that held up trousers once his brother's, and he listened to the protesting grumble of wind within his bowels. In a slow glissade his stomach caved in and turned halfway over—it seemed for one moment that he had no stomach at all, only a head going up like a balloon, buzzing and bounding through space up and up, till it burst in a bubble of blackness and left him standing with his back braced tensely against the bricks of the wall. His eyes felt dry, with a burning and granular dryness.

"Ah'm *really* hungry now," he thought, and the thought frightened him, for in this city men could not beg on the streets even covertly.

He tried mooching twice. The first moochee gave him a half hlled sack of tobacco. But the second looked around for the law, and Cass ran into an alley. He went down the alley only a little way, and he came to a grab-can where the coal-oil had dried.

Now came the night-hours, when men walked up and down. All night Cass went through streets and alleyways, smelling and pawing and stooping over.

"Look!" (His belly seemed now to whisper its need.) "Look in that *big* can, down below." He tried to turn the can on end, to dump its refuse out, but he lacked strength. So he dug deep down, blindly groping beside high-piled ashes till his fingers sank into something soft and warm. When he pulled his hand out it was caked to the wrist, with human dung.

Cass did not feel disgust this time. He saw his hand with eyes which were dry and burning, and no longer capable of disgust. He smelled, with a nose which nothing could now offend. He scraped his fingers halfheartedly against ashes and fence. And Belly whispered, "Look! Look *behind* the ashes!" But there was nothing behind the ashes to eat, there was nothing there save a few drifted leaves. So Cass sat down on the leaves, between the high-piled ashes and the fence, and he pulled his cap down low over his eyes, and he slept.

Early the following morning he went into a small bakery on Durango Street, to beg for bread. The woman behind the counter looked at him for one moment as though she thought he might strike her; and then she looked sorry for having thought that. But she had just given the last of the old stuff to the mission, she said. "The-Jesus-Feeds-All mission. 'Cause that's where they're feedin' the homeless now, an' it's where *you* ought to go."

Half an hour later, in the rear of a delicatessen on Zarzamora Street, Cass pulled a half-loaf of raisin bread out of a can. Save for one small corner, it was untouched by coal-oil. In the bottom of its crust were small toothmarks, so that he did not eat all the way down despite his hunger.

"Ah'd like to get me tattooed sometime," Cass planned as he gnawed in the alley.

A while later Cass had a great piece of luck. He found a head of lettuce the inner leaves of which were still fresh and green. That *was* luck. It was in back of a fruit store that that happened, and he hung around the place for an hour after the finding in the hope of another head. A boy came out of the store carrying a crate of bananas, but he put the crate on a wagon, and he hauled the wagon to the corner, and then he turned that corner out of sight.

On the evening of Cass's second day in San Antonio the garbage cans were sprayed again. So it was then time to be moving on.

He had had his fill of San Antonio. Or rather, not his fill.

He returned to his wheelless passenger coach and found two men sleeping where he had slept. When they wakened he jungled up with them over a fire near the Soupline tracks. Both men were older than himself, and they seemed unwilling to speak much to him. But they gave him potatoes and coffee and a cut of plug-tobacco. Toward midnight a westbound stock-run began humming the rails, and all three rose from their fire to go. Cass saw the headlight a mile down the track, heard her working steam with the brake-shoes slack. Then she whistled, once, the headlight began growing larger every second—and he raced with the other 'boes to catch her before she gained such speed as to make catching difficult or impossible. He swung up a ladder, cracked a seal —and dove.

It was warm in the reefer with the other two. They pulled the trap down over their heads, shoved a spike in the lock to prevent the trap locking, and slept.

Hours later, under floodlights far ahead, Cass saw six bulls in slickers come out of a Harvey Café. They walked limned sharply against those lights; they laughed as they went toward the tracks. Across the thunder of approaching wheels their laughter, like six bells in storm, tinkled thin and silvery. As the first car rolled beneath the lights the first of the bulls swung himself up its ladder; climbing, his body swayed and powerfully flexed as though on hips forged of rock and rubber. Then easily as five jungle-cats, with the same steel swing of rock-and-rubber torsoes, the others followed and advanced.

All six were young men; they were all of them hard. The one who led drew a flashlight; the others gripped small colts. Their high-heeled boots had steel-spiked soles that they might not slip on the icy spine.

Other men saw.

A quarter of a mile away, from where they crouched on a rocking roof, they saw and ran. Caps yanked low over their foreheads, bodies bent in challenge to the slant rain beating, bums raced down the narrow spine away from the men who walked in light. The cars were coated with ice and rain, they ran in mist and a swaying dark. The planking, as though in alliance against them with rain and bulls, kept buckling beneath their feet. Between cars a four-foot gap—no time to measure gaps tonight—just *jump!*

Already the Hood-beams were bathing the cars that made up the train's center section. *"Jump you lame-leg son of a bitch, jump or we'll shove y'over."*

At the side, autos waited. The six on the top shagged the 'boes down the side, into the arms of their deputies. The bounty on bums was a dollar a head here; the detectives split with their aides. No use playing 'possum tonight, lousers—deputy's baby needs new shoes.

Some of the bums huddled stubbornly in reefer pits, thinking no bull would trouble to come down after—even when a flashray made their darkness bright. Such a bum didn't know what a bull was getting just for climbing down in after him. And when a bull did come down it went worse with the bum. Working methodically and with devastating thoroughness the police yanked men out of reefers like dish rags out of deep sinks. Then, with a car packed to the hood, with a deputy on each running board and a constable on the fender, they raced toward the city with sirens blasting the January sky. The only chance a 'bo had was to keep traveling back in the hope that by the time the last cars came under the lights the train would have gained such speed as to force the bulls to abandon it.

Cass heard the wheels begin a steadily-rising roar.

The homeless had a special fear of this place. It was here, near Uvalde City, that the hungriest jailhouse and the crudest bulls in all southern Texas were located. There had been an epidemic in the place, and its fame had spread among transients far and wide as a place sedulously to be avoided.

Racing against the racing wheels, the bums ran toward the cab's green light. Fifty feet down one narrow board—a blind leap then into rocking space—and fifty feet to the unseen gap once more. Through fog Cass saw the green sidelight eight cars ahead. Someone behind kept treading his heels, and one ahead was lame. Then the dark split, and the men in hoods were bearing down. Men on the cab car! "*Jump you club-foot son of a bitch, you're holding all of us back.*" The deputies appeared to the 'boes like an army with flashlights approaching through mist—bums veered and stumbled, Lame-Leg missed, and the others saw, and the wheels went up and the wheels went down; and four raced ahead where there had been five. When the bulls started firing, none of the transients paused; two got to a ladder and scrabbled away into mist. One flung himself over the side and then lay very still till they picked him up. Cass ran on—till steel clanged against steel inches to his left. Then he flung himself blindly down a reefer pit, grabbed cold iron as he dropped, and let go with both hands.

His fall was broken. Feet first he smashed down onto a softness. He thought of dead men, of snakes and of dung—"Who's in here?" he asked, looking down at the thing on the floor at his feet. There was no reply. He saw a girl or a woman, he couldn't tell which, with something or someone dim bending over. Then a match scratched, and a voice called out. He saw a Negro face two feet from his own, then the match died, and the calling ceased; there was no sound then above that of the wheels.

"Whyn't she git out o' mah way, 'stead o' layin' stretched out right in mah way?" Cass asked. He discerned the face on the floor. The woman was white.

"Now you sure done it. Skwar down on her belly you hit, wid her belly big uz a barrel." The Negro flapped his lips hurriedly, one on top of the other; his voice was that of a northern Negro. "White boy, you ort git slapped clean to Jesus."

To Cass it was all unreal as nightmare, for the thing had

happened too quickly to be understood clearly. He had only run from men who were enemies; but apparently he had just killed two poor reefer-bums, a woman and the child she carried.

The Negro cupped a brief flare, in the basket of his hands, over the face of the stricken bum. When her eyes opened he asked, "How are yo'? Are yo' hurt bad, yo' think?" For reply her eyes shifted accusingly to Cass's sooty phiz bending above her. His face had eyes that seemed almost closed now, and a mouth like that of a small boy getting ready to cry. "I know who to blame for this all right," her eyes seemed to say to Cass.

"Ah'm right sorry, Miss," Cass said, feeling genuinely solicitous for the small white face on the floor. He saw that she was a girl in her twenties. Her face was pimpled, and coated with coal dust; on the left side of the throat ran a twisted pink scar tissue, like a scar left by scalding water. He saw her clutching at her pain till she tore her skirt at the crotch; he thought of the black girl left alone on the prairie. "Ah'm always doin' wrong," he thought. "Sometimes ah mean it an' sometimes ah don't." He felt a helpless bewilderment. Then he looked again at the girl, to where her fingers clutched her pain, and all his innards seemed suddenly to sag ... blood was there slowly, at the deep seam there, darkening blue cloth. Her fingers fumbled where pain like a burning girdle bound her now; the dark matting between her thighs was becoming dyed with a red wetness. The match flickered out.

The Negro spoke sharply.

"Take her head, I've got her feet. We've got to get her out of this hole perty damned pronto." The acrid odor of blood rose pungently in the rocking chamber.

When Cass lifted her head she began screaming again; and frightened as though a dead woman had screamed, he fell forward and almost dropped her. He braced his back against the steel screening, and shut his eyes for a moment to steady himself. The screening was wet with snow or rain; the car was rolling fast.

"Quick! We're pullin'!"

In the tiny chamber the Negro's voice rang and reechoed. Cass fancied that in the darkness then the womb of this girl was already opening, gaping red and terribly.

He had never seen a child born, he had always feared to be near such a sight. His fingers, weak like a drunkard's fingers, kept slipping and fumbling about her neck as though momently he might let her fall. He had no strength left. From hunger and idleness his hands had become hands of cotton. The Negro flung the woman over his shoulder much as one would a half-filled flour sack, and in a wink of an eye was clinging by one hand to the grating's top; he began butting the trap-door with the back of his head.

"Should ah come up theah an' open it fo' yo', mister?" Cass asked.

With one sharp and peremptory push of the head, the trap flew back wide to the sky. Slant rain flecked again into Cass's face, into his eyes and down his ears. The Negro and the woman were gone. Cass imagined them, over his head working cautiously back, the black man bent and swaying beneath the burden . . .

Minutes later shadows darkened the opening over Cass's head. The Negro was coming down once more, and the woman's arms were about him. From his shoulder her face descended reproachfully on Cass. Cass stood looking up with hair in his eyes, understanding that it was too late—too late because he had made it too late. When he reached the floor the Negro brushed Cass aside.

"Couldn't make it. Couldn't take a chance the way she's moving now. Have to wait till she slows, that's all."

Cass climbed the grating to close the heavy trap. He tugged manfully, but he was weak as noodle-water, and the swinging hood seemed to weigh more like a thousand pounds than the one hundred and fifty that it was. Then recalling with something of shame what the Negro had done without use of his arms, Cass strove heroically; with both fists he caught hold and strained frantically upward till it actually came halfway—then his fingers seemed to melt, the hood balanced for one split second above him, he ducked—and it crashed. There came a small click from the outside then; and the reefer was black as pitch.

The Negro started climbing when that small click came. Cass watched from below with a desperate hope.

"You ort to get slapped clean back to wherever you come from," the Negro called down, and descended as quickly as he had gone up. Cass didn't have to be told what he'd done.

Slam a steel reefer all night from inside, nobody walking the spine will hear. Shout till you're hoarse and beat the sides with a shoe, nobody outside will hear a sound. Might as well just lie still, save your breath, hope for luck. Maybe they'll unload the car at the next division point; maybe a brakie will look down in. Maybe he saw you jump down and knows all the time that you're sealed there. Maybe someone else saw; maybe a yardman or maybe the shack; maybe some bull or maybe some switchman. Maybe a hostler will peer down and say, "Did we have you scared for a minute, boys?"

And maybe you'll stand for three weeks on a siding and get shipped three times across the state of Texas before someone looks down in. But by then it's a little late of course. More than one brakeman has opened a reefer long-sealed to find on its floor just two shoes, a rag, and one skeleton.

The wheels roared, rails sang and a long smoke poured. To Cass it seemed that the wheels were singing a song full of mockery. "*Ho! Ho! We were waiting lang. Ho! Ho! We've caught three more. Lousers, lousers—caught three more!*" The wheels ground to a stop, waited like live things very still; and then, with monotonous mockery, rolled on.

It was cold in the reefer. Cold and dark. Cass measured the night by the times that the wheels stopped. Measured the hours by the song the wheels sang. The woman slept. This was Del Rio perhaps, perhaps Sanderson. In the musty air of the chamber the smell of the white woman and the smell of the black man mixed. The woman had an odor faintly like something sour; the Negro smelled salty-sweet. Cass felt his head wobbling with weariness, then the Negro said, "Matches." He was standing above Cass with his shirt unbuttoned; Cass stood up quickly to find him a match. As he fumbled he was surprised to notice that the Negro was only a boy no older than himself.

"Here—matches."

The Negro took off his shirt to make a pillow for the woman's head. Squatting, he tore the lining out of his shoe and made a torch of it in the second before the match failed. The woman looked up in terror, and then pain pulled her mouth into an oblong "O." Cass cringed at her howling. It was as though he were being struck for what he had done. He held the torch above her, and it trembled in his hand. The Negro wiped a jack-knife on an unclean rag . . .

The thing which Cass saw cut free that night in the S. P. reefer chamber looked like nothing so much as a length of pink sausage at first. Then it went black all over and looked like nothing at all. Holding it awkwardly, the rude torch burning in his hand, Cass felt that he held so much filth. He had a crazy desire to touch the small flame to the thing, to stomp it down into the cracks of the flooring, into the darkness there. He wrapped it in a wet newspaper instead, and he laid it down in the corner.

The Negro tried to staunch the woman with his cap. The floor became a cess-pen running with blood, stinking of urine and strewn with rags. When Cass touched the rain-wet screening he fancied he touched blood even there. Once, being either too dazed to turn her head or too weak to lift it, she vomited down her own breast. Pieces of stuff dribbled from the corners of her mouth. Trying to retch a second time, her head merely bobbed weakly. Cass saw that her right eye kept crossing, being too weak to focus.

"She ain't hardly no older'n me or you," he said to the Negro. And now the woman became so quiet and still Cass thought for one moment that she were dead. Then her mouth gaped, slowly, and she began to breathe heavily. Cass sank into the corner opposite with the thing wrapped in paper. The pit began to stink as though a dozen mangy curs had drenched the door knee-deep.

Once in the night the mother woke, and the Negro asked Cass for the matches once more.

Cass said, "Here—Matches," thus giving the other a nickname along with the box.

In the corner the child, dead as decay, moved with the long car's swaying. Sometimes it seemed to raise itself, sometimes it rolled toward the wall. Once, when the car buckled violently, it worked whole inches toward him just as though it lived. Cass thought then that, it being so strangely dead, it knew whom to blame for its death. He felt that it would crawl like that soon again, that in hate it would bite him with small teeth like a rat's teeth. He lacked the courage to rewrap it in the paper. He just shut his eyes, and let it bounce, and listened to its mother's muttering. As he listened there came briefly, out of a meaningless babble, clear words.

"I dreamed the mines were burning. I saw them all aflame. Let me go now to the place I used to be."

After that she fell once more into babbling; after that she slept.

"She got on in Sabinal right before dark," the Negro said, "I was in a empty up front when she come down the track. When I seen how she was I helped her up, an' she gimme a cig'rette. 'Goin' to Laredo,' she says, 'ol' man's in the jailhouse down there again.'" Then a shack come along an' told us we'd better duck an' stay ducked, that federal men was comin' on in Uvalde. An' they sure come on, didn't they? That's when we found this reefer. It was jest gettin' dark then." He talked on and on, until the words mixed in Cass's brain into a mumbling as meaningless as the mother's.

With a start Cass came awake, he did not know what had waked him so suddenly; he could not return to sleep. He remained tense and strained, in spite of himself, as though he were waiting for something; he didn't know what. His uneasiness increasing, he climbed the grating with the futile notion that the trap might not have locked after all.

Cass recalled the other time he'd been sealed in. That had been only three months before, but it seemed now like three years. And now he could feel nothing save his own utter weariness and his own great guilt. Thirst, shame, and hunger were less now than his guilt. Every time his eyes closed and his nerves relaxed for a second, his brain leaped up shouting, "Look out! Look out! You'll be getting a boot if you don't look out!"

And guilt hung like a dark stone about his neck, heavy, heavy like hunger, . . . and all utter weariness dragging him down, . . .

down into . . . darkness and cold hunger, heavy, dark, down and heavy into . . .

When the reefer was opened out from above all three slept. In the bluish light of a flash-ray a stubbled face looked mildly down. Mountain breeze with fog-laden night wind off of prairie, and a looking-down face all covered with stubbles.

"Jeezus K. Reist. What a vile stink. What y'all been doin' down there anyhow? *Say*, is thet a *womern* y'all got down here?"

Matches shook the girl gently, and Cass picked up the small thing in the corner. Then, Matches and the mother first, the unnatural parade went up the grating. When the brakie saw the stillborn child in Cass's arms, his mouth went eggshaped with amazement.

It was yet dark night. From the roof of the car Cass saw two Mexican hostlers knocking cinders and ashes from the fire-box of a dead engine. They were dressed to the ears to keep off the heat, and fire played weirdly upon their features. Cass wondered whether the fire-box which they were cleaning was the one that had pulled them from San Antonio. If it was they had been in the reefer but six hours. He followed Matches and the brakeman down the tracks to a little suburban freight station.

There in the silent depot west of Ysleta they stood looking down at the suffering woman. The scar tissue on her throat had turned to a pasty gray. "It's longer than mine, but mine went deeper," Cass mused, holding the dead infant in one hand and tracing his own scar with the other. The brakeman put a coat beneath the mother, lying along a hardwood bench; then he walked toward the door backwards, his face still thick with wonder.

Cass wished desperately to rid himself of the thing in his hand; when the woman half-opened one eye he held it out to her with a tentative gesture. But the eye closed and the Negro spoke angrily, "You ought to get bounced back to where you come from, that's what." He took the body from Cass and wrapped it at the feet of its mother. "I've got to get out o' here, now," he said. "Ain't nothin' else I can do, an' I'll sure get in deep trouble if I stay. That dumb shack'll bring the law back with him. So you'd best scram with me, clown." He stuffed the shirt which the girl had used for a pillow into his pocket. "Mebbe you figger on walkin' alone?"

The question was a challenge.

"Well, yo' comin'?" he persisted.

"Yeah, ah reck'n ah'll trot along with y'all fo' a space," Cass answered.

Outside it was raining again. On either side of the tracks stretched the prairie, half-seen under fog. A cow-bell tinkled, near at hand and coming nearer. The Negro drew a battered pack of cigarettes out of his pocket and offered one to Cass.

"I took 'em offn her in the depot," he explained. "All we done for her was worth it, don't you think? 'Speshully you." He smiled a little at his jibe, as only very tired men smile. Cass had to grin a little too; he'd sure been a clown all right.

"But mebbe she'll die," he thought, "Mebbe that feller in jail is waitin' on her. Mebbe he was plannin' to git out 'fore the kid was born. Mebbe . . ." He made a wry face and spat. In the darkness the spittle caught a clump of scrub cedar and hung long and whitely in mist for a moment. Then it dropped. Beside him the Negro plodded along like a sick mule in a muddy furrow. Twice they paused to light cigarettes. After they had had three apiece Cass suggested timidly, "Mebbe we ought to save some fo' later on. Them's the fifteen-cent-a-pack kind ah think." The Negro walked on for several minutes before replying. Then, "Say, yo' know why they made Camels in the first place?" he asked.

Cass didn't know.

"To keep niggers an' Jews from smokin' Ol' Strikes, that's why."

They both laughed, without strength. It was a good joke—"Niggers an' Jews." You could turn the joke around if you wanted to, too, if you smoked a different kind. Only when, in his mind, Cass tried to turn it around, the thought blurred oddly and skipped away.

Matches stopped, stood on one leg like a heron, braced one hand on Cass's shoulder and slipped off his right shoe; the one from which he had torn the lining for a torch. He wore no socks, and Cass saw that the loot was encrusted with a brown and fish-like scale. He rubbed it with his knuckles till brownish chips brit-tled olf onto the S. P. ties.

"It itches," he said. "It itches like the crabs."

Cass volunteered advice: "Y'all ought to wear a white sock on that, on *anythin'* like that.'

When they reached El Paso they found the streets almost deserted. But morning was breaking over Juarez; and an empty truck came rolling by as though to herald an empty dawn. Neither knew where this city's breadline, if any, was to be found; they walked aimlessly.

They stopped in a doorway while Matches took off his shoe again to scrape his knuckles against his toes. Behind him, throwing a sickly greenish glow across a flight of uncarpeted stairs that led up to nowhere, an unshaded nightbulb still burned feebly. Once a woman passed the door, head down and hurrying in the rain.

"I'm tired as a old sick hound," Matches said as he scraped. "Aint you?" Cass said, "Yeah. Yo' look tired kind o'. Reckon last night was a mite too much fo' yo'. Mahself, ah ain't been eatin' so reg'lar o' late." He looked up, and there was a woman there with them, standing as though she had already been there for several minutes. Just standing beside him, looking, down at the same sick black foot at which he was looking, her face framed in a shawl and with one bright raindrop trickling down her cheek toward her open throat. A white woman, tall, smiling a strange half-smile. Under her arm were newspapers wet as her cheeks; and green flow from the night-light bathed her head as she stood. As though his foot then were something obscene Matches thrust it hurriedly down the throat of the shoe. Cass's eyes followed the slow raindrop down the cheek. In the long moment before it came to her throat he became conscious of his own increasing excitement. Though he did not see that throat until that drop came to it, yet his heart pounded before he saw, in anticipated horror. And both himself and Matches saw the same thing at the same moment: *Pink scar tissue down the side of the neck like a scar left by scalding water*—and terror hit both with one blow, they ran wildly out of the hallway and down the street.

At the corner Matches caught up to Cass. They stood together peering back through the rain, but there was nothing behind them save the grief-stricken houses on the long Southern street; and one dark doorway looking blindly out upon a mist-wet world.

"Holy Creepin' Jesus, man, didn't she *look* like her though?" Matches gasped. He was breathing heavily and favoring one foot as he stood. "But I only got scared 'cause you did, that's why. I didn't even think about that other till you turned rabbit on me like that. Holy God-'n-Jesus man, I thought I'd never catch you with this leg of mine. You shouldn't ought to scare a fellow that way. Why, she were only some little scurve who lived in that place, that was all; even if she were scarred up a little."

"Ah guess mebbe ah had that other on mah mind a little still," Cass confessed. "She sho' gimme a turrible fright for a minute."

His heart was still racing; they lit the last of the cigarettes together. The morning fog was lifting, and the sun came through.

"If I jest had a sock," Matches complained, "a sock like you said. I think that'd keep it from rubbin' some, don't you? But I always get the dirty end of the stick. I shouldn't of tore out that linin'."

Cass perceived that weariness had stripped his friend of the self-reliant air which he had seen in him the night before. Matches seemed, of a sudden, devoid of all will. When Cass asked him how old he was he replied, "Nineteen, I guess."

Cass said, "That's how old I am too I guess."

They were walking down a street lined with old elms, and at the end of the street they came to a park. It had a picket fence going around and around, and swings for small girls and slides for small boys and teeter-totters for bigger children. Cass could not remember ever having seen anything quite like this park before. They found a gate and entered there.

It was noon and growing warm. The boys found a stretch of dry ground beneath a tree, and Cass lay down. The small grass bent itself between his fingers, long shadows trembled in the light.

"Ah'd better shake this shine," Cass cautioned himself.

Surreptitiously, Matches tried bathing his foot by wriggling his toes like fingers beneath the still dripping boughs of some nearby winter shrubbery. He did this a long time, then declared his foot healed and lay down beside Cass.

"But a sock. If oney I had a sock now," his eyes closed as he muttered, and in a moment he was sleeping soundly, one arm in a ragged sleeve outflung and the other shielding his eyes; as though even in sleep he feared to be struck.

"Ah ought to git me a coat fo' the night that's cornin'," Cass thought, watching sun-shadow between half-closed lids. Sun-shadow made him think of wet lengths of yellow ribbon stretched flat aslant the grass to dry. Some lengths were narrow and some were quite wide, some intertwined and became one, then wriggled into many, all yellow-wet and delicate across green shadow-grass.

Matches wriggled his toes in sleep. Cass's own feet had gone sockless for months, he too was very tired; but just as he felt himself dozing off he became aware of someone coming toward them. A silver badge above pointed boots swung up a winding cindered path twirling a club on a cord like a swagger-stick. Cass saw the boots coming, shoved Matches once and fled; from behind high shrubbery then, he watched: Boots nudged Matches till he rolled over groaning like a sick man. Sweat on his forehead gleamed in the sun, his open mouth drooled saliva in his sleep—he woke with a jerk, with his eyes bugging out. There was, for one moment, no flicker of recognition in them.

"This is white folks' park, nigger. Get goin' 'fore I fan yore fanny."

Boots twirled his club-on-a-cord significantly, boy-fashion, threatening.

Cass waited on the street for Matches. He'd like to josh the nigger a little now. But when Matches rejoined him they walked on in silence, and Cass said nothing at all.

On a street lined with radios competitively blasting the air into splinters, they sat down on a Keep-Our-City-Clean box. Both were hungry enough to chew their own tongues, but they were both too weary to think consistently even about food. Cass rested his feet on the curbstone and watched the gutterflow swirl past. Much was being borne on that tide; a frayed cigar-butt came past first, then a red beer-cork; and then, its pages flung wide in a disgraceful death, a copy of *Hollywood Gossip* came by. It lay flat on its back, a whore-like thing. Cass sniped the cigar and the magazine, crushed tobacco onto a dry page, and rolled a rude cigarette. Smoking, he glanced at the dry pages of the magazine. One page bore a picture of Douglas Flatass, Jr. in a stove-pipe hat, hugging two girls in one-piece bathing suits. Out of this fellow Cass fashioned four long cigarettes, but the figures of the girls in the bathing suits he preserved, studying them as he smoked. A small frown came between his eyes; he squinted narrowly. Six weeks without a haircut, three weeks without a shave—he had not had a square meal for weeks and he had not slept lying down for five full days. He tossed his head back jerkily, flouncing hair out of his eyes, and he ripped one of the paper girls up the middle. He had an odd feeling when he did that; and after he had rolled another cigarette he looked through the book for more girls' pictures. But there was no other dry page, and he began to feel more tired than ever. He offered Matches a cigarette, but the boy did not take it. He merely sat holding his kinky head in his hands, and would not even shake his head to say that he didn't wish to smoke now.

Cass recalled vaguely as he sat that a day or a week before he had eaten meat in some place where there had been fog on the streets. Or he had not eaten meat. He couldn't remember; and he couldn't remember the name of that place, though his mind sought it sleepily and long. Somehow, much seemed to depend upon the remembering: Chicago, Springfield, St. Louis. Memory was a jumble of steel rails, city sounds, sunlight on boxcars and fog on a half-forgotten street. So he dropped the magazine in the gutterflow, wiped his nose on the back of his hand, and poked Matches.

Apparently the encounter in the park had taken the last bit

out of the Negro, for he walked beside Cass now as though he were half-helpless. When Cass turned, he turned; when Cass paused for traffic, he paused; when Cass hurried forward, Matches hurried forward beside him. Only once as they went did the Negro speak coherently.

"Bummin' takes everythin' out of a feller, don't it?" he asked as they turned a corner into Mesa Avenue.

Cass agreed readily that it did. "Yeah, sho' do. Bummin's knocked all the tallow clean out o' mah pole." To himself he thought, "Ah better shake this shine."

When they reached the next Keep-Our-City-Clean box Matches wanted to remove his shoe again; but his fingers slipped around his ankle like a little child's fingers. So Cass took it off for him, kneeling as the other sat. He pulled a wad of newspaper out of the box and padded it into the shoe's torn places. Beside him a bare-footed Mexican boy, holding a small brown girl by the hand, stood and watched with a cynic's air. A woman with furred shoulders went by on high heels, her head in the air and her nose sniffing elegantly, as though about to spew green phlegm sunward. As he struggled to get the shoe back on Matches' foot someone behind him spat toward the gutter over his shoulder; he saw the gob, like a speckled bug, being borne away on the current. People were gathering behind him; it was time to be getting on.

They had not gone half a block farther when Matches stopped and complained, half-accusingly, to Cass. "It hurts. You just made it worse you did. Now it hurts worst. You ought to get slapped clean to Jesus." They could not stop, there was no place here to stop, and Matches continued to complain with a rising irascibility.

"If oney I had a sock. A *white* sock, mind you. Have *you* got that kind?"

That was the last thing he said to show that he knew that Cass was still with him; after that he seemed slowly to lose awareness, he became like a man mildly drunk or doped. Cass had not known what havoc the simple fact of overtiredness could work. Only a few short hours before he had almost feared this boy; now there plodded beside him only a sick pickaninny who depended on him, Cass, to lead him about and to put on his shoes. Cass felt something of a mild responsibility.

Matches stopped dead still and planted himself directly in front of a bespectacled youth with books in both hands. The boy looked frightened at Matches' glance; and when Cass looked at Matches he too became a little afraid; Matches' eyes were fever-bright and burning hollowly. Cass took his arm, but he wouldn't budge an inch.

"*You.* Gimme that sock." He took Specs by the lapel, and the boy dropped a book. When he straightened up, after retrieving it, his voice quavered shrilly as a frightened school girl's.

"Saaaay—I'll call a cop on you, nigger." And he raised his voice in a long wailing plea, "Ohhhhh, officer!"

This time *two* silver badges, two rows of brass buttons, two pair of pointed boots shining in the sun.

"Here, niggers—at it again? All right, Smitty, take 'em both along."

Cass cocked his head, half-unable to believe what he had just heard. Slowly then he understood: a white man who walked with a "nigger" was a "nigger" too. He recognized the park bull as the other bull took his arm, and he said, "Ah'm not no nigger," but the bull made no reply.

Cass wasn't afraid, somehow. He was a little too tired to be afraid. Going to jail was all a part of this life; no one escaped it for very long and he'd been pretty lucky for a long time now. What he didn't like, what got him by the short hairs, was that crack about being a nigger. He saw the big park bull start reaching for Matches when Matches was still five feet away, and Specs stood in between. The boy ducked wildly when the cop's paw came over his shoulder—to seize Matches' shirt and pull him free of the sidewalk with a yank which ripped the sleazy cloth down to the navel. Matches came so straight forward that his head would have rammed the cop's Sam Browne belt, had not the cop stiff-armed him with his open palm.

Cass glanced at the bull who was holding his wrist.

"Ah'm not no nigger," he repeated; but the cop didn't seem to hear.

With the eyes of the gathering crowd upon himself and Matches, Cass thought of his scar and turned his head away; as he turned, Matches screamed, like the black girl had screamed.

"You got no right! You got no right!"

It was shameful to see the Negro so, his shirt in tatters so that his navel showed through, screaming nonsense at a cop as though he had lost his mind. A man in the crowd laughed, harshly, and a girl fled titillating. "Oooooooo—what I *saw*." The big bull started shaking Matches, to stifle that foolish screaming in the street. Matches' arms flailed stiffly against the brass buttons. A ragged end of his sleeve caught the cop's star and left it hanging lop-sidedly.

"You got no right! You let me go!"

Someone behind Cass said, Quit shakin' him, officer, he's only a kid."

"You got no right!"—the fingers clawed weakly upward, the club-on-a-cord whizzed in a gleaming circle a foot above his head, the fingers reached up for it, and the club came down. It came down slantwise across the temple, with the hissing sound of a large stone thrown through a thin paper wall—a brief sound, sharp and ripping and cold; Matches stood very still for one long moment. He had stopped screaming rather suddenly. A dark star appeared on his temple, and his head began sagging a little, like a wounded fighting-cock's head. Hands caught him under the armpits as he fell; white hands held him tentatively, offering him out to the bull like a limp dishrag.

Cass whimpered.

"My, wasn't that *brave*," a woman mocked from the crowd.

As the bull half-carried and half-dragged Matches toward the patroil a boy's voice called him.

"Oh, Officer."

This time the cop's eyes were shifting uneasily. Without fixing his gaze on any one face he asked, "Well, who wants to see me?"

No reply—till he turned. The woman's voice came again:

"No one, officer my dear. Who would? You smell most awful vile."

"Who said 'at to me?" he bluffed loudly. "Who said 'at, huh?" His face looked ready to burst with its bluff. Then he saw laughter starting and got inside the patrol with Matches to escape it. The other officer followed with Cass in front of a chorus of catcalls and jeerwails. Cass heard only one thing clearly: just as the door slammed someone shouted in, "Niggerlickers—that's all cops is. That's all they do—that's all they *can* do. Big tough niggerlickers, and that's all they *do* do."

Matches' eyes opened, but he did not speak. On either side of him sat a bull. Cass, sitting opposite, watched the Negro revive and wondered whether he understood all that had happened.

Although his own hands were free, Matches' were thumbcuffed; Cass was torn between regret for having walked with the Negro, and with pity for seeing him beaten.

The big bull guarding the door looked over to Cass and spoke warningly. He was still out of breath, and a bit bewildered, it seemed.

"This'll go mighty hard with you two boys. Mighty hard, I can say that now. Almost a riot call it was, an' a riot call al'ays goes harder"—he gasped for breath. "Lots o' trouble you boys made— trouble in the park first . . ."

His rump-like face was streaked with sweat. As though to reassure himself of the penalty they were certain to have incurred, he spoke to the other bull.

"A riot call ai'ays makes it twicet as bad, don't it Arthur, huh?"

Arthur nodded. He was thin, and freckled, and looked unhappy.

"See what Arthur says? Ya almost instergated a riot, that's jest what I'm sayin'—an' ya'll get ninety days each fer it sure, or elts"— he gasped again for breath—"or elts I'm not yer witness!"

In spite of exhaustion, Cass went sick with fear then. He hadn't reckoned on ninety days.

"He jest wanted a sock on account his foot is so bad," he said. "Honest, mister, that foot look ready to drop off'n his laig."

The silver badge looked at Cass with a huge and expression-less, a moon-like wonder. The big thick brain behind the eyes began to move slowly, like a heavy door opening onto a room long closed. Then his face looked cunning-cruel, as understanding at last came into it. And he guffawed. Thwacking his thigh resound-ingly he yawped his face so near to Cass's that Cass smelled the foulness of his breath like the breath from a privy.

"He jest wanted a sock! He jest wanted a sock! Hey, Arthur, do ya get it, Art? He jest wanted a *sock*, an' ain't that what I given him?" He went off into whole gales of laughter, his body shaking to its very fingertips. "Say, Art—d'ye get it?—He jest wanted a sock!" Arthur smiled a bit wanly, a bit indulgently, and said nothing at all.

"Ho! Ho! Ho! He wanted a sock, a *clean* sock—an' ain't that jest what I given him? Ho! Ho! Ho!"

Outside the late afternoon sun was waking trembling checkered patterns on low stone buildings rushing past. They were going to have a place to lie down.

They were going to jail; they were going to eat. They were going to have a place to lie down.

Cass said, "Ah'm not no nigger," and looked over to Matches accusingly.

Matches only smiled. Then, "You're ridin' jest the same, ain't you?" he asked.

But the little bull named Arthur only sighed.

9

I had no money to pay my fine
Not a friend to go my bail
So I got stuck for ninety days
In El Paso County Jail

Oh such a lot of devils
The like I never saw
Robbers, thieves, and highwaymen
And breakers of the law

They sang a song the whole night long
Their curses fell like hail
I'll bless the day they take me 'way
From El Paso County Jail.

"Goddamned if I don't think you *deserved* ninety days, hookin' up with some young shoke that way. Me, I hates them sons of bitches. You wouldn't catch *me* ridin' a reefer, or walkin' down a street, or doin' *nothin'* with *no* nigger, North or South. Say, kid, I wouldn't let a jig smell the hole where I crapped in a year ago eastertide. I hates them black sons of bitches so bad as soon as I smell 'em my left nut gets tight. And say, kid, don't you even know what comes of nigger-lovin'?"

Nubby O'Neill crossed his booted toes under him and rolled a cigarette deftly with one hand; the only hand he possessed. A highly-feigned hatred of everything not white and American was the high-point of Nubby's honor. Cass sat hunched on a blanket wishing he'd been put in with somebody else.

"Don't you even know what the rules is, sonny? Well then, lemme wise ya. Five hundred licks on the fanny is the fine here fer nigger-lovin', jest one hundred more than fer Mexican-lovin', which is twicet as bad. Ain't you never been in a real jail before, son? Five hundred swangs—an' it sure looks to me like you're a great nigger-lover just by the way yer sittin' there with yer head hangin' over an' yer fanny gettin' cold. Say, son, don't ya know what comes of nigger-lovin' in Texas?"

"Ah couldn't tell there was nigger in that reefer till ah jumped down in, mister," Cass lied desperately, "an' when we got into the yards the law pulled us both, an' I told 'em, hell, that nigger ain't no friend o' mine."

"Hey, Mr Bastard!" O'Neill shouted, "The Breathin' Jesus-God—Did *you* hear *that*?"

The next cell said that he had heard that. O'Neill spoke more quietly to that cell.

"Well then, tell this old boy in here what I would of done if I'd found some ugly black sonabitch in the same reefer where *I* wanted to ride in, North or South."

As though it were being read from a book, the next cell made answer.

"Reck'n the judge would just have made that ugly black sonabitch hit the grit."

"*See*," O'Neill accused, "an' that's what you should of done. Only ya didn't, so o' course you got to take yer five hundred swangs." He jumped to his feet and announced, "Court's in session, gennelmen."

The five other prisoners of tank ten piled out of their cells and into Cass's; no cell-doors here were locked within the cell-block. They held their belts in their hands, and Cass went so cold with fear that he felt his heart swinging slow, like a heavy pendulum in his breast. Then all the blood of his body seemed pouring through his throat in one thick dark stream; he tried to plead, to cry out or weep, but his throat closed with his fear. Nubby yanked him by the collar to his feet.

"Sheriff,' O'Neill ordered, "bring in the prisoner of this court."

Somebody whirled Cass three times around, then shoved him out of the cell and into the narrow bull-pen.

"An' now yer arrested," the sheriff informed him, "an' yer standin' in court, an' yer guilty as hell—an' if the judge says to hang you we just got to do it."

O'Neill hemmed and hawed and rubbed his chin with his stump. "Gennelmen," he pronounced solemnly, "I've just learned somethin' downright disgraceful. The prisoner has just confessed it to me what he is. This here is a nigger-lover standin' 'mong our midst. He is very strong on anythin' black, just so long as it's plenty stinky. He finds 'em in boxcars mostly, he says, down in reefer bottoms in where he has most his luck. When I asked him just now he said he is es-spesh-uffy great in nigger whores with soft shankers on their behin's—" the judge paused for the sheer effect of the pause, pointed one hairy finger at Cass and barked, "*You.* You kiss niggers' arses. I seen him doin' it, gennelmen. I was there. So now we got to give him ten thousernd kisses on *his* tail. With the belts, gennelmen."

Ten thousand was the largest number that Judge O'Neill

knew; Cass took him at his literal word and trembled visibly. Then he whimpered. He stood there whimpering with his hair in his eyes, and a gray prison light bathing his head from above.

"Not *really* with belts, mister? Not *really* with a belt? Ah don't love niggers, ah swear ah don't, ah don't kiss no niggers' arses." Cass had to catch a sob between his very teeth before he could continue his defense. "An' ah don't look for 'em anywhere—why," he groped for words, "why, ah *hates* them ugly black sonsabitches."

By this assertion the court seemed somewhat mollified; into the judge's face came a slow relaxation. These were good words his prisoner was speaking, this plea had an honest ring. He sucked his tongue for a minute, speculating on the possibilities for the prisoner receiving money or tobacco from some outside source in the future, and then announced the verdict.

"O.K., son. You look like a white man all right. Only don't get arrested with a nigger in Texas again, take my word. If the law don't lick you for it, then someone elts will. You was just lucky in gettin' a merciful-kind judge like me this time, that's all."

O'Neill addressed his court.

"The red-headed pris'ner is put by me on probation now, with a suspended sentence of ten thousernd swangs on his left butt an' five thousernd swangs on his right. Sentence is suspended on account he is so young an' all, an' this is his first offense, an' he is a white man. Court's adjourned."

On Sunday morning the early flushing of the thundermug in tank ten would waken the deputy's family, where they slept directly below, on that one morning of the week when they wished to sleep late. It was flushed by hand, with a bucket; it thundered like Niagara through conduits and sewerage. For an hour after Hushing, it made strange seeping sounds. Therefore the prisoners had to wait, uneasily restraining themselves, till they heard someone stirring below them. The chief deputy rose at nine-thirty to build the fire on Sunday morning; not until that time could the men relieve themselves. Cass learned of this on his first Sunday morning in the tank. He rose in that January dawn, used the bowl, flushed it and returned to his blanket. The noise of the flushing wakened every man in the cell-block, but only O'Neill admonished him.

"If I wasn't so tired we'd have court on you right now fer doin' that," Nubby muttered from beneath his blanket, "but you just wait till Joe Spokes gets up here. You won't be getting no breakfast this mornin', son."

And Cass didn't. At eleven o'clock Spokes' son came up with four troughs of oatmeal and cornbread, and said simply, "Paw says some 'un done it agin. Y'all know who 'twas better'n paw er me, so here's four troughs, an' four is all y' get." So Cass watched the others eat, being hungry enough to clean the thundermug, inside and out, for one small nibble of cornbread. No one offered him a nibble; he did not expect anyone to do so. O'Neill sat cross-legged in his corner balancing his trough precariously between his right knee and his stump, digging in with his one good hand. Cass hoped desperately that the trough would spill, but it didn't. The end of Nubby's stump was callused with small red bumps hard as stone.

Although Nubby O'Neill was from South Chicago, yet his right forearm bore the legend, tattooed in hair above the stump: "Texas Kid. His Best Arm." He insisted that this stump was of greater service to him than was his good arm, and to prove his contention he bashed in the bottoms of tobacco tins with one short blow of the nub. "There!" he would chortle, exhibiting a dented tin to Cass, "How many men is there could do that with a whole arm? Could *you*?" Cass would wag his head sadly, to express grave doubt, and would make a half-hearted effort to dent in a tin with his fist.

Nubby slouched all day on his blanket, his back to the wall, singing idle songs. He wore a pair of Spanish boots badly out at the heels, a gypsy's bright bandanna, and a great gray stetson with three holes punched in its top. From the shoulders up he looked much like one of those fake cow-punchers first brought into popularity over a generation ago by William S. Hart astride a pinto pony. From the shoulders down, however, Nubby was clad only in a pair of the county's overalls stuffed into the battered boots. His appearance was thus that of a man who had seen too many Western movies in adolescence.

"Know what I'm in here for, son?" he asked Cass on one of their first days together. "Indecent exposure an' malicious mischuf—that's what *I* done. Drank too much cerveza in Juarez one night an' leaked on the streetcar all the way comin' back acrosst the bridge. The car was full of spiks an' I just didn't like it, that was all. I hates spiks pretty bad too, ya see. That was why I left South Chicago mostly, on account of niggers an' spiks movin' into Stony Island. Right in the aisle I leaked all over an' some of 'em on the car only laughed. Even one of them cholo gals laughed a little—now what d'ya think o' *that*, son? Only, when we acrosst the bridge on the Merikun side a cop grabbed me—a smart Mexican-lover. Say, ya think *you'd* have enough gut on yer little inside to do what I done that time?" Nubby stretched himself out on his blanket, clacked his bootheels over his head and asked, "You want to hear the song I made up about myself that time in Ciudad Juarez?

I made it up right in here, settin' right in here on top this ol' tore blanket the mornin' after they brang me in."

In a vile wail, raucous as a sick raven's, he began to sing for Cass:

> *Oh I've seen the lights o' London*
> *I've seen the streets o' France*
> *I've seen a man get ninety days*
> *Fer unbuttonin' down his pants.*

"But that's only the first stanza though," he apologized, "I'm gonna make up lots more later on. Only I'm gonna get out perty soon so I s'pose I won't finish the nasty thing anyway. But I still got eighty-four days to do anyhow, so I might as well finish it at that. Say, Red, we'll get out t'gether about if you only got ninety days to do—what d'ya say we mope along t'gether a while? I'll give up my good-time an' wait fer you, Red."

It was the first time he had addressed Cass by any term other than "son" or "sonny" or "Kid"; Cass was duly grateful.

"Only I might get twelve days good-time 'stead of only six; good-time fer behavin' myself ya know—an' then o' course I couldn't give up all *that* to wait for you. So ya might have to travel all alone after all then. But if I get twelve—say—I don't like to travel much alone on account I can't lick everybody I meet with only one mitt. Sometimes I got to scrap some perty tough customers ya know, an' then I'd need you on account yer so ugly. So, how about it, Red? What d'ya say? You look like a white man to me all right; an' I'll bet I could make a *real* white man out of you, too, if you'd stick with me a spell."

Before Cass could reply Nubby was off again as though his tongue were unhinged.

"Only I might not wait eighty-four days to get out at all. Fact is I might get tired waitin''most any day now an'bust out of here like a whore out of heaven. Some night last part of nex'week mebbe. Then o' course ya'll just have to travel along without me—unless you want to cop a mope *with* me. *Say!*—mebbe I'll cop a mope on the very last night. That'd be a swift one all right, wouldn't it, Red? Say I'd break out a hour before Joe come up to spring me—just fer the downright meanness of it ya know, that's all. Say I'd go downstairs an'make Joe's fire fer him, an' when he got up, why—there I'd be, makin' his fire fer him. That's just the way I am though, Red—here t'day an' gone t'morrer. That's Nub O'Neill, an'I guess you'll find it out."

Cass was flattered at Nubby's proposal that they travel together after release; he felt that something was expected of him now.

"How would y'all do that, Judge?" he asked. "Break out ah mean."

Judge O'Neill winked broadly.

"That'd be tellin'. It's fer me to know an' fer you to find out. *Say*, Red, you want to hear a song I made up once? The name I call it is 'The centypeed an' the scorpyun havin' a intercourse.'" Want to hear?'

Cass expressed genuine eagerness. Nubby wetted his lips and sang. His voice was wholly execrable.

> *Oh, the centypeed clumb on the scorpyun's back*
> *An' his eyes bugged out with glee.*
> *He said, "I'm gonna make you, you poison sonofabitch,*
> *Pervided you don't make me."*

Sliding easily then into prose, Nubby spoke low and confidentially.

"Say, Red, ask one of the boys what happened the last time Joe Spokes put a nigger in this tank 'stead of upstairs in tank three where they belongs. Go on, Red, just ask one of 'em once."

Obediently, Cass questioned a boy seated on the Hoor of the opposite cell.

"What happened the last time Joe Spokes put a nigger in this tank 'stead of upstairs where they belong?"

The reply came swiftly; it was ready-made; as though the same cloth had been used several times before.

"Ol' Nubby like to've killed that young shoke."

"How'd y'all do it, Judge?' Cass asked with but feeble curiosity.

"Busted in his head with *that*—" Nubby pointed dramatically to the heel of his battered boot, and added, "Did it alone too, boys didn't I, mostly?"

Unanimous assent. Then:

"Say, Judge, tell that boy in there 'bout what you found in the Mex 'legger's shoe."

Nubby grinned proudly and explained briefly.

"They brang a Mex 'legger in here one afternoon way last fall, an' he said he was Hat broke. He give the court a half-dollar, Mex, an' said that was all he had. Well, I wouldn't believe no Spik nor Cholo if he was swearin' on his mother's grave—I went through him up and down, crosswise an' bottom-side up. But I couldn't even find a empty tin of terbacco to dent in. He moaned the whole time I was friskin' him, so fin'lly we let him go with a couple good swift kicks in the arse. But after a while I begun noticin' how he kept his shoes on when he went to bed. So I made him take 'em off, an' he'd been in here three weeks already, an' I slit open both soles, an' in the left was a wad big enough to choke a Stony-Island flatfoot."

"How much?" Cass asked; the others replied in chorus:

"*Thirty-three dollars an' twenty-nine cents—Amerikun.*"

Nubby swelled his chest. "Yeah. Every buck was Amerikun. So I took it all off him right away on account what right has a spik got anyhow with Amerikun dollars on him? Well, I'm not the tight kind, I guess you'll find that out all right—I bought these boys three bucks worth o' black-eyed peas an' gave 'em four ready-made cigarettes apiece besides. Didn't I, boys?"

"Sure did, Judge."

Nubby glanced across at Cass. "I'm savin' the rest, though. Joe Spokes don't know nothin' about it o' course, so don't go shootin' off yer trap when his kid's up here."

"Say, Judge, tell that boy in there about the time that Mex 'legger said, 'Do your stump ever hurting you, Meester Nubbee'— an' you knocken him cold with the heel of it then, so when he woke up you ast him, 'Now who you reck'n my stump hurts most, Meester Ferdinando Speek?' And he says, 'Me, Seenyor, mostly.'"

But Nubby refused to tell this tale at all. In a wholly unexpected outburst of modesty he roared, "Be still about me all the time in there, you lyin' little sea-sucker makin' up lies all the time in there—one more an' you'll get biffed colder'n the Mex did with my stump—only I'll use my boot on *you*."

Utter silence, from all quarters, till Nubby's feigned ire was appeased. Smiling then, one eye half-shut, he pointed his stump toward the boy who had spoken, half-seen across the bull-pen. The boy was bent over as though he were playing with something on the floor; Cass could not tell what.

"See that boy acrosst the way? That's Creepy Edelbaum. Just look good at him fer a minute now. He got only one nut an' the brain of a child. He's a half spik, half Jew, an' three-quarters Creek

Indyun. He's feeble-minded a little bit too I guess—Ain't you, Legs?"

The boy looked over to Cass, and he was blushing between the bars. "Yeah, I guess so," he said. "A little I guess."

"Creepy! (We all call him Creepy on account he's my punk.) Hey! Creepy! Stand up!"

The boy jerked violently to his feet, and his face was ablaze with guilt: shame had left two bright spots burning there, one on either cheek. His face was white as anemia, it was angelic and girl-ish and long; he was over six feet, lean as a rake, and he looked like an elongated milk-of-magnesia bottle. But he did not look feeble-minded.

Nubby pointed commandingly to the thundermug at the end of the narrow corridor; the bowl stood in a pool of unmopped night-filth there. Creepy began scrubbing industriously around it, under Nubby's capricious foremanship. The Judge explained gen-teelly to Cass.

"My bowuls again. They're about to move again, I guess."

Creepy scrubbed hard, both inside and out, for Judge O'Neill demanded absolute cleanliness of others. The boy worked bend-ing over at an angle of ninety degrees, so that his hip-bones jutted out of his frayed corduroys like the hip-bones of a starving cow. Without straightening his back or turning his head, he spoke to Nubby.

"I hung yer spoon *facin'* the wall 'stead of 'way from it after I dried it this mornin', Judge. Is it all right that way?"

O'Neill deliberated. Gravely he observed the spoon in the iron holder above his head, hanging toward the wall; it was the first time he had noticed the spoon hanging in precisely that posi-tion. Although he was disturbed by the fact, he decided to concede the point and append its moral to his underling. At first he spoke patiently, like an elder brother. "First thing I know, son, you'll be hangin' it *upside down*. Don't ya know there's always the right way to do a thing, son—an' then there's the wrong way? Well now, this time you done the wrong way. Henceforards an' after this, do the right way. Hang it like other people does." His voice quickened, and lashed out. "An' now quit yer everlastin' babblin' an' get that seat dry—I can't hold in till they spring me, can I? *See*, yer wipin' the *wrong* way with the brush, *nobody* does that way. Say, I got half a idee to make you wipe *me* jest fer that."

The boy's livid pallor deadened to a muddy gray, but he said nothing, only scrubbed the harder. Nubby winked at Cass.

"Yus, my boy, that's exac'ly what yer gonna do after this. Creepy, you are now Official Wiper of Tank Ten, El Paso Country Jail—on account of I'm the judge an' I appoint you."

The cell-block roared with laughter, and one cell stuttered out, "W-when C-Creepy gits really g-good at wipin', we'll all wipe C-Creepy with our b-belt buckles. H-how'd you like a nice b-belt-buckle wipin', Creepy?"

The steel rang with laughter.

"Spokes'll raise hell with you boys if you don't quiet down a bit," the trusty in the run-around warned, leaning on his broom.

Creepy didn't know whether Nubby meant the appointment in good earnest or not; he daubed ineffectually at his eyes with the back of his unclean hand, and the laughter about him redoubled.

"Why, Creepy," Nubby said solicitously, "I'm simply 'ston-ished at you startin' in to cry just 'cause yer 'lected to be Chief Shtunk. I'll bet there ain't a man in this tank but wouldn't give up half his cornbread in the mornin' to be Chief Shtunk in here. Why, it's a honor—don't you know? Say, fellers—*ain't* it a honor to be big shtunk in here?"

Cass lay face-down on his blanket shivering with cold. He was sick with pity for the bending boy; he was cringing with fear of the laughter around him. Yet he laughed, loud as any. He was afraid not to laugh.

Above the thundermug some wag of another day had inscribed in black crayon a simple observation: *A flush here is better than a full house.*

And an arrow pointed downward so that none should miss the jest.

There was nothing to do, nothing to do; each day they were cold, every day they were hungry. In the mornings, water stood frozen on the floor. In the afternoons Spokes let one man into the run-around to sweep. But all the rest had nothing to do, afl the rest watched the one man sweeping, each one wished that it were himself who had something important to do like that.

Every night Creepy tittered quietly to himself, tossing and distressed. One night Mr Bastard went into the cell where Creepy lay giggling; the giggling ceased, and Creepy called out:

"Judge! Nubby! Make him quit it now, Nub."

Mr Bastard skipped softly back to his own blanket, laughing low, and a ripple of low laughter rode from cell to cell. Nubby shouted from across the bull-pen:

"Hush up in there, One-Nut, or I'll come into you myself.'

And this was no vain threat. During the first two weeks that Cass slept in the jail, Nubby went into Creepy's cell four times.

On such nights Cass sweated in terror, remembering the man in the park in Chicago, fearing Nubby as he had feared that man. As it turned out, however, Nubby never molested Cass; although

Cass came to know him well, came to be his friend, there was never this between them. Among Nubby, Creepy, and Mr Bastard, however, there developed, within Cass's first weeks in the jail, an intense rivalry. And on the Saturday morning of Cass's third week in the place this rivalry culminated in open battle.

On that morning Creepy Edelbaum was unable to clean the toilet seat for Nubby, to wash his trough after breakfast, or even to hang up Nubby's spoon. He lay on his blanket, smiling crookedly up. When he tried to rise, he fell. No one knew what the matter was till Joe Spokes, turnkey and chief deputy, came up with the breakfasts. He opened Creepy's trousers and glanced at the groin: the boy had ruptured himself in the night. Cass's heart went sick at the sight, the boy looked so helpless lying there.

The chief deputy, kneeling, spoke to the boys grouped around him, looking down over his shoulder. Cass saw him touching the boy's scrotum.

"Nothin' seeryus, boys. Nothin' contayjus. He won't git no worse. Oney jest don't bother him no more, you boys, he got to tay right still till it go back into place." He rose to his feet with his hands on his hips and stood tooking down. "Yore a nasty little rat, ain't you, son? Yore a Jew-boy too ah'll bet—ain't yo'? Who larned you all them nasty tricks—the rabbi?"

Creepy shook his head, and Nubby spoke quietly, "Don't lie, son—don't lie at a time like this about what you are."

"I just meant I didn't know *who*," Creepy said, and the boys and the deputy laughed together.

When others laughed at him Creepy summoned a foolish grin and kept it till such laughter died.

But no one bothered Creepy any more, because of Joe Spokes' order. Nubby released the boy from all of his former duties, and imposed those duties on Mr Bastard. Toward Creepy Nubby became almost motherly in his concern; when Creepy wished for water he had but to say so and Nubby would bring it. When cornbread and turnips were brought up at three o'clock, Nubby fed him like a child. Nubby forbade him even to stir. And no one save Nubby could tend him.

After breakfast of the second day of Creepy's illness, Nubby tossed two shirts to Bastard to wash, and Bastard refused pointblank. He was bigger than Nubby and built all in one piece like a brick backhouse. Sometimes when he tried to speak his lips moved and no sound came; then he would strain his throat far forward and redden with effort. But this impediment not even Nubby had dared to mock, till now.

When he tossed the shirts to Mr Bastard, Nubby stuttered exaggeratedly.

"W-wash th-th-them th-th-there sh-sh-sh-shirts f-f-f-for m-m-m-me."

Everyone in the tank laughed; for they had few chances in this place for laughter. With a single motion Bastard ripped one shirt from sleeve to hem (the shirt was frail and his hands were strong), and he had his fingers on the collar of the second when Nubby got to him. Nubby's eyes were very wide and his face was white as the toilet seat after Creepy had finished scrubbing, but Bastard's eyes went to slit-like points, and his face was a bag ready to burst with blood.

There is nothing quite so terrible to see as a fight in a blue-steel jailhouse. There is steel and stone all around, up, down, and across. You fight between steel hinges, iron spoonholders, projecting bolts, on a gray stone floor. There is no one to cry, "Stop!" no one to shout, "Foul!" no one to say, "I guess he's had almost enough now." There is only a trusty grinning through the bars offering to bet on the winner. "Boys, I'll put up two sacks o' Bull Durham on the boy with the boots."

By sheer weight alone Bastard forced Nubby to the floor. Nubby's stump waved in the air as he fell. Bastard straddled him, seized him by the hair and cracked his head against the floor. Nubby's hair was long and black. Five times Bastard slammed his head against stone. Then a blue foam came to Nubby's lips and his eyes went wild with pain. Mr Bastard stopped to look up. He was puzzled, being afraid to get off and afraid to stay on, afraid to beat the judge wholly unconscious, yet afraid not to, . . . he brushed sweat off his forehead with the back of his hand, grinned at the ease of his victory and raised himself up a little, as though about to ask the trusty what he ought to do next. In that second Nubby let him know what he ought to have done next, with the toe of his boot. He caught Bastard squarely at the base of the belly, and the boy caved in like a jack-knife snapping. His face bunched with agony, his teeth clenched; for one moment his whole body was paralyzed with pain. For one long moment he crouched over Nubby like a man of wood, his torso bent slightly forward and his fingers spreading wide. Then Nubby shoved him off and rolled him backward, yanked him by the hair to his feet and skarved his head against the nearest hinge, until Bastard screamed wildly, like a woman. Blood boiled out down the back of his neck, and Nubby paused for breath. Bastard crumpled, slowly. Nubby helped Raridon pick him up and assist him back to his blanket.

Had Nubby lost he would have ceased to be judge of the tank, and fines would have been collected by Bastard rather than himself.

After a while Nubby made a bandage for Bastard out of the

shirt that had been torn in two. He daubed the blood off the boy's hair with a wet rag and tied the bandage neatly around. In return Bastard gave Nubby a shirt of his own to compensate for that one he had ruined; and an hour later he began on Nubby's laundry. In the morning he hung Nubby's spoon. Cass marveled at this turn of affairs, until night came. When night came Nubby left his own blanket and went into Bastard's cell.

And Creepy Edelbaum lay on his back, smiling crookedly up. In an undertone, with a jerk of the thumb, Nubby assured Cass that Creepy would become increasingly jealous of Mr Bastard, and that when Creepy and Bastard both recovered, there would be a grand fight.

Although Joe Spokes would not tolerate a severe kangarooing of any white and Protestant American, he permitted the court to make the most of Negroes and Mexicans. Since Nubby was treasurer of the court as well as judge, such permission implied the right to take anything or everything that a Mexican might possess and to beat him into the bargain. Funds went straight into Nubby's pocket, and were never seen again. Consequently every black or brown boy brought in was, for Nubby, "fresh meat an' fish," as he himself termed it. In return for Spokes' permission Nubby acted as stool. Spokes kept him in tobacco and stamps, and he answered whatever questions Spokes put to him.

Cass awoke one winter night, and out in the corridor the nightlight burned dimly. Bars stood against the light straightly and tall. Cass heard the sounds that men make in sleep. At first he did not know what had waked him. Then Raridon, a boy in for vagrancy, shrilled out suddenly into the stillness.

"Judge! Nubby! Wake up! Fresh meat an' fish fer you!"

Keys jangled and feet came pounding. Cass ran out into the bull-pen with the others as the great bolt clicked.

Mr Bastard, scratching himself in underwear, mumbled sleepily for only Nubby to hear, "If it really *is* meat this time I just hope the judge'll buy us some *real* meat with the dough. I'm g-gittin' plum sick o' livin' on t-turnips an' c-cabbage all the time." Then the jumble of their voices stilled, for they heard Joe Spokes speaking on the other side of the door. They listened with their ears cupped to the wall. They could hear Joe Spokes laughing.

"He's friskin' him now," Nubby whispered, "he must've found somethin' valooble on him or he wouldn't be laughin'." The outer door opened and Spokes shoved in a Mexican boy in ragged knee-breeches.

"Mejicano!'"he ordered, "Aqui, Mejicano."

It always took Big Joe longer to open the tank door than it did to open the outer doors. The door to the tank was opened by an air brake locked in a box on the outer wall, and the key to the box, much smaller than his other keys, usually eluded him for a minute. His inevitable remark to the boys as he fumbled for this key was, "Got to be awful keerful with you men t'night. Pris'ners is smarter'n sheriffs ye know."

But Joe did not say this this time, though all of them waited to hear.

All Joe did this time was to wink at Nubby as he went out, after the Mexican was inside with them. Nubby winked back, the door slammed, retreating keys jangled; then all stood silent, heads down and listening, till the last great door closed down below and no sound could come through. Nubby's grin came off then as though it had come off for all time.

"Court's in session," he announced. "Sheriff, bring in yer man."

The play-pretend of the underdogs aping the wolves on top, the man-child game at once so terrible and so ludicrous had begun again in tank ten.

Their prisoner was small and lithe; he faced the court with a friendly white grin. Nubby handed Raridon the rules of the court; Raridon was bailiff by virtue of his being able to read. His voice sounded like a small boy's reciting in a classroom. Nubby frowned a heavy self-import.

"These are the rules of the kangaroo court. Any man found gilty of braking into this jailhouse without consent of the inmates will be fined two dollars or elts spend forty days on the floor at rate of five cents a day, or elts he will take fifty-five licks on the fanny and get the thing over with. Every man entering this tank must keep cleaned and properly dressed. Each day of the week is wash day excep' Sunday. Every man must wash his face and hands before handling food. Any man found gilty of spitting in ash tub or through window will be given twenty licks on rectum west. Each and every man using toilet must flush with bucket immediately after's. Man found gilty of violation gets twenty-five licks on rectum east. Throw all paper in the coal tub. Don't draw dirty pictures on the wall, you may have your sister come visit. When using dishrag keep it clean. Any man caught stealing from inmate of this tank gets 500 belt-licks on both rectums. Every man upon entering this tank with a vener'al disease, lice, buboes, crabs or yello glanders, must report same immed'ately. Any man found violating any of these rules will be punished according to the justice of the court.

"Anything not said here will be decided by the justice of this court. The judge of the court can search everywhere. He can search anybody. The judge could be treasurer too, if he wanted. The judge is Judge O'Neill."

Joe Spokes' son had written all this for Nubby, in a large hand; and the Mexican boy had understood not a word of it all. His face showed that not only had he failed to understand, but that in all probability he had never been in a jailhouse before. Cass surmised that Spokes had pulled him off a boxcar for the sake of the feed-bill.

"Me Ilamo Salomon Rivera, pero me dicen 'El Diamante Negro'—si."

After delivering himself of this the boy laughed pleasantly up at them all. Cass interpreted: "He says his name is Salomon Rivera, but folks call him 'The Black Diamond.'"

When Nubby began searching, the boy showed no sign of fear; obligingly, he turned out his pockets to assist the hunt. The pockets were full of holes; through one a firm brown thigh showed. In his stetson and boots, but with neither shirt nor pants on, Nubby looked, beneath the dim nightlight, like something at night in a madhouse. He searched everywhere, but found not even so much as a nickel sack of tobacco. He ripped open the lining of the boy's cap.

"Sometimes you could find somethin' valooble som'eres," he said, "fifty or a hunerd dollars or a diamond ring maybe."

He could not believe that there was nothing to be found, and drew off his belt.

"Savvy this?" he asked, dangling the belt before the boy and adding in an undertone to the others, "there's more'n one way t' make a cholo talk." He swung back on his heel as though about to strike with the strap. The boy whitened then, and with one swift gesture yanked off his shirt and handed it to Nubby. A gift. Nubby hung it between the bars of his cell and pointed to the ragged breeches. Without hesitation the boy obeyed. Nubby hung the pants beside the shirt. Then he looked around him; and the belts closed in.

And now the long beating began, with only the cold bars listening. Cass closed his eyes, feeling tired and ill. Each bar had a cold and watching face, each bar stood singly and alone. It seemed to Cass there was no sound now in the whole world save the crash of a leather belt on flesh in El Paso County jail. There was only an indrawn breath in all the world to hear. And a low, indrawn sobbing. In the silence between the lashes he had a smell as of something burning in his nostrils; at first he did not know what it was. Then he realized that it was blood which he smelled, and the old weakness came upon him so that he had to grasp bars tightly, in both hands, to keep from fainting. The Mexican boy began to cry out whenever a belt came down; but his head jerked forward with every blow so that the cry came forth half-choked. The flesh on his buttocks became black and blue; then one raw red strip hung down. Raridon held his head to steady him against the impact of Nubby's blows.

"Hold 'is head down there!" Nubby roared like a bronk-buster whenever the boy stumbled forward; "If you can't ride 'im I can!"

While Nubby flogged, the others stood in a dull-faced line behind him, a belt in each one's hand, each waiting his turn. Like sand-lot semi-pros at batting practice. Creepy counted shrilly, from where he lay.

At his forty-fourth count Nubby's arm weakened, but he finished out his fifty, and Raridon took his place. Cass then moved into the position of head-holder, and Nubby kept the count. Raridon was a stronger boy than he appeared. Although his wrists were thin as pipe-stems, his palms were broad and his arms were long, so that he needed no large muscle to inflict wholesale havoc now. Then, somehow, it was Cass's turn, and everyone was looking at him, and Nubby was looking closest of all.

It did not seem possible to Cass to strike the helpless boy; and yet, in a half-daze before Nubby's glare, he found himself unloosening his belt. Mr Bastard stepped back to give him a little more room.

"Oh, boy," Raridon chuckled in anticipation—"Boy *oh* boy— watch this ugly red-head bear down on Mexy's arse now. Start funkin', Mexy! Yore arse is goin' clean through the floor in a second!"

Cass swung lightly the first three times. One hundred and one; one hundred and two; one hundred and three. And three times was all that he did swing lightly.

"Hold it!" Nubby barked. "Stop right there. It's what I been suspishunin' ever since you bust in here—yer a Mexikunlover, that's what. You love 'em just like you do niggers an' yer sentence is unsuspended right off. So get down in his place now 'fore I beat yer belly blue with a boot instead of a belt."

The Mexican boy stumbled nakedly onto his blanket and lay there crying softly. For a moment, as he bent over with his own buttocks exposed, Cass was secretly proud that he had not swung hard like the others. Then the belt came down, and he was all regret. Mr Bastard was beating him, and Nubby was holding his head; every time the leather came down he pinched Cass's ears and gritted between clinched teeth:

"Mexikun-lover, Mexikun-lover. Nigger-Mexikun-nigger-lover.'

In the minutes that followed pain taught Cass that he must never again treat a black man or a brown as he would a white.

Nubby released him after twenty-five lashes.

"Can't be *too* hard on you, son," he explained, "bein' as we're trav'lin' t'gether." He tossed Cass a ready-made cigarette and added, "but it just goes to show you how tricky them spiks can be. You took twenty-five lashes fer that pepper-bellied lascar and now I'll betcha my shirt he won't give you so much as a single bite of cornbread fer doin' it, wait an' see."

On the first morning after the beating Nubby told Cass to return the boy's shirt and breeches, still hanging between the bars of Nubby's cell. Cass found Salomon lying naked and shivering; he leaped to his feet when he saw his clothes, begging Cass humbly with outstretched hands. As the boy put his clothes on Cass saw blood dried on the floor of the cell. He himself had not bled. An hour later breakfast came up, and Salomon came limping into Cass's cell with two chunks of cornbread in his hand. Without a word he laid these in Cass's lap, and left. Cass divided with Nubby, and Nubby said not a word.

Nubby was well satisfied with himself. He had put down an insurrection, he had secured himself a new boy, he had shown a Mexican who was boss in tank ten, and he had given a white man an excellent object lesson on evils of Mexican-loving. Later in the morning Salomon sang:

> *Una noche serena y oscura*
> *Cuando en silencio juramos los dos*
> *. . . Las estrellas, el sol, y la luna . . .*

Creepy and Mr Bastard had never been in jail before; both were in their middle teens. Nubby O'Neill was twenty-eight and had done time in two state penitentiaries. He had lost his hand working on a conveyor in a reform school in Southern Illinois when he was thirteen, and since that time had divided his life between West Texas and Chicago. One day Joe Spokes brought him a copy of Zane Grey, and Nubby sat cross-legged with the book for a week; he read with a painful slowness. Then, on a Friday night, he finished the last page and declared it to have been an excellent story. Indeed he grew so enthusiastic over *Riders of the Purple Sage* that he forbade Salomon to sing any more of his "Chilli-fartin' cholo songs."

"*Amerikun* songs is all what's sung in number ten tank from this day on," he announced, and gave Salomon to understand by waving both his book and his belt at the boy.

After that Salomon was silent from morning till night; but Nubby substituted for him by singing them all a song he claimed was his own. It was, he declared, a "real *Amerikun* song—an' I call it the Blind Child."

> *They tell me that tonight, papa*
> *You wed another bride,*
> *That you would clasp her in the room*
> *Where my poor mother died,*
> *That you would bid her press a kiss*
> *Upon your throbbing brow*
> *Like she my own dear mother did—*
> *Papa, you're weeping now.*

Nubby's offense, indecent exposure, made him the only actual malefactor in the tank; the others were all more petty offenders. Creepy, Mr Bastard, Raridon and Salomon had been pulled out of boxcars for the sake of the feed-bill; the jail officials received sixty cents a day from the county for each prisoner. This sum left such ample margin for profit that when every tank was not full to capacity the officials felt that they were losing money with every passing day.

And every passing day brought hunger, till hunger was a living wound in the gut. For Cass, as with the others, the fact of confinement greatly intensified pain: there was nothing to do, nothing to do. Nothing to do but to listen to the wolf howling behind your navel.

It was so in all jails, in those of the North as well as the South, in Dakota or Ohio the same as in Texas. Every day the boy Salomon complained quietly, always half to himself. "Yo tengo hambre, companeros," he whimpered, as though he thought they were all somehow concealing food from him.

Cass gripped bars in both hands and listened to his bowels grumbling. His belly was still there all right, but it felt as flat and as thin as though somebody had been stomping upon it. Somebody stomping in boots as sharp as his father's had been; as pointed as Nubby's had become.

It grew cold in the jail. By standing atop the thundermug the boys could see a cold rain falling. At night they slept in all their clothes and wrapped their blankets about their heads despite hordes of lice. In the afternoons, when the tank was the warmest, they pursued lice across the blankets with burning matches. When a louse was caught he crackled once, and died.

Two days after he had regained his feet, Creepy caught the nettle hives. His body became one itching mass from toe to head. All day and night he scratched himself furiously, his mouth clenching and jerking into a thousand agonized shapes. When Spokes' boy came up with the meal-tray Creepy opened his shirt and showed the boy his chest. A livid red rash covered both breasts and ran down to the navel.

"Ah'll tell paw," the boy promised after having satisfied his curiosity by touching the rash through the bars.

In the evening Spokes came in carrying a small spray-gun, in appearance like a fire-extinguisher, and offered to spray Creepy with it. The spray was used as a disinfectant and rat-killer, so Spokes thought it only fair to give Creepy warning.

"It'll singe yore hide a mite, but it'll cure it ah reck'n," he assured Creepy. Creepy declined, for he had witnessed the spray-gun's potency against vermin, and his rash did not happen to be itching him at the moment.

But a minute after Spokes had left he began scratching again. Nubby, watching from a distance, took the occasion to cheer the boy's spirits.

"There's a sunny side to everythin', Legs," he said. "See, you can't quit scratchin' long enough now to fool with yerself, so maybe you'll get to be a real man soon; if you stay sick long enough. It's a silver linin' you want to took for, Legs, not always the gloomy side."

Sometimes Cass fancied that he would never get out of jail, that something would happen to him and he would never see sun and daylight again. After three weeks in the place he could no longer imagine himself as being free, so strange a thing did liberty then seem. Something would happen: he would catch some strange disease on the thundermug and die before the week was out; or Joe Spokes would be shot by a Mexican and the county clerk would misplace the records. Then he would grow old in this jail, and would never be free again.

At such moments of doubt the wolf in Cass's belly seemed to howl out of hate as well as from hunger.

But when your belly starts crawling up the inside of your neck, just to see if your mouth is still there, a long drink of water will push it down for a while. Warm water is best, and the boys heated a gallon every morning, after their meager cornbread breakfast. They made a small fire in the corner of Raridon's cell, fanned off the smoke so that those downstairs would smell nothing, and drank it before it cooled off. Cass drank warm water in the El Paso County jail until, like the others, he became diarrheal.

In the last week of February he came to his twentieth year.

He made a calendar on the wall: twenty-one days became twenty-three; he had sixty-seven to go. Then, sixty-six.

He thought he would never be free again. But Nubby sang every day for him; he passed whole hours listening to the tinny din of Nubby's nasal tenor:

> *On a cozy little chain gang, on a dusty southern road*
> *My late-lamented pappy had his perm-unent abode.*
> *Now some was there fer stealin', but my daddy's only fault*
> *Was an overwhelmin' weakness fer crim-inal assault.*
> *His phil-osophy was simple, it was free from moral tape—*
> *See-ducshun is fer sissies, but a he-man wants his rape.*
> *The list of daddy's victims was em-barrasin'ly rich,*
> *And though one of 'em was mammy he couldn't tell me which.*
> *Now I never went to college, but I got me a degree—*
> *I reckon I'm a model of a perfect s.o.b.*

Big Joe Spokes was a hard old man. They were all hard men. The sheriff, the deputies, judges, lawyers, and preachers: all were callous old men. They all seemed to live without deep feeling. They all knew the things that were done in the jail. They knew, and they scarcely cared. Those who cared somewhat blamed the boys themselves. These men made a hard jest out of suffering, even their own.

"Ah think thet one-arm boy is goin' after the stuttery one of late. Leastwise he ain't pesterin' the kid who's sick no more. Well I figger thet stuttery boy got it all comin' to him all right, he uz always too pert to suit my likin's. Say, y' reck'n it'll larn him to steal rides on the Santy Fee?"

They laughed together.

Once, for nine days running, tank number ten lived on an oatmeal and turnip-green diet. Each boy lay on his blanket without complaint, without tears, waiting for time to pass. Sometimes from outside they heard the chimes of the First Methodist Church coming to divine service. The second Sunday in March came on the fifth day of the turnip-green diet, and all thought on that day, since it was Sunday, that there would be a small cut of meat for supper. But it was turnips again, and cornbread. They were all sickened of such thin swill, yet only Bastard had the courage to complain when Spokes came up with the meal-tray.

"H-Holy s-sneakin-Jesus, Mister Spokes, w-when we gonna git a little s-salt pawk er good ol' sow-belly er somethin'?"

The boy kept trying to grin through the bars. Spokes was shoving tin troughs through to Nubby.

At every meal it was Nubby's self-delegated duty, as judge, to assign each man his trough. None ever presumed to take a tin until Nubby had pointed out the proper one for each to take. He was capricious in this process, and none of the boys ever knew who was going to be pointed out first, and who was going to get next to the most to eat. (It was always peculiar that, after he had appointed an eater of each ration, that it was always Nubby's own trough which remained the one most full.) Now, as he aligned them, feigning unconcern, he calculated sharply out of one corner of his eye. Then he assigned the next to the largest to Cass, the next to Creepy, the next to Bastard, and the last to Raridon. Spokes waited until the little ritual was over. Then he answered Bastard.

"Y'all want to come down to the commiss'ner, son?" he asked. "Y'all kin tell him what yore wearyin' of. It's him what got the big say-so—ah oney take his ordahs."

The commissioner was a county judge, as every one knew, so Cass poked Mister Bastard to make him be still. County judges were all pretty much alike. But Bastard misunderstood that nudge, and the quietness of the deputy's voice had misled him.

"Sh-sure would, Mister Sp-Spokes; if y'all don't mind."

Spokes fumbled for the keys to the pneumatic lever a minute, and then the tank door opened slowly. Bastard stepped out into the run-around—and the keys came down like a spiked club on his head. Blood spurted from the half-healed wound back of his ear, he crashed like a blind man against the concrete wall, holding his head in his hands and gasping with shock. Spokes followed with the keys. "Thar! Larn me how to run mah jailhouse, will ye?" The keys cut into the back of the naked neck—"Thar! Tell me my own business, eh?—Now git back in yore kennel 'fore ah lose mah temper an' cut the livin'—out o' ye."

Keys do not knock a man out, but they cut and slash fearfully. Bastard stumbled to his blanket with blood from half a dozen wounds darkening the side of his face and neck. He lay down, moaned for an hour, and after a while slept.

Cass saw the boy called Bastard sleeping. He lay on his back with his face upturned, and his face was unwashed of its blood. Two thin streams had come together to coagulate in the lacuna of the throat; to form a dark and terrible necklace there. With his every breath that dark necklace trembled, like a strung locket's trembling. Cass looked away. He felt sick and helpless.

"Paw shouldn't of kicked Bry'n so hard," he told himself.

In the night Cass heard Bastard waken, heard him fumbling about in darkness for something.

"He might find his trough all right," Cass thought, "But there won't be no turnips in it now no more." He had seen Nubby eat half of them and forcibly feed the rest to Creepy with a spoon. Cass wondered whether the cuts that Bastard had received would leave many scars or only one. "Ah wisht mine was on back of mah neck 'stead of on mah mouth," he thought almost jealously.

Before that night was past Joe Spokes came up a second time. There were three deputies with him, and all were half-seas over. The boys heard them roaring together on the other side of the outer door. It was Nubby who made the proper guess:

"They've raided another still, I'll bet my breakfast with any man here. Say! Mebbe we'll get another Mex 'legger!"

The possibility of another thirty-dollar kangarooing caused Nubby to pull on his boots frenziedly. The other boys remained apathetic, for they knew that Nubby did not spend money for supplies any more. Nubby was saving his money, he said, to get his boots repaired when he was released. "A man like me just can't afford to be feedin' a hungry mob 'ike you an' buyin' 'em cig'rettes," he said whenever the hint was dropped about spending some of his money.

Nubby was disappointed that night, for Spokes brought in no prisoner. Spokes had found a still, but had lost its owner; he had come up only to let the trusty into the cell-block with the others. As he hauled down the lever in the box on the wall Cass saw that he held a bottle in his left hand. The trusty dodged past him into the cell-block, crouching in fear that Spokes might let him have the bottle over his head as he ran past.

When Spokes tried to shove the lever up he was too drunk to raise it all the way with one hand, and he refused to give up his grip on the neck of the bottle in his fist. His deputies clustered drunkenly about him, mauling each other like playful bears, and among them they finally got the lever up into place. Spokes leaned against the wall as the door closed, and laughed a little at the boys looking solemnly out at him from their cage.

"Say," he asked, "where's the monkey what took a thrashin' this afternoon?"

"Here, Mister Sp-Spokes," Bastard replied obediently, coming forward into light. He was hitching up his trousers, and one side of his face was still unwashed. Big Spokes looked him up and down, an expression of amiable curiosity in his eyes.

"Wouldn't a shot o' tequila make up fo' thet beatin', Monk?" he asked, holding the half-filled bottle out between the bars, "Ah didn't mean to beat you *bad*, son."

When Cass saw the bottle, and smelled it, the desire for drink made him tremble all over. He wanted to reach out and snatch the bottle away. But Bastard did not even reach for his gift. "It sure would make up, Mister S-Spokes," he said, "them keys s-sure p-packed a wal-wallop."

Spokes' face darkened, and he roared like a drunken bull at the boy.

"Y'reck'n it *would* make up, eh? Well goddamn it—ye'll play hell a-gittin' it!"—and he crashed the bottle into a thousand fragments against the bars.

After the officers had left, laughing and lurching down the stairs, Bastard said, "I knew he was just kiddin' when he sh-shoved that t-tequila right out at me like that."

Cass tried to reach some of the liquor as it spilled down the floor, but neither his tongue nor his spoon was quite long enough.

A single spoonful would have helped.

For the next three days Mr Bastard's attempt to complain to the commissioner and the consequent loss of his turnips was a running joke in the tank. Even Joe Spokes laughed the next few times he came up. "Any complaints t'day, anybody?" he would ask, looking at no one in particular; and the boys would giggle and repeat the joke among themselves for an hour after. Even Mr Bastard began to laugh at it a little. But the turnip-and-cabbage diet continued until the second day before the trials.

On the second day before trials a grand jury came "to investigate conditions," and on that day the boys got meat and milk and potatoes three times.

"Any complaints to make, boys?" the foreman, a tall fellow who looked like a hill man, inquired.

There was no complaint. Joe Spokes was standing in the runaround holding his key-ring in his right hand.

> *Oh, the only friend that I have left*
> *Is Happy Sailor Jack;*
> *He tells me all the lies he knows*
> *An' all the safes he's cracked,*
> *He's cracked them in Seattle,*
> *He's robbed the Western Mail;*
> *It would freeze the blood of an honest boy*
> *In El Paso county jail.*

Cass thought, "Mebbe ol' Nub ain't such a bad hat after all. Ah guess mebbe he ain't so tough as he takes on sometimes. Ah guess he wouldn't jump no real white man less'n he got awful sore at him. He don't never bother me. An' he sure kin scrap all right wunst he gets his Irish up."

10

DURING HIS LAST week in the El Paso County jail Cass lay for
hours each day on his blanket, thinking of a different place. Eyes
closed, he saw the great prairie once more. He saw a dark old
house on Chihuahua Street, and a road where Mexican children
had played. He saw a dusty doorway where once a lilac bloomed,
and he seemed to smell the windy smell of clouds across the earth.
He remembered how as a boy he had played in the sun in the summer; how wind had gone wailing through the white nights of winter; how dead leaves had drifted in the brown months of autumn;
and how in one springtime all things had been troubling to him.
He opened his eyes. The grayness of the ceiling four feet above his
head came down like a weight upon his lids; that ceiling seemed
part of a high dark wall, as a Bible's covers once had seemed. A
stench that a thousand imprisoned men had left hung in the air
like a low gray pall.

"Ah want to go home," Cass thought to himself, forgetting that he had never really had a home. He was not so far from
Great-Snake Mountain now, he kept telling himself; three coun-
ties to cross, that was not very far.

All one night he lay wakeful, remembering, regretting, hoping. In a few days he would be free once more. Should he then
return to the North? He thought of Chicago, of its million faces

and its hostile doors, its frightened people and its hungry streets. He asked himself if Nancy wished to see him again as much as he wished to see her. He wondered, and could not tell. All that night he lay wakeful, with thoughts of Nancy and freedom. He thought that these last hours were, perhaps, the unclean fringe of his transient life—that when they were past life would, somehow, become secure. Somehow or other, he wouldn't have to keep moving all the time now any more.

Then it was morning, and it was April, and Joe Spokes sent up four breakfasts instead of six. When the boys saw that there were but four troughs they knew that two in the cell-block had been freed by the grand jury: on his last day in jail a man received no breakfast. So they all shouted at once through the bars at Spokes' son, the second they saw the troughs.

"Who's the two gittin' sprung, Junior? Am I? Is one me? Who's out?"

Junior referred to a slip of paper with which his father had furnished him. He held it upside-down for a minute, pretending to be unable to read; then he reversed it and tried to read the blank side. The boys waited humbly, till he had had his fill of teasing.

"The troughs is one fo' the guy you guys call Bastard an' one fo' Jew-Boy Legs,—he ain't well enough to git out anyhow,—an' one fo' Raridon, 'cause he lies to Pa faster than a dog kin trot, an' one fo' thet godderned screw-me-down copper-belly cholo who Pa say he ain't neper gonna leave go."

Nubby winked at Cass, and Cass returned the wink. But it was whole minutes before he fully realized that he was free . . .

Sitting on the inside of the railing in a musty courtroom, Cass waited with Nubby to hear a judge tell them that they were free men. Cass saw Matches sitting on a bench on the other side of the room, with four other Negroes. Matches grinned, a fulsome, white, spontaneous grin, and waved one hand. Because Nubby was at his side, Cass feigned not to see. It had all been the dirty smoke's fault that he'd been snatched in the first place.

"Soon's we git out," Nubby said, "we'll buy potatoes an' onions an' bread. Then we'll jungle up in the scrub."

The judge resembled an old frog, for when he spoke he croaked.

"This mo'nin' yer lives is beginnin' again, boys," he informed them. "Find a job som'eres an' stick hard to it. Work hard as yer able an' you'll both get ahead. Good-bye. Good luck. God bless yer."

He reached one hand down on them as they stood, and his eyes looked rheumy. The boys shifted their caps from their right to their left hands, and shook the old man's fingers. Cass distrusted old men. It seemed to him that they always lied.

They came out together onto a sunlit street. How strange it seemed to Cass to walk freely once more. How sweet it was just to breathe! He felt that they could not walk swiftly enough, could not breathe too deeply, and he began to run. Nubby tried hard to keep up beside him. They walked and ran until they reached that broad highway that leads away in a curve toward Presidio County.

When they became too tired to walk farther, and it was growing gray dusk, they left the highway to cut across toward the Southern Pacific. They walked through tight-waisted Spanish dagger and cabbage-headed sotol cactus till they reached the tracks. In the low scrub there they built a fire. The prairie stars came out, and a small wind whispered by.

Cass lay looking up into the night while Nubby poked potatoes about the coals. "Want to hear a song I made up once, Red?"

Nubby asked. "It's all about a tom-cat an' a pussy-cat?" Cass said nothing, for he didn't want the quietude of the night disturbed by Nubby's wailing. But Nubby took his silence for consent.

Cass felt that he wanted to sing something too, to shout out something in joy; and yet something hurt all the while. It was as though outwardly he rejoiced, yet inwardly still sorrowed, secretly, to himself. Nubby pointed at the sky. "Sure lots of stars up there t'night, ain't they, Red?" "Yeah," Cass agreed, gnawing a potato, "Ah oney hope ah kin stay out under 'em a spell now."

And an old wonder came over him, and an old fear.

"Ah'm Cass McKay," he told himself, "Ah bin in jail. Ah got kin-folk hereby, an' mebbe ah'm goin' home."

He fell to sleep thinking of his father.

In the middle of the night he woke with fear like a hand at his heart. For a moment he thought he was back on his prison blanket; he sat bolt upright, sick and sweating. Fear held his heart for a full minute before he understood where he was. Then he saw a small light from a ranchhouse or barn shining to him from far in the distance, and he felt reassured. "Ah was in there a long time," he told himself as though only now understanding, "but they've let me go now." But the little light went out as he watched, and before he fell to sleep once more he felt afraid of something again; he did not know quite what.

Shortly after daybreak he was aroused by Nubby. Nubby had sighted a jack-rabbit and was howling and zig-zagging crazily over the prairie after it, his right arm flapping in the wind and his left hurling clods. Cass joined in the chase. He hurled a jagged rock at two bounding ears, and then held his breath in fear that the rock might hit; but it missed by a foot, and the next moment the rabbit was gone. The boys returned to their jungle.

"Whew!" Nubby gasped, "first one of them things I ever missed—but I did clam it once, I guess, right square in the back of the neck. He begun limpin' a little after I thrun it, betcha she'll think he's been nibblin' the sotol-cactus, he'll seemed like to me. Say, when he gets back to his missus I'll be wobblin' that bad."

About seven o'clock a green-fruit train came piling up the grade, and they hopped a coupling as the cars began gathering speed on the downslope.

"Ah'm not trav'lin' much further," Cass shouted at Nubby over the din of the wheels, "cause ah got kin-folk this side o' Great-Snake Mountain. Reck'n ah'll stay on with 'em for a spell."

Nubby glanced at him with something of dismay. He had a genuine need of an able-bodied companion. An hour later, in an empty reefer, he showed money to Cass.

"Forty-two bucks in that left boot, Red," he said, counting in the cool dimness. "I guess I must of kangarooed twelve Mexes in that jailhouse before you ever bust in. Didn't have much luck nohow after you come in. But now if you wants to go home to Maw-maw, like a pukey baby, go right ahead. I ain't stoppin' ya. But *I'm* goin' to Chicago to get my tattooin' vamped up. I know a place on Van Buren Street there. An' we could have a real time in Chi too. I'd make a real man of you, Red, on this dough in Chi. Yeah, an' when our money's gone I know a place I could get us some more. That is, of course, if you just wanted to. I could learn you lots, Red. 'Course if you don't want to know nothin' I'll just have to find some'ne elts to get tattooed with on Van Buren Street that's all." He offered Cass a ready-made cigarette; Cass took it before replying.

"Ah'm plum sick o' bummin'. Ah never wanted to in the first place, oney mah ol' man got in bad in our town. Reckon that's all blowed over now though, an' ah got a sister ah ain't even seen fo' three years."

In Valentine the train stopped for an hour. Nubby bought bread and beans, and they ate on the outskirts of the city. When they were finished he gave Cass another ready-made cigarette, and they walked back to the train in silence.

It was growing toward evening when they crossed the Presidio County line; the train began to slow toward the roundhouse.

"Y'all better hop off with me here, Nub," Cass suggested, rising. "They break this man up here. Be mebbe three-four hour fo' there'll be 'nother man out—'less there's somethin' on the Santy Fe befo'. Come on, Nub, ah'll show yo' mah home town."

Nubby rose, as though with misgivings, and would go no farther than the Southern Pacific freight depot with Cass. The depot was darkened but for one small light burning beneath a green shade in the ticket office. Nubby slouched crookedly against the baggage car in the darkness, jingling the coins in his pocket. He gave Cass his hand.

"Yer sure lucky to have kin-folk," he said, "all I got is my brother Elmy, an' nobody knows where he is." There were tears, either feigned or real in Nubby's voice, "I guess Elmy maybe died of bein' mean by now, like all my folks done."

Cass mumbled, "Glad to've knowed y'all," and turned down Nevada Street and toward the town. Over the mountain hung a high hood of night-dark. The mountain snaked four times, then rose, in one sheer point, into the high hood.

As he walked through the dusk Cass passed a young orchard, and the odor of cherry and wild plum came to him mingled and fainting together. Somewhere to his left a drowsy dove was calling low and patiently. The great moon came over the edge of the prairie, and the velvet dark came down.

As he came into town Cass saw Clark Casner, the Santa Fé ticket agent, hunkered up on the courthouse steps. Cass remembered this lank ribbon of a man, so full of sighs and sleepy blinkings. Clark sat with his thin knees supporting his chin, poking a yellow toothpick between his teeth. Cass stood above him, saying who he was, and the agent began nodding his head mechanically. He replied nothing at all, merely shifted the toothpick. Then his legs flung out, he was off the steps and pumping Cass's hand.

"Why, dammit all, boy, yore Bry'n McKay's brother,—hain't yo ? Damme, ah wouldn't have knowed yo' from third base. Y'eve shore put on size since ye' tuk out o' town, hain't yo'? How long now is thet? Ah guess po' Bry'n was still around then, weren't he?"

"Five years," Cass replied, and then wondered why he said five instead of the three that it was.

"Well, son, yore brother was a good boy, 'cause ah knowed him 'fore he went oversea. An' mebbe you was a good boy an' yore sister was a good woman, ah dunno 'bout *that*—but yore pappy was the meanest man that ever hit this town, an' in mah time we've had lots o' bad hats here. But ah don't spec' ah have to tell *you* 'bout yore own paw, do ah, son?"

He peered into Cass's face, to read there what he could of shame or fear or pain. Cass averted his eyes; he wanted to ask Clark Casner something. Something a hundredfold more difficult than asking a stranger on the street for a nickel.

"Ah don' know what 'came of mah ol' man, ex-actly," he confessed.

The ticket agent perceived his embarrassment and tried to help him.

"Well, he's better off'n Bryn." He paused to spit out the toothpick—"Ah guess y'all know th' old song:

Here is to Huntsville, the land of blue skies
Where the wild wind blows and the bulldung flies.
If ye've never been to Huntsville . . ."

He checked his tongue abruptly, seeing that he was not being taken quite as humorously as he had intended. But Cass remembered the jingle about the state penitentiary, and he added its last line for Clark—

Never go to Huntsville—it's the back door to hell—

and he walked away with shame like a plunging sword within.

As he passed the Poblano Café a girl tapped on the window from the inside. It was smoky in the place, he saw men drinking there. He waved his hand at the girl, saw that it was not that Pepita to whom he had once brought customers, and passed on.

Moonlight was misting Chihuahua Street when he came in sight of the house. It looked like an old and dark-cowled nun kneeling in prayer beneath great stars, the moonlight a halo about her bent head. How quietly it waited there! And the memory of his last night in it came upon him.

A lamp burned in the kitchen and men were talking on the porch. Cass leaned on the gate, he listened intently; voices came to him in a slow curving murmuring, in a wave that broke and fell, never falling quite to silence, never rising quite to clarity. The air smelled of punk, and the men were laughing.

And suddenly something other than that laughter was strange. Suddenly something unheard was changed, and something unseen was hostile. Something here that had once been friendly was friendly now no more. He felt ill. He almost wished that he had gone on with Nubby.

Someone was coming toward him. A woman, a girl—then it was Nancy, for he knew her stride, and his heart leaped up the path before him. How firmly his sister walked! How strong her stride! He felt that the gate was swinging beneath his hand even though he knew it was closed. His throat constricted a little when Nancy spoke.

"Who is thet there?" she asked.

For a moment he could not answer; he lifted his face to be recognized, instead. In the dimness he could not see Nancy's face clearly, and he waited for her to come closer to see his. But she paused in the pathway, and her voice changed, till it was like a quick whispering there.

"Y'all kin come in fo' a dolla'," she said in that flat hard whispering, "a pahty cost but a dolla'. Hev y'all got a dolla', fella?"

The men on the porch had stopped laughing to listen; so he only shook his head.

PART THREE

Chicago

The "dangerous class," the social scum (lumpenproletariat), that passively rotting mass thrown off by the lowest layers of old society, may, here and there, be swept into the movement by a proletarian revolution; its conditions of life, however, prepare it far more for the part of a bribed tool of reactionary intrigue.

THE COMMUNIST MANIFESTO

11

CHICAGO'S SOUTH SIDE seethed in the spring of 'thirty-one. Unemployment demonstrations, eviction riots and strikes shook the city. In the dress shop where Norah Egan worked there were three wage-cuts in the month of March, and another was threatened for April.

Norah Egan hadn't worked in the shop very long, and sometimes it was hard for her to breathe in the place. All the tall windows were kept tightly closed here, even when green April came, because when they were opened the lake wind whisked across stacks of blue bungalow aprons and white morning frocks, and blew the frocks on the top to the door. And the door was pretty dirty, for it was hard to sweep between the machines. There were so many machines here, you see, that's what made this door so hard to sweep. There were so many machines, and the loft was so small, and dirt on the door didn't matter much anyhow. No one would have thought that any one man could ever have gotten ninety big sewing machines into so small a room.

On one of the machines a belt was loose, so that it kept slipping and slapping all day, from morning till night, slip-slop-slapping all day; till it made some of the girls want to cry out or scream something.

Norah Egan wanted to scream or cry out because she hated

the shop's hurry-up sounds. From where she sat in the loft's far corner she sometimes wanted to call out something or swear, right in the foreman's face. "It's loose, Sheely. Why don't you tighten it? Why don't you fire me? What time will it ever be quiet in here?"

Maybe that was what Norah wanted to ask, something without much sense in it like that.

But Norah didn't even so much as ask for a glass of cold water, far less yell out at the foreman some nonsense about the shop's hurry-up noises. Instead, she set her teeth down tight into her nerves and forced her thirst back down her throat; and breathed in the odor of doth that was new mingled with the smell of rancid sewing machine oil and the smell of sweat from ninety bodies bending and bowing all about her.

Spindles went here, bobbins too, up and down and up and down. Yet it wasn't the slapping of the belt nor the incessant drone of many spindles, nor yet a low cloud of sweat-stench about her that Norah Egan minded most. What made things so hard, from the very first day, was not having water from morning till noon and then not from noon until the power was closed. That's what made things so hard. From her very first day.

There was a sink behind a partition near the shipping room on the second floor—but it took six minutes to get down there and six to get back, that was the hitch. Twelve whole minutes, and who could tell what a foreman might do in twelve minutes? Oh, you'd get his permission if you asked it all right. Sheely seldom refused his girls such small favors; only when you came back your machine was locked up and your pay was waiting, with five percent off for the cost of cashing your check. That was the hitch *there*. (But maybe it wasn't all Sheely's fault, he had his orders like everyone else; he had his orders, and three kids at home.)

So you learned things from others, you waited and watched. You learned that the best way to do was to drink all that your stomach could hold in the morning and then try to slip-sneak down to the sink a minute before the others at noon. Now, there were only twenty minutes for lunch here, so you had to eat quick—but get downstairs first. Take your sandwich with you and chew in line behind the faucet, get it all down before it's your turn so there wouldn't be dry crumbs left in your teeth all afternoon. Don't stop to talk—chew! Ninety other girls got thirst too—don't push, we still got nine minutes—Don't shove, shovin' won't get you water no faster—*Say!*—Quit shovin' back there an' let a girl drink! Say, don't *you* push *me*—Twenty whole minutes for lunch.

It's kind of tough all right, at first. But you get used to it after a while. If you're tough. Only, Norah Egan wasn't so tough. And that was the hitch *there*. She was small, and slight, and had always had someone stronger to take care of her. She had always had someone, and now she had no one, and a loose belt kept slipping and slapping all day.

Norah would have liked to be one of the pressers, for pressers had only to iron, fold and pin, and they earned eight dollars a week. Only Norah knew that it would be of no use even to ask Ed Sheely for such a job, because Ed Sheely didn't like Norah very well. Norah kicked too much, from the start. She kicked when he gave her organdie to sew, instead of being a little grateful to him for giving her something to do. Organdie was the hardest to handle of all the materials, and it paid least of all. It was so stiff and so thin it made your fingers numb just to work with it an hour, and if you weren't very careful it tore. That was bad, when organdie tore. The garment had to be bought then, and the retail price paid for it too. Six bits out of your check then, sometimes a dollar, and you finished the garment at home. And since you got only half a cent a dozen for ruffled organdie collars and cuffs, mistakes came rather dear. But for French seams you got five cents a dozen—just ten times as much and no harder to handle. So Norah wanted to work with French seams sometimes, and when she never got anything but gingham and percale and organdie, she kicked.

Once she kicked about the windows being kept shut, and once about the dirt on the floor. First she wanted this, then she wanted that. Then she raised a stink about the sink downstairs, that Sheely shouldn't count the time it took to get down there and back. And then she said that Sheely was favoring one of the girls with French seams. But she never said one word about a belt being loose, and she never asked anyone to tighten that belt. That slipping sound went too deep for speech. And she never seemed to realize that Sheely had three kids.

Through March, and all through the brief green April, Norah's weekly checks ranged from four dollars and ninety-five cents to seven dollars and fifty cents. That was the busy season then, and they were locked in each night till seven-thirty. Ed Sheely punched the time-clock for them at five-fifteen, and then he locked the doors.

"Got to do accordin' to law," he said every night, gulping in apology after the doors were locked.

Norah wanted to punch out her own time, and she didn't want to punch it until she'd finished work. So she kicked. And Sheely gave her organdie just to shut her up.

In the first week of that June work began to slack a little in the Sunshine Frock Shop. For that week Norah drew only four dollars. Next week it was two and a quarter. And the week after that she had no work at all, just walked in every morning and sat at her machine with her basket empty beside her chair, to wait for Sheely to give her something to do. Organdie or muslin or anything at all.

And every day of that hot week Norah sat doing nothing from morning till dark. Just sitting and waiting and looking down at her palms, and once in a while looking outside at two telephone wires hanging limply in the heat.

Norah saw Sheely give work to his favorites whenever work came in, and once when he walked by she said, "I'm still workin' here, Ed."

"You only work on French ruffles," Ed answered, and kept right on walking.

Sometimes girls about her looked at Norah sidewise after that, wondering when Sheely would give the blonde kid a little something or other to do. Norah saw that look, what others were hoping a little, and she wanted to toss back her head and shout at them all: "*You* don't have to feel sorry for *me*. Not a one of you. I can take care of myself O.K." Only Norah couldn't, she never had. There had always been someone stronger, and now there was no one; and she had never had to rush so, just to *eat*, in all her life before.

When only three or four in that whole dim loft were working, then Norah Egan didn't feel quite so badly. But one day everyone she could see had something to do for at least an hour; everyone but herself. Everybody made at least lunch-money that day; everyone save herself. Herself she just sat doing nothing at all, and looking down at her palms. She smelled woman-sweat like a dirty pall all about her, scuffed her shoes through the dirt beneath her feet; wondered about the weather, when days would grow cooler; wondered about room-rent, how she would pay it; wondered about

Sheely's three kids, what they looked like; and then she wondered how soon times would get good again. That was all on a stifling Friday morning, and there was a small off-season rush, and Norah was hungry a little.

When the power was closed at noon that day she didn't have much worth washing down with water, so instead of going downstairs to the sink with the others she went straight on down to the first floor and then straight on out the door. She took a leisurely stroll along the outer drive, saw a boy picking dandelions behind the Field Museum, watched red and green roadsters going up and down in the Nash display on the boulevard, looked at bonbons in a Fanny May window, chewed gum and held her hands on her hips; and she didn't go back to the Sunshine shop at twelve-twenty-five as she should have.

On Monday she answered an ad for work in a dress shop on West Lake Street. And she was hired so quickly, given machine and basket and cloth and shears so fast, that she should have been at least a little suspicious. It wasn't until the week was out that she learned she'd been hired only as an apprentice. For the week's work she was given the apprentice wage: fifty-six cents. Eight cents a dozen for seven dozen aprons turned out in that whole sultry week of July. So that was the hitch *there*. She quit the place feeling a little bewildered and wishing that days weren't so hot.

The day after Norah quit the Lake Street shop she saw the same aprons on sale for a dime apiece. She saw them in Woolworth's on North State; she stood looking in the window with her half-dollar wage in her palm. And it seemed to Norah Egan then, in that moment of looking at those aprons through a plate-glass window on North State, comparing the pink with the mauve and the green with the blue, while strangers passed and traffic crashed, that from somewhere far far up above her there came down the drone of many spindles. Up, then down. And Norah looked up to see what that sound was, but it was only the Lake Street L rumbling around the loop.

Every day then, all through late July and August, Norah followed the Help-Wanted-Female-Gentile column. Every day, at the bottom of a whole row of little trick ads, she read the little trick ads of the Lake Street shop. And wherever she went other people knew tricks, and she didn't know any, and most things had a hitch. But Norah found all the ads out after a while. Each morning she walked from Thirteenth and Dearborn to the *Daily Times* building to look at the want-ad column posted outside the pressroom. Each morning she went from office to office, from house to house, all through Chicago's blazing summer, pounding the long Chicago pavements, knocking in the early forenoon heat at a million hostile Chicago doors.

Once she got a job washing windows, way up on the Northwest Side. But she didn't wash the windows very well because she was hungry a little; and the woman who had hired her said there was nothing else to do, after she'd seen how Norah had done the windows. Norah got thirty-five cents from her though, and a cup of coffee before she left.

In the first week of September a small ad appeared in the *Herald*:

WANTED: DANCER. EXP. PREF. APPLY HAUSER'S
RIALTO.—S. STATE.

Hauser himself was out front barking when Norah answered that ad. He was a paunchy person with a red shoe-button mouth wearing a black and mountainous derby far down over both ears; but he treated Norah like a gentleman ought, and he gave her a dancing job.

Norah had danced in high-school a little; only this wasn't that kind of dancing.

The Little Rialto offered both white and colored burlesque to adult audiences only. Herman Hauser pointed to enlarged photos on either side of the ticket cage, those on the right being of white girls, and those on the left of black. Above his head a star-bordered sign swung in the State Street breeze:

HOT PEPY BURLESK! NO MINERS ALOUD!

The job paid seven-fifty a week, so Norah did just as she was told. She had grace and looks, and she learned quickly. Herman patted her shoulder, approving.

"You'll be at the Haymarket some day," he assured her, and took her about the waist.

Norah's photograph had been outside only two hours, when the shoe-shine boys and newsboys of the street noticed the change. Half a dozen of them were waiting for her when she came out at the end of the afternoon show. One jumped up on his shine-box the minute he saw her, and began barking in imitation of Herman. Norah saw him pointing, heard the sudden shrill clamor of boy-voices mocking, and fled. But they flocked after her on either side, all the way down to Ninth and Dearborn.

"She dawnces ona dime, gents; she shakes that thing! Hey, Nick—look at it shake!" Nick slapped her on the rump as she walked and ducked quick as a cat when she turned on him. "Look at it shake! Oh sister!" They followed down to Ninth and Dearborn.

After that Norah never used the front entrance any more. She used the alley-exit until the job was ended. And it ended within two weeks.

Had Herman been less simple the job might have lasted longer. Norah was having a cigarette in the dressing-room with two of the other girls when Herman walked in without knocking. But he always came in without knocking, he had never feigned that his trick was not deliberate. Why should he? Whose show was this, anyhow? What was this here anyhow? Is this the Drake Hotel or something private here anyhow? Norah tossed a towel across her shoulders, but he had caught the wavering sheen of the light on her breasts. She felt the flare that resentment was lighting in her eyes—and then, because she saw that that flare was pleasing his eyes and mouth, resentment flared to anger. Spirit—that was it. Norah Egan had spirit. How Herman loved a spirited woman!

Norah's head flung back, and she gathered into one word her whole indignation.

"*Schwein!*"

The other girls had tittered to hear that word on Norah's tongue, for Norah had learned it solely from Herman; as all of them had, every day they had danced for him.

"*Schwein!*"

It had been surprising then to see that Herman became neither excited nor angry; he just stood above Norah looking down sheepishly, didn't say so much as one word—only smiled a little as though to conceal how much he was wishing that one of the other girls had just said that to him instead. Then one stubby finger went under the towel, the unclean nail of it touched a tip. That was when she had let him have it: right across his smile with the back of her hand so that the upper lip cracked and left blood on her knuckles. Whew! It had rung out like a pistol shot in that tiny room. The other girls had stopped tittering, and Herman had gone scarlet. But he hadn't shown anger, even then. He had just kept looking down as he might have on an ill-behaved child, reproving her mildly, in an offended voice, over a broken lip. He shook his poor wronged head a while, licking the lip with his tongue, and it seemed to take every ounce of his self-possession just to keep from choking up.

"Oh, Egan, I am so surprised at you, always for two weeks you being such a good llttie girl, and now you do this because I tease you just one time . . ."

Norah felt suddenly sick within: not at the sight of the blood of the man nor at the reaction from her anger, but rather at something she sensed beneath his words. Something that, under his words' sweet warmth, hissed and was cold. And she could not quite bring herself to apology.

"Don't you think now, Egan"—he was sterner now—"Don't you think now you should be saying something to me?" He did not want to fire her. "Think only a minute now, Egan . . ." and Norah hadn't wanted to be fired. Yet she just sat there looking down at her palms and wishing she could say something real friendly now. But when she looked up it was too late to speak, for Herman was gone, and the job was gone with him, and the other girls were all saying how foolish she'd been and what will you do now, honey.

Norah dressed and went out the rear entrance. It took longer to get to Harrison Street through the alley, but she didn't want to take any chance on the newsboys. Walking up that dim passage, Norah had tried to console herself a little: it had been a dirty job from the start, she'd been sick of it from the very first day. There were better jobs. She'd find something decent pretty soon. Only, something inside told her maybe she wouldn't. Something said: "Go back and say that you're sorry, Norah. Say anything that he wants you to say, but get that job back before it's too late." Only it was already too late, of course, so that was simply silly.

The next morning Norah went to the County Free Employment Bureau on Dearborn. Behind a desk a woman dressed in black bombazine said, "There ain't nothin' here this mornin', dearie," and Norah just stood there and kept on waiting, even when the woman repeated that there was nothing at all this mornin' dearie. Norah said, "You got to give me somethin', anythin', that's what you're here for." She had been told that this was the way that people got jobs. The woman appeared startled, because most people went away when you said there's nothin' at all this mornin', dearie. She fumbled papers, coughed, looked at the girls waiting on the bench against the wall, glanced at the line of boys filing into the boss's office with applications in their hands.

"You mean you know someone?" Black Bombazine asked, but not too loud.

Norah said, "No, I don't know *nobody*. I just want a job. My uncle lived in Cicero, but he's dead two years. I'm broke. I ate once yesterday. I can't make a loan."

"But I got nothin' at all this mornin', dearie. Whyn't you try Direct Relief on Wabash?"

"I been there twice now. They gave me an order, but the stuff didn't come, an' now they told me I should come here. They said you'd give me somethin', that this was the place."

"Dearie, whyn't you try the place on South Mich?"

"I know about that too," Norah said. "I want a job. The place on South Mich is for whores."

Black Bombazine blushed and then dialed swiftly. She whispered something into the phone, and she frowned, and she looked up all smiles. Then she dialed again. She frowned again. She pleaded over the wires. She scribbled addresses, she dialed wrong numbers, and finally she said, 'I guess this is your lucky day, dearie.'

Norah Egan had a job again.

Every morning now she sat, with twenty other women and girls, in a room on the fourteenth floor of the Montfield building. She listened to a booster-talk for an hour, was given carfare and a black briefcase, and rode out to the West Side. There was shaving soap in the black briefcase, and shaving cream in tubes, and shaving talc in tins, and razor blades, and three different colors of toothpaste, and two different colors of hair tonic, both guaranteed, and four different colors of toothbrushes. Her commission was twenty percent, and her territory the whole West Side from Division to Twelfth.

"Garages are good," Mr Marcus, Sales Manager, advised Norah on her first morning. "Hit all the garages, tire-shops, battery-places—places like that. Don't bother no barber shop though. Don't take 'no' for an answer, neither. Be pers'nable."

Mr Marcus gave her a little book to study at night. It was called "Personality In Salesmanship."

One girl on the force made as much as twelve and fifteen dollars every week, and she told Norah exactly how she did it.

"I'm friendly with 'em, hon, that's all, you got to get up close when you talk. Don't be afraid to take his hand even when it ain't washed. Smile. Get up close."

This was all a part of "Personality In Salesmanship," Mr Marcus assured her. He added that not all of the best ideas were printed in the books.

So Norah got up close. She smiled. She did everything she was supposed to do.

Yet at the end of two weeks she had earned only three dollars over her car-fare, and more than that had gone for lunches. But she decided to try it another week, and be just as personable as possible. Norah knew she could smile. She knew she was rather pretty, in a light blonde-babyish way.

On a Thursday afternoon, and that was the second Thursday in September, she strolled into the office of a garage on Division and began spooshing her line at a mechanic lolling in a swivel chair with his feet on a desk. She had just begun spooshing when a tall fellow walked in and said he'd take two tubes of toothpaste; then he asked the price of razor blades. And then he took a look at the briefcase, and Norah smiled, and he said he needed shaving talc badly. Norah got up a little closer, and the closer up she got the more he ordered. Toothpaste. Hair tonic. How about pomade? Norah made out his order while she talked, and before he was through the order came to three and a quarter. Her hand trembled a little when she handed it to him to sign, and the fellow in the chair guffawed like a mule. That was when Norah caught on—when he laughed. She looked at the tall fellow just to make certain, and he began grinning. She got out as fast as she could then, and it seemed to Norah that laughter followed, as the shoe-shine kids had pursued.

You got to be friendly: Norah knew now what that meant. It meant that to earn more than expenses you had to sell more than shaving soap.

When she told Black Bombazine why she had quit, the woman was horrified. Then she admitted that some jobs were that way, in these times, and men were all devils anyhow. And then she added a word.

"But I really don't think a young woman like yourself, Miss Egan, with no one to help you as you say you haven't, a girl without even a college education even—do you really think you can afford to be quite so *demanding* in the type of work you prefer? Do you know, Miss Egan, that we have young women registered here with degrees from the University of Illinois? and Purd*ue*? And Holy Name! Not to mention a number of business colleges, and St Swithin's Academy—girts who are wilting to start from the ground up, as it were. In these times, you know, dearie, we all got to take what we can get and be satisfied. You should know that by this time, dearie. So I'm just that dreadful sorry. You can drop in early part of next week, but I wouldn't say now just what good it'll do you, dearie."

Norah didn't go back there, but she did return to the Little Rialto. She returned to tell Herman that she was sorry—and would he give her just one more chance? He was out front barking, like the first time she had seen him. The megaphone at his mouth seemed a part of that mouth now, a kind of funnel-shaped extension of it. He tipped his derby when he saw her, and went on barking.

"Stella, the little dawncin' girrul! This show ain't decent, foiks—don't come in! She dawnces on a dime an' she shakes all she's got! She dawnces on one leg an' then on the other—"

Norah worked through traffic until she reached him. "How's gescheft, Mr Hauser?" she asked. There were men and women passing, white and brown and biack.

"Fine, Egan, fine," he lied, wondering why in the worid she had stopped.

"Good enough to give me my job back again?"

It was funny, watching the look that came over him then.

Watching his expression, Norah recalled an oid story-book thought: "I weep for you," (she said this to herself while watching Herman's sorry look) "I weep for you, the walrus said, and deeply sympathize."

That was just the kind of a look it was.

"I am so extremely sorry," Herman said, "but I gave last week to everyone a one-dollar cut. Even to myself I gave. So how could I be paying you seven-fifty like before?"

"I'll work for six," Norah said simply. "He knows a lot of fast tricks," she thought, "most everyone knows some, but I don't know any yet."

He was having his fun out of this, too; she could see with half an eye. The shoe-button mouth looked as pleased as it had the time it had caught her without a brassiere. And somehow, she still felt half-naked with him. She wished he'd grin or even laugh out-right, instead of always keeping the corners of his mouth pressed down that way when they wanted so badly to turn up. Then she saw that he was still waiting for words she had failed to speak two weeks earlier.

"I'm sorry what I said that time, Mr Hauser, I didn't mean it really, you know." She had the feeling that this paunchy little man in front of her held her life cupped, like his blue megaphone, in the palm of his pudgy hand: he could throw it down now, or toss it away to the street, or crush it under his heel, or merely blow through it; she had this strange feeling while waiting for him to reply, and she didn't quite understand how one person's life could be at another's whim.

Herman's eyes twinkled. He'd gotten his apology from her, and it felt good to get it. He'd taken her down off her high horse, and now he'd take her down a little more.

"Why, Egan," he said, feigning astonishment, "you ain't afraid you'll have to start hustling your bustle, is you?"

She saw it then of course, that that was what he'd been aching to say all along. For fifteen minutes he'd been playing with her just to say that, and get even. He wasn't going to take her back; he'd just been having a little fun. To get even.

She turned away, in order not to give him the further satisfaction of seeing her eyes.

Spindles went here, bobbins too; fall rain came and fall wind blew. Belt slapped. September passed.

Something had come loose all right.

Back in her little room in South Dearborn, after that whole long summer had passed, Norah went to her window to look down at the street far below: a littered, shadowy street, black children played now in its shadows. Something about its desolate aspect made her think of the face of some sightless thing: it seemed with blind eyes to look up, it seemed no sun ever cut its shadows; dimly Norah Egan perceived, waiting in one darkened doorway, the dim form of a woman. Waiting.

Nigger street. Nigger street in September. Nigger, stay in it, it's where you belong. "I hate nigger kids," Norah told herself listlessly.

Norah Egan, free, white, female and twenty-one, alumna of Cicero high-school class of 'thirty-one, Norah wasn't thinking now that just because she was hungry she might go downstairs and stroll slowly past strangers. Not a bit of it, for there wasn't the slightest need of that. She wasn't nearly that hungry yet, and she told herself firmly that she wasn't.

Yet.

•

Out of a two-bit flop on Wells Street, Cass and Nubby O'Neill slipped into the Wells Street night. Arm in arm down darkening streets they scurried toward a dime dance-hall. Like two amorous terriers in pursuit they trotted to where women were.

"Ah aim to dance with that little Swede Signe," Cass told Nub.

"I've seen worser-lookin' frails than that un," Nubby replied, "only I ferget where."

They kept their silence then, all the way down to Clark and Center. Then they turned to the left, went two flights up a musty staircase, and entered a room which was all moving shadow and red crepe paper and dim blue light. Nubby bought tickets, handed half to Cass, and dropped a warning word.

"Take care that Swede ain't diseased, son."

Cass went wandering through the colored fog, the string of tickets dangling from his hand, until he found the plump little person named Signe. It was the fourth time that week that he had been here to "dance" with the girl. For fifteen minutes they clung together, Cass paying no heed at all to the music.

The music was only a river of sound in his brain, a tom-tom pounding which sanctioned, somehow, the slow thrusting of a knee between the girl's thighs. She held the tickets in fingers enclasped behind his neck; at each pause in the pounding she ripped one more off the string. In return for this privilege she wriggled, pressed, and suddenly jerked. In a corner he slid one hand down to her buttocks.

"I told you twicet now you can't do that here," she admonished without malice. "Every time you come up I got to scold. Maybe you want to walk toward the park? We'en buy apple-taffies on the way."

Cass nodded and followed her through the fog. As they came out onto the crowded street the girl paused next to a vendor of pop. "I'm thirsty, Red," she announced, and the vendor looked hard at Cass. Cass's nickels were numbered; but he bought two bottles of a thin pinkish lymph and thought, "Damn the cost anyhow."

"I oney wisht it was bananer-cream soda instead," the girl complained after taking but one peevish sip. "Whyn't you just ast me first did I *want* pink?"

They stood on the curb appraising each other, in mild unconcern over yellow straws. She saw a pair of bushy red brows, a crooked gray scar, and a ten-cent tie of several hues; he saw a spoiled mouth and a waspish air, a bloodless face above a sleazy green dress.

"Ain't you gonna buy nothin' but this dinky pink pop?" she asked before she had half-finished the bottle. "Ain't I even gonna have peanuts even?"

At the Center Street entrance to Lincoln Park Cass bought a lone bag of peanuts. They sat deep in shadow to eat them, and Signe dug into the bag with such ready fingers that he felt a mild alarm lest she take too many. Out of the corner of his eye he glanced down into her small cupped palms: she had taken five. Then he saw that she was counting too.

She counted up to four, popped the two smallest into her mouth, and looked to see how many remained. There were three.

"But they're the stale kind," she pouted. "Whyn't you get fresh, on account of I don't *like* stale?"

Cass thought, "When the money's gone me an' Nub got to hoist a joint somewheres. Nub says so. He's done it afore so ah guess he knows how. Ah guess his dough's most gone." He regarded Signe longingly, thinking of bushes behind him. "But a man needs dough to make a gal like this," he concluded to himself, "an' everybody got to take a chance oncet in a while."

"You could buy them apple-taffies now," she said, crossing her legs, "or you could buy gum 'n we could just chew it."

"Ah like you," Cass said; the girl looked at him blankly.

"If ah could jest buy somethin'," Cass thought, slipping one hand here and the other there till his arms were about and between her like prongs, "ah bet ah could make her tonight."

She let him have his way with her, passive and disheveled, for several minutes. Then:

"If we ain't gonna have them apple-taffies, why, then, let's go back 'n dance."

"Tomorrow night we'll have apple-taffies," was all he could think to say.

"You been handin' me that fer a week now," she answered. And all the way back to the dance-hall she sulked.

Late that night, in the two-bit boarding house on Wells, Cass complained to Nubby. They stood in a two-by-four garret-like room, and neither felt ready for sleep.

"Ah could have made that little Swede," Cass said, "oney ah was broke."

Nubby sat crosslegged on his cot. Above his head a small night-light burned feebly, casting a sheen across his boot toes. He removed his right boot and fumbled in his sock for something.

"That's the way with these cheap scurves every time," he said, "what you an' me got to do, Red, is to pull us a job. Then we'll get us a couple *real* flooseys."

Cass sat on the edge of the other cot. He watched Nubby fumbling in his sock, until he found what he sought. Then he slipped the boot back on and stood before Cass with a five-dollar bill in his hand.

"This is about all what's left out o' my kangaroo money, son. I must have kangarooed forty-six guys in that jailhouse before you ever bust into it." He regarded Cass closely. "But we spent it all together, didn't we, son? We got my boots soled an' my tattooin' jazzed up, an' you mooched a little now an' then, an' we got through the whole summer—Didn't we, son?"

Cass nodded. He wanted to say that he'd done a little kangarooing once or twice, and that Nubby might have nothing at all now had it not been for the help of others in a jailhouse tank. He wanted to say that the money should have gone for groceries in the jail; he wanted to say that he too would like to be tattooed sometime. But he said nothing at all, he both feared Nubby and depended upon him. He knew that Nubby wouldn't let him crawfish out even if he wished to, now that the money was so nearly gone. Cass didn't want to be alone in the world again, ever.

"Yeah," he agreed, "We spended it t'gether awright ah guess—but don't call me 'son' no more, Nub. It hurts mah feelin's perty bad sometimes, an' you ain't so much older'n me anyhow."

"Mebbe not. But I seen twice as much an' got most the brains, besides havin' all the gut there is between us. You ain't gettin' cocky just 'cause you mooch a little here an' there, are you, son? 'Cause there's lots bigger things than that a man got to learn before he's a *real* white man; I've told you that before."

Cass stood up slowly and advanced. He shoved his face within an inch of Nubby's, and replied with the whine suddenly gone out of his voice.

"Y'all been talkin' on all summer now 'bout how much you seen an' what you done an' all the tanks you been in. Well, ah ain't been in oney one jail, an' mebbe ah ain't seen so much—but ah sure got gut! Ah'm *all* gut! Ah'm a Texas hell-roarer! Y'all don't even know what the sheriff back home used to call me!"

Nubby backed up just an inch. No, he didn't know that. Then he saw that the boy was bluffing a little, and he smiled inwardly. The boy was coming along pretty fast of late.

"'Bad-Hat' is what he called me there! Bad-Hat on account ah'm so bad! Don't *never* call me 'son' no more."

Lovingly, Nubby fingered his bill. He had kept it in his sock so long that it smelled wholly vile now. During their summer together he had shown Cass this bill several times, and each time its odor had seemed stronger to Cass. Nubby spoke resignedly, fingering his love.

"Well, I s'pose I might have knowed you'd turn on me sooner or later. I've done my best to make a white man out of you, but you got no more use for me now. I could've learned you how moochin' is only chicken-dribble comparin' to what we could've got, with my brains an' your guts. Why, I could even of spent this fin on a drunk fer the two of us. Only I see now you don't want to go 'long with me now no more an' if I spent the fin I'd be broke—an' then where'd I be? I wouldn't have someone to help me earn it back an' you'd be off somewheres gettin' drunk off somebody else. Maybe I *could* get it back by moochin' o' course—but you know how I like moochin'. I got too much pride in me fer that game, son. An' besides it's only chicken-dribble comparin' to what we *could* get." Nubby glanced down at his fin. His face held a pious and wistful light beautiful to see.

Cass's eyes went rubbering about the room as though seeking some hidden thing in its corners. "Ol' Nub ain't got the *slight*-test idee how tough ah been in mah time," he mused. "Me an' ol' Olin'd make Nub look like chicken-dribble."

"Ah didn't do so bad moochin' down State the other mornin', Nub," he said aloud, "six-bits—that's lots more'n jest chicken- dribble."

"You was talkin' pretty loud a minute ago, wasn't you, son?"

Cass looked at the fin in Nubby's paw. He thought of five-dollar bills, many five-dollar bills, fifty-five fins all rolled neatly together, each one his own; each one rather smelly.

He thought of two white girl-hands, cupping peanuts in their palms.

"Yore jest callln' me 'son' now to get me riled, Nub," he said reproachfully.

Nubby laughed shortly, and spoke hard.

"Don't stall me, son. Is it yes or is it no? Do we get high together? Or do you sleep in Lincoln Park tonight? Say, don't you figger you owe me *anythin'*?"

Cass gulped, so that for a moment he could not reply. "What night you been figgerin' on, Nub?" he asked, wholly without heart. Nubby had his answer ready before Cass had finished speaking.

"Tonight's as good as any I know, Bad-Hat," he said; and then it was Cass's move.

"Well," Cass temporized, "O' course there wouldn't be so much cash as on Sattiday, an'..."

Nubby cut him off.

"Wednesday night is perty good too," Nubby said, "an' so long as yer gettin' kind o' anxious to go, we might as well spend the fin fer a rod an' get high Sattiday instead. No use us wastin' time, *is* there, Bad-Hat?" He took Cass's hand before Cass could offer it.

"They used to call me 'Scarface' sometimes too," Cass said, without seeming so sure that they really had. Nubby's fingers felt damp to his.

As they went down the musty staircase Nubby spoke over his shoulder, but Cass didn't hear his words very distinctly. Then they were downstairs, walking past the desk where the night-clerk sat.

"We won't be back tomorrer, Droopy-Drawers," Nubby barked at the old man as they passed, "We're movin' into a high-class hotel." Nubby waved the clerk a brief farewell.

"So long, Old Cootie-Chaser," Cass added, with a similar wave.

The old clerk failed to wave in reply. He was hoping that neither bum had left seam-squirrels on his cot. He would have to wash the crumbs out with naphtha in the morning if either had.

Wells Street windows were darkened now. On either side the tenements, like lean old beggars waiting in a row, stood bowed above the street. Cass saw the unclaimed children of Chicago's tenement-town begging and selling. He heard a young boy offering himself to a pervert in front of a cheap hotel. He saw a Negro girl on a doorstep who shot out her tongue like a snake as they passed; and he saw an aged white woman who tapped her hps and smiled horribly, in an unnatural invitation.

"Don't we need a heat or somethin'?" Cass ventured to whisper in Nubby's ear after they had boarded a southbound car.

"That's right where we re goin' now, Red. To get us one big blow."

Nubby knew every dive, every joint, every hole-in-the-wall from Twenty-Second and Wabash (The Four Deuces) to Sam Hare's Delis in Morton Grove. And he sat so silently sullen all the way into Blue Island that although there were questions Cass wished to ask he forebore out of a fear of being mocked.

On Western Avenue in Blue Island Nubby led the way into a pool-hall. A clock on the wall read 1:55. Cass waited in front, watching an Irish boy and an Italian playing rotation, and wishing that he had fifteen cents for a pack of Camels. He was tired of rolling his own all the time, a nickel a sack, like some hick from the country.

In less than five minutes (the clock had not quite reached two) Nubby came out wearing a crooked grin on his face and a portentous bulge on his hip. His silence and sullenness had vanished; he was almost bursting with information.

"They gave it to me fer four bucks," his voice was amazed at his fortune—"four bucks an' four bits an' a dime an' two nickels, an' then the one they call Turk thrun in the jimmy to show he's all on the square."

They paused in an unlit cranny between two stores and Nubby withdrew the bar from his hip.

"Here," he instructed. "You take the wreckin'-bar an' I'll take the heat on account it'll be my job to keep off bulls from you. That's the main job so it's mine. Slip it down yer pants, Bad-Hat ol' boy, make a hole in yer pocket an' keep holt of the end so's you won't drop it front of the police station an' make a noise like afternoon of Judgment day."

"Migosh, Nub, you don't give me credit fo' knowin' *nothin'*," Cass protested.

Nubby tucked him under the chin. "Is oo angwy wif papa again, Weddy-Weddy?" he asked, "Don't oo even want papa to tell oo how to do?"

Cass brushed Nubby's finger away. "Are we gonna go, Nub, or ain't we?" he demanded irritably. Nubby laughed and hooked him by the arm. As they stepped up into a westbound bus Cass felt the steel of the bar glide against his thigh.

"Poke me when we get to 146th," Nubby instructed after they

were seated, "I always got to catch up on my tighteye before I pull a job." Nubby feigned sleep, his mouth hanging wide and his eyes so tightly closed that they wrinkled.

Cass thought, "Bluffin' again. He's jest as skeered-like inside as me, any time. He wouldn't have the guts to pull what me an' Olin done once t'gether."

When they piled out of the bus in Harvey it was drizzling. They walked south to 154th and turned east.

Nubby's boots went clicking swiftly along the pavement; he never discarded these, El Paso winter or Chicago summer. Twice a year he had them resoled, and every dime he could spare went for a liquid polish called Brownglow. He seldom used this polish without remarking to Cass, "Brownglow, it's my own special brand."

"This is a good ol' street," he commented, increasing his stride a little, "I was raised in this neighborhood. When I got to be fourteen me an' my brother joined the Boy Scouts, Eagle Troop Sixtysix, an' our first really good deed was to roll a old drunk guy comin' down this street. We knew how already then, Elmy an' me. That was in the war-time, an' we was pertendin' he was a spy till we finally got to thinkin' he really was, I guess. Every night fer a week we waited fer him in the alley, an' fin'lly we got him. Honest, me an' Elmy was like a couple young coyotes in them days. Elmy was six years oldern' me, an' he sure learned me lots. Only sometimes I think I ain't got as much gut as I had then, an' then I feel sad. We weren't scared of nothin' then, us two. Elmy always stuck up fer me too, even against the old man sometimes. We'd go home about once a week an' the old man'd kick us both out an' cuss from here to Gary." Nubby laughed lowly, in recollection. "We stole a streetcar out of the Hammond barns one night, after the motorman got off, an' we run it fer eight blocks clear to the end of Hammond like hell on wheels, with Elmy bangin' the gong with his heel an' throwin' on the sand an' singin', an' me swingin' along the straps like a little monkey in the zoo-house an' all the cops in Hammond chasin' us down Homan Street. I guess it must of been the Fourth of July, 'cause I remember hearin' firecrackers goin' while we was ridin'. We went to St Charles fer that, me an' Elmy, an' that's where I got my nub. But we learned a lot down there, if I got to say so myself. If I got to say so myself I ain't been caught fer a lot of things since. Only sometimes I wonder where Elmy is, if he ever comes around the old places any more, if he ever got caught much since."

It was a street lined by small stores: two real-estate offices, a grocery, a butcher shop, a bakery. In each small nightlights burned.

"Real-estate offices has always got a safe-full," Nubby divulged. "They collect a couple er ten thousan' dollars at twelve o'clock on Sattiday night an' then they hide it all in a little tin safe 'cause all the banks is closed by then. Only I got nothin' to crack a safe with tonight, so the real-estate places is out. Come on, son, don't slow down an' don't start gawkin', make off like yer goin' some'eres real fast. You got to learn how to case a joint just by walkin' past it real fast; that's how first-raters does."

They walked on for two more blocks, until Cass noticed a store that had no nightlight burning. It was a delicatessen on the other side of the street. He pointed.

"Fer Christ's sake, son, don't *never* point a place like that. Honest, son, you gimme the weak-trembles sometimes. Seems like you don't learn quick er somethin'. A place like that ain't good fer cowcrap. People sleeps in the backs of them kind with four burglar alarms an' a dog an' a janiter an' nothin' inside the register but plugged pennies anyhow. We want some place where ain't no light lit, where ain't no dog, where ain't nobody sleepin'. And where is lots of the ol' McCoy."

They walked on in silence for several minutes, Cass reflecting all the while.

"Say, Nub," he finally said, "Ain't that butcher's place back there like y'all say we want? All *ah* ever seen o' butcher shops never had nothin' in the back 'cep' a ice-box mebbe, or a place to kill roosters that's all. Ah reck'n they don't have no dawg neither, on account the dawg'd eat up all the sausages on 'em, don't y' reck'n?"

The logic was irrefutable, but Judge O'Neill did not wish to appear hasty. He deliberated the matter now with his practiced ponderosity.

"They was a light burnin' in there, son."

"But they're lights in 'em *all*, Judge."

"Just to investigate conditions then," Nubby compromised curtly, "like the gran' jury done that time." At the corner they turned and walked back on the other side of the street. By the butcher's clock, hanging directly under the nightlight above the register, the time was 3:25. They slipped into the alley and around to the rear.

"Only got a hour before light now, so we got to work fast," Nubby hissed. "First thing you want to do now, Red, soon's I get the window high enough up, is to douse that light up front. Don't go stoppin' an' gawkin' around to see is somebody gonna see ya doin' it, 'cause if ya do, then, sure enough, somebody *will* see ya. So just tiptoe up soft an' slap her head off, same as ya would a old whore what's give ya clap." He perceived Cass's trembling and spoke more gently. "Tomorrer night we'll go up to the dance-place, Bad-Hat. Betcha that little Swede of yours'll be glad to see her man come 'round again, eh?" He nudged Cass, and Cass tittered. "But tonight we both got to take our chances, you the same as me, Bad-Hat. Need a cig'rette?" Cass thought of a hundred dance-tickets, all in one string, all his own. He lit a cigarette and inhaled deeply.

"I guess you seen where the cash-box is settin' all right," Nubby added. "So I'll wait here an' head off bulls, on account it's my roscoe and I could shoot straighter anyhow."

"Ah seen it, where it was," Cass acknowledged.

With a stone scarcely larger than a pebble, Nubby broke the window. Neatly. The sound of its breaking was so brief that for one second after Cass was uncertain that it had really been broken. A small round hole above the catch was the only evidence of the stone's course. Nubby began working the window up against its second catch while Cass held the revolver.

"If someone comes up sudden on you, Red," Nubby cautioned while he strained at the sill, "don't shoot 'em dead right off. Just shove the steel against his neck for a second an' give him a chance to reach for the roof. When ya let him feel cold steel right up *against* him like that, then he'll know ya mean business all right. An, when ya get inside—'member—the button that opens the box is the one way down farthest over. Always."

As the lock gave the window groaned out piteously in the early morning air; both men stood as though paralyzed. Cass whimpered softly. Then, "Bust 'er with this, Red, an' remember— she give ya buboes an' crinkums an' the bloody-blue flux is why ya doin it." Cass disguised his whimper with a faint tittering, and lowered himself inside with no especial grace. "Once a fellow called me Hell-Blazer," he said hollowly, "on account ah copped a shirt off a line for him in New York." Nubby handed him the jimmy with a final word of warning.

"If anythin' goes wrong, son, I'll meet ya front of the hotel day after t'morrer. Remember: front of the hotel, in the afternoon."

In the unfamiliar dark Cass smelled old meat. He groped toward a long crack of light in the wall. The wall was a thin partition, he found, for it wobbled when he shoved against it. Once he stumbled face-forward, stumbling through darkness and old-meat smell, and hit the floor with outspread fingers into a heaped soft-sharpness. He smelled the soft-sharpness, ran his hands through it, let it trickle through his still outspread fingers. Sawdust. Mechanically, he brushed his clothes of the stuff. Then he struck a match and saw, by holding it in the creel of his hands, that he stood next to a pile of crates stacked behind the partition's end. Through boxes he glimpsed the cash register standing in the full glow of the nightlight. Boy! Would he bust that! He edged around the crates, strode up the inside of the counter, and smashed the globe just like Nubby said to do; then he punched the lowest key on the right-hand side.

Money. Bills. Pennies and nickels and dimes and quarters and half dollars. Packets of quarters, packets of halves, packets of pennies and nickels and dimes.

He cocked his head on one side and he gaped, with his mouth hanging wide and his shoes full of sawdust.

Then he said, "Oooo"—like a small boy spying a bright coin in the gutter.

He'd gone along to prove himself game, he'd gone along on bluff—and he'd found money! Dimes and dollars and halves and quarters. He'd found it all, so it all was his. *All* his. Tentatively, as though fearing it might disappear like a dream, he picked out one dime, brought it close to his eyes, rang it once on the counter— and then he went half-mad: he scooped up furious handfuls, whole handfuls fell to the floor; he dropped bills, bent to retrieve them, banged his head twice on the counter in bending, padded on all fours down the length of the counter to recover one nickel, and came all the way back, on his knees, padding, with the jimmy still gripped in his hand.

Cass had not really known that men actually got money by robbery: he had heard so often of robbery, yet it had always seemed unreal and not quite to be believed. And now it waf real. Now he knew that it was *truly* so. He'd come because he'd been afraid not to come. He'd found it all. It was his.

Sweat from his forehead stung the corners of his eyes, and he had to keep blinking it out; it coursed down both sides of his nose until he felt it on his tongue. With one hand he clutched the jimmy, unaware that he still held it, and with his free hand he grabbed, reached, and stuffed. He picked out pennies, crammed in bills, dropped to all fours to retrieve a dime; his eyes were almost closed, but they glinted a little with avarice. Only a flush on his cheek bones betrayed his excitement now.

And strangely now Cass remembered a bill that a man in a park once had shown him; he thought that every one he took now was a twenty. And when he had gotten every one, he clawed under the counter and found two nickels. Then crouching through the dark, fouling himself against the counter's projecting points with every step, he stumbled toward the rear. Behind the partition he tripped over the same sawdust pile which had floored him once before, and then he rapped with the jimmy on the window with such force that the pane cracked down to the sill. He was panting like a switch-engine and trembling like a leaf; he had sawdust down his neck and his hair was in his eyes. When he was half-way out the window, one leg in and one leg out, the jimmy slipped from his hand and clanged to the concrete. Clearly it rang out, in a narrow canyon between stone walls, then bounded away down the stone slope of the alleyway like a toy fire-engine clanging away. As always when violently excited, Cass heard no sound; he saw, and understood, and heard nothing at all. He gasped, "Nub! Nub! Ah gotten it *all*—a hundred dimes an' a hundred dollers an' a hundred—Jesus, Nub, run!" But he himself seemed unable to move until Nubby moved, and Nubby was standing terribly still holding Cass's sleeve, watching a jimmy-bar dance on gray concrete. Steel clanged against brick a foot over their heads, and Cass thought, "Some 'un jest threw a brick at me." Then someone big was right in front and little sparks were coming from between Nubby's fingers; and whatever had been big in front wasn't there any more.

Cass ran zig-zaggedly.

As he turned into 154th Street he slowed to a walk with the frightening realization that, a second or an hour before he had heard two shots and one in reply. Three shots, clearly. That was all Cass remembered hearing—the thought sent his mind black and blank with fear. And when that blackness lifted he was sitting in the rear of a northbound bus, his eyes fixed on a slowly-lightening street, his body itching with a slow-drying sweat. Morning was breaking, it was raining again, and a street-sign said Sixty-Third and Cottage-Grove.

He transferred west to State and stood on a corner among half a dozen Italian laborers, trying to screw up enough courage to hail a taxi. He felt he was attracting the attention of the Italians by keeping his hands stuffed in his pockets; so he tried holding them carelessly at his side instead. But that made him nervous lest a pickpocket be among the laborers, who looked much like Mexicans to him. So he stood, in the chill Chicago morning and the dim

Chicago light, a thinly-clad hulchy-shouldered hick with his fists going in and out of his pockets every fifteen seconds, with a lurking look in either eye. Once on the streetcar the problem of what to do with his hands was half-resolved for him. The car was crowded, and with one hand he had to hang onto a strap. He hung on all the way to Chicago Avenue, being afraid to leave the car south of Madison because of the big white police court on Eleventh Sreet.

Daytime! Morning! He'd gotten away!

Pride like a mounting tide was in Cass then, his blood began singing a boastful song.

"Tough," he told himself, "tough *and* smart. That's Cassy McKay now ah reck'n all right. Ol' Olin Jones, he was tough some too; oney Olin wasn't so smart. Ol' Olin had to get along on chicken-dribble." Cass stopped as though arrested by a sudden thought; "Crimps! The Jesus-God!—Ah got to git me a gun fo' this day is over, so's if that one-arm squinch show his puss around callin' me 'son' an' all, ah kin blow him clean to Jesus. Ah'll dust him off, he come askin' fo' slice o' mah cash. Smokin' gun-muzzle, that boy's likely to wake up in the morgue, he comes messin' 'round mah country."

Then the thought occurred to him that perhaps Nubby O'Neill was already on a slab in the morgue; and he sobered just a little.

Sitting on a bench facing the curve of the lake at Oak Street, Cass passed a pleasant hour sacking his mind for suitable nicknames for himself. He felt he deserved some mighty tough nickname now—all first-raters had tough names.

Cassy McKay, roughest, meanest, smartest mav'rick since Billy the Kid, sat slouched on a bench at the Oak Street beach fingering his pockets and thinking of names.

"'Texas Kid'—that ain't so bad. Oney Nubby got that one already, an' it ain't hardly mean 'nuffo' me anyhow."

"Bad-Hat" was the best he could come to, and he decided to have this tattooed in red across his chest sometime. "So it'll look like the very drippin' blood of hell an' Jesus," he assured himself

Passersby observed a gawky country kid with his knees hunkered up to his cheeks and his eyes almost closed, his hair catching fire-glint in sun, and his mouth hanging open. October beach-Hies encircled that hair as though seeking some warmth of its blaze. Flies droned lazily, and Bad-Hat snored. Terror had exhausted the Texas Terror.

A low wave-lapping lulled him in sleep. Once he woke with a start and stared with unseeing eyes at the lake, muttering half-aloud, "Ah gotten clean away, that's jest what ah done. Ah didn't get caught—no *sir*. Ol' Nub got his arse plugged mebbe—mebbe Nub plugged the bull. Ah jest don't know an' ah don't give a whoop. Hopes they both get plugged, that's what. Serve 'em both right that would. Smokin' gun-muzzle! Ah gotten clean away!" He fell to sleep once more, and he dreamed he was riding with Nubby O'Neill in a boxcar. The floor of the car was covered with straw, and he was showering Nubby with bills. All twenties. The straw became darkened and littered with them, the car was full of falling bills. Nubby was grinning crookedly and clutching everywhere. And suddenly Cass heard himself saying, "Oney ah'm not gonna give *you-all* none, you done them boys in the jailhouse wrong," and with one movement he scooped it all up and jumped out of the box into a rushing darkness.

When he awoke, the lake that had been so smooth when he had closed his eyes was rising in sleek-barrelled swells, gray, foam-less, and growing; clouds had came across the sun. A little black girl was trying to launch a cigar-box onto the waves; and October felt aged and gray.

The shouts of the black girl had wakened him. Each time she launched the box it would be picked up on an incoming billow and hurled far up the beach; then she would run, screaming with joy, to retrieve her craft and try once more.

"Skinny black bitch—but wait'll ah get me mah big blow. First thing ah do is gonna be to get me a coupie o' them nigger cops out in Englewood, with both guns a-blazin' like Wild Bill Hickok's."

He rose and walked, swaggering oddly from the hips, into Lincoln Park. He wanted some nook or corner now where he could count his money. He'd count it all carefully, and wad it up tightly, and put some of it where no one else could find it. Then he'd get a shave and a haircut, eat a big meal, and perhaps get tattooed. He would get tattooed all over, chest and arms and back, just like a sailor. And then he'd go up to Clark and Center, and he'd dance all night with Signe. He dismissed the thought of Nubby with mental bluster: "Jest a little side-windin' shtunk, that's all *he* ever was. Jest 'cause he yinged them boys in the jailhouse he thought he could ying Texas McKay. Well, he never got mah meat, an' ah reck'n he's learned some different now."

He could find no corner which he felt was sufficiently safe for the counting of money. His dimes and quarters were accessible, it was the uncounted bills which irked him.

He had his shoes shined on the street, and he tipped the boy a dime. In a second-hand haberdashery he espied an oversized straw hat from the previous season; it flaunted a green band, so he bought it. He weighed himself three times in the course of one block; he bought peanuts and a pack of gum; at a streetstand he ate two hot tamales and three hot dogs. As he was buying an ice-cream bar from a vendor at the corner of State and Ontario he caught sight of himself full-length in a plate-glass window.

"Whew! Jest looka me!"

It was the reflection of a rather huge cave-chested fellow, licking a chocolate ice-cream bar under a dazzling lid. For the first time he noticed that his nose didn't occupy quite as much of his face as it should, because it turned up and was flat. He gazed at it enraptured, till the bar began to run down his fingers; and when he continued on his way he was full of a self-satisfaction as greasy as the bar. He began licking and lapping with renewed vigor.

In a drug store he bought a roll of adhesive tape, intending to tape the bills to his body in the first convenient lavatory. He passed a place with curtained windows, walked past twice before feeling certain that it was a speakeasy, and then pushed in without giving his timidity a chance to chasten his boldness. He waved to the bartender, because he knew that was how Nubby would have done, and he walked to the lavatory in the rear. On a toilet seat, closeted, he counted out five fives, two tens, and nine singles. He added these several times, each time with a slightly different result, and each time with an increased pleasure. A warm glow filled him. He tested the texture of each bill, and he regretted a little now the tip he had given the shoe-shine boy. He wanted to get even more money than this. Oh much, much more than this.

He wadded the two tens, and four of the fives, and five of the singles into one tight, tiny knot. He wetted the money at the faucet to make the knot tighter, tinier. Then he opened his shirt and inserted the pellet into his navel. Nubby had shown him how to do many things. He bound it up and across and back, and patted it twice to make sure it was tight, and observed the light growth of down on his chest. Perhaps, if he shaved that fuzz there once or twice, it would begin to grow long and hairy and black. The tape made his belly appear to be bandaged, and even policemen and thieves hesitated before ripping a fresh bandage off a boy's belly. He put the remaining fin in his vest pocket and the singles in his shirt and pushed out of the closet. He'd have a drink now, and then he'd find little Signe, buy her everything her heart desired, and dance all night.

But he wouldn't spend all his money at once; he'd spend it just a mite at a time. Like Nubby. That way he'd make it last a long while, until he could get a lot more. He wouldn't give people dime tips any more, either; and sometimes he might even walk off without paying at all.

At the counter he stopped for a glass of beer, for the fellow behind the counter looked friendly. It was good beer all right, it slid down smooth as okra. He looked around, and he saw it was a nice joint all right. There was music coming from somewhere, soft-like kind of, and a couple other young fellows were having a drink. They looked like good fellows all right. They were from Iowa, one of them told him; so he set them up to a stein apiece because he was from out West too. When the drink was down he said, "Texas McKay, that's hombre"—and he spat clean over the cuspidor. They were swell fellows; it was a gold cuspidor. There was a couple sitting all alone, without anything to drink in the corner, so he waved them to the counter to have a shot on him. They sure made a nice couple all right. It was a nice place. That guy behind the counter was a swell guy.

After four straight shots, a sour and a solid stein, Cass decided he ought to lean against something. Against something close, right away. After he had leaned against something close for quite some time he became aware, with a slow and blinking awareness, that he was leaning against something close inside an L station. Somehow, this did not seem quite fair; somehow it seemed just a trifle improper. He'd tried to remember leaving the speak, and he could not remember. He tried to find out why he had to go over to Clark and Center, and he couldn't find out.

Directly in front of him a monkey-faced woman was sitting behind a wire cage taking dimes, and somewhere far, far up above her a tiny bell kept tinkling, tinkling. It tinkled whenever somebody passed. Someone would pause in front of the cage, the old woman would yank a blurry white cord, and then—the far-up small tinkling. This did not seem quite fair to Cass. And it seemed just a trifle improper, too.

He shook his head slowly. This helped a little, so he shook it faster. It helped make the white cord a little less blurry. His nose picked up odors, but his brain could not distinguish . . . it occurred to him that this place smelled like the monkey house in Lincoln Park on a Sunday afternoon in August . . . The old woman herself looked sad as the mandrill. He commenced wishing ardently, albeit still dimly, to give the woman a fare through the bars of her cage . . . She would take it as the mandrill took peanuts that day. So he grabbed the thing against which he leaned and shook it, quite slowly, three times to the left; then he shook it, very fast, to the right. It made a pleasant noise, and it wobbled. But it would not come loose, no matter how fast he shook it.

Little Norah Egan saw him doing that through her compact mirror while powdering her nose in the Eighteenth Street station. He was fumbling over the peanut machine, and when she took his arm he grinned a knowing grin calculated to conceal the fact that he did not remember her very well. He felt that he must not

let Whoever-This-Was think for a moment that he had not recognized her on sight. That would hurt Whoever-This-Was's feel-
ings; it wouldn't be fair, because she knew him so well. The woman
in the cage regarded Cass closely, and pulled the bell harder to
express a growing doubt. Then, through a fog, Cass seemed to
remember. He said, "Hel-lo, Shiggna littl' girrul—let's eat pea-
nutsh 'n apple-wasshies!"

On Eighteenth and Indiana Officer Gerahty saw them
approaching. Norah was keeping him on the inside within the
shadows of the buildings; but he weaved a little with every third
step, so she had to keep shunting him straight with her shoulder.
Gerahty looked the other way until she got him across.

She hadn't wanted to cross State at Eighteenth: she never
liked Gerahty to see her have a customer. But Customer had
insisted on crossing there, and he was too big a lout to argue with.

Gerahty looked the other way so long that a cabbie leaning
against Thompkin's restaurant window started laughing.

"Somebody's payin' Gerahty these days even if the city ain't,"
he called to someone half-seen across the street.

She heard men laughing, and she wanted to run. The drunk
on her arm said, "Did ah get me *tat-tooed?* and she answered,
"We'll see up in the room, daddy."

Laughter followed. On the staircase up to her room the drunk
took a notion that she was going to thrash him; he kept telling her
that he'd pay her this time, that he wouldn't try to heel out. With
every step he paused to assure her of this; that made it hard, he
was such a big lout.

"Letsh dansh like we used," he said, "Letsh take a walk too."

Norah hoped that the Dago girl on the second floor wasn't
peeking through the crack in the door again. To see the trouble she

was having with this one. Girls who picked up drunks were called hay-bags, and straight-hookers wouldn't even talk to them. Pimps called a woman a hay-bag when to call her a whore would have been flattery. Landladies would house a straight-hooker willingly, but would tell a girl to get out if they learned she was a hay-bag. But Norah took a chance because it was such a good-paying trick; and everybody had to have some fast trick to get by these days.

"I'll rook him fast if I once get him inside," she told herself. "I'll have to be fast because Gerahty saw."

Once she'd told Gerahty to go to hell, and he'd hit her between the eyes. It had served her right for talking back, and the Dago girl on the second floor had laughed with Gerahty at night on the stairs. Gerahty'd take it out in trade with that dirty Dago, but never with herself. He said he didn't like blondes was why.

He'd said his wife was a blonde was why. On the night that they laughed, they'd laughed at her.

When she got the drunk inside he lurched uncertainly past the low dresser, twice put his hands like a shield in front of his face, plucked twice at a scar on his mouth's left corner, and flopped across the bed on his belly into a snoring sleep with his arms outspread.

Norah searched his clothes methodically; they looked like a hick's clothes, they smelled second-hand, and in his vest-pockets she found a five-dollar bill folded over upon itself many times and bound with a rubber band. No small change. No ring. No silver belt buckle. Only the fin.

She rolled him over to see what he had in his shirt; there was nothing but the fin.

And suddenly someone was there in the room right behind her, walking up slow-like right close behind her. Norah tried to slip the fin into her slipper; she knew it had to be Gerahty then.

Gerahty grinned. He held out his hand with a black kid glove on it.

"We'll split it," Norah said. "It's all he's got."

Gerahty smiled. He just kept holding his hand out, smiling. Norah didn't have any black tight gloves like that.

He got pretty close and Norah thought, "He'll sock me quick-like, like that other time." So when he stopped smiling just ever so little she put the fin down into his glove.

When Gerahty started going away she said, "Help me get him downstairs. He weighs a ton. He smells high."

Gerahty grinned.

He said, "So do you."

Gerahty always said funny things.

After he was gone she went to the drunk on the bed, took his jacket from his shoulders and picked his straw hat off the floor. She hung the hat on the bed-post, and she put on the jacket. She sat huddled in the jacket's folds, in the rocking-chair by the window, and rocked slowly, like a child, back and forth. She heard a streetcar stop on State, stop and start up and clatter away. Once the woman in the flat below sang out in a long whiskey soprano, but a rushing of water across the hall drowned out the song.

> *Sweet Blonde baby, I'm in love with you*
> *You made me cry when we said good-bye.*
> *Sweet blonde baby I'm in love . . .*

She couldn't hear the rest of the song until that water-rushing stopped. She listened to noises on the stairs, sounds from the street and creaking sounds all through the big house.

Once the drunk on the bed stirred, and muttered in sleep. Once she felt a nameless dull aching, where her breast used to be.

And she ceased to rock, and she slept.

Footsteps cautiously across the floor woke her when gray morning came. The drunk was standing by the window looking down; in the early morning light she saw the scar on his chin and thought it was dirt there. She watched him looking, and wondered what it was that held his eyes in a stare; as she watched he paled and drew back out of sight of the street. He grew so white for a moment that it made her a little afraid just to watch him. Then he turned toward her.

"Y'all got to keep me here a spell, ah reck'n," he said.

In the dimness it was hard to tell just how high this mug still was. No use getting him sore though, or he might sock her. He wouldn't have been the first and he looked pretty tough. But he didn't look as though he knew many tricks.

"I don't keep nobody, ballsy," she told him, "I get along O.K. all by myself. Gum-bye, please."

It was hard to tell. Maybe the bastard wasn't still high. He kept picking at his chin all the time and she wished he'd stop doing it. He was kind of red-headed, and he talked like some kind of kike. Norah didn't like kikes. She shrugged off the jacket and handed it to him. Maybe that was what he was waiting for. Maybe that was why he was standing that way with his head cocked off to one side and looking like a down-in-the-mouth hound.

"Ah'll pay y'all," he said; he spoke sadly.

That was horsecrap, Norah knew; they all told her they'd pay. But she wouldn't say no, because then he might sock her. So she just sat silent and looked down at her palms. On the left one a tiny crevice ran in an arc down from her wrist to the base of her thumb. Something had come loose all right. If he tried to hit her, she'd yell like fury.

No, he wasn't sober even yet. He kept creeping up to the window, and then stepping back out of sight.

He saw her watching him and he guessed her thought. He went straight to the window and ripped the cord off the shade; he laid it straight out on the floor, glanced over at her, and began walking its length without stepping off once.

"That proves you got cash I suppose?" she asked.

"Oney proves ah'm sober," he mumbled; and walked it again without stepping off.

"Only a little more flat then sober, eh?"

He fumbled inside his vest-pocket a minute, then grew pale about the mouth again.

She shouldn't have said that to him, she thought. He might try to sock her now.

"Y'all kin hand over that fin," he said, and added slowly, "Hay-bag."

Hay-bag whore. Everyone hated a hay-bag. She was in for it now, kikes had hot tempers.

"I had to give it to the cop, daddy. It's his cut. Don't get sore. Take it out in trade."

"Ah'm too hungry to get sore," he answered, "an' ah don't feel like tradin' right now."

She went to the dresser and tied her hair into a tight yellow knot behind her head. It was cold in the room. Too cold for October. But behind the dresser were nine sticks of wood and eleven lumps of coal. Big lumps, little sticks—she had counted both kinds when she'd put them both there. One kind was little and one kind was big, and she wouldn't let on to a soul what she'd hid there.

And then, sometime when she was all alone, she'd burn up a part of it in the stove. Not now. Not all of it. Not any of the big lumps. Just some of the little ones when she was all by herself. It'd be all for herself then. She'd have it all.

From where she stood she sensed again that the drunk was afraid of something. Maybe police; maybe his mob. No, it wasn't for her he was sticking around here; it wasn't even for his fin. He was afraid, that was all. And her own fear faded a little.

He was standing by the window with his straw hat on lopsided; the hat was too big for him, his ears alone saved it from slipping down.

"Ah've more money, Blondie," he said, and it surprised her to hear his voice sounding friendly. He was calling her "Blondie" now, but he'd called her Hay-Bag at first. So he wasn't so hard, he was kind of soft. He was kind of soft and kind of nasty; and the soft-nasty ones were the ones she feared most. They were the smartest and meanest, both at once. But she wondered whether he'd called her Blondie more for her eyes than for her skin, or for her hair more than both eyes and skin put together. She looked in the mirror, but she coutdn't tell for certain.

"Y'all behave yo'seff an' ah'll give y'all a smell o' real money," he boasted, "but right now get yo arse downstairs an' bring me back beans an' coffee with some o' my fin. Don't spend it all. Ah'm hungry."

So he still thought she had it. The soft-nasty ones were the meanest. Norah didn't move an inch from the dresser.

"I gave it to the bull I told you," she said. She wasn't so afraid of him any more. She'd stay far enough away so that he couldn't sock her, and she'd talk back a little perhaps. She'd like to get even for what he'd called her before.

"Ah got more," he said in the soft-friendly voice.

She knew the answer to that. She spoke into the mirror.

"Don't tell me you got more, lunk, 'cause I been all through you. You're flat as a matzoth, an' it's time to scram. Hop off, beat it. You smell like a sniffer. But say—if the landlady asks you questions downstairs, don't say you was tight when you come up here last night. She don't like it much."

She heard him coming toward her, and turned to face him. Maybe he was sore about being called a sniffer. Maybe he wanted to sock her now. The soft-nasty ones were the kind that socked you. Sometimes they were the worst. He was coming up to her pulling up his shirt. What the hell. And he'd walked a straight line. She saw two thin white strips binding his navel. The tape was dry and brought the flesh with it as he pulled; he had to loosen it with spittle. When both strips were off he picked out a pellet that looked like one of the oversized spitballs she used to make in high school. When he unrolled it she saw enough there to keep a man with a woman for almost as long as just about any man ever feels like keeping any woman around.

On the top was a ten, and when she took it he said to her, "All ah want is fo' y'all to keep me here a spell. Ah jest don't want to go downstairs fo' a spell. All ah want is to stay up here fo' a spell. A man with a gun is lookin' fo' me. Get it, Blondie?"

She hesitated, and then she got it, her eye on the ten on the top. "It'll cost you a penny for this, lunk," Norah Egan said.

12

DURING THEIR FIRST days together Norah and Cass did not exchange many words. He gave her money, she bought what he ordered, and they quarreled like children over the change. For three days and nights each kept his own silence, save for dickering over the cost of groceries. But on the third night they spoke long.

Cass had small desire to caress this girl; she had no desire to be caressed. At night he lay on one edge of the bunk and she on the other rail, like two diffident adolescents.

"First he called me Hay-Bag, but now he says, 'Blondie'," Nora thought suddenly, waking in the night. "That means he's get-tin' ready to put over a fast one."

"Ah don't like bein' alone," Cass thought, drowsing in the night. "Ah wonder how sister is."

On the third day a police squad sirened up to the house, Norah watched him close. He looked pretty scared when bulls came down the hall, and she had her own alibi all ready; but the cops were looking for somebody else, some woman who'd helped turn a neat job down-state.

Norah wondered then whether this lunk himself had ever pulled anything very neat; whether he might not pull a neat one again pretty soon. She'd have to be careful as long as he stayed. She'd have to watch all he did pretty close. He might be a junkie, sometimes you couldn't tell. Maybe his cash was running out already: and that was what she'd have to watch closest of all.

On the Saturday night of their first week together he walked out on her. Just grabbed his straw hat off the dresser and walked out in the rain without so much as an aye, yes, or no. Just like he was sore about something and had walked out instead of socking her.

He had often stood at the window, looking down; and now Norah looked out of the window and hoped he wasn't gone. She stood concealed behind the curtain, and she saw him crossing the street in the rain. He was walking fast with his shoulders hunched, and rain was running off the brim of his hat. It was a straw hat, a little too big. She wished he had turned up his collar.

He came back, in less than an hour, with a box of candy and a bottle of cheap perfume. Twenty cents for the candy, she guessed, and fifteen for the perfume. For Christmas, he said, and threw them on the bed instead of handing them to her like a gentleman ought. Christmas in October. Then he pulled two more packages out of his pocket, and these were both just for himself. One was a cigar-store Ingersoll that must have cost almost a dollar, and the other was sotol straight in a half-pint bottle. Where he'd gotten sotol he wouldn't say; all he'd say was that he'd paid ten bucks for the eighty-cent watch. She could tell that he'd had a nip on the way by the way he began to talk about himself.

He had ridden all over the louse-ridden country, he told her, had bummed from El Paso to Niagara Falls, from the Falls to Tacoma, from Tacoma to Shreveport, from Shreveport to Chicago and back to El Paso; and here he was back in Chicago again. He'd ridden boxcars East and West, North and South so many times, he said, that now it was all kind of mixed up in his head; so that he no longer remembered just where he *had* been. But his name was

Bad-Hat wherever he went, and he treated his women right. So she could start calling him Bad-Hat any time now.

Norah only said, "Horseguts, I'll call you Hick. An' you ain't been west of Whiting"; but she didn't say that very loud, and he didn't seem to hear. She sat on the bed with the perfume and candy and tried pumping him to pass the time. She tried to do a little lying herself. She wanted to say that her folks had been movie actors, or something big like that, but he wouldn't be interrupted for a second.

He just kept spooshing his line all over her.

His spoosh was about a pal of his who'd helped him pull a job or two, and how they had been living for six months, like two millionaires, in a big hotel on the North Side. He had forgotten the name of the hotel, but the pal was a judge from Texas . . . Well, the judge had once or twice pulled a shirt off a line and run like the devil when the dog started barking, but he'd never pulled anything really big, he'd never known very much till the hick here had taught him a little.

Hick had jimmied the window and cracked the cash box while the judge silenced the sound the way Hick showed him how. The judge had watched in the ailey white Hick cleaned out the place—"An' mah name is Howlin'-Coyotee McKay," he finished, "an' that's how ah always works. When we come out in the alleyway there wasn't a sound, an' we split it right there underneath the flash 'cause ah'd tuk a fancy to the lad. An' he went uptown an' ah went down, an' ah ain't seen mah gonsil since."

"Who you hidin' from? What's a gonsil anyhow?"

"Gonsil's a punk, Blondie, an' ah'm hidin' from po-lees o'course. Who yo' s'pose—a lan'lady? Bulls been troublin' mah tracks fo' two years now an' ain't never caught up yet."

"How come then you go out and get high in an L station if you're runnin' from bulls?" She had him at an advantage now, for his eyes could scarcely keep her in focus.

"Who's runnin' from bulls? Ol' Nubby got a rod."

"Who's Nubby?"

"Who y'all s'pose? The judge."

"Who's the judge?"

"'Who's the judge?'" he mocked, "listen at her—'Who's the judge?' The judge is Nub, who y'all think *is* judge—me?"

He laughed, and his laughter was half-nasal.

"Well, what if the judge is around? You just said you split with him fair an' square."

"Jest kiddin' y'all, Blondie, that's all. S'posed to meet ol' Nub front of hotel—oney ah copped a mope instead. Smart, eh Blondie? Get smart, kid—watch mah smoke an' all y'all see is ashes."

Norah thought, "He's swifter than he looks maybe. An' maybe he knows more fast ones than I could count. Maybe he'll slip over a fast one pretty soon. Maybe I'll come out on the dirty end of this stick too."

"Where did you see him?" she asked, "He ain't in the house that I seen. There's lots here, but no judge."

"Seen him first mo'nin' ah was sober, standin' 'cross the street, lookin' up an' waitin'."

"Seen him since?"

"Twicet since, in the same spot lookin' up. He ain't sure."

"Figurin' to hide out till he's too old to chase you? Must be a mighty hard-bitten boy to scare *you*."

She had him straight now. And she wasn't going to be rooked by every bastard with plunder in his eye who came along.

"No, ah ain't scared. Oney Nub got a rod an' don't care fo' nothin'."

"Well, where's *your* big blow?"

"Ah left it down in the Big Bend country. Ah'm always fo'gettin' things."

She'd have to look around a little, while he slept later on.

"Ah'm fixin' to get me another one. Ah'm figgerin' on a long cut short."

"What's your name? Shtunk?"

He didn't seem to notice what she called him now. She'd like to call him a downright son of a bitch to his face because he was such an ugly bastard. She had to ask him a second time what his name was, and all he answered was, "What's yours?"

So she said, "Stella."

"Stella what?"

"Stella Howard."

"An' mine's Two-Gun McKay from West Presidio an' mah middle name is Hickok. Ah don't like no Mexican-man, but them Mexican gals like me. Say, gal, they call me Bad-Hat down where ah come from. How long yo' been hay-baggin'?" he asked, and Norah made no reply.

"Hay-baggin' don't pay, Btondie. Y'ought to get in a good game. With me. With your looks an' mah brains we'd clean up in a hurry."

After a minute Norah rose from the bed. She brushed the box off the pillow onto the floor so that the small chocolates rolled in a dozen directions at once, under the chair and under the dresser. Then she went to the table and drank out his sotol without taking breath.

She wanted to strike out at something, to hurt something as she had been hurt.

"Y'all talk sometimes like mah sister used," Cass told Norah one morning.

There was resemblance in the voices, both were low; likeness too in the way Norah walked. But there resemblance ceased. Norah was not so tall as Nancy, and she was not so handsome. She did not appear to be a full-grown woman. Her mouth was a pouting child's mouth, and all her ways like a child's. Her bearing alone betrayed what pain she had borne: she went about without speech, never laughing, always complaining a little. She found it difficult sometimes even to smile.

Yet, as Cass boasted to her of places he had seen and of things he had done, there grew within her the hope that this man might not try to possess her.

On their fifth night together he spoke softly to her, and she said out to him that she did not desire. He let her be then without persistence. Norah felt a little grateful for that, for a minute.

"You're a gentleman," was her spoken praise for him. "He's got something up his sleeve," she thought after a minute.

And so he stayed on untroubled by his ignorance of that motive which most strongly kept him from leaving.

Of what he had told her of himself with his tongue, the scars of his body told her yet more. She had heard, with never a spark of emotion, that his father had been cruel. Of cruelty she had learned something herself. But on the night that they had been a week together he stood half-undressed in the light, and she saw two furrows cut into the flesh like two thin pink hoops around his shoulders. His back was turned, outside it was raining, he did not know that she saw. Pity surprised her that time. For one long moment, pity held her like love. But she struggled free, she would not be held.

She feared that which held her lest she be pinned by it.

After the light was out that night he told her of his earlier days; he spoke of West Texas and the cities of the North. He told her how life on the road differed, South and North, West and East. Then he told how he had once been beaten in a brothel in New Orleans; when he told that a strange thing happened. Norah reached out her hand and with one finger touched the line of the scar that ran down under his chin, traced it down in the darkness to the top of his throat, felt the blood of his body pulsing there.

Although this thing which the girl did was small, yet to one like Cass it was very much. He took her hand, and he held it as he once had held Nancy's hand. And when he released it, love for her was in him. He turned to her slowly, as she turned toward him . . . After a while she gave him her memories. At first her voice was flat and hard, as Nancy's had become; but as she spoke on, it softened somewhat, and she spoke more swiftly. She told him how long hunger had driven her, how shame, cold and mockery had driven her. She spoke of high school days. She told him how she had danced in a little burlesque house, of all that had happened before that time and what had happened to follow.

Then she tried to tell him of something else, something he did not quite understand because of a sudden huskiness in her voice. She broke off, and being helpless then to do otherwise, she wept. Cass did not attempt to quiet her, albeit it seemed to him that sobs tore her throat's flesh. He could only hold her and feel the whole body shaken, and it seemed to him that her heart bled from ten thousand wounds. Sleep alone stilled her tears.

But as she slept at last and he lay yet awake, Cass felt a bond growing that grew ever stronger.

Nights of peril . . . nights of love; . . . days of hiding . . . nights of love.

Then fast-passing weeks, fraught with peril though they were, were yet for Cass happier by far than any he had ever before known. Indeed, the very dally peril in which he now lived added something of a shadow zest to his new manner of existence. In short order Norah taught him to read and write once more, and to do simple calculations; these were achievements that gave him a new confidence.

He had first begun to feel fully a man after effecting an escape at Nubby's expense; dally now he strengthened that feeling. Norah's nearness gave him strength, was at the root of all he now felt. It was her affection which melted shadows in which he had crouched for too long: the shadow of shame, and the shadow of fear. To be without these was to come into sun. It was to find himself, in one day almost, rid of a pain so old that beneath its weight he had become almost unaware of its heaviness. Pain had been with him much as it is with a man who loses a leg: he had become so used to an aching that he had ceased almost to feel it. His head felt clear for the first time in his life.

Such a sudden coming into the sun, after the night that had been so long, gave Cass moments of joy which were, in a manner, ecstatic: he would prance half-naked across the floor, singing, laughing, chattering, teasing. He would imitate for Norah the speech of mountain folk. He shrugged off self-consciousness like an unclean hood. Norah would laugh at him in these moments;

but sometimes as she watched his face while it smiled or laughed it would seem to her that it was unwashed of something adolescent. The film of puberty was still upon it. Sometimes, while eating, he picked at his scar: then she would draw his fingers away from his face.

And he talked constantly. From morning till night he wagged on and on. He spoke of everything that drifted into his mind—of what someone back home had once said about Northerners, or of the automobiles cruising in the street below, or of some man or woman he once had known. There was no stopping him. Since he seemed to require no answers save those himself supplied, Norah soon came to pay little heed to the streaming of his tongue. Sometimes he scribbled on paper a long column of figures, added them, and then insisted that she add them also in order to see whether his total had been correct. He had an implicit faith in whatever answer she gave.

He realized now that heretofore he had been ill. He had been ill and he had not known. His head had been clogged with darkness, and now it was clear. He had always been aware, dimly, of a darkness in the back of his brain, it was only now that he could look back and see, clearly, that he had been dimly aware.

Nights of peril ... nights of love; ... days of hiding ... nights of love.

13

When Cass had but ten dollars left in his pocket, he bought, with half that sum, a small Smith and Wesson.

The purchase was not hard to manage. The house held half a dozen gunmen, any one of whom was willing to sell anything he possessed, from his body to his weapons or his woman. Cass bought the gun from a punch-drunk whorehouse lackey on the second floor, and he bought it with Norah's knowledge.

When the remaining five dollars had dwindled to two and a quarter he left the house alone, at night. For the first time in his life he went toward danger without fear. He had a job to do, and he was going to do it well. He had found something worth fighting for, and he was going to fight. In the only way he knew how.

On State and Congress he hailed a cab and directed the driver straight west on Lake. He sat hunched up in the rear, watching the fare roll up on the fare-clock. When the clock jumped to two dollars and five cents he jumped a little with it. Then he composed himself by drawing his gun, patting it, and muttering a low assurance to it.

"Ah'm Tex McKay an' ah take mah time. Ah treat mah woman right."

When the clock reached three-sixty the driver turned his head for further directions. "Let him feel cold steel an' he won't make trouble," Nubby had counseled.

So Cass pressed the steel of the barrel into the flesh above the fellow's collar, and gave him several directions. The car swerved wildly toward the curb, the cabbie grabbed the wheel in panic, straightened it out and kept it straight, then listened to his customer's directions. Cass spoke low and right in his ear, so that the fellow's lips began to quiver as though he were either about to curse or to cry. "Don't holler," Cass warned, then added, "Turn right at the next corner an' park."

After the fellow had turned right, and parked, his customer spoke again.

"Now open up or ah'll open you-all up."

The cabbie opened the till without a word and came out as Cass ordered. Cass heard his own voice then: it was steady. It told the driver things without actually saying them. It told the driver it wasn't afraid of the job it was doing. It told the driver it didn't mean to be caught.

"Whyn't you guys ever pick on a Checker or Yellow?" the cabbie asked. "I can't even make gas-money these times." He was a little man, unshaven and ragged.

"Shut up," Cass said. "Shut up or ah'll bash yo' head into a goddamn blood-puddin'," and he felt pretty tough when he said that. When he had gotten everything there was in the till, even to the nickels and dimes, he made the driver climb into the seat again.

"Nubby'd knock him cold now or else cop the cab," he told himself.

But he himself seemed unable to do either. He hadn't the heart to hurt the trembling cabbie and he couldn't drive the cab. So he said "Git out," and the driver stumbled out again. Then they walked into the alley, and for a block and a half Cass prodded him to make him keep on walking. The fellow stumbled, muttered under his breath, and sobbed something about a wife. In the middle of the second block, on the spur of the moment, Cass stepped back into darkness.

It was hue and cry then. He'd done a foolhardy thing, the alley was blind. He clambered over two fences and roused a dog before he reached Lake Street again. He caught a car atmost in the middle of the block, grabbing it as he would a swaying boxcar; and he was going east. As he stood in the darkness up front next to the motorman he heard the long wail of the police-siren rising to the west. It rose in a shrill, wild warning, then died to a whisper, thin, trembling, still penetrating. He left the car and ran in a half-slouch beneath the shadow of the Lake Street L. A train thundered overhead, and Cass mounted the steps two at a time. "Ain't nothin' more ah can do 'cep' keep goin' as fast as ah can," he panted—"all ah can do now is keep goin' an' hope." As he paced up and down on the half-deserted L platform a squad car flashed beneath him going east, siren screeching. Cass could tell when that squad overtook the streetcar by the way its siren broke off in the middle. Then it was coming back: coming back straight west on Madison.

His train rolled up, its broad doors opened wide, he was inside in brightness, he was going swiftiy. He picked up a copy of the *Herald-Examiner* from a seat and hid his face behind comic-strips all the way down to the Loop. Not untll he was back in the heart of the Loop did his courage desert him. He was mingling with an after-theater crowd on Michigan when he realized, in one sudden moment, that he had escaped, and when he realized this fully the reaction took him.

He wanted to run—he could scarcely suppress the desire to race wildly, screaming, to go zigzagging aimlessly down the boulevard, to run shouting up the staircase to the room, to get away — to get away . . .

So weak with shock was he that twice on the staircase he had to sit down to rest. He sat with his head in his hands, and he whimpered. He rolled his head between his hands and pounded his temples with his fists to quiet the wild throbbing there. When he walked onto the room Norah rolled off the bed and switched on the light. She took one look at him, and went for the whiskey. His shirt was drenched with sweat, and his face was so pale that its freckles stood out like moles. He sank into a chair and tried to open his collar, but his fingers fumbled helplessly about the collar's button. Norah opened it for him, held a whiskey glass to his lips, and took off his shoes. His socks were as wet as though he'd been wading. She sat up with him until he ceased to tremble, and by then it was too late to go to bed. Before that morning had passed, they moved. Just walked out and didn't come back. Took the first clean apartment they found, a two-room affair off Erie and Huron, near the old watertower.

He had gotten forty-one dollars, and the sum lasted them three weeks. Then they moved again. Norah didn't have to sit up half the night feeding him whiskey the second time; that time they moved the minute he came in. They took another furnished apartment two blocks away on a street whose name, by a coincidence which pleased them both, was the same as his own: Cass Street.

After two forty-dollar hauls Norah began to call him her "forty-dollar man."

"I'll go out with you, hon," she said, "Maybe I'll bring you luck an' well clean up big." She spoke half in jest, and he answered in jest.

But she persisted in the suggestion until he said, "Promise y'all won't shoot nobody if ah buy another rod an' we go out t'gether to Cicero some night?"

"I used to live in Cicero," she said. "I know that town like a book."

Then she promised, solemnly, and he bought the gun.

The first robbery which they committed together was of a small drugstore on Irving Park Boulevard. When they entered there was no one in the store but a clerk, a chinless fledgeling with a ptomaine eye; Cass covered him while Norah emptied the till. She took her time, as he had told her she must, emptying everything into her purse. She left the store first and made her getaway south. Cass left just one minute later by the drugstore dock. Not until late the next afternoon did they see each other again, when they met in the River Hotel on North Ctark.

Cass arrived first, just as dusk was coming down on the river. This was April dusk, and he recalled, standing by the open window, the dusk of another April, in another place. Along the river far below little lights began to grow. He saw a light creeping slowly beneath a bridge. He stood watching in darkness until he heard Norah's knock. Then he switched on the light and hurried to the door.

"I got no idee how much I got, hon," she said the moment she entered. She tossed him her purse, stretched herself on the bed and added, "I was too lazy to count it all. I think it's a lot this time."

She watched him narrowly while he counted. He licked his thumb with each bill he touched and she said, "You lose time spittin' on your hand every time you count a dollar." He had to begin all over again then. She felt a little bit glad that she'd annoyed him.

As soon as he finished she asked, "How much?"

"How much yo' reck'n?" He felt like teasing her now. There was more than he had expected.

Norah Egan pursed her lips, frowned, and deliberated aloud, "I seen three twenties on top when I opened the register, so I s'pose there's—oh, let's see—seventy-five—eighty bucks about—yeah?"

Cass replaced the bills, zipped the purse shut, and tossed it across to the dresser. Then he sat down beside her on the bed.

"How much yo' reck'n?" He put one arm about her.

"Well, a hundred say then . . ."

"Gettin' wa'm, Blondie."

"Eighty-five?"

"Cold."

She sat straight up, her eyes brightened and narrowed; it seemed to Cass that she was already exulting, and he wished that she wouldn't look quite so anxious. He wished that she were half-feigning such eagerness.

"Jesus Christ, Red, tell me you ain't kiddin'."

He could not see how well she was feigning.

"'xac'ly four dollars under five hundred, hon. Ah've not yet counted the silver."

His voice sounded lifeless.

Easy come, easy go.

Get smart like us, yokels—it's smart to be smart. Some day we'll be snatched, you say? Well, being snatched and being locked up are two different things, yokels. You got to take a chance no matter what you do, don't you? And the bigger the chance the bigger the rake-off. You got to be smart, it's smart to be smart. This is the town to make fast jack; if you can't do it here, why then you're a yokel.

Cass and Norah would lie abed every morning till ten, they

would idle pleasantly through the forenoon; then, if the day was warm, drive along the lake or through the park, in the evenings they sometimes took a bus ride, because Norah didn't enjoy driving the car at night. Too much traffic. Some nights they'd go to a movie, some nights they'd stay home and read, and play the victrola. Cass would read aloud to her from *True Romance*.

Norah invented a pet name for him which she used only on special occasions. "Lunky" she called him; and he called her "Kitten."

"He called me 'Haybag' at first," she thought, "but now he calls me 'Kitten'." And yet she was pleased to be called such a name, for she felt the name had some truth: she knew that her grace was both young and feline; she knew how cruelly, yet how smoothly and softly, she could yield this man her body. She became aware of a new lightness in her limbs; she felt again how supple her young strength could be. Sometimes, after dark, she danced for him a while; and such moments of night were for Cass strange and still beyond any moments he had ever before known.

He saw her once standing nude in a subdued blue light, her hair undone and transformed by a lamp's glow from its daytime yellow to a strange dark blue: it cascaded down her shoulders like a living blue torrent. She saw him watching and closed her eyes, to sway indolently with head backstraining, her hands on her breasts. Bathed as she was in blue cloud and black shadow, she seemed to Cass to be swaying in sleep and in dream. Behind her a darkened wall panel formed for her body a frame that meltingly became a part of herself: to Cass it seemed that that panel was no longer oak, but was instead some fragment of night struck to solidity and wood for one brief passing moment. When she ceased to sway it would fade back into night, into stuff of shadow, stuff of dream.

"Star an' Garter stuff, Kitten," he said; and he could have bitten his tongue the moment he said it. She opened her eyes slowly, looked at him half-incredulously, and then stepped quickly out of the light. She never danced for him again. Nothing he could ever say could make her dance for him again.

The happiest moments of that spring for Cass were the long walks he and Norah took along the lake. Once they were sitting among the white rocks that form the breakwater in a long curve below the boat harbor, and he told her that she resembled the lake because it was at night that both were most alive. Below them slow waves washed quietly, all that night; and there was a strangeness about white rocks and slow waves that Cass had not felt since a lilac bloomed, in a dooryard rain, one spring night seven years past.

"The lake's a little hard to catch on to, Kitten," he said. "First ah figgered it made me feel so homesick-like 'cause it was always so unnatural damn big, jest like ah thought y'all made me feel homesick fo' mah sister 'cause y'all were perty like Nance. Oney it weren't the bigness at all hardly, Norah. Wasn't 'cause the lake looked so big anymore that it was 'cause yo' seemed like Nance. 'Cause ah've gotten kind o' used to the bigness now, got used to yore pertiness even—but ah still have that feelin' ah cain't hardly deescribe 'bout y'all an' the lake. Like ah could jest git drowned in you someway, or elts mebbe get drowned swimmin' somewhere out there. Do ah talk screwy, Kitten?"

"A little, yeah. Only say some more anyhow, 'cause it all sounds like somethin' I read once. It's nice. I'd like to read books again like I used."

"Well, ah cain't any more stop feelin' the strangeness of the lake than ah could stop lovin' y'all. It's that strangeness that gets me, Kitten—not the bigness. Jest like ah love y'all not 'cause yore eyes is brown, oney jest cause it's *you*, Norah."

She turned to him, being pleased, kissed him lightly, and laughed low.

Sometimes they rode the bus-tops together, and then her hair blew lightly against his cheek. His arm held her closely, her head lay on his shoulder; he would feel the pressure like velvet of her bare arm and firm thigh.

How happy Cass felt in such moments of closeness! If he but shut his eyes his head swam with happiness; there would be a strong sweet singing all through him, as of the blood in his veins rejoicing in its own flow. Once from a bus-top he felt like calling out to some strangers walking below him, "Poor blind ones down there! Look up to where Cass is! This is me, this is Cass—up here with Norah! Kitten loves me—she and I sleep together! Every night I kiss her, it's just me that Kitten loves. I'm Cass—you remember? This is Norah, and she loves me."

Sometimes when he lay by her side in the night Norah was already sleeping; he would think to himself as he felt himself dozing, "I'm falling asleep now—and when I wake up Pa will be just coming in from the kitchen, Bryan will be asleep right here beside me, and Nance will be fetching wood for the stove" . . . But when he awoke it would still be Norah beside him, his head resting on the carpet of her hair. Everything around him would be warm and clean and bright, on the floor a new rug, deep and dark and soft. The breeze that comes off the lake in the mornings of summer would be rippling the curtains ever so gently; gently so as not to wake Norah. Then it would seem to Cass that all this was so good that there could be no dark smoke-filled places anywhere in the world. It would seem that nowhere could there be a dim room with dirt for a floor, where once a small boy had lived in fear of a father.

It was dream-like now, in this place, to recall it.

One morning Cass was wakened by shouts and cries from the street below. Raising his head from the pillow, he saw grotesque shadows racing down a long red fence, jumping up and jumping down, waving monstrous arms over headless bodies, first running this way, and then, all with one motion turning, racing back in the direction they'd come. For a moment the red fence itself seemed to be moving. Cass became deathly afraid. Ever since the time in Great-Snake Mountain when he had seen a crowd pointing and shouting as though all out of one mouth he had been afraid, above all else that he feared, of a mob.

"Norah!" he called, "Wake up! Look downstairs. Somethin's up!"

Norah opened her eyes, swung her legs lazily to the door, and stepped, still yawning, into blue-tasseled mules; leisurely she went to the window.

"Just a bunch of Reds puttin' on their act," she reported, "Niggers an' white guys listenin' to a nigger talkin' from a car, an' a whole gang of sheenies runnin' up an' downstairs draggin' furniture into a house."

Coming back to the bed and seating herself beside him, she combed his tousled morning head soothingly with her hands.

"Scare you a mite, Lunky?"

"Jest a mite," he confessed.

Behind her thin night-dress he felt her full breast's young warmth, its soft fall and rise.

"That's the third time this week."

"What's the matter with them folks anyhow?" he asked.

"Bunch of dizzy kikes I guess, that's all."

He plucked at his scar, and she drew his fingers away from it. "Don't do that, honey," she asked. "It looks awful nasty."

Norah didn't like kikes.

Norah and Cass disliked moving so frequently. Both wanted some place where they could live without absolute secrecy, some place where they could stay a year, if they wished, without having to move once. Norah found such a house. It was on Orleans Street, a big three-story frame building owned by a woman named Josie Hill.

They had lived on the fringe of Chicago's vast underworld. Now they moved into its very heart.

The house on Orleans Street was known from coast to coast as "a safe hole." Here lived men and women whose whole lives had been given to beggary and theft. Cass and Norah came to know Lon Costello, an old man who simulated a racking cough as a livelihood and hence was known as "T.B." There was Lon's partner-in-crime, a little half-witted jew known only as "Stir-Nuts." There was Anthony Brown, known as a "dinger"; he twisted his right arm out of shape every morning, and returned, his arm back in position and his pockets jingling, before the day was done. He was a young Alabaman who claimed that his true profession was gambling, and he was only "dinging it" to get a gambling-stake together. His most frequent boast was that in the winter of 1929 he had dropped five thousand dollars in a single day at Tia Juana.

Others here were transient: each day new faces came and left. The owner of the house was an elderly woman who bore on her face the marks of a lifetime of furtive living. Lon Costello told

Cass that she had bought the house with the proceeds of twenty years of work as a "D.D." She had begged, playing mute, from city to city and prison to prison, until now in her dotage she owned a house. To Lon her success in life was enviable. He would have married her at the drop of a hat; but she would have none of him, he said.

Anthony Brown assured Cass that he would, with a few days' training, make an excellent "wire"—a pickpocket. Lon wanted to teach Norah "The Black Hood" act, but Norah objected strenuously. "The Black Hood" was a woman who sat with a baby in her arms and a cup by her side, in some neighborhood where the danger of arrest was not large. Lon offered, for a ten percent cut of the proceeds, to find the neighborhood, the baby, and the cup. He was full of such projects, and when he was refused he only laughed and proposed another "squawk."

There were sluggers and gunmen here, mostly stolid, uncommunicative fellows who had a silent contempt for the beggars, dingers, and squawkers about them. Cass classified himself among the gunmen; but it was odd that, without question, the gunmen seemed to put him into the same category as Lon Costello and Anthony Brown. He soon learned that Norah and himself were not yet of the elite of this world. Showing his Smith and Wesson at every opportunity somehow failed to impress. Talking loudly seemed to bring quiet smiles.

On the second floor lived a "throwout," a fellow who could throw his joints out of place at will; he was a card-sharper on the side, and offered to teach Cass rare card-tricks at a dollar a trick. This card-sharper-throwout was an Assyrian with a long tragic face, and he held a social position midway between that of the dinger and the gunman. Others in the house called him "Ashes" and looked at him a little in fear. Cass went to him to iearn, despite Lon Gostello's counsel not to go near the man. Lon hated to see anyone spend a dollar on another man's project while he himself had so many better ones for sale.

For hours each day Cass sat with the Assyrian trying to learn sleight-of-hand. He was far too awkward, and after two weeks he abandoned the idea in favor of a simpler trick which Lon offered to teach both himself and Norah free. Every morning all through that summer Norah and Cass sat with Lon or Anthony Brown learning idle games across a kitchen table. Across the table sunlight slanted, and the cards slapped softly from hand to hand. Through the open window the roar of the L curving toward the Loop became a familiar sound. Children fought and played in the street below, and peddlers cried out from the alleys. This was Little Italy, and the streets were alive with dark folk from morning till night, and all night long.

Outside the window lay the city, basking under sun or sleeping through the summer night. Down to the Oak Street beach the Italians took their children. Cass and Norah followed them down and slept in each other's arms on the shore.

This was the tragic meeting-place of men, the brief city sprung out of the prairie and falling again into dust. This was the gathering-ground between the years, here humans bred for an hour and died. Some of these in this place wore pants, others wore dresses. Some here were hairy and some were hairless, and all went down to the beach together, talking, beneath great stars, in a tongue ten million years younger than their brains. Thus the eons of spawning in the teeth of decay, ten million years of defeat and lusting, war and disease and conquest, had at last brought them gabbing to this place. They would eat pink popcorn balls here, have dreams at night, ride streetcars a while, and die, and decay; and call the dreaming living, and call the decay death. Mingled with the sand of the Oak Street beach was the dust of men who had bathed in the lake ten thousand years before Eric the Red. And Cass McKay sat upon the sand, a skinny man in a blue bathrobe, reading *True Romance*.

"Y'all are shore one sweet kid," he said to Norah Egan, fondling her hand. "Ah'll bet y'all'd like some p'tato chips right now, wouldn't yo'?" He came down hard on his southern accent, for he knew she had come to like its sound. He knew because she mocked it.

"Ah sho' would," she said, and they laughed together, two human things in the city.

"Let's go down to the Chink place on Wentworth," he offered, "an' eat up all their chop suey."

Thus passed one summer for two people, with card-games in the morning, sun-baths in the afternoon, and love-games at night.

One rainy morning in early September Norah went downstairs to do the day's shopping; in the store on the corner she bought meat and butter and eggs, but when she opened her purse she lacked several cents of the sum necessary. She had to make an extra trip then, in order that they might have ham for breakfast. When she reentered Cass was squatting cross-legged on the floor with Lon Costello and Anthony Brown. They were playing three-card monte, and nickels and dimes littered the rug. The little Jew called "Stir-Nuts" was standing above them, looking down and giggling half to himself.

Norah paused in the doorway and crooked a finger to Cass. Without rising he reached in his pocket and rolled a half dollar toward her across the rug. Then, feigning laughter, he called carelessly, "That's all there is, Blondie. There ain't no more."

And so, as soon as their supper on that night was done, Cass put on a yellow slicker and looked over to Norah; she was sitting on the edge of the bed, tugging away at high black galoshes.

He went to her, kneeled, and forced the boots over the little brown slippers; she ran her fingers through his hair as he knelt.

"How about the dishes, Lunky?" she teased, "You ain't gonna leave 'em all dirty like that I hope."

"Hell with the dishes, hon. Mebbe Lon or Stir-Nuts'll do 'em." And they went.

Norah drove slower than usual that night, because of the rain. Despite the swift little wiper the windshield kept clouding up every few minutes.

"God*damn*," Cass swore, "Looks jest like a second deluge." He pronounced "deluge" "de-loog."

"Ol' floodgates jest opened an' let down a deloog. God*damn*."

"Coming down too hard to last very long." Norah spoke curtly.

He tucked her collar in tightly about her throat. It was the second time they had used the car for this purpose; they were driving west on Lawrence past a cemetery which reminded Cass of the old French graveyard along Basin Street in New Orleans.

He had developed a habit of reading street-signs aloud; when the red traffic-lights stopped them on Damon he spoke abruptly into the windshield, peering narrow-eyed through the rain on the glass while he plucked at his scar.

"Hmmmmmmmmmm. Save With Ice. Hmmmmmmmmmm. Save With Ice."

When the green light flashed, Norah flooded the engine; they lost twenty minutes under a gas-station shed then, waiting for the engine to dry out. She drove without speaking all the way into Cicero. There they parked three blocks south of the Western

Electric plant, on the same street in which Cass had robbed a cabbie of forty-one dollars ten months before. It had been on that occasion that he had learned what an excellent street for his purposes it was: unlit save for gas lamps burning askew, and lined only by vacated cottages.

On the corner a blue and white Neon sign said "RUGS"—a drug store, with the "D" broken out. A slant rain blurred the sign a little now. This was their hoist.

Outstretched branches held leafless arms across their way as they walked toward the sign; drops flicked in their faces with every breath of the whispering wind. A bare-headed boy pulling a small wagon came down the street bawling to the blind windows, "Ice creeyum bars! Ice creeyum bars an' popsickuls!" About them the slant rain ceased, and the wind became more like a faint passing murmur than a wind.

Cass walked by the place first, his head in his collar and his collar turned up. Norah waited five minutes, then walked past more slowly, pausing a moment in front of the rows of cheap magazines displayed in the window. She raised her eyes but one second, then passed swiftly on: in that second she impressed on her brain the store's interior almost to its last detail. Her eye for detail was keener than Cass's. It took him ten seconds to observe what she could see in the wink of an eye.

"If we have to go different directions," he said as they met on the corner, "hide out somewheres on Clark till Wednesday, then come up to the hotel in the afternoon. If it ain't safe by Wednesday get word to Regan where yore stayin'—Ah'll pick it up from Regan; he's the night clerk now."

Before entering they held a final consultation: the tall one was the owner—the Jew with the mustache and hornrimmed glasses.

"Ah'll take him," Cass said, "on account ah don't like Jews."

The boy at the fountain didn't look much like trouble, Norah would take him and then fish out the till. If a customer or a cop walked in that would be Cass's work. Norah would come in after him and leave first; he'd give her a minute to get to the wheel.

Cass waited at a newsstand across the street until he saw that the store was deserted of customers; then he recrossed and sat at a white-tiled table with his scar turned toward the unseeing wall. When the fountain clerk brought him water he ordered a malted milk.

"An' put in a choklut floater," he added.

The container was purring about on the mixer when Norah drove up. Cass could hear the car's motor running when she opened the door, and the sound seemed as soft as that of the container on the mixer.

"A lemon coke," Norah said, and she said it casually. Cass rose from the table and sauntered slowly toward the rear; he felt that Norah had timed herself well. He saw her fumbling about in her purse as though for her change, heard the mixer humming smoothly, heard the wind rising outside.

When Cass got back of the prescription counter Norah pulled her Colt from her purse and spoke steadily. "This is a stick-up." She heard Cass's voice, strangely hard and ringing behind glass as she covered the fountain-boy. She heard a door close, and a key turn, and she forced the boy farther back, placing herself against the till. The boy kept making frightened white faces in front of her; his mouth kept jerking his underlip sidewise. "We won't hurt you, son," she assured him, fearing that he might decide to scream. She saw that his face was thickly pimpled, and added, "I'll bet you eat lots of sundaes on the Jew boss, don't you?" The boy stopped making faces then and merely stared stupidly. She heard Cass's voice, coming nearer, and caught the flash of his yellow slicker.

"A cinch, Blondie! A cinch!"

She sensed his exultation, knew that he must have the druggist locked in the lavatory.

As he brushed past her she saw the side of his face that bore his scar. In that hasty moment it looked to Norah like a loose and grayish ribbon hanging out of the corner of his mouth. The light made it look like that, so gray-like and loose.

"A cinch, Blondie! A cinch!"

He covered the fountain boy in her place, and tried to joke with the boy to calm him. Norah banged open the till, and Cass caught the glint of silver beneath the light. He saw sweat standing on Norah's forehead under her little gray hat; a dime rolled across the floor at his feet. She was scooping bills into her purse, the malted milk was slopping furiously all over the mixer; outside the rain was beginning again. Cass heard it tap against the windows, and he smelled the drink on the mixer. Norah zipped her purse shut, slid around the edge of the counter, and was through the door. Through the fountain-mirror Cass saw her go; then he leaned leisurely across the counter, the .45 flat beneath his palm on a cold marble surface. He would drink a mouthful of that chocolate malted before he left. That would impress Norah. He was Bad-Hat McKay, and he took his time, and he treated his woman right.

"Git that offn the mixer!" he roared. "Pour it! Quick!" He saw the boy's fingers fumbling for the button, saw them find it at last. The boy slopped half the milk out of the container, and a long shadow passed the side-window. The milk was spilling over the glass's edge, the Jew in the lavatory kicked the wall.

"Ah said *quick!*" he repeated—and the boy dropped both glass and container; Cass heard the glass break, saw the boy begin trembling with fright.

He said, "Don't holler," and looked in the mirror when he said it. He saw the door behind him begin opening, and he thought that that door would never get quite open. Then the mirror fogged and blurred, as though wet with steam or dew. A plain-clothes bull with his rod in his hand, and behind him a glass door closing slowly.

In that split fraction between decision and action Cass saw, reelingly reflected through mirror and door, the figure of Norah stepping into the car; he heard the purring of the motor, and knew that she wasn't going to wait. Then her figure was gone, and the motor was gone, and a red taillight winked slyly through darkness and rain.

Cass could not have turned when the door opened behind him; he could not have whirled, firing, and so have fought his way out. Cass had not the courage, not an ounce of such courage. He did not dare now to move even one small finger. And then fear took him so that he felt all his innards sagging and cringing; a weak urine ran down his leg, leaving him sick and strengthless. The gun in his hand slid off the cold marble surface with a small silver tinkling, down into a sink with a half-sunken coca-cola glass, and one soapy cup, and a long-handled sundae spoon.

In that moment Cass thought of two white-girl hands, cupping peanuts in their palms. He counted, slowly, up to four. And hands took him from behind.

14

When a man starts suddenly out of sleep to find himself lying atop cold iron on the upper bunk of a windowless cell, he is stunned for a moment. For one long moment he doesn't know where he lies. Then he touches a ceiling just by lifting an arm or hears the stirring of another in the darkness beneath, or hears the tread of the tier-guard far down the tier—he remembers then so that his heart pains, beating faster.

Yet even when everything comes clear once more—the long ride with the siren wailing—what the young lawyer said to the hard-eyed jury, what the old judge said to the young lawyer—even then a man must wonder, not quite understanding. Remembering boyhood, early yearning, love and hope and pain, he cannot wholly understand what has brought him to this place.

Cook County jailhouse, say you're there. One to fourteen for robbery with a gun. First-offense, white, male, native-born. Say that's what you are, say that's what you're serving. Being first-offense, native-born white like that helps a little. It can even keep you from getting ten to fourteen. All the same, even one year is a hell of a stretch, even where ten months of good conduct equal twelve. After you stare through an opening in a blue-steel door for a week, ten years and ten months mean about the same thing. Before a month is out you feel that you've done a year. Not only heart-hurt and hurt all the time: hurt because you're cold, hurt because your bunk is crumby, hurt because you're worried over some woman outside. And you're hungry. Say for ten months, every night, you lie down hungry. In the middle of the night you wake up—and you're hungry. Hunger is a dry hand, say, squeezing on your gut. And there's nothing you can do but think, "Tomorrow morning at ten I'll get oatmeal to eat." No use standing up, no use whimpering, no use cursing your cell-mate or walking up and down; no use bawling out through the bars, "I'm hungry, Guard, I can't steep I'm so hungry." Guard doesn't care much. So you lie still and take it. You take it until it seems there are two on your bunk: yourself, and your hunger.

Then come faces of men you have hated, men you have fought, men you have tricked; memories of faces that will not let you be, but come in throngs in the night in the dark, in the cold. Faces of men, faces of women, faces of children and strangers and friends. (Beautiful rough-hewn faces of men, sweet-mouthed level-eyed faces of women.) The faces of friends hurt more than faces you hate, if you miss them more than you hate the others; but if you have no friend, and hate some one face pretty much, then that hurt is even worse than the other.

And when you can't sleep you try to forget whatever pain it is that hurts most, hunger or love. Think about something else, remember something funny. Some joke you heard or some place you saw or something you did, or some job that you pulled. Remember all the places you've been: Cincinnati, Seattle, Niagara Falls; remember how the colored spray looked from the Canadian side, all green and yellow and red like that under the colored floodlights? Only you can't remember clearly because your belly is flat as a washboard and twice as cold, and you're thinking that if it hadn't been for one piece of bad luck you wouldn't be in here at all.

Cass tried to remember places: Harrisburg and Joplin and East Texas. But when he got around to thinking of Oklahoma City he recalled an afternoon when he'd been sitting on the courthouse steps in Pawhuska up in the Osage country, when one of those little brown Osage girls had come past. She had walked slowly, yet lightly. So it was no use, it all came back to Norah. Night and day, Norah Egan.

"She cain't come to visit, on account of they'd snatch her," he consoled himself daily. "She could write me a letter, but it seem like she don't. If she goes broke she can sell the car, but she won't get half what it's worth."

And night and day a dull pain filled his heart, a pain which seemed daily to draw him back into darkness. Into the back of his head came again the old feeling of being, somehow, clogged; he felt the old numbing darkness coming back, and he was helpless, in this place, to fight it. With Norah not near he was helpless in most things. He felt that he was losing a part of himself, some vital part. And his mind, as though swathed with many dark bandages, would admit few memories but memories of Norah; would permit few thoughts to escape that were of her. Sometimes, surreptitiousiy, some reminiscence of Nancy, of Bryan, or of his father would creep in, crawl weakly about for a minute or two—and then he would recall Norah in a yellow dress or how she had looked when asleep . . . Night and day, day and night, in an endless river of memory. . . . Norah had leaped a tiny stream flowing between two great white rocks, she had jumped lightly across, in a yellow dress. She had had a peculiar way of jumping, just as she'd had her own way of speaking, of laughing, of singing, of dancing and thinking and smiling. She had never said, "Good morning" to him, but always, mocking, "How you-all this mo'nin', suh?"

Cass, remembering small things Norah had said, words he had disregarded once, now remembered them all, each one, with a pain that racked him like a skewer turning in his bowels. Seeking release from his memories he often went to the opening in his door to try to talk to the tier-guard or a passing trusty.

"Ugh-hugh," the trusty would say. "Yep, I guess you're right about that, sonny"—and would keep on walking by. Then Cass would try to talk to his cell-mate, or to the prisoner across the corridor.

Day and night merged together slowly, until there ceased to be days that were different from night. The men slept. Each morning at four they heard the tier-guards change. Bootsteps coming up, bootsteps going down. Men here hardly knew the night from the day save by bootsteps going down. They rose, they walked, they spoke low words; they hardly knew that the night had ceased.

Twice each day two prison cooks and a kitchen-guard came up the tier rolling a little white two-wheeled wagon before them that resembled a street-cleaner's wagon. Before each cell they left a ladleful of slop in the opening. Usually it was cold slop. Sometimes there was bread in it.

For an hour every afternoon the men were let into the bull-pen for exercise. They paced up and down swinging their arms, or stood staring at each other without speech. There were some who had been in the jail for so long that when their doors were opened for their hour of freedom they would not move from where they lay. Cass came to understand such men more and more. More and more, as time passed, he would have to force himself to take advantage of the bull-pen hour. Before his term was up he would be as these others.

After the bull-pen hour had passed the great door would slam behind him, and a blue-steel rod would shoot across the top of his cell, double-locking his door. The rod was operated by the tier-guard, with a single motion double-locking every cell on the tier. Cass became used to its sound, came eventually to await it; before the end its sound would give him peace. For an hour after hearing it, its slamming would, somehow, solve everything; its finality leave no room for doubt. He would forget then, and sleep for a while.

Sometimes the men heard voices come up from the brickyard far below; they bent their heads to the wall, listening. Each man stood next to his own gray wall, each stood in gray sack-cloth, listening. Sometimes confused human cries came up through the walls into darkness.

Cass's cell-mate was a half-demented weasel who was serving six months for a crime against nature. It was his constant boast that, through abundant virility, he had for many years earned a living as a male prostitute. His speech consisted solely of this boast, until Cass wearied of hearing. When the man's term was up, in Cass's third week, Cass was heartily glad to see him go; even though it left him alone in the cell. For two months Cass was alone, and his only conversation of those months was with an Irishman confined across the corridor. Cass could see into this cell, and all that the two men in it did. Of the two he seldom saw more than the one, however, because one lay all day with his face turned toward the wall, coughing regularly. The odor of a sick sweat on his body at times pervaded the entire tier. The sick one's cell-mate was a hairy devil named Conlay Costigan; with the sick man Conlay waged unceasing warfare. He harangued him for hours every day, upbraiding him for his illness. Cass wondered why the head jailer did not have the two separated. Costigan never let the tier-guard go past without calling through the opening of his door, "Cleary! Hey,

Cleary, ye pitiful ould louse. Misther Cleary then Sor!—An' would ye be so good as to say one word now to Jayler to get me out o' this pin wid this sick boor layin' here? Would ye now, Misther Cleary plaze Sor? The man smells verra fould indade Sor . . ."

But Cleary would pass on, for he had heard the same plea a thousand times; and Costigan would peer over at Cass.

"Jay-ler thinks me an' Billy Moore should be in thogether, being as we're cousins, in for the same rap. But that's just the jay-ler's opinion, lad; between Billy an' me is now no love whatsoever. An do ye not think I've a right to my health, lad? Must I get ill with yellow glanders p'raps, just 'cause Billy here did not care for his self in his yout'? Lord only knows what Billy has got."

Cass once called out to the tier-guard, "Put number forty in with me, Cleary." The old guard looked over his shoulder at Cass's eyes in the opening.

"Don't worrry about that hairy ape, sonny," he advised. "He wouldn't get sick if you shot him. An' anyhow that T. B. is goin' to the hospital tomorrow. Had it straight from the chief this mornin'."

But the morrow and a week of tomorrows came and went, and no one came to take Moore away.

Cass scratched a huge heart on his wall, plunged an arrow through its center, and wrote Norah's name beside his own above the arrow. It took him a full morning, using the edge of his spoon, to make the heart; and in the afternoon, after the bull-pen hour, he added bleeding drops beneath the arrow and its wound.

On a night in Cass's fourteenth week, a prisoner went mad. The hour was late, between twelve and one, and most of the men had been sleeping for hours. The fellow wedged his head into the opening of his door and began screaming nonsense into the corridor, like a rooster cackling upon catching his head in the wire netting of a butcher's coop. "Friends!" he called, and the voice was an old man's voice, "Friends! Wake up quickly and see what I'm doing! Pick-a-lee! Call everyone now to come look at me quickly. Peter! You Petey! You rascal! You thief! My son is a thief, he steals, then he lies. Come here once, you devil, and I'll trounce you good. Good friends, kind people—say where is poor Peter? Come look at poor Petey, he steals and he lies and his nose is all snot again. Pick-a-lee! I say, pick-a-lee! There is no bread any more, good people, that bread was all eaten long ago. Pick-a-lee, you Peter! Pick-a-lee you Pete! Pick-a-lee! Pick-a-lee! Pick-a-lee!"

Cass saw the shadow then, grotesque as a baboon's shadow. Someone on the north end of the cell-block began cursing the racket, and across the corridor Conlay Costigan added his curses.

Then a whisper, awed and terrible, went up and down the whole corridor.

"The crazy-house—they're takin' him to the crazy-house. It's twice as big as this an' it's way out west in Dunnin'."

The jailers had to saw a bar off the door before they could free the mad fellow's head to take him away. Cass did not sleep the rest of that night for thinking of his father.

He lay awake on his bunk, and all old faces, all familiar eyes and figures returned. The giant figure of Sheriff Lem Shultz striding down Nevada Street in the sun, waving a greeting to all he saw; the strange dark man named Benjamin Cody staring down into a fire and praying as he stared; the eyes of the Mexican girl Pepita; and the smoldering eyes of his sister.

"Ah shouldn't of spoke so to sister that time," Cass thought.

There was no desire in Cass to return. It was Norah Egan he

wanted now. Where she was was peace, and home, and all things that meant well to him.

"Mebbe she writ a note an' they don't want ah should have it," he thought. Yet he knew that even in a note she would be unable to say even so much as, "I sold the car," far less to speak of where she was or of what she was doing. Weekly, he feared being taken to the Thursday night show-up at Eleventh and State.

"She'll leave word with Regan, where she's hidin' out," he told himself.

He remembered how his life had been before he'd met her. He counted the times he'd been beaten or mocked, how often he'd gone hungry or cold. It seemed all his life before that meeting he had gone hungry and loveless and cold. He had been sick in an open boxcar once; no one had come near to help. It had never mattered, any time, until he met Norah. He had fought then to keep what she had given him. He had put down fear, that he might have her love. He had fought hard as he had been able, in the only manner that life had taught him. Life had taught him that there were no rules: everything went, fair or foul, below the belt or an inch above it: if you wished to live, to feel that you too were a man no different than other men, then you packed a heat on your hip and you got what you could. If you didn't take chances, then you lived in a flop. You begged, you whined, you averted your eyes. You were always half-hungry. You went without love.

Because she was all things to him Cass felt now, lying face downward on cold blue steel, because she was his, he would continue to fight when he was released. The girl was his, she was all life had given him; and he would not now let her go.

His, Cass McKay's. And never anyone else's.

And the life of the jail flowed on, in a slow muddy stream.

Cass reckoned the interminable days by a calendar drawn on the wall: he watched the morning hours crawl across his cell on a shaft of gray light filtering in from somewhere high above, to trickle imperceptibly across the floor all afternoon, finally to worm out beneath the steel door in the evening. Then he made a cross on his calendar, for another day had passed. Sometimes he had a cell-mate for a day or a week, and sometimes weeks went by without one.

In his third month, when 1932 had become 1933, he reached his twenty-second birthday. He called to Costigan across the way, "Today ah'm twenty-two!" but the surly fellow made no answer. Cass called out to the tier-guard, "Know what day t'day is, Cleary?" But Cleary kept right on walking.

In the middle of January Cass had a cell-mate for three days. A husky young Pole was shoved in one afternoon while Cass was lying half-asleep on the lower bunk. Cass wakened with a start when he heard Cleary's voice.

"Here's comp'ny for you, Red."

Cass sat up blinking and said, "Hello." For reply the other flicked his tie across the spoon-holder in the manner of one well used to jails, spat against the far wall, and swore softly to himself. Then he sat down on the bunk, shoving Cass's legs against the wall to give himself room.

"You sleep upstairs, kid," he said while unlacing his shoes, "Get up there now. I got to sleep."

Cass made no move.

"Say, fella, you unnerstan' English? Where you from?"

Cass elevated himself, slowly and ominously, upon one elbow.

"Mah name is Bad-Hat McKay"—letting each word fall like a ten-pound weight on the other's ears—"An' ah come from the

Big Bend Country. Some folks call me Two-Gun, an' some just says Bad-Hat."

But the other did not appear even faintly interested now. Cass leaned on his elbow, waiting, until his whole side ached with the effort. Then he lay down once more and returned his feet halfway to their original position. The Pole spoke sharply then, "Whyn't you stay down in the Big Bend? How do I know I won't catch syph from livin' in here with you? What you doin' up North anyhow? God, you don't look like you got good sense." He shoved Cass's feet back to make more room for his buttocks. Cass remained supine. The fellow rolled a cigarette and returned the tobacco to his pocket without offering it to Cass.

"I asked you once now—what you doin' North? I don't want to have to ask you twice."

"Ah come up lookin' fo' work is all."

"Kind o' work?" His tone was now that of an employer inter-viewing a prospective employee. Cass thought hurriedly.

"Show-business work," he answered, and was surprised to hear himself say it. "Ah make all the burleykyoo houses North an' South." He was bewildered to find himself on the defensive, he wondered whether Costigan across the way was listening.

"Don't lie, kid, you ain't never had a job nowheres, not all your life you ain't. I think I'll start callin' you Jizz-Lips on account your mouth is so big. That's we call a big-mouth kid in my neighbor-hood—Jizz-Lips. Say, if you come from Texas like you say you do, then answer me somethin' quick. If you don't answer quick, then I'll know you're just lyin'. Why is times so hard down there that you had to come way up here lookin' for work? Don't you know there ain't no jobs up here for punk kids?"

Cass thought it wise to reply.

"Spiks got all our jobs down there. Ain't no work left for a white man in the Big Bend country."

It was the explanation which Cass had heard most often. The other reflected for a moment, then spoke gravely.

"Well, they ain't no spiks in my neighborhood. There never was that I remember. But we always had hard times. We never had enough to eat. I never had a square meal till I started coppin' bikes with the boys. How you figger that one out, wise-guy?"

His tone this time was one of propounding a riddle; the solution came easily to Cass.

"Niggers then. Niggers is why. In Texas it's Mexes an' up here it's shokes. Say, didn't ah see twenty nigger cops out in Englewood? Didn't ah see twenty dinges with mailbags draggin' letters all over the derned post-office one day?"

Cass was a little proud of this explanation, until the Pole flared up at him. He leaned far over the bunk and shook a warning finger within an inch of Cass's nose.

"Say, Jizz-Lips, Englewood is my neighborhood—an' nobody ever seen a nigger cop in my neighborhood. You're just lyin' again is all." He waggled the finger to emphasize his challenge, "An' you didn't see no nigger mailman carryin' any letter of mine around, I'll tell you that to your nasty peckerface."

Cass said, "Cleary'll get after you, you talkin' like that to me." Then, placatingly he added, "Mebbe it wasn't in Englewood I seen 'em."

Cass had the uneasy feeling then that Englewood was no more the Pole's community than it was his own.

"You ought to be more careful what you say, Jack Ugly," the Pole warned, "cause I got one terrible temper. You'll just have to be watchin' yourself night an' day while I'm in here now, if you're figgerin' on gettin' out alive. Lucky for you I'm not in long. I'm on my way to Joliet. You sleep upstairs as long as I stay."

Cass felt that this fellow was gaining the upper hand much too easily. Evidently the fellow didn't quite realize how tough Cassy McKay really was. In an effort to retrieve his waning prestige, Cass patronized.

"Well, fella, ah don't know as ah blame y'all fo' gettin' all blowed up—reck'n ah'd get sore too if some 'un said ah lived in niggertown. Yeah, ah hates 'em perty bad mahself. Fact is ah don't s'pose there is many folks hates 'em quite so bad as me."

The other disputed the point.

"No, ain't nobody hates 'em like you 'cep' me. I hates 'em worse'n you or anybody else. Now get upstairs."

Cass wondered where Nubby O'Neill was. He climbed onto the upper bunk without protest, and lay down. He lay down slowly, so as not to raise dust out of the moldy blanket. He wished to sleep, but the other continued to plague him with questions.

"You got a girl, fella?"

Cass answered with pride. "O' course. Ain't *you?*"

The other would not commit himself, seeming more interested in Cass now than in himself.

"What's her name?" he asked.

"Norah."

Immediately the Pole feigned an elaborate astonishment. "Norah—*Norah* did you say? No kiddin', kid? Is Norah *really* her name? Why say, you know I used to own a yeller hound name of Norah—an' *that* bitch didn't even have a tail! Can y'imagine such a thing happenin' right in here the first day I come in?"

From one of the cells came laughter, tow. Cass could only summon a sickly grin and hope that the man wouldn't go any farther in his assault upon another man's honor. So he said nothing, and the other stretched out on the lower bunk, and snorted in contempt.

'Hmmmph—Norah. How many times you scored already?"

To Cass, the whole cell-block seemed waiting for his reply.

"Ten or 'leven or twelve mebbe, ah reck'n," he said.

"Hmmmph—ten or 'leven or twelve sounds just like more lyin' to me. What you say they called you, fella? Lyin' Sam the Bullcrap Man—is that what you just told me they call you down South?"

Cass saw that there would be no end to his persecution until he defended himself. He would have to prove to the whole tier that there was a man in here with this hunky. He rolled off the bunk and came to his feet in the center of the cell as though about to commit red slaughter. He stood above the other, a dim figure in the dim cell light, tugging at his belt and looking tough. He didn't feel very tough, tugging that way, but he closed one eye, as Nubby would have done, and he spoke out of the corner of his mouth.

"Jest in case you ain't heered," he drawled, "mah name ain't Lyin' Sam. Ah'm Texas McKay, case you ain't heered."

Their eyes held for a moment, and then Cass's shifted; and when he spoke again his voice betrayed his fear as nothing else could have betrayed him. "'The Texas Cracker' is what some folks call me too," he said, yanking now almost desperately, "On account ah'm from Texas jest like ah said."

"Don't apologize," the Pole answered, "Texas Cracker, eh? Well, I been to Oklahoma, an'! know all about you cowboy crackers. Lots o' brotherly love down in that country—if your pants is pressed. It's 'Hello, brother!' if you got a buck or two, but 'On your way, louser!' when you're broke. Oklahoma stinks. Nevada stinks.

So I guess Texas must stink too. Everythin' down there bites, stings, or got a thorn on it."

"Y'all cain't talk bout mah home state thataway."

The other rolled over on his side as though preparing for rest. "An' you stink too, fella."

Cass climbed quietly back onto his bunk. Maybe the fellow was going to sleep now. But he had scarcely settled comfortably on his blanket when the Pole began again.

"You cowboy crackers think 'cause you got a different smell than a nigger that you're better some way. You Texas loomps got nothin' else to brag on so you brag 'cause you got a different o-der. Me, I got nothin' at all against niggers. They ain't never bothered me none. An' lots of 'em I've knew had twice as much brains an' guts as any Oklahoma cowboy *I* ever seen. Lots more than *you*. I know niggers got six times as much brains as you got. Fact is I kind o' like niggers. We all come out of a hole, didn' we?"

"But ah thought y'all said yo' *didn't* like 'em," Cass protested.

"I've changed my mind since hearin' you talk."

Cass tried to think clearly. There was something wrong here, and he didn't know what it was. He would be glad when this fellow was well on his way to Joliet.

"Ah guess if we was down South *now*," he finally said, "Y'all'd find out somethin' 'bout guts an' whose got 'em. Y'all wouldn't talk so high an' mighty 'bout niggers down *there*. Not where ah come from, no sir yo' wouldn't. We'd whip somethin' out o' yo' fo' talkin' thataway in mah home town."

"Sure you would—you an' a hundred other cowboys. An' that's the only way you *could* do it, too. An' they call you tough guys 'Texas crackers,' eh? Well fella, you know what *I'm* gonna call you?"

Cass made no answer. He was not especially eager to learn more.

"Well, I'm callin' you the Texas *Crapper* an' you're callin' me 'Mister.' Mister Joseph Novak. Get it, Jizz-Lips up there? *Mister* Novak."

He waited, while laughter surged, then persisted quietly. "I asked you do you get it or don't you get it?"

Cass got it. He got it when he heard Novak's feet hit the floor, and saw the Pole's broad back coming out of the bunk below. Cass spoke quickly then. "Ah got it," he said. The back withdrew.

"You can start sayin' 'Yes-Sir' right now then. 'Yes-Sir, Mister Novak'—like that. Say it."

"Yes-Sir. Mister Novak."

And for three days Cass said "Yes-Sir, Mister Novak" and "No-Sir, Mister Novak." For three days the Pole gave him scarcely a moment's peace. Cass did not speak unless he was spoken to, and he slept on the upper bunk. After Novak was gone he felt as free, for an hour after, as though he had been released. He hoped desperately that he would not be given such another cell-mate.

With every passing day, it seemed to Cass, the stench of Costigan's cell-mate grew stronger.

Once Cass woke in the night half-strangling for breath. The odor of sweat in the cell-block lay like a blanket about his lungs. He sat bolt upright, head back-straining, clawing at his throat for breath. The odor lifted a little, like a slow gray curtain lifting, and he rolled his head in his hands in relief.

"Phwat in God's name makes ye *sweat* so, man?"

Costigan was speaking to the man below. Cass heard Billy Moore waken and stir in his place. A listening silence seemed to fill the cells. All down the tier the cells were listening. Cass could tell by the indrawn silence there. Costigan spoke challengingly, as though to provoke reply.

"Ye've kept me from slape five nights runnin' now wid the terrible sick smell of ye. Will ye niver die an' lave a man in pace?"

The listening dark closed down. Someone on the other side of the bull-pen gripped the edge of his bunk and tossed about upon it until it groaned and rattled beneath him. Then he stopped, the sick man spoke; his words seemed to struggle among themselves as they were spoken.

"Ah, but ye're a crool hard man, Conlay Costigan, to spake so to a man railly dyin'—railly in truth a-dyin'."

It was the voice of one groping through fog, unseen and unseeing. Cass was aware of a hurrying shadow swimming aslant the wall of the long-lit corridor. Eager for any excitement, Cass went to his door. Perhaps the tier-guard would beat up Costigan.

But the guard only spoke to the man below.

"Leave off yer chatterin' now, Billy Moore, an' try to get you some rest. God knows 'tis rest you're needin'."

Moore defended himself anxiously, in a kind of fevered desperation.

"'Tis not I what's doin' the talkin', Cleary—'tis the great scut of a black Dublin rat above me, him what woke me out of the first true slape I've had in long weeks now, him wid his unclane an' mockin' spache. Ah, Misther Cleary Sor—"

The voice broke off, with anguish or disease; then resumed in a long nasal whine thick with self-pity.

". . . an' me a dyin' man."

Cass saw Costigan lurch half his body over the bunk's edge, thrust down one great and hairy paw to clutch Moore with fierce sure fingers.

"A scut it is I am, ye bitch's bastard?"

The long tier murmured, and was still. Costigan jerked Moore up tih their faces almost touched.

Cleary spoke quietly.

"Put the man down now, put him down fast. You've a sorry record enough, Con Costigan, without addin' to it in here. Put him down, I said."

Costigan heard. Deliberately, he spat in Moore's face, and dropped him. And to Cass it seemed then that Moore was sinking his teeth into his tongue, in impotent fury.

"That was a perilous bold thing to do," Cleary admonished. "Don't you know that should the dyin' man but spit upon you now in his turn, then surely he would bring you to the grave with his-self? Don't you know this, you great foolish fellow?"

Cass laughed. He had never heard the superstition before. He felt that Cleary must be speaking merely in order to impress Costigan.

Costigan only guffawed, to show he was not quite so simple as Cleary thought him, and Cleary turned to go; but even as he turned Moore cried out, and he had to stop. Cass had never heard a voice in deeper pain. It was the voice of something tortured in sleep and unable to waken. The voice of something lost in darkness.

"Tis a true tale—a true tale—I'll be dead in a week, cousin Con, yet I'll spit in ye're face e'er I go—an' ye'll thin be as dead as I." He laughed wild laughter. "Ye'll be as dead as I soon enough, cousin Con, ye huge black turd from a Dublin whore."

Cleary waved a hand at Costigan, then he spoke to Moore like a man to a tired child. Cass was surprised to hear Cleary's voice, that it was not unkind.

"We'll get you into the hospital tomorrow, lad, and in a month you'll be as well and fine as Costigan hisself is now."

Empty words. There was no room in the hospital for Moore. He was going to die for want of a cot to lie on; and none knew it better than Cleary.

For two nights thereafter Costigan held his peace, fearing a quarrel that might deprive him of his "good-time"—the days deducted each month from sentence during good behavior.

On the third night Cass could scarcely sleep again for the smell of sweat in the narrow place. Finally he ripped a square of material off the pocket of his prison shirt and placed it over his mouth. The device helped; he felt himself sinking slowly toward rest. Dark waves seemed closing over his head and the tattered rag-bag of his fatigue seemed turning quietly to soft dark down—when Moore coughed. Moore coughed the long rack-splitting cough that rives the bones of the body and brings bright blood boiling into the throat. Cass woke, and heard Costigan in a shout-ing rage.

"Ah, ye offal—ye foul thin offal! Ye filthy slum-begotten Ulster pickpurse—"

Silence, fearing Cleary. Cass tiptoed to his door, peered over into Costigan's cell, and waited. He heard Moore settle to rest again, heard the strained breathing become regular and easy, knew that Moore slept once more.

He was about to turn back to his blanket when he discerned Costigan's dim figure moving, slyly, over the edge of the upper bunk. He saw Costigan bend his great head over until his mouth was six inches from Moore's ear. And he coughed like a sick steer. Moore woke with a suddenness that started him coughing anew, and Costigan threw himself back on his bunk, chuckling to himself. His chuckle, cunning-cruel and sly, reminded Cass of a hare-lip, and of Olin Jones' faint laughter. So he laughed a little with Costigan.

The Irishman had found a new pastime. He never wearied of his jest. Repetition never diminished the pleasure it afforded him. Indeed, he found it sport well worth staying awake for. Whenever he heard Moore breathe easily, he leaned over, chuckling in anticipation of his joke, and coughed down Billy Moore's right ear. The sick man would waken, fuming, and Costigan would throw back his great dark head until the whole tier was loud with his laughter.

Cass was wakened every night. He could sense Moore's hatred, like a thin living current across the corridor, every time the man tried to curse—and coughed before he could find his voice. All through the long nights the two lay caged together in darkness. Hate became as a fog about the mind of each, until both groped in perpetual night. Hate gnawed at the heart of each, until both lived in perpetual flame. Hate consumed the very spirit of each; till the blood cried out for blood.

Then Moore began to sink, and the mocking cough of Costigan sometimes failed to stir him as he slept. He slept for longer and longer intervals with every passing day, till consciousness came only as a passing thing to him. When his jest was thus rendered ineffective, the harassed Costigan was driven to the brink of insanity.

On a Tuesday forenoon in July, on the day that Cass's term was up, the doctor came. "I guess them pills didn't work again," he said, looking down at Moore.

Cass peered through his door. He could see the doctor on one knee beside Moore's bunk, but of Moore he could see nothing more than a pair of unlaced county shoes.

"This man's ready for the hospital all right," Cass heard. "But we'll prob'ly have to bring him back next week. We can't spare space over there to those that space can't help."

An hour later an intern came down the tier, pushing a low stretcher. When he reached Costigan's cell Cleary hurried up, bawling at Costigan hulked in a corner. "Lift that man out here— and do it quick."

Costigan came out of his corner like a colossal gray-breasted spider. Scowling, his mouth twisting with sullen resentment, he placed one shoulder beneath the dying man. Before Costigan reached the door Moore slid to his feet.

It was the first time Cass had glimpsed the man's face. It was a long, womanly face, dark, and woefully emaciated. He stood in the center of the cell, facing Costigan unsupported, and Costigan stood grinning across at Cleary. The intern put a hand on Moore's shoulder, but Moore shrugged it off. He was swaying a little, and Cass heard his breath coming harder.

"Well, your health seems to be returning, Billy Moore," Cleary said, and he laughed uneasily.

And then to Cass Billy Moore's face seemed suddenly liquid and aflame, as a face seen behind a fire. Moore's eyes stormed with the last vestige of his passion. In a last writhing of his hate his lips clenched, and could not speak. He spat full in Costigan's face, whirled completely about, and lunged face-forward across his bunk.

His head struck iron with a dull-ringing sound; his left leg scraped against the stone of the door. The white-coated intern kneeled slowly then, as though his legs ached. He rolled Moore over, and held Moore's wrist, and bowed his head deeply against Moore's breast. Then he rose and took Moore's ankles. Costigan stooped to take the head. Cass saw Conlay Costigan bending down.

As he straightened up Cass heard him cough.

And late that afternoon Cass was released.

"She's left word with Regan," he told himself.

15

HE CAME OUT of the Twenty-sixth Street exit of the county jail at three p.m., wearing the same yellow slicker in which he had been arrested. Ten months in county had aged his eyes: they held now that chastened half-shuttered look which only long pain can teach any man's eyes. The corners of his mouth had come down till the lips looked almost stern.

Strange sunlight struck his eyelids, new street-sounds struck his ears. He yanked his cap far down over his forehead to shut out the sun, and he walked a bit faster to get past the sounds. He caught a northbound car on Kedzie and stared at strangers like a child riding on a car for the first time.

He did not know of the World's Fair opening until he came down South State. On either side hawkers sold patent medicines, World's Fair flags and World's Fair flowers, World's Fair souvenirs and World's Fair balloons, patent cork screws, patent razor blades, patent cameras, patent ties, patent hose, beach balls, pocket-knives, patent salves of diverse cures;—and on every corner World's Fair pimps watched for World's Fair cops with one eye, and for World's Fair prospects with the other. Radios extolled the glories of a World's Fair two blocks east, and thin children begged from store to store.

Children, like hawkers and whores, peddlers and pimps, had

to watch for cops with one eye and for prospects with the other. Sometimes a cop caught a hawker selling contraceptives along with his razor blades; sometimes a cop caught a twelve-year-old begging too openly.

Cass had forgotten something of the suffering in this city, and what he had forgotten came back to him with redoubled force now. Almost it was like seeing South State for the first time; his eyes were opened by unfamiliarity: a street of misery unspeakable.

He had known long of hungering thousands here, of Chicago's maze of graft and rackets, of its gangster politicians and its crooked mayors. But never before had Cass seen its hunger-ridden streets decorated with flags, nor its whores selling tin souvenirs. He had known long that the price of common bread here, was, for thousands, degradation. That here, just in order to eat, thousands lived in fear, furtively, with lust, shamefully.

And now the city itself seemed a whore, selling a tin souvenir.

Now the city had been made to wear a painted grin and a World's Fair smile, in order that business (which had been ailing somewhat) be made whole once more. "Boost and buy!" the papers bawled, and radios along South State reechoed the frantic plea: "Boost our city! Buy! Buy! Buy!" The papers pleaded and threatened, mocked and cursed; then they cajoled: "Oh buy! Only buy!" The radios sobbed. The *Tribune* demanded: "Buy! Give! Buy! Give!" (Small boys who beg grow up into thieves, small girls into dollar-whores.) 'But say, ain't the Enchanted Islund perty, dearie?' "*Boost the fair! Boost the mayor! We want dollars, we don't care—Just Buy! Buy! Buy!*"

But it seemed that some people no longer had money, because they had spent it all like water, or had been altogether too thrifty, or had invested unwisely.

(Just as in the final stages of syphilis a dying prostitute is given an urethral smear, so did a World's Fair now seek to conceal the decadence of a city sick to death. This city was trying with noise and flags to hide the corruption that private ownership had brought it. The *Tribune* was its smear. The *Tribune* gave glamor to its World's Fair reportage, but said nothing of homeless thousands living in shelters, not a word about women being forced into prostitution under its very nose. The *Tribune* printed pictures of Buckingham fountain, of merry-go-rounds and royal weddings, but had no space for warning its readers of an epidemic begun at the Fair. Publication of such a warning would have saved many lives, but it might also have hurt World's Fair receipts. The *Tribune* was the World's Fair's pimp. Its concern was for the money-bags of Lake Shore Drive, of Winnetka and Wilmette; it had no concern for truth. Systematically it fought, as always, any change in an order of society so beautifully calculated to permit the plundering of the millions by the few, so ideally suited to enhance private interest at the cost of the masses: the system which requires of each generation that millions be slain in wars for world-markets.

The *Tribune* calls such killings: "A war to end war," or "A war for democracy." Its editors spew "patriotism," "love," "kindness," "brotherhood of man,"—the white piously resigning themselves to the approach of another war whose sole purpose will be that of profits for just such men as the *Tribune*'s editors and owners. The *Tribune* prints false news, doctors its news, distorts its news, shouts "America First!" And the little lackeys of the copy-desk, the little bootlickers with pencils behind their ears, when told to doctor news from Russia or Red China—the little lackeys obey. The lackeys have homes in Rogers Park to pay for.)

In front of Hauser's Little Rialto Cass saw the paunchy

person with the red shoe-button mouth; he was standing beneath a black derby, bawling through a blue megaphone.

"She dawnces on a dime, gents," Herman bawled at Cass as he passed. "Stella the little dawncin' girrul—Don't come in here boy—it ain't decent."

And Cass recalled in passing that Norah had told him of this place, of how she had danced on its stage for a while. He wondered how long the money from the drugstore hoist had lasted, and whether she had sold the car. He hurried west toward the river. When he came to the hotel across the bridge on Clark he turned in.

The dapper clerk behind the desk greeted him heartily.

"Well, fer Chrise-sake, I thought they hung you last fall—" They shook hands over the counter. Cass tried to make his voice sound casual when he asked, "How's mah girl, Regan? What'd she leave here fo' me?" His casualness betrayed his concern. And Regan didn't know where Norah Egan was, far less how she was. She had been in only once, and she had said nothing to him.

"Alone?" Cass forced himself to ask.

"No, it was a party up on the third floor; there was a whole gang here that night I never seen before."

So Cass exchanged cigarettes with the fellow, talked a while, boasted a while, laughed and had a drink on the house, and left.

He walked west to Orleans Street, to the old frame house where his summer with Norah had been spent. A tall man stopped him on the steps.

"You want a room?" he asked.

Cass shook his head. No, he didn't want a room. He was looking for his wife. He was just out of the hospital, and her name was Norah Egan, or Stella Howard.

"No frail here by either name," the tall man said. "I'm the landlord. Who are you?"

Cass asked for Josie Hill, for Lon Costello and Tony Brown. Then for the little Jew named Stir-Nuts. They would know where Norah was now.

"No, I don't know them folks, kid. Old Lady Hill got bumped by a truck on Taylor and Halstead last March. Well, she was gettin' perty old anyhow y'know. Too bad."

Cass came down the steps feeling troubled, for he didn't know where he ought to go next. There was a Chinese restaurant on Westworth where Norah and he had sometimes eaten in that summer, and there perhaps he would find her now. She would be sitting alone in the rear where often, in happier times, they had sat together. He would ask the Chinese boys if she still came in if he didn't hnd her already waiting.

On the Wentworth Avenue car Cass watched the women boarding every time the car stopped. He felt that at any corner Norah might board.

For three hours he sat in the little restaurant waiting for someone familiar to enter. Someone of the old mob, or perhaps some girl who'd lived in the house on South Wabash. But Cass didn't want to go back to the house on South Wabash; and he could not understand when not even the owner of the restaurant remembered Norah clearly. He had thought that everyone remembered *her*. The longer he sat the harder it became to fight off the loneliness coming around his heart. When he felt unable to merely sit quietly here doing nothing, he rose as though knowing decisively where he was going next. He could not let himself feel that he didn't know where to look.

He returned to dim streets they had walked together, hoping, by some chance as dim as those streets, to meet someone he had once known. He walked both sides of Huron, from Clark to the lake and back again, looking up at lighted windows, peering in at names on door-bells. Then he tried Erie. Then he tried Ontario. When it became so late that the benches along the beach were deserted of lovers, he spread his slicker out on a bench and slept.

In the morning he returned to the house on Orleans Street and rapped on every door from the fourth floor down. But the old mob was gone; no one in the whoie building had ever heard of Anthony Brown or Lon Costello or of an Assyrian throwout named "Ashes." On the way downstairs Cass met the landlord coming up. He redescribed the little Jew Stir-Nuts. The landlord seemed annoyed.

"I'll tell you what you do, sonny," he counseled. "You go over to the five-hundred block on Clark, an' there's a little kind of kike or sheeny that looks as batty to me as you say the guy you want is. Maybe he's your man. But anyhow, even if he ain't, don't come lookin' back here no more. Your man ain't here an' your wife ain't here, an' folks don't like to have you bangin' their doors at all hours. It scares some of 'em perty bad."

Cass wished that older men would quit calling him "son."

"The Jew sells the *Examiner* over there, sonny, an' most everyone on the street knows him."

Cass walked back to Clark and found a hunchback sitting at the newsstand at the corner.

"You the paper guy?" Cass asked, and the fellow nodded swiftly.

"I'm the *Examiner* guy," he said, "but the paper-truck is late." Cass's heart went sick. There was only the place on the South Wabash to return to, and it was hard to return there. It held too many keen memories of his earliest days with Norah, as well as holding the fear that she might be near there again—that he actually might find her there.

When he got off the streetcar three blocks from the World's Fair gates he stopped in a restaurant for coflee. He piddled his spoon about a cup for a while, and the coffee grew cold, and he left. He walked south feeling ill, and came to the house. His fear, as he went up the steps, was as strong as his hope.

The door was locked. He pushed the buzzer savagely, heard it ringing clearly within, and waited. A frowsy Negress opened. Cass removed his cap and entered. He took one look around, and he laughed a little. The place had been so thoroughly remodeled that he scarcely recognized it. It was a high-class brothel now, no longer a cheap rooming house. The hall and stairway had been varnished, and overstuffed easy chairs lined both sides of an entrance-room. Two high-school boys waited, smoking cigarettes held in long holders, lounging in easy-chairs.

But no one here had ever heard of Norah Egan.

"As a mattah o' fac'," the Negress informed him, "there ain't no nachal blondes like you say workin' here any more. All blondes we got now is dyed uns."

At the corner of Seventh and State Cass counted his money. Of five doltars given him by the county he had three dollars and twenty cents remaining. His desire now was to get dead drunk for a week, but he fought the desire down.

"Ah reck'n ah'll have to git out o' town after this whenever ah want to git high," he counseled himself. No, he couldn't afford being arrested for drunkenness now. He saw the star-bordered sign of Hauser's Little Rialto, and remembered again that Norah had danced there.

"Won't do no harm jest to *ask*," he told himself, and he waited in front. He didn't know quite what he was waiting for, whether to see a show, or to ask for a girl who once had worked here, or both.

The house had not yet opened for the afternoon, and the ticket cage was empty. But a door was open and into it Cass peered inquiringly, to see what he could see . . . and up a dim aisle came two struggling forms, viciously tugging and pulling at each other.

"Loud Mout'!" one bawled, and Cass stepped back in amazement, "Out from my showhouse, Loud Mout'!"

Cass retreated to watch from a safer distance. Halfway in the door and half out the pair ceased to struggle. Instead they stood with noses touching, hurling obscene threats, waving arms, each shaking a fist in the other's face. One held an empty basket in the hand that was not a fist; he wore a white jacket and cap. The other was short, with crimson jowls and fists like hams. He looked like the boss, and he talked like the boss; and every two seconds he grabbed for the basket.

"You are a Loud-Mout'," he announced, as though unaware that he was repeating himself. "You are a Loud-Mout' *schreihaus* Dane"—and he tried again for the basket.

The white-jacketed one tossed the basket a dozen yards up the aisle, followed it with the white cap and jacket, and strode off south on State. The little man with the voice went into the ticket-box and closed the door behind him. Cass came to the opening.

Inside the cage Herman was replacing his derby above his ears.

"Are you-all the boss?" Cass asked.

"Well, if you just seen what I done to that fatass Dane I'd guess you'd know who's boss." Herman was still blowing from excitement. "The show ain't started yet," he added.

"Ah'm lookin' fo' mah girl—"

Herman stared, not understanding. Cass gulped.

"Ah mean she used to work for y'all an' her name was Stella. She's mah wife. Ah cain't find her. Ah jest come out of a hospital. She's a blonde."

"I don't knowin' from nothin'," Herman said. He had something more important to do than to hnd stray blondes for their State Street sheiks.

"Her whole name was Norah Egan. She was a blonde. Mebbe you fired her fo' talkin' back?"

Herman remembered then. "Ahhhhhh,' he ahhhhhed. "Whyn't you saying who you meant in the first place?" His face darkened with challenge. "Sure I fired Egan. You don't like it maybe? You could stuff it, if you don't like it you know." He came out of the cage to thrust his pugnose into Cass's face. "I fire *all* loud-mout's from out my show. Didn't you seeing what I just done to one loud-mout'? He will come back some day next week and ask can he have his old job back and I will be telling him what I told Egan. She come back and says she will work now for less and will not talking back to my face any more and—"

"When'd she come back, mister?" Cass cocked his head to the side expectantly.

"Well, I just told her I would not take her back again even for thirty-five cents a week, on account I have a better dancer now who will not talk so back to my face and—"

"But when was that, mister? Jest last week?"

"Two years ago was all this happening." Herman had quite recovered his poise, and he spoke more quietly. "But how should I know where at you could find anybody? And do you know what I think Egan was doing the time she come back here already?"

There was an eager gleam in Herman's eye; then he seemed to check his tongue, for the gleam faded. "Did you say *wife?*" he asked as though suddenly appalled.

Cass said, "No, ah didn't say 'wife'," and turned away. He felt as sick as though he'd been hit below the belt. For half a block he walked, slowly slouching, thinking dimly; then he paused, and he turned back.

Herman was inside dusting the seats. He dusted with his right hand and held in his left the basket which the vendor had tossed down the aisle. Cass waited in the doorway until Herman glanced up.

"Kin y'all gimme a job, mister?" he asked, "ah don't talk back, 'cause ah got no loud mouth."

Herman glanced up. "Whyn't you say what you wanted in the first place? Or ain't you the same guy?"

"Ah wasn't sure what ah wanted."

"Did you say 'wife'?"

"No, ah didn't say 'wife.'"

Herman sized him up. The fellow didn't look like he'd talk back, but he did look as though he might steal nickels on the side.

Up and down, from the worn brown shoes to the torn brown cap and the slicker rolled up under his arm, Herman appraised him for what he was worth. No, this boy wasn't so classy like the Dane.

Ten months in County leaves a man with a pallor like a gray talcum sprinkled across his face. Herman needed a hard man. Out of a cautious nature now he said, "I got no job for you, sonny." He saw the gray-faced man gulp, and he looked a little closer. Herman distrusted handsome men as unconditionally as he admired pretty women. Experience had taught him, and his logic was rude; a handsome Dane had made trouble among his dancing-girls, and this fellow was no Dane. And he looked too ugly to start woman-trouble. No, Stella wouldn't flirt with this one. Being ill-favored and honest himself, Herman made the unconscious assumption that ugly men were more honest than handsome fellows. To Herman, honest men were fighting-men: Cass's mouth bore a battle scar. Only fighting men bore such scars.

"You could sell tonight for me, if you wanted," Herman said, "I'll buy you hot-dogs an' beer next door. O.K.?" He handed Cass the basket, with the white jacket hanging across the basket-handle. That was all.

Herman Hauser bought him hot-dogs and beer twice a day for a week and a half; every night he checked up on Cass's receipts. At the end of two weeks Cass received six dollars, one full week's pay; and he settled down to the routine of the first steady job he'd held in his life. But Herman never conceded openly that Cass had a job with him. Each pay-night he appeared mildly surprised to find Cass still with him.

"You could stay on this next week," he would say in handing Cass his six dollars, "but after this week I got to cutting expenses."

With this threat over his head from week to week, Cass worked for Herman Hauser for ten months. Through the fall and the early part of the winter he vended stale candies and peanuts along the dark aisle. On the stage girls danced, shrieked, undressed, and retreated with leering woggles. Men in the seats strained forward to see. If Cass blocked one's view for a second he was cursed. Negroes barked at him, "Get out from front o' mah eyes!" and he moved humbly on down the aisle. He watched a talentless comedian slogging about in oversize shoes until he wearied of watching. The piano made a tinny din, and a sixty-year-old scurve off the street sang a ballad of love in the country.

Ten cents was the price here both night and day, and you could stay just as long as your flesh could bear it. You could smoke on the main door, you could hiss from all corners. If you felt in the mood, you could hiss yourself hoarse here. There were no ushers to hush you, and the girls on the stage would merely bend a bit toward you over the single footlight, and without trace of bitterness hiss in return. You could drink out your whiskey in the very front row and smash the bottle agreeably on the concrete of the aisle—if you felt in that mood. For ten cents, one dime, the tenth part of a dollar, you could as a patron of the Little Rialto do all but three things: you could not urinate behind the piano; neither could you clamber nervously over the footlight and there attempt rape while the girls were dancing, you had to wait till they finished and earn a kind of consent; lastly, and this most emphatically, you could not come into the Little Rialto to sleep. Before you dozed for three minutes you would be roused if you tried it. Herman Hauser himself would do the rousing.

He would come tapping your shoulder gently. You would not persist then if you were wise, for Herman enforced this ordinance with a severity against which there was no defense. Had he not, the Little Rialto would have been transformed overnight from a theater to a day-flop, for out on the street strolled transient thousands, each man of whom loved deep sleep like warm food. Since buying the Little Rialto Herman had fought off hordes of wandering men; sleep-hungry legions had he repelled. Since the price of the flop-houses round about was uniformly twenty-five cents, and Herman's seats were well-nigh flealess, the attraction was practically irresistible. Only, poor as it was, Herman preferred show-business. Poor as it was.

Herman stood out front and barked, and as he barked he

peeled his eye. All those fellows who approached his cage with an aspect both soiled and slumbrous Herman followed within. Once inside, if the customer spread out his coat and slumped suspiciously far down thereon, Herman would come tapping gently, pointing to a sign none but he could see, and whispering a low warning, "No slipping please."

This was the time the customer might very well start staying awake, for Herman warned only once. A second offense was to him sheer defiance: he would yank some poor fellow out of sleep by the collar, haul him into the aisle by the front of his shirt, and rush him bodily onto the street by the seat of his trousers. The only hard ones for Herman to handle were those whose brains were inflamed by dope. If a man had nothing but whiskey or beer inside him Herman could handle almost any man's weight. But on one occasion a six-foot-four-inch Negro came in walking on his toes and slumped quietly into a seat behind a beam in the very last row. Herman assumed that he was merely sodden from cheap rye or Shipping Port, so he tapped the Negro's shoulder— and business began to pick up. The fellow rose out of the seat like the black djinn from the bottle, and had it not been for the immediate assistance of Cass McKay, Herman Hauser might well have been strangled to death under his own roof. After that Cass told him how to distinguish between red marijuana and colorless whiskey; where whiskey loosens a man in muscle and brain, marijuana tightens until something snaps. And men with whiskey in them do not walk on their toes, airily.

All in all, Herman's Little Rialto was a boisterous little temple enough, a dim-lit, ill-smelling, tinsel bordello, one moment like a tottering pier as the footlight rocked in its socket under laughter like waves that came crashing—and the next second silent with a silence receding, till Cass could hear the recoiling of breath in throats all about him.

It soon became Cass's duty to whisper, "No sleepun here." But the actual rousting remained Herman's work.

To Cass it seemed that the colored company here had the more verve, that their humor had a sounder ring, that much which they did was both fresh and spontaneous. In the black troupe was a veritable dynamo of a man named Dill Doak. He was a muscular, bullet-headed man of Cass's age, as black as the ace of spades and with a bass voice which flickered the gas flames behind the exit signs when he sang *Asleep in the Deep*. By his limitless energy he electrified others; his energy was such that it amounted to an intelligence in itself. By his spontaneity and drive he made the black show more popular, even among white patrons, than was the white troupe's performance. And this Dill Doak had a mind as keen as his body was strong. Although on the stage he was a light-footed, dance-loving, song-loving, rubber-limbed mappet, full of a rich, black belly-laughter, yet offstage he spoke and acted in a way in which Cass had never seen or heard a Negro speak or act before.

There was no compassion in Cass for the chorus girls, white or black. They worked like Trojans, ten hours a day and twelve on Saturday, six and a half days a week. And they earned seven dollars.

Cass scarcely saw them after a while; after a while he saw only a continual shaking of loose breasts (breasts made loose by pawing and shaking); he saw only the graceless clogging, and painted clown-lips, and the old men who strained far forward to see. They watched with their aged mouths pursed.

"The seegars is fi' cents, gen'nelmen," he barked. "The chewin' gum is fi' cents, the peanuts is fi' cents, the pop is fi' cents, an' the big choklut-almond-raisins bar is fi' cents."

On his evening round he put aside candy and peanuts to sell cigarettes and magazines. Older men bought cigars or cigarettes; boys bought candy and the *Paris Art* magazine.

When Cass stood at the head of the aisle after the lights came on for intermission, Herman's customers saw a loosely built man with close-set eyes, his hair combed straight back from his forehead with a fine-tooth comb. The magazines they bought from him were "For Lovers of Nature Only," according to a warning printed in red on their covers.

"Somethin' speshul fo' men only!" Cass barked, "Fo' fifteen cents what 'riginally costed fifty! Across the street it's still fifty, gentlemen—what a bargun! Money back if unsatisfied—but what he-man wouldn't be satisfied with this," he flung back a cover to display a two-page print of a half-dressed girl on a bed. "Now," he concluded, starting up the aisle, "who's first? Oney nine copies left, so speak up fast, first come first served. Fo' fifteen cents what costed fifty an' money back if unsatisfied—somethin' speshul fo' men only!"

Each Tuesday night was amateur night, and Thursday, when souvenirs were given, was ladies' night. But Saturday night was "Win a Lucky Garter Night," and this event often packed the house till twelve o'clock. On this night six men in the audience holding lucky tickets were privileged to go on the stage and remove, each from the knee of one of the white choristers, one gaudy garter. There were six girls in the white chorus, and Saturday night was all theirs. There was no black show on Saturday night. And Herman saw to it that on Saturday night no Negro in the audience ever got hold of one of his "lucky" tickets.

Cass came to hate them all save Dill Doak.

Had it not been for the hope of seeing Norah once more, for planning against a day when he might again see her, Cass might have gone back on the road. But he felt that she could not be far from the street, wherever she was. Sooner or later he would find her, or he would see someone passing who knew where she was. And when he found her again he didn't want to be broke, he didn't want to be on the bum then. He wanted to be able to take care of Norah. So he saved against that time. Every week he saved one dollar. On his one night off, rain or wind, he walked streets of the Near North Side: Erie and Ontario, Huron and LaSalle and Cass.

When he rose from his dressing-room cot at seven he built a fire in the boiler-room downstairs, dusted backstage, dusted the seats and swept down the aisle, and mopped the stage with warm water and suds. At nine o'clock he put out the signs, and the pictures of black and white dancing girls.

During the day he built up the fire before each performance. The boiler-room had never been cleaned. Years before the building had housed the Helping Hand mission, and there still hovered above the ashes in the basement something of a dim religious light. Ashes had been piled to the ceiling in every corner; on wet days the sewer backed swirlingly into the middle of the floor and spread to the corners and seeped down the walls. Bedraggled gray rats would be left lying belly-up in front of the furnace grate when it receded. Cass would toss them by their tails into one common burying ground, in ashes. Sometimes as he groped for the llght halfway down the rickety staircase there would come a swift scampering from below; then he would know some rats had survived the last rain. Sometimes the globe burned out, and he felt a little afraid to go down; but night was cold and fire was low, and he had to go down. He would go stepping high, with a flashlight in his hand.

If the fire smoldered and died in the night he would have to scout through the alleys for kindling in the morning. He would run down deep snow-ruts, his collar upturned, his big feet sometimes tripping over a tin can frozen in ice. Behind some Loomis Street store he would find a crate, usually filled with rotten or frozen fruit; he would dump the fruit out and race back to the show-house, passing waiting milk-wagons as he ran. By eleven o'clock, when Herman walked in in his heavy overcoat, the Little Rialto would be warm, the aisle would be clean, and the stage would be ready for its props. The props were always the same, save for Saturday night. Cass was prop man, janitor, vendor, errand boy, occasional rouster, and, when Herman's throat was sore, barker. He stood in front with the blue megaphone then, in Herman's overcoat. And he bawled like a young bull just freed of the barn.

Often during those first months Cass could not sleep well on his cot in the dressing room. He would wake up thinking himself back in the El Paso County jail; the hardness of the cot and the stuffiness of the room, thick with the odor of stale sweat, made him have this waking-fear often. He would rise in the night and walk the narrow aisle, sick at heart for Norah Egan. He would pace up and down as he had in the bull-pen in County. The dark old stage behind him stood, at three o'clock of a winter's morning, like a dirty-curtained tomb; and each single seat as though death had been sitting there. Each seat, like each bar in a jailhouse tank, stood singly and alone. And even in daylight, when girls perfumed the air, there always remained something of death in the place to one who had seen it deserted at night. At night, after cheap perfume had faded a little, and girls had gone home, and laughter had died, then a death-smell crept into the little house, and Cass would wake up afraid.

Cass sat in the front row and held his head in his hands. Sitting so, he would think of Norah Egan, of her life and of his own. Sometimes he felt that they had both been robbed, some way, and he did not understand quite how. But whenever he thought of one man robbed by another, he thought of somebody in boots. He was an ignorant man. The real world he never saw. Daily he saw suffering and want, but he saw through a veil of familiarity. What he saw he took for granted. He could not trouble himself, one way or another, about any better or happier world. He had become too hardened to pain and to suffering. His heart had become callused. He could see no farther than Herman Hauser. All those faculties which might have enabled Cass to see farther than the end of his nose had been dulled; they had been dulled into atrophy by hunger and cold and frequent humiliation. So Cass had not only gone hungry and cold, but he had been blinded to that which had robbed him. He knew he had been cheated: he had been cheated of Norah Egan. And sometimes it felt as though it were someone behind him who kept cheating him all the time.

He had but one strong desire: he wanted Norah Egan. He wanted to place his life firmly on earth, and he wanted to live it with her.

In the middle of January came a change: Cass had to learn a new line. Instead of carrying chocolate bars and magazines through the aisles, he stood out front and bawled the new line through Herman's blue megaphone.

"Hot peppy burlesque goin' on inside, folks—chase them

blues away! See all the little dancin'—shakin'—singin'—squirmin' laydeez! See 'em do the World's Fair fan dance! See 'em doin' it! See 'em dance on a dime! See 'em do the Gilda Grey! See 'em shake an' see 'em wobble! *Every mussel in movement every minute gennelmen—First she dawnces on one leg an'—*"

It was cold standing outside in the middle of January. Herman bought him a fancy red cardboard hat, high as a hussar's and trimmed with silver braid. It was purchased to rival the hat of the uniformed barker at the sixty-cent burlesque across the street; but it failed to keep Cass's ears warm. He wore his yellow slicker, and for gloves he borrowed the huge dangling things that Dill Doak wore on the stage. These he always had to return before Doak went on, however, and Herman never liked to see him run inside to return them. So when he saw that the barking job was fairly permanent, Cass bought himself a pair of mittens. He spent little, and only when forced to do so. He was saving for Norah, a dollar a week.

He became proud of his big blue megaphone, of his line, of his gloves and, most of all, of his fancy red cardboard hat. After he had conquered an early diffidence, he became proud of his barking, too. Full of self-import, he strode up and down. Oppressed with his responsibility, he marched back and forth in front of the ticket cage, the January snow flaking the front of his slicker. Herman liked his bullish voice. He taught Cass to drop much of his Southern accent, and let him bawl away.

After the months spent in selling inside, Cass was glad to get out on the open street. The pounding of the great drum inside, the shrill singing from the stage, and the hard laughter from the seats came to him but faintly where he now stood. He was glad not to hear it, he was happy to be free of the faces inside; here there was more to see and to hear. From where he now stood he could see the whole street. And sometimes as he barked, watching faces thronging past, he would think suddenly, "Norah will come past! Ah'll see Norah again!"

Once, just as he was turning his head to speak of some triviality to the blonde in the ticket-cage, he caught a glimpse of a passing face that sent his heart into his throat. For a long moment he stood half-dazed, his megaphone dangling from his hand and his eyes staring after a slender girl walking slowly. He lurched awkwardly up to her, caught her sleeve—and his heart sank like a sudden sock in his breast. The camel in the ticket-cage stared at him in amazement, but he was too shaken to explain.

"Step right up, gennelmen," he bawled. "When yore three feet inside the door yore six thousand miles from home—See all the little dawncin' girruls—See 'em shake that thing, see 'em squirm, hear 'em sing—Hottest show off the World's Fair grounds.—Don't come in here, boys, it ain't decent—Somethin' special fo' gennelmen oney inside, an' every seat is a dime until the show closes! See 'em shake that thing! See 'em squirm! Hear 'em sing!"

PART FOUR

One Spring in this City

In place of the old bourgeois society, with its classes and class antagonisms, we shall have an association, in which the free development of each is the condition for the free development of all.

THE COMMUNIST MANIFESTO

16

"You don't have to building fire any more," Herman Hauser said in the first warm week in May, "so now you're getting five bucks per—O.K. by you, Red?"

Cass protested feebly.

"Five bucks ain't much fo' a man, Mist' Hauser. Barker 'cross the way gits twelve an' a half."

Herman eyed the uniformed fellow at the sixty-cent burlesque across the street. Through a maze of traffic the springtime street-steam was rising from between street-stones.

"That guy is taller than you by an inch an' a half. An' he can't sleep backstage like I let you doing, either, I bet. I save you room-rent every week—don't you realizing?"

Cass realized. He realized too that in a dozen places he could rent a room for four and a half dollars a month.

"Ah'd rather keep on gittin' mah reg'lar six bucks per then an' not sleep backstage no more," he said, sensing Herman's chronic distrust of him.

"Well then, I been thinkin' I would rather not have you sleeping backstage any more then, either," Herman parried. "There is already too much sleeping back there with those niggers."

He laughed at his wit, so Cass laughed with him.

So it was in that spring that Cass came to have a room of his own. It was not very clean, it was not very large, it had but one chair, and its window was small; it was smelly, and dark, and at night it was damp. A poor thing in all—but his own.

And it was on East Ontario, overlooking State.

This was the second World's Fair spring in the big town by the lake. Cass had been renting a room for a week when the exposition reopened. On the opening afternoon, while a mayor was standing atop a platform in the midst of the shambles, Cass was pacing up and down in front of the Little Rialto three blocks away, barking; and listening to a mayor's voice reproduced through a street-radio over his head as he barked.

> *This is an event to be remembered as the climax of man's ideals. There is not a business which will not profit by this epochal event. The bettering of economic conditions will increase our attendance. An historic milestone on our national journey toward greater and finer and better things for our people.*

But Cass McKay could drown out any street-radio, and he resented any rivalry, even a mayor's.

> *Here y'are gents—hottest woman-show off the grounds, first she dawnces on one leg an' then she dawnces on the other— Oh she shakes like jello on a frosty mornin'? Between the two she earns her livin'! All she wears is sleeves an' two beads o'perspiration, —if y' can't see through them yore too old to come in here, Stella the little dawncin' girrul!*

World's Fair spring in the big town by the lake. Over on Michigan Avenue the people were going in one gate and the people were coming out of another; and inside the gates was chaos. Nude dancers, wind-tunnels, Indians, Byrd's South-Pole ship. Dante's Inferno, Miss America, alligator-wrestlers, Lincoln's cabin, flame-divers, a five-legged cow beside the House of David, *pigs ships temples villages gorillas clocks artillery cats dogs camps*—a zigzag riot of fakery, a hash of hot-dog stands and shimmy shows lapped by the lake. There were college-trained men pulling jinrikishas past gyp gambling joints, there were hundreds of Negroes scraping for tips, there were cane-sellers, peep-show houses, prostitutes, trinket-vendors, dinosaurs, punch-drunk pugs, a proboscis monkey . . . and a mayor, on top of a platform. He was standing right on the very top of the platform, in the very center of the nightmare, and he was bawling a line for Big Business.

Cass stopped pacing and cocked his head, listening hard as he was able; and he heard a president's voice.

The most critical days of the national emergency have for the most part passed. I am fully convinced that this exposition will create a demand for the latest products of science and industry. I am fully convinced that this exposition will aid in the strengthening of national morale. I am fully convinced . . .

"She got the stuff that makes the young men old an' the old men young!" Cass roared in challenge. "Yo' can put ever'thin' she wears on a letter behind a two-cent stamp! If y'aint been in here y've led a sheltered life!"

The millions who visited the exposition of 1933 must have seen in it, as I did, an inspiring demonstration of courage and confidence. Those who will come to the exposition of

1934 will see how abundantly that courage and that con-
fidence were justified. They will see evidence of the recovery
that has been brought about. They will see signs pointing the
way along that upward path upon which we as a nation
have set our feet. I am fully convinced . . .

That night ten thousand kids in Tenement Town were sleeping when it rained. When it rains in Tenement Town sewers back
up into basement Hats. AH over the World's Fair City, World's
Fair spring or World's Fair summer, ten thousand kids slept in
homes damp as kennels. Ten thousand kids didn't have enough
to eat. The World's Fair playground was a city of ten thousand
hungry half-sick kids searching the alleys of Tenement Town, a
welter of diseased slum-streets. Sick kids sold papers, sniped tin-
foil out of gutters, shot crap in hallways. Sick kids all over the
World's Fair City, all through the World's Fair spring. No room
to toss a ball around on these streets; these kids didn't race on
Tribute bicycles or *Daily News* roller-skates. No room for bikes in
Tenement Town; no time for roller-skates or ball. But room for
selling papers, room for shining shoes, time for working all day in
N. R. A. sweat-shops.

The Polock kids chased the Dagoes and the Dagoes chased
the Jews. The Wops slunk behind fences on either side of the
Loomis Street alleys and slung milk bottles over at each other's
heads. They're half sick from birth, so they grow up bad. Black
kids, Wop kids, Swede kids, Hunkey, Litvak and Chinese kids—
the skinny tough dirty knockabout kids that had to knock down a
fence to get into the World's Fair playground.

Or look at the Irish around the old gas house, around the
fourteenth ward. A hard-working tribe that is, when sober.

Contractors, steel-workers, truck-drivers, ward-heelers, mailmen, and cops, and two-bit politicians. Only there isn't much contracting being done just now, and the steel-workers are talking strike again, and the city is behind with the cops' and the mailmen's pay again, and the two-bit politicians are playing the races, and some of the truck-drivers are scabbing to pay the rent; and some of the ward-heelers are learning to pimp. The high-school kids from '31 and '32 and '33 and '34 are still waiting for work, any kind of work. They booze while waiting. Their old men booze too. The ex-contractors and the ex-cabbies and the ex-truck-drivers, the Dagoes and Hunkeys and Polocks and Jews.

Look at Young Finnegan this spring, now that the World's Fair springs have passed. He'll be eighteen in August, if he lives that long. Gets six dollars every Saturday night for fighting at White City if he wins in six rounds. Otherwise he gets only four. Fin earns his suppers during the week by pimping for the house on Twenty-second and Wabash. Finnegan's big sister works upstairs, that's how Fin got the job. Mamie's up there now with five other girls, and that's how the Finnegans get along. Finnegan'd like to go home, he'd like to take Mamie home with him, only he can't. When Fin's old man started throwing D.T.s at two o'clock in the morning Fin's old lady leaned out of the window yelling bloody murder. The old man, and he hasn't worked since '29, started after her with a bottle of Hill and Hill in one hand and a six-inch can-opener in the other—Finnegan tossed the old fool downstairs on his fanny before somebody got hurt. So what? So the old man bounced all the way down on the fanny, two steps at a time, and when he hit bottom the Hill and Hill broke, and something inside the fanny broke too; he couldn't get up, and he couldn't lie down. So he sits up on top of three pillows all day now with a steel brace beneath him, a bottle of Hill and Hill on the medicine stand beside him, and a brickbat across his feet. He's waiting for Finnegan to open the door, and he won't let Mamie in either. Because Mamie would steal his watch and drink up his Hill and Hill and fight with the old lady and spit out the window.

But they all booze, they all fight, and there are a thousand Finnegans. With so many dollar-women there couldn't be less. Even a mayor has to pimp a little now and then to make ends meet: for the Chrysler outfit, or Standard Oil, or any other big-business scurve who has the money to pay. You understand. That's what the mayor was doing over on that platform three blocks east. That's what he was doing there all the time he was talking. Pimping for the old whore called Chicago Business, painting her up for her last big Saturday night. Sure the mayor's a pimp: a pimp for Big Business. Ask the city-hall bunch, they'll tell you things.

"There is not a business which will not profit by this colossal event. There is not a business . . . profit . . . colossal event . . ."

Sometimes visitors to the Fair saw puzzling incidents on the way back to their hotels. Late at night, after a day spent on the grounds, they saw old men, like unclaimed curs with tentative claws, pawing in garbage barrels or ash cans; or they heard voices of children begging from some unlit doorway. The *Tribune* had nothing to say of this, for the *Tribune* was owned by the pure-in-heart, and the pure-in-heart averted their eyes. They were good Christian editors proud of their paper, of the greed-inspired lies and the sweet christfablings and the star-spangled spew that they termed "editorials." They were proud of their souls, for their souls were clean; and proud of their churches, for their churches were large; and proud of their schools, for their schools taught conformity; but proudest by far were they of their Fair, their great

Century-of-Progress slut stretched out on a six-mile bed along the lake with Buicks for breasts and a mayor standing up to his neck in her navel making a squib-like noise.

(Be pure in your hearts, be proud yet a little while, wave your flags, sing your hymns, close your eyes, save your souls, go on grabbing. Get all you can while yet you may. For the red day will come for your kind, be assured.)

The women who walked the World's Fair streets lived with two dark fears: the fear of disease, and the fear of police. Of these the latter was often the larger, for illness gives warning where police do not. And the police beat the women as well as the men; the police-women beat them.

Fear of hunger, fear of cold, fear of blows, fear of men; fear of health officers, fear of jail, fear of hospitals, fear of sudden raids in the night. "But *say*—ain't the enchanted eye-lund pertier this year than last, dearie?" Around the World's Fair grounds that spring prostitutes walked the streets all night. From all over the stricken land they came, in the wake of the great exposition of progress. (Flies to the dungheap, women to the Fair, and the star-spangled banner will make a soft wipe-rag soon.) Of these women and girls there were some few who secured employment on the Fair grounds as waitresses, as "sticks" for gyp gambling joints, or as dancers in peep-show houses. But these were only the few and the highly fortunate. Others spent their days in Grant Park lying about among old men and boys, like men mooching nickels and dimes down South State, like men sleeping in louse-ridden charity flops when a night was cold or rainy. Thus there sprang up a jungle in the depths of Chicago's rumbling gut, a charnel-dump next to Donnybrook Fair; the city fathers could not heal this condition, howsoever they tried. Their jails were already overcrowded with petty-larceny thieves, vagrants and beggars. When a few were driven off or jailed the ranks were shortly replenished with new hordes of incoming transients; there was little to do but to let them stay and pretend in the papers that they were not there. Yet these were women who might have been mothers, and these were men who might have been men. Over their heads as they lay in the grass nightly a red, white, and blue sign flashed above them:

A CENTURY OF PROGRESS. BIGGER AND BETTER THAN EVER.

One Sam Philips, black as ink and Alabama-born, was in Chicago only two days when he got picked up on South Prairie Avenue by Sergeant M—— of the South Park Police. Sure the boy looked suspicious—he was in rags, and had no place to sleep, and he was a nigger. So what? So M—— says, "Run, eight-ball, or I'll put you in for vag." Sam Philips didn't know very much, he'd only been in town two days. But Sam did know that he didn't like jails, and that he could run pretty fast all right. "Two hundred yards I'll give you," the sergeant offered—and black Sammy Philips just took it on the lam. He ran twenty feet; M—— dropped to one knee in the proper manner and let her flicker, one through the legs and five through the belly—but he got his promotion, so I guess it's all right.

Bill Becker got married in '26. One kid. Two kids. Bill's wife's name was Katy, her folks didn't like William. Three kids. Four kids. And sure enough, in the week that Cermak was shot in Miami, Bill lost his job at the Western Electric. Eighteen months later, on the day that President Roosevelt asked a microphone, "Aren't you better off this year than last?" Bill went into the bathroom and opened both wrists with Katy's best sewing scissors. "Look, Katy hon," Bill woke her at three in the morning and turned on the light so that she could see better, "Look, hon—now why don't you do it too?" Katy said afterwhile she didn't blame him a bit, it was all mother's fault, Bill had always been good to her.

When the Italian girl came up the steps the woman in white said she didn't remember. "I come for the job you promised last fall. Papa says I can take it now. I'm almost nineteen now you know, so I guess I can take it now all right." The woman in white could tell sixteen and a half at a glance, but the girl did look like she could take it all right. "O.K., dearie, hang the old skirt there. Keep the foot-pad straight and get two bits for the towel. Put the dough in your slipper, don't take off your apron till you got your money, and when the big bell rings get out through the back. Tony'll show you where."

Well, let's forget it. Let's listen to the mayor, that'll make us all feel better. Let's just not look around. Let's just look at the flags and the purple totem-poles and the ritzy red roadsters going straight up and down in the Nash tower on the boulevard. Let's listen to old Sam Insull telling how much he loves his country, or to Charley Dawes how much he loves it too. Well, old Sam can start all over now, and Charley can keep right on goin'. You know, for a while there some of us thought Sam Insull had really done something wrong in using the mails that way, but of course we just didn't know. We know now that he didn't do anything wrong at all, that he had our country's best interests at heart all the while. We know now, since the courts freed them both, that Sam and Martin aren't just two smart fellows who took so much that lots of other smart people felt that Sam should have a little help. No, really, Sam ran off to Turkey because he likes Turks.

Cass McKay barked beneath a World's Fair banner all that spring and summer. One evening he went to the Fair. He went because it was his evening off, and because Dill Doak asked him to go.

Dill Doak was an unusual Negro in several respects. He never spoke to a white man with servility, and he could not be patronized. He addressed Herman simply as "Hauser," and Herman called him "Doak." He was a far shrewder showman than Herman, and Herman knew this well. But that Dill was anything more than a shrewd showman Cass had not known. It was not until after he had spoken a number of times with Dill that Cass began to realize that Dill was somehow wiser than himself. He read much. Often Cass saw him backstage between performances, seated on a prop, brooding over the foreign-news page of a daily paper. Cass could not understand a Negro who became heated over a war being fought in South America. Daily he sought to prove to Cass, with newspaper clippings, that in South America the United States was at war with England "by proxy." Cass didn't know what "by proxy" meant; but nevertheless he listened to Doak, and sometimes read the clippings. Cass felt a need of companionship that was almost like a hunger; inwardly he was grateful to Doak even for speaking to him. This, however, Cass would never have admitted to himself. On the evening that Dill proposed walking over to the Fair it did not occur to him to refuse to go because Dill was a Negro. When white men gave him a passing glance as they passed down the street together Cass had a tug of conscience, which he allayed by assuring himself that "Dill ain't jest a plain every-day nigger. Even Herman has to do what Dill says sometimes."

That evening at the Fair remained in Cass's mind as one of

the most chaotic of his memories. Later on he recalled only a topsy-turvy confusion of color and sound: houses, radios, lights, smells, voices.

"Holy sneakin'-Moses," he exclaimed as soon as they were inside, "ain't this somethin' *bee-yootiful?*"

"Looks all kind of mixed up though a little, don't it?" Dill asked doubtfully.

For the first time since he had come out of County, Cass forgot himself for a few minutes.

> *Sally Rand*
> *Lost her fan,*
> *Give it back,*
> *You nasty man.*

Dill sang.

But that evening ended abruptly, as others of his evenings had. They came to a concession where three Negroes were perched in cages; for ten cents anyone could hurl a baseball at them. If the ball struck the proper mark the Negro was automatically dumped into a tub of water beneath the perch. Dill walked by without stopping. Cass paused, and had to walk fast then to catch up to Dill. A few minutes later Dill said he wished to leave. Cass was still eager for sights, but his companion's sudden lack of enthusiasm dampened his own spirits. After they were out on the street once more Dill seemed reluctant to converse. But Cass chatted on about everything that came into his head.

Cass fancied himself an unusual fellow, because he was from Texas and had been in jails; he sought to impress the fact of Cass McKay's uniqueness in the world upon Dill.

"Ah've sho' seen a heap o' these United States in mah time," he boasted. "Have a cig'rette, Dill? Yeah, ah've been inside more jail-houses than ah got toes, ah reck'n—Oney don't never tell Herman 'bout that, ah never mention jail to him. Jest the same, in mah time ah carried a rod. Y'all didn't know that, did yo', Dill?"

Dill hadn't known. Cass whispered confidentially: "Real reason y'all see me standin' out front every day is to keep crooks from hoppin' the ticket-cage. That's what Herman hired me for in the first place, y' know. That megyphone is oney a blind. Herman don't care if ah *never* bark, jest so long as ah don't go strollin' away an' give that John Dillinger a chanst at the ticket-box. *That's* what Herman's payin' me ten bucks every week fo'."

Cass fancied too, since he was white and Dill black, that Dill must be a little flattered at his company. Dill would sometimes come out of the show just as Cass was bringing in the signs for the night, and then Cass would call out, "O.K., Mist' Hauser, if ah leave now?" Herman would usually nod, and Cass would be released. He would have Dill's company for two blocks, up to Van Buren. On that street Dill turned west and Cass continued north.

In their brief walks they spoke of many things. Once Cass said, "Noo Awlins—that's mah town. Lots of life, lots of pep, an' that's what ah go for. Ah kin have a bigger time on six bits down there than ah can on two bucks up here."

Dill became angry that time, so that Cass never mentioned New Orleans to him again.

"New Orleans," Dill answered, "is a sewer. The South is a sink, and cities like that are its sewers. The South is rotting. Wherever you go, in any large city, there are thousands of stalls with women and girls in them," he glared accusingly at Cass, and it was in that glare that Cass read his anger—"Don't you think it's a sign of decay when women can be *bought?*"

Cass said, "Course it ain't *right*, Dill. But it's that way *all* over, North an' South. An' ah reck'n there al'ays was stalls everywhere an' likely al'ays will be."

Dill spoke confidently. "It hasn't always been, and it won't always be, and it isn't all over. In Russia this is already a thing of the past. We must change the order of things here too."

Cass did not know whom Dill meant by "we," and he lacked the curiosity to ask. He was thinking of Norah Egan, and he was growing sicker every minute.

"Ah wish ah hadn't spoke so to sister that time," he said to himself.

Back in his Ontario Street room that night he stood looking down at the street betow. The lake wind was whisking papers along the dark curbs. A policeman passed twirling a nightstick, and a streetcar crept like a cat down State. And as he stood so an old memory returned: he seemed to smell, faintly and far off, the odor of burning punk, and to see again white sunlight across a dusty road. And then the bitter face of his brother tooking down.

"Nothin' but lies they told. An' they won't speak truth to you-all neither."

That was true, of course, he knew now. People atways lied, he had learned that. They lied to get even, or they lied to live. Almost everyone had to lie, one way or another, just to live. For someone kept cheating all the time, you had to cheat back or be robbed. As Bryan had been robbed. As Nancy and his father and Norah Egan and himself had been robbed.

There was someone who cheated, and all men were robbed.

•

On one of the first warm evenings in June Cass went with Dill Doak to a gathering of white and Negro workers in Washington Park. Riding South on a State Street car, Dill spoke to Cass of his own people. He disliked Negro ministers, he said, because they preached humbleness to his race.

"These ministers use religion to *stabilize* things—and things are so rotten they ought to be dumped in the nearest garbage-can, 'stead of bein' perfumed. To hell with humility, meekness—I believe in *fightin'*."

Cass remembered a little of the Negro's lot in the South, and he understood something of Dill's resentment. Down South, he remembered, it was always as though the black folk were thinking quietly to themselves, but saying nothing. He remembered Negroes speaking among themselves on boxcars and becoming suddenly silent at the approach of any white. Sometimes Cass had had the feeling that Negroes, everywhere, were listening to some strange new thought, sometimes half-unwittingly, sometimes eagerly. They were hearing strange words, yet half-feared to look where the speaker stood. With eyes straight ahead, they feigned for a white not to see, not to hear. Yet the whispers persisted, always true, always counseling; and in the end, they knew, they must listen.

When they reached the park it was night. The trees stood bowed over two thousand human heads, and above the trees slant flood-beams spilled. The heads were black or the heads were white; flood-beams lit fair hair or hair that was kinky. It was night in the park, and these were the people. Overalled workers, with wives looking worn, formed a great listening circle on the grass. Behind them, on benches, sat a thousand more; behind the benches workers stood ten deep. And all eyes were on a platform built among the trees from which a Negro was speaking.

Cass and Dill spread their coats on the grass and leaned back, listening. Cass cocked his head a little to the side to hear better. The speaker was saying that he was sixty-eight years old, and that he was the son of a slave. So, too, had he been a slave, he said, for he too had worked all his life for nothing. Into the world with empty hands his father before him had come; with empty hands he had died. So too had himself come, so too would he soon die. He had nothing left but his children now, and these he did not wish to live and die as his father and himself had lived and died. Bosses, black and white, had stripped him of all he had earned in a lifetime of toil, he said.

"Even the old must revolt! Join hands with white workers in the fight for unemployment insurance—forget them little ministers who tell you 'be humble,' 'be humble.'"

Cass heard the crash of applause about him like a sudden hailstorm through the trees. Dill's big hands seemed bent on breaking themselves against each other. Then fists shot upward into light—black fists, white, and brown—and everyone was standing up and singing. Cass did not quite understand all this.

After the singing and hand-clapping had died a young white man came to the platform. He spoke in a quiet, well-modulated voice, and said that he too believed in revolution . . . so long as it was bloodless.

"I believe in that bloodless revolution which for almost three years now has been swinging the country steadily toward permanent recovery. There is no need of bloodshed . . ."

"What of San Francisco?" someone up near the speaker shouted, "What about Minneapolis?"

The speaker answered glibly. "Unavoidable," he said, and a low booing began before he could say more. The booing persisted until the speaker held up his hand in a plea for silence. Then he invited anyone who disagreed with him to come up to the platform if they wished to refute him. A young Negro girl passed through the light and stepped onto the stage. The speaker assisted her up and stepped aside. The girl spoke briefly.

"Ah've worked in sweatshops since ah been twelve," she said in a high firm voice. "Since ah been twelve ah've worked in 'em, an' that's eight whole years. Ah nevah got a chance to go much to school because of 'em, so ah nevah learned to use big words"—she glanced at the white man standing beside her. "Ah nevah went much to school, but ah did learn one thing this gen'elmen here *nevah* did," she paused for breath and went on "—*What's good fo' the bosses ain't no good fo' us!*"

Cass thought the applause then would never end, and he was puzzled to know why the girl's simple assertion should have provoked such wild cheering. It was minutes before the white speaker could begin again. After he had finished, the chairman, a Negro, leaned over the railing of the platform and scolded the crowd roundly for their discourtesy.

Other speakers followed. Cass was bored. Some spoke of charity beans, of overcrowded conditions in shelters, some of evictions, and some of families that had to live in damp basements. One told how the Republican party, by chicanery and bribes and hypocritical promises, had gained control of the black vote in Chicago, and then had sold the black people out. Another spoke of the muddle-headedness of the Garveyites, Negroes who had a scheme to take the black race back to Africa.

"Africa or America," this speaker declared, "it doesn't matter where the Negro lives, he will be exploited in one place just as thoroughly as in another; he will be exploited till the day when the workers of the world take over their earth."

An elderly Irish woman described the wretched shanties for which workers were forced to pay high rents. A young Jewish girl spoke of the discrimination against both Negroes and Jews at employment agencies, in schools, at bathing beaches, and told of the methods used by police to crush protest.

Cass wished to leave now, but Doak was rapt in the speakers' words.

A short stocky Negro took the platform and called for a vote of protest against the legal lynching of the nine Negro boys framed in Alabama on a rape charge. He explained how the lives of these innocent boys could be saved only by a mass protest of workers. The Southern white ruling class were determined that the nine should die, in order "to set an example" to the Negro masses of the South. He then proposed the motion of protest, and the audience endorsed it with renewed cheering.

Cass rose. "Let's go, Dill," he said. "They talk sech lawng words that it don't all make sense."

Nevertheless, Cass went again several times to the Washington Park forums. At heart he would rather have got dead drunk on his evening off; he would have enjoyed that more than sitting on the grass with Dill, listening to something he did not understand. But it wasn't much fun getting drunk alone, and it cost too much anyhow. And he feared to be drunk, lest it mean six months making brick in the bridewell for him because of his past record. Dill seemed to be the only man now who had time for him, and Dill wouldn't drink. So Cass went to the park for want of something more interesting to do. Often he wished that he had Nubby O'Neill or Olin Jones for a friend once more.

"Me an' Nub was sure two tough boys for any bulls to handle," he assured himself in his loneliest moments.

He left the show each night at one, walked with Dill north to Van Buren, and then continued north alone, to Ontario. Usually he was back in his room by twenty minutes after one.

He enjoyed this brief walk, after the long day. At one A.M. streets were still and air was purged of thronging thousands. From twelve to twelve he barked until his throat hurt; from twelve to twelve the Little Rialto rang with laughter and stank with the odor of unwashed men. Before the day began once more Cass had this quiet walking-time of release. It gave him a few minutes to gather himself, to breathe deeply, and to wonder whether he would ever see Norah Egan again.

One night he was crossing State just north of Erie when a woman called from close behind him.

"What a second there, Red. I got to talk somethin' to you." Cass's heart leaped like a fountain—but when he heard the voice again he knew it was not Norah's. He stopped in the middle of the track to look back, and he saw a woman's form dimly outlined in a doorway.

"You callin' *me?*" he asked.

"Yeah. Come on over here. I got to talk to you somethin'."

"If y'all want talk with me come over here an' say it."

There was only a low tittering for reply; he turned to go. But before he had reached the opposite curb the woman spoke again.

"Aw say now, don't go runnin' off on me like that. I'll bet you worked real hard today in the little nigger showhouse, didn't you, Red?"

She giggled, and repeated, "Didn't you, Red?"

"One of Herman's girls drunk," Cass thought, "How'd she get 'way up here ah wonder."

"Is that you, Ruby?" he asked, naming one of Herman's white choristers.

She didn't reply, so he crossed over and asked, "Y'all want ah should see yo' home, Ruby?" He stood under a lamplight, peering into night-dark.

The voice from the doorway became suddenly impatient.

"Oh, fer god's sake, hon, don't stand there gawpin' like you don't know what it's all about. You ain't *scared* of girls, are you?"

Cass stepped out of the light. His curiosity was aroused. But no more than his curiosity. He took two steps toward her, paused and said, "No, ah ain't scared of girls, but ah ain't, . . ." and a fist like steel smashed across his nose, fist-steel hit him twice below the heart. Cass threw up his hands in panic-defense—and then he was flat on his back in the doorway, and the hand on his mouth was a stump of a hand, and a face grinning down was Nubby O'Neill's.

For one moment Cass thought that Nubby was going to cut his throat in that doorway.

"Didn't think I was still around, did you, son?"

Cass could do nothing but writhe helplessly. He was so shaken by fear and shock that he did not hear Nubby's words clearly. Not until after a full minute had passed did he realize that Nubby was not hitting him. Nubby was only laughing low above him, and the girl, whoever she'd been, was gone.

"Ah'm terrible sorry, Judge," Cass pleaded, "Honest to Jesus, Nub, ah didn't mean harm that time. Jesus strike me dead ah didn't. Ah been huntin' all over town for y'all, Judge, every day ever since—Honest to Jesus Christ in Heaven above so help me God—ah'll pay y'all the dough—every cent—int'rest—ah never spent a dime of it—oh let me up, Nub."

Nubby cracked him across the mouth with his stump for answer.

"Goddamn yer dirty dollars, anyhow. There's nothin' tight about me, son, an' never was. Is money all you *ever* think of, Red, just *money?* And did I ask you fer any? Did I say I was after you fer a couple measly bucks? Why, goddamn you, I got more in my poke right this minute than you'll ever see in all yer life if ya live a hundred years."

"Ah guess y'all didn't shoot that cop after all, did yo', Nub?" Cass asked.

Nubby cracked him across the teeth with the stump again. His teeth rattled with the blow. Cass whined, "Why y'all do that, Nub, if yo' don't care about the dough? What yo' sore about, Judge? Couldn't y'all let me jest set up a spell, if yore not really sore?"

"You stay down an' I'll tell ya why I'm sore. Because yer a trayter is why I'm sore. I'm so sore I might do somethin' terrible 'most any minute now, so don't get me no sorer. Five times in two weeks now I seen ya walkin' with a nigger so black he looks like a rain-cloud comin' down the street. How come you doin' me this way, son? How come you ferget how I slap hell out o' you once fer messin' with them ugly black sons-a-bitches? You fergit 'most everythin' a body tries to learn ya, don't ya?"

He grazed Cass's nose, already battered, with his stump; it didn't hurt so much this time, but it was frightening.

"Why goddamn it, son, yer a downright dis-grace to me— that's what it's cornin' down to. Why, I cried almost when I first seen ya doin' me that way, after all I learned ya. Oh I've tried so *damned* hard, son. An' this is how—you—do me—"

His voice caught. He was on the verge of tears, Cass felt.

"Ah'm right sorry, Judge," Cass repeated earnestly, beginning slowly now to realize his error with Dill. "Ah won't do y'all that way no more. Ah guess ah jes' forgot how bad them niggers could be."

Nubby rose then, cautiously. Cass brushed the dust of the

doorway off his trousers, and began to feel a little glad that he'd found Nub again. Nubby turned him around and brushed dirt off the back of his coat.

"Nice coat yer wearin', son," he commented.

Cass said, "Yeah—an' y'all are still wearin' them boots, even up here, aint yo', Nub?" He laughed nervously. Good ol' Nub. He sure must have plugged that cop all right.

"Come on down to the corner, son, an' I'll buy you a beer. You don't deserve it hardly, but I just like you so much I got to do you somethin' after lickin' you like that. An' I could have licked you bad, I guess ya know. Only I didn't—I just let ya go."

Cass hesitated then, taking over-long to finish the brushing of his cap.

"I got to talk to ya, son," and Nubby took his arm. "I like you all right, son. I ain't sore about nothin'."

Over a stein of beer at the corner tavern Nubby said, "I've gone pretty straight, son. I ran into Elmer one day last winter, an' he got such a good job now, runnin' a elevator somewheres, that I've went straight."

Nubby paused, to shut one eye and probe Cass with the other. "Haven't *you*, son?"

Cass said, "Yeah, ah reck'n so."

Cass never walked with Dill Doak again. The Washington Park forums became the merest fly-speck in his memory. And Nubby came past the show-house, with a wave of the hand, almost every night. On Cass's evening off they drank together. When Nubby drank too heavily he siept on Cass's cot, in Cass's room, and Cass siept on the door. Cass was careful not to get too drunk.

•

In the first week of November Cass saw Norah Egan. She was stepping off a curb in a streetlamp's glow, he caught the dash of her blue coat slantwise through traffic. A light blue coat, a street-lamp's glow—and a streetcar clanged in between. Cass heard his heart begin storming in his throat. The car wobbled its rump with gathered speed, clanging as it wobbled—to leave him standing in the middle of South State with Norah in his arms. And her eyes so wide with fear or surprise that he could not even bend to kiss her.

"I seen you comin', Red," she said, and she took one small step back. Cass waited for her eyes to lose their fear. They were looking up at him as they had in their earilest hours together, with a wild fear of being struck.

"They sprang me, hon," was all he could think to say; and then he could only stand and say nothing at all, with a sickly grin smeared over half of his face and both his hands holding hers.

An auto curvetted past, blasting horn-wrath at them.

"I seen you comin', Red. Only I didn't know it was you. What you got on your head anyhow?" She spoke hoarsely and then looked down at her palms, imprisoned in his. But when she looked up she smiled a little, so he stooped to kiss her then.

"It's a show-hat ah got on mah head," he said proudly.

"Kissin' on the mouth ain't healthy, Red," she cautioned, and her voice sounded small and wan. She spoke without emotion, with a weak half-smile. Cass took her hand and took off his hat. He led her across the street.

"Ah'm the big shot here," he said, waving the hat toward the Little Rialto. "This is where ah work, Blondie, an' that there is mah boss. Ah work here. This's Mist' Hauser." He took the trumpet from Herman. Norah gave Herman a sidelong glance, and leaned against the ticket-cage. "How you doin' in there, hon?" she asked the bobbed-haired camel within. Herman Hauser coughed into an unclean handkerchief; he looked once at Norah, and once at Cass, and then at the camel in the ticket-cage. Cass strode up and down in long coltish strides, the horn at his mouth.

"See the World's Fair bubble dance, boys! See the hottest girl-show off the grounds! Last show about to begin!"

When he noticed that Norah was speaking to the ticket-taker instead of watching him admiringly, he stopped and went to her. He put his arm about her waist, and he grinned over at Herman. Herman was folding a handkerchief carefully, preparatory to placing it in his left-hand hip pocket.

"See, Mist' Hauser, ah found Blondie again."

Herman remained absorbed in the handkerchief's folds, and Norah wriggled free.

"You shouldn't never walk off right in the middle like that," Herman said at last. "Not for noting you shouldn't walk off." And Norah said, "Don't, hon," wriggling free.

Herman placed the handkerchief in the pocket.

"You should be acquainted by this time how bad for business is women standing leaning in front. Fined I could even be getting."

He shook his head sadly. "Did you say *'wife'?*" he asked sternly.

Six dollars a week was pretty much.

"I guess I'd better be runnin' along now," Norah offered.

Cass held her hand, not quite understanding.

"Y'all wait inside for me," he said.

Herman turned away as though in disgust. When he reached the door he spoke over his shoulder.

"Tickets is ten cents, Red," he said.

But he didn't even like it at ten cents, Cass could tell. He let Norah's hand go, and he went to the ticket-cage. She restrained his hand when he reached for his change.

"Ain't you *sore*, Red?" she asked, looking close.

He always had been a queer customer. You never could tell what he really wanted, and what he might be going to do next.

He shook his head, handed her the ticket. No, he wasn't sore. He just wanted her to go inside and wait.

"I got a room down the street. We'll go up when I'm through, an' we'll talk."

She looked close and then stepped back, just an inch; and she didn't take the ticket.

Cass cocked his head to the side and looked down; he saw her eyes widen, and he saw her fear returning. He spoke slowly. "Ah swear to Christ ah ain't sore, Norah. Don't look so scared, hon. Why—ah ain't been sore one single second even. Ah been workin' an' savin' an' layin' by, the whole time. We'll get *married*, hon."

He broke off, and she laughed a little. She caught it, of course, when he said that.

He'd marry her all right. He'd get her alone up in that room and slap the *soopreme* hell out of her, that's how he'd marry her. She knew. She knew them all. They all tried a trick or two to get even, and they never forgot when once they got trimmed. If once you slipped over a fast one, by thinking faster, they'd get even if they had to bust a gut to get even. If it took two years to do it, they'd get their own back.

"I don't want to get married yet," she said, "I got another date. But I'll come by an' see you sometime, an' then we'll talk."

She twisted one hand free. The camel in the ticket-cage tapped on the window. "You're lettin' customers go by,' she warned.

"Come in here, Red," Herman called from the door, and Cass took two steps toward him; then Norah started in the other direction, and he turned to follow. She was walking fast, he had to run a few steps to catch up. He took hold of the sleeve of her coat because she wouldn't stop, but kept on going a little faster all the time.

"Why y'all actin' so silly, Blondie? Don't yo' want to get married?" He clutched at his hat to keep it from toppling.

"Nope, I'd rather go it alone, Red, that's what I want. I might get you in trouble. I might—well, you don't need me really, an' you got a big job now—an' I never did need no one y'know."

"But ah do need y'all, Norah. Ah been workin' an' savin' an' puttin' by."

Same old spoosh, same old lunk. And the soft-nasty ones were the meanest.

She was getting out of wind. They had walked almost two blocks, and she had a stitch in her side.

"You don't need me an' I don't need you. Better get back on the job, Red. I got a date. I got a new boyfriend. I'm gonna meet him, I guess."

He drew her into a doorway then, and would not let her go. He saw that she was lying out of fear, and he had to be sure that he knew what she feared. This street where World's Fair flags had flown was cold and empty now. The door of a beer tavern across the street opened and drunken music crashed briefly forth. Cass could see people in there, men and women drinking together, and he heard a child's voice laughing past him; then the laughter was lost.

"I only got twelve bucks out of that drugstore, Red—can y'imagine there wasn't no more'n that?"

"Ah'm not askin' what y'all got," he protested, groping blindly for her fear. "What ah'm askin' is y'all should come back to Herman's till ah'm through, an' then we'll go up to mah place."

That was the third time he'd handed her that. Well, if lying wouldn't get rid of him, then the real thing would.

"I'm sick, Red. Bad sick. You'd catch somethin' from me. I been in Venereal House since May. I ain't right yet."

Both barrels like that she let him have it. He lifted her chin to see her eyes, and he stood for a long while looking down. It took him a while to understand, but he got it after a minute. After a minute, he saw she spoke truth. He shook his head then, and he let her chin go. She thought she'd gotten rid of him then for sure.

Only she hadn't, she'd only thought so.

"It don't really matter none, hon, 'cause y'all could get well again."

He said that funny-like, as though he were swallowing. She looked at him a second, then took his arm.

"All right, Red," she said. "You win. Let's go."

All the way back to the Little Rialto neither spoke. When they got in front of the place and saw Herman barking under the big sign Cass said, "Sit in the back row. It won't be long now till ah'm through. We'll have a drink across the street before we go up to the room."

"I can't drink nothin' but milk these days, hon," she said. She touched her throat with one finger, looking wan. She took the ticket from him and added, "You know, I really thought fer a minute you was sore about somethin'?" As she went through the door the border of her coat caught on the door's corner; she stooped, unhooked it, and was inside. Cass saw Herman walking around the ticket-cage with his eyes on the ground as though he had just dropped something. He encircled the cage twice, picked a penny off the pavement, and glanced up at Cass. Cass stood apologetically, appearing solemnly repentant. "Ah just *haid* to cut out after her when she tried walkin' off, Mist' Hauser,"; he reached for the megaphone, but Herman did not surrender it so easily.

"I got to cutting expenses tonight, Red," he said without a trace of anger in his voice. He raised the trumpet to his mouth, and he barked out into the street:

"Hottest woman-show on South State! See 'em shake that thing! See 'em squirm! Hear 'em sing!"

Cass didn't move until Herman paced away. Then he followed one step behind.

"Y'all mean yo' don't want me to bark no more t'night, Mist' Hauser?"

Herman took the horn from his mouth.

"You come back next winter, Red. You can build the fire for me like you done last winter. Remember?"

"But ah could jest sell mags an' gum still though, huh?"

Herman shook his head and went on barking. Cass followed, up and down, one step behind, back and forth in front of the ticket-cage.

"Could ah sell if ah came back t'morrer night?"

Herman shook his head. He went to the cage, spoke low to the faded blonde within, and draped a five-dollar bill over Cass's left wrist.

That was how Cass understood that his show-job was through. He knew Herman wouldn't do that unless it were through. So he folded the fin neatly, without a word, and hitched up his belt with one hand. Herman said, "Leave the hat, Red. Good luck."

"Ah couldn't keep Blondie right on six a week anyhow," Cass

consoled himself. "Now ah'll get me a good job." He shoved his fists down his pockets to show Herman he didn't care. "S'long, Dutchy," he said. "Here's yore tinny tin hat,"; he flipped the hat carelessly toward its owner.

Norah wasn't in the back row, and she wasn't up front. But backstage the black girls were in a tumult the minute they saw him. "How come you chasin' white gals through here all the time?" they asked in chorus, and the mulatto in the corner threw a slipper at his head. "How come you bust in here when y'ought to be bar-kin'?" the little one called Queenie asked, and then they all laughed together. Dill Doak pointed to the alley-exit. "She walked out that way, Red," he said, "an' she didn't even stop to say she knew me once."

Cass started north up the alley, and then he turned south. At the end of the alley he looked both ways down Harrison, but there was no woman in sight. He fumbled for his cigarettes, and wished that he'd gone the other way.

"Ah reck'n ah'll take out o' this pesthole direc'ly," he told him-self, strolling slow and smoking, swaggering a little from the hips. "Ah been here too long a'ready. Ah had some good ol' times here, an' ah didn't leave much undone. But ah can't even get high in these parts no more without takin' some awful chances. Ah miss mah sotol pretty bad too ah guess. Ah guess ah got too much life in me to hang around one place so long. Ah guess ah ought to be movin' on."

He rested one moment against a billboard advertising some product too indistinct to be clearly discerned now. He flicked his cigarette butt into the street, and he blinked at the street lamps burning all in a row. He looked in each direction down Harrison Street, and he looked both ways down State.

"Ah guess ah shouldn't of said that to sister that time," he said half-aloud.

And he whimpered against the billboard.

All that late November afternoon low clouds hung over the World's Fair city. All that November afternoon the air was still; till the day was like a calm gray evening.

A Polish policeman surveyed the sky from one front window of a southbound Clark Street car. "Too warm yet for snow," he said to the motorman, "looks more like rain to me."

The motorman was old, he did not reply; he just thought to himself: "Rain or snow or mist or sleet—all's one, once they touch the street. What's that? Who spoke? Wife has been dead now for twenty years and here am I still waiting. And it's going to snow. Or rain. Well . . ."

Half a mile to the east, under a green-gray cloud, the lake lay a dark blue curtain stretched smooth and tight to dry. So smoothly, so untroubled did it lie that the fog above it seemed to be flattening out every small wrinkle, ripple, and crease in the dark-blue smooth-tight curtain.

"How warm it is for November," thought men on the streets hurrying home to warm suppers, and some of them said it aloud. "How dark it is for the daytime," they said. "Who can tell, perhaps it will snow tonight?"

Within the houses women looked out of windows the while they cooked under small yellow lights. "How warm it is for November!" they said. "How dark it is for the daytime!" Then they put forks and knives on the cloth, while water ran in the sink. "Perhaps it will rain tonight," someone said over the telephone, "It may perhaps even snow. Who can tell?"

The low-hanging clouds seemed ready to open, all that day.

They looked like fat gray cows trailing single-file: it seemed that the snow they withheld might be warm milk in white udders.

And just as the small streetlights came on, the first flakes began to fall. First three, then four, then many fell.

Beside what had been a World's Fair grounds Cass and Nubby O'Neill came to lounge as the November night came down. Save for the glow of their cigarettes one might not have noticed two men standing in shadow.

"Don't call me 'son' no more, Nub," Cass asked, "Ah'll jest call you 'judge' like before, an' you'll jest call me 'Two-Gun.'"

Nubby spun his cigarette in an arc toward the gutter.

Cass spun his cigarette in an arc toward the gutter.

"Nope," Nubby answered, "I can't do that quite yet. I can't trust you enough now to be givin' out fancy tough names. You got to show me you're a real white man before I start callin' you *anythin'*."

"Ah didn't know no better before, Nub. Ah was jest a dumb kid then."

"Well, I'm tellin' you now then, son, an' for the last time: no *real* white man ever runs off from another to join up with some nigger. You got somethin' to live down with me, son, before I can let you hold a gun of mine again. An' I'd never trust you with a dime again any farther than I could thrun a battleship."

"Ah'm not so afraid-like ah was before, Nub. Ah jest got scared that time. Ah ain't told yo' half what ah done since that butcher shop hoist. Yo' wouldn't believe it all, all ah done since. But if ah told you *some* things ah done ah' bet you'd call me Two-Gun *then* all right."

"Maybe I would an' maybe I wouldn't. An' maybe my heels is gettin' run down again an' I still got too much pride to mooch." He glanced inquiringly at Cass, and Cass cocked his head a bit wist-fully to the side.

"Sometime, Judge, if we come back here together next spring, sometime mebbe when we got a little extry cash on hand—ah—ah—"

"What's eatin' on you son? Spit it out!" Nubby spoke impatiently.

"Well, ah'd like to get me tattooed sometime in that place you said on Van Buren."

Nubby nodded ready assurance.

"O.K. That's the first thing we'll do when we get back next spring. Maybe by that time I'll be callin' you 'Hell-Blazer'—how'd that be, son, eh?" He nudged Cass in the ribs, and Cass blushed faintly.

"That'd be swell if you oney could, Judge," he said. "Ah could even get it tattooed on mah chest then."

He blinked at a street lamp, with flakes falling slantwise past its light. Stoplights down the boulevard flashed from red to green. It was time to be getting on.

Afterword

by Nelson Algren

ANYHOW, THERE WAS a little piece, a little advertisement, and I forget where I saw it. It must have been in some neighborhood newspaper. Maybe it was in the *Saturday Review of Literature.* Maybe some small magazine. Anyhow it said that the Writers' Circle, 3600 Douglas Boulevard, is interested in manuscripts. So when I got back to Chicago I went over to 3600 Douglas Boulevard, which was the Jewish People's Institute, and I went to this little group and the guy named Murray Gitlin—he was the club director there—had a lot of young people in trying to write. He wanted to write himself and he was very friendly. He was a very friendly guy. I didn't have a typewriter at the time and my brother-in-law wouldn't let me use his, but Murray gave me his in his office. We were up in Albany Park then, up on Lawrence Avenue, so in order to use the typewriter, I'd ride the Kedzie Avenue car to Douglas Boulevard and transfer over. It was about an hour's trolley ride. I don't know what he used while I was using it, but he gave me the corner. And either I wrote the letter to him or at any rate this letter I wrote about my hassle in this gasoline station got into his hands and he said, "This is a story; make it a story." So I did and called it "So Help Me" and I sent it to *Story* magazine, which I hadn't heard about, but Murray Gitlin knew about *Story*, and they took it and published it in 1933. Because they took it, I got a form letter from Vanguard Press. I was twenty-four and I got this letter from Vanguard Press: "Are you working on a novel? We are interested in a novel on the basis of this piece in *Story* magazine." I had nothing else to do so instead of answering the letter, I rode to New York. I was so used to hitchhiking by that time, I was so used to walking out the door and getting on Route 66—it was just as easy as getting into a car, and although I never knew exactly what route I was going to take, I never had any trouble. By that time I was a professional transient so I knew all the places to go by then. So I rode to New York. Some kids—two guys with a lot of bedding in the car—picked me up and they were going to New York by way of Niagara Falls. I said, "All right, I've never seen Niagara Falls." So I came down. We saw the Falls and it seems to me I helped them somewhere along the line. I think I helped to buy food or something. I think I helped buy gas once or twice. Anyhow we came down the Palisades. That was the first time I saw New York. And I went right up to Vanguard Press and met James Henle. And he said, "What'll you need? What would you do? How would you write a novel?" I said, "I'd go back to the Southwest." He said, "What would you need to do that?" I said, "I need thirty dollars a month." I mean I knew it would cost that much. You get room and board for twenty dollars a month and that leaves ten dollars for tobacco and so forth. And so we made a deal. He gave me ten dollars to get out of town and a promise of thirty dollars a month for three months, a total of one hundred dollars.

I wrote in *Somebody in Boots* on that. I didn't finish it in three months, but I delivered it. It was delivered in 1935. That was the only work I did between graduation and 1936 when the W.P.A. opened up. I got married in 1936 and the book wasn't a success at all, so I didn't try writing another novel until 1940 . . .